1.85

DREAMS OF PASSION

Rebecca leaned toward him, and his hands grasped hers. He would not allow her to pull away. Instead, he drew her to him, his eyes blazing in the moonlight. "And what are *your* dreams, little Cat-Eyes?"

You are my dream, she almost cried, but her throat was so tight she couldn't speak. She could only stare up into his face—that beloved handsome face. He hesitated a moment, bent down closer, and then his lips sought hers.

Tentatively, she kissed him back. Tasted the sweetness of his mouth. He gathered her into his arms, bent back her head, and ravished her mouth with his kisses. His lips were hot. Demanding. Unrelenting. . . .

BESTSELLING ROMANCES BY JANELLE TAYLOR

CRIMSON DESIRE

BY
KATHARINE
KINCAID

ZEBRA BOOKS
KENSINGTON PUBLISHING CORP.

ZEBRA BOOKS

are published by

KENSINGTON PUBLISHING CORP.
475 Park Avenue South
New York, N.Y. 10016

Printed in the United States of America

For Richard, With Love

"Where can I go you will not follow?
You claim the wilderness as you claim my soul.
Between us, there can be no secrets
For where I am you are—my beloved savage!"

Prologue

August, 1793

Dear Aunt Margaret,

By the time you read this letter, Papa and I will be on our way to the Northwest Territory—the Ohio Country! This news may come as something of a shock to you, but considering all that's happened—Mama's dying so suddenly of fever—I think it's for the best.

Please don't worry! Two years have already passed since General Arthur St. Clair was defeated by those awful savages, and his replacement is Anthony Wayne, the war hero.

You will remember how he stormed Stony Point and took it away from the British after everyone said it was impossible. We shall be in good hands with him. Of course, everyone *now* says he's grown too old and gruff and gouty for frontier warfare—some even say he is mad! But Papa says he's exactly the sort of man to give the savages what's coming to them.

The only thing I regret about going is having to give up our plans—the ones we made while Mama was still alive. But who knows? Maybe the Ohio Country is full of suitable husbands! If not, I won't forget Philadelphia. Think of me when next you meet a handsome, refined, young gentleman, like the ones Mama was always telling me about. Maybe I'll get to Philadelphia someday after all. I hope so. Affectionate regards.

> Your niece,
> Rebecca McDuggan

One

Rebecca awoke with a start in the smoky close cabin. Something warm and heavy and alien lay across her chest. A sour stench filled her nostrils. For a moment, she wanted to scream—then thought better of it. She lay there feigning sleep and slowly collecting her wits. It could not have been anywhere near morning. Papa was still snoring, asleep on his pallet of skins and pine boughs, the shadows dark and deep on his side of the cabin. Her own skins were shoved down near her feet, and she could just make out the scent of pine warring with the stale odor of leather and sweat.

Then the thing on her chest began moving, groping for her breast. "Take your hand away, Will," she hissed.

The hand, having found its target, squeezed and kneaded instead. "Come on, Becky. Y' know ya like it. Y' want it as much as I do!''

The hulking figure of a man leaned over her. In the glow from the dying fire, with his bristling black hair and beard, he looked like a grizzly bear. He smelled like one too. Didn't he ever wash? she wondered. His entire body, or what she could see of it, naked from the chest up, was covered with crinkly black hair, and peeking out from beneath his beard was his most prized possession—a necklace of fingers. Human fingers they were, seven dried and shriveled fingers taken from the neck of a dead Shawnee warrior.

Revulsion churned her stomach. "I said, take your hand away, Will!" She spoke a little more loudly this time, hoping he'd take the hint. In a moment Papa would hear them; then how would Will explain this unforgivable breach of hospitality and friendship?

Instead of moving his hand, Will bent down closer. "Aw, Becky, I bin itchin' to touch ya like this since y' first come to the wilderness last autumn." He thumbed her nipple roughly, sending a spasm of pain, not pleasure, through her body. Was this what lovemaking was—a painful violation?

"Y're enough t' drive a man wild, you are. Yur tits're as big as apples, an' that hair—that bee-oo-tiful red hair . . ." His breath reminded her of bear's grease, let sit too long in the sun. She tried to squirm away from him, but he pinned her down with his heavy body. "Lie still, dammit! There's no need fur all this fuss—y' ain't got nobody else, have ya?"

Then he gave a throaty chuckle, already knowing the answer. "Aw, Becky, Becky . . ." he moaned. His body began to move against her. She could feel the bulge of his manhood hardening against her thighs. "I got what ya want, little red-haired spitfire—right here in m' drawers."

Panic rose in her throat. "Papa!" she called sharply and was rewarded with a groan and a movement from her father's pallet. Will's meaty hand clamped down over her mouth. "Shut yur trap, will ya'?"

Papa was a heavy sleeper, but surely he'd heard them! Struggling to breathe against Will's foul-smelling hand, she listened intently. Papa seemed to be turning over, to be settling himself more comfortably. Oh, Papa, no! she begged silently, don't go back to sleep! But the stillness in the cabin was breathless, an almost palpable living thing.

Will ground himself against her, breathing hotly in her ear. "Think yur too good fur a plain old back woodsman, do ya? You, with all yur book learnin', an fancy ways—I done told yur Pa he shouldn't have let yur Ma go an' spoil ya! Book learnin' in a woman is wasted—only sharpens up her tongue."

She swallowed a gasp. Those were almost Papa's exact words! She'd heard them often enough while growing up, back home in Pennsylvania, but there had always been the sweet reasonable voice of her mother to overcome his objections. "Now, Angus, we want our Rebecca to marry well, and there's plenty of fine young gentlemen in Philadelphia—only a day's ride away—who'll appreciate what she has to offer."

Grief tugged at her belly. If only Mama had lived to prevent this misguided adventure! Then her grief gave way to hurt; had Papa and Will gotten so familiar they'd finally come around to discussing her future? But what about *her* feelings, *her* wishes, didn't they count for something?

Will's voice came to her again, thick now with lust. "Won't do no good t' fight it. Yur Pa an' me has come to an understandin'. He won't stand in the way of you'n me gittin' hitched—all y' have to do is tell him yur willin'."

Willing! She'd never be willing! Sheer rage made her buck against him, but his hand stayed clamped over her mouth. His body all but crushed her. "That's it, little spitfire, rub up against me!"

She felt him reaching down to undo his breeches, and a moment later, he was pulling up her skirt. She grasped the first thing that came to hand—his full bristly beard—and pulled as hard as she could. Will began to swear under his breath. "Little spitfire! Little she-cat! After we're hitched, I'll learn you some manners!"

Then her foot brushed against something hard

and cold. Papa's skinnin' knife! How could she have forgotten it! Papa always slept with his musket at hand, leaving his knife for her, in case of prowling Indians or animals. Opening her tightly clenched knees, she stretched out her foot to draw the knife closer. She had to let go of his beard to take hold of the carved wooden handle, but at last, she held it firmly. Carefully, lest he should suspect something, she slid it out of its leather sheath.

Will mistook her movements for the beginnings of reciprocated passion. He took his hand away from her mouth and attempted to kiss her, slobbering in her face instead. "That's it, little spitfire! My own sweet Becky! I knew soon as I seed them big green eyes and that flamin' hair, red as fire, you was hot blooded as they come—a reg'lar little spitfire!"

She brought the knife in close to her body— almost wedging it between them. Very deliberately, she pricked his broad belly with the cold sharp blade. "Do you feel that, Will? Do you?" She shoved the blade upward a fraction of an inch. "You'd better get off me or I'll cut out your liver!"

He recoiled as if bitten by a snake. "Why, you little—" Words failed him, so complete was his astonishment.

"Spitfire?" she inquired sweetly. "Yes, Will Simpkin, that's exactly what I am, and you best not forget it. This—" She waved the knife under his nose. "I always carry it, and I know how to use

15

it. If you ever dare touch me again, I'll geld you with it!"

Lord forgive her for telling lies! She hoped Will wouldn't notice that the knife belonged to Papa.

Looking down at her, angry and incredulous, Will shook his head. "If that's how you want it, so be it—but let me tell you somepin', miz high falutin' Becky. The day'll come, you'll change yur mind. You got cravin's jus' like I got! I knows it and your Pa knows it, y're ripe fer the pluckin'. So I kin wait! Yes, I kin wait—cause skinnin' knife or no—my day's comin'!"

It was a long speech for Will Simpkin, and if a grizzly bear could have dignity, for one small moment he had it. Then, he spoiled it by adding, "If it weren't fer yur Pa—sleepin' easy in trust—I'd take ya right now, willin' or no. That little bitty blade don't scare me none."

Trust! He didn't know the meaning of the word! And the knife *had* scared him. She knew there'd be no more trouble out of him tonight! She pulled down her homespun skirt. Thank heaven she'd at least had enough sense not to change to her clinging nightdress when she went to bed! Then she turned over quickly. The mere sight of him disgusted her. If only she didn't still smell him!

Will grunted and moved around, *sounding* exactly like a grizzly as he got comfortable in his own pallet on the beaten earth floor. Soon, the only sound was Papa's deep throated snoring, but

Will's angry comments hung in the silence like the cloying odor of his unwashed body. So she was ripe for the plucking. Was that what it meant—the nameless longings that swept over her, hot as an August wind?

Oh, Papa! she thought mournfully, how could you betray me? Encouraging such a brute!

It was an old argument between them. Papa thought that at seventeen it was close to scandalous she wasn't yet married—safely bedded down, as he put it. He blamed her mother for putting too many free-thinking ideas in her head. Now that Mama was gone, dead from fever last summer, gone also was the bright promise of an extended visit to Philadelphia. Here she was in the wilderness—the Ohio Country—instead of in the home of her mother's wealthy Philadelphia family! This very spring she was to have joined her vivacious Aunt Margaret, who thought it barbaric that she'd thusfar been forced to spend her life on a small farm in rural Pennsylvania.

Yes, here she was, and here was Will, the only other person they'd seen in the seven months since they arrived! Dear God in heaven, was this to be her destiny—to be pawed at and grunted over by the likes of Will Simpkin?

She nestled into the pine boughs, her thoughts heavy as lead. There was a sudden rumble of thunder. Another rainstorm was sweeping down on them, the first drops splattering loudly on the rooftop overhead. Did it always rain for weeks on end in the springtime in Ohio? Tomorrow was the first of June, and winter seemed hardly over!

But no grizzly bear of a man will ever have me, she promised herself. Somehow, someday, I'll get to Philadelphia!

Then she thought of leaving Papa, and her heart turned over. All his life, Papa'd dreamed of seeing what lay west of the Alleghenies, as she'd dreamed of seeing what lay further east. Even if she could find a way home again, how could she go off and leave him?

She remembered the depth of his grief, the silence into which he'd retreated, after her mother's death. Afraid he might die too, she feigned a sudden interest in the Alleghenies herself.

"So 'ee've a hankerin' to see bears and injuns, now, have 'ee?" Those were the first words he spoke after weeks of silence. His blue eyes lit up, and his endearing Scottish brogue actually lilted. Under the straggly red beard—unshaven since the burial—color came rushing back into his pale leathery skin.

In that moment, her future was decided. "Yes, Papa," she'd said.

So all the way down the Ohio on a rickety raft from Fort Duquesne, they journeyed, then all the way up the Muskingum past the juncture of the Tuscarawas.

And now, here she was: in a cramped hastily-thrown up cabin without even the most simple comforts—a chamber pot or a goose tick quilt. And the rain beat on the clapboard roof with hard angry fingers.

Papa and Will were already gone by the time she got up the next morning. She heard them tramping around, Will muttering, "Ain't it a woman's place t' git some hot grub in our bellies?" and Papa's pert reply, "Time enough to train her when the lass belongs to 'ee."

But she stubbornly refused to budge. They could gnaw cold jerky and discuss her all the way to the salt lick, as far as she was concerned! She lay there until she heard the bolt fall into place as they left the cabin, and then, she lingered awhile longer and surprised herself by falling back to sleep.

But now, I must get up, she thought, yawning and stretching. Laziness was sinful; so Mama had always said. She rolled off her pallet, stood up, and brushed off her skirt. Her muscles were stiff and sore. For all the merits of pine boughs, highly touted by Will, she surely wished Papa would get around to building a proper bedstead! Will himself claimed he had one in his own cabin upriver. He said he built it to please his future wife. She wondered; had he really built a bedstead? He didn't seem to be especially handy, having no other interests but hunting, trapping, and killing

19

Indians when he got the chance. In any case, she didn't care if he had or hadn't. *She* never intended to sleep on it.

Going to the cabin door, she unbolted it, stepped out, and was immediately confronted with a circle of dripping trees. But the air was clean and fresh and had a heavy fecund odor. She breathed deeply—savoring the freshness. Maybe summer would bypass spring entirely. This morning seemed warmer than usual, and trees and under-brush appeared to have grown denser, more close together during the night.

She looked now at the trees, and a shiver ran down her spine. Would she ever get used to the limitless wilderness pressing in around her like some menacing beast?

The trees stood silent and dark in the still gray morning, their roots twisting and turning, their vines reaching out as if to grab someone. Nothing really moved—in fact, the stillness was eerie—but the sensation that she was being watched, that unseen eyes followed her every move, made her feel prickly all over.

"Wilderness jitters," Papa called it, but even knowing that her fear was common to new-comers did nothing to dispel it. Bears, cougars, wolves, and numerous other four-footed creatures lurked in the surrounding forest, but the animal she feared most was a two-footed one—man.

Shawnee, Ottawa, Delaware, and Miami—there

might even be one or two other tribes, she was uncertain of their names—hunted across this land. For centuries they had fought one another over it, but now, a common enemy had forced them to unite. She and Papa were that enemy: settlers who were either brave enough or foolish enough to think they could hack out a foothold in the Ohio Country. True, they'd seen no Indians through the long cold winter and spring, but almost three years ago, on a snowy morning in November of 1791, the entire army of General Arthur St. Clair had been wiped out by the united tribes—led by a Miami chieftain with the peaceful name of Little Turtle.

Evidently, this Little Turtle had never heard of the Land Ordinance of 1787 that opened up the Northwest Territories to white settlement. And no doubt he was as unimpressed as she was by the man who had been sent to replace St. Clair. How could she and Papa ever have thought Anthony Wayne to be such a great hero? How could they have thought it was safe to come here?

All Wayne had done so far to prevent another uprising was to build a few widely scattered forts, not one of which was close enough to do her and Papa any good. But she could hardly blame the savages for wanting to hold onto this fiercely wild and beautiful land. A savage land for a savage people. She'd let them have it—gladly!—if only Papa didn't love it so!

She clasped her arms around herself, peering

21

cautiously into the trees. To the east, a faint pinkish smudge heralded the sunrise. On the other side of the mountains, invisible through the forest, lay civilization and safety—the home she had left behind. Would she ever see it again? Would she ever see Philadelphia? What did life hold for her in this harsh frightening land?

The feeling of being watched, of not being alone, grew stronger. But I am alone, she assured herself. Papa and Will had left hours ago. It would be several days, at least, before they returned from their journey to that far off salt lick.

Well, what was she going to do today? She ought to clean up the cabin, but the remembrance of stale smoky air further tainted by sweat and leather stayed her. Then a delicious thought occurred— why not take advantage of being alone, free of Papa and Will? Chores and responsibilities could wait; she'd do something she'd been dreaming of doing—take a bath and wash her hair!

The idea of being alone in the wilderness abruptly lost all its fearfulness. Anticipation bubbled up in her—a bath! A lovely sweet-smelling bath after months of furtive rubbings with a scrap of cloth dipped in icy-cold water! Looking up, she saw that the tiny patch of sky overhead looked almost blue instead of gray. The faint smudge in the east was deepening to a rosy blush, the dewy mist already evaporating. Why, the day *was* going to be a warm one! It might even turn out to feel like summer! Why not, she thought daringly, bathe outside in the big oaken barrel they'd brought from home?

She rushed inside the cabin to rekindle the fire. She'd have a bath in heated water like some fine Philadelphia lady! And she'd use the last tiny sliver of scented soap she'd been hoarding for just such an opportunity. Of course, Papa had warned her last evening to stay quietly near or inside the cabin, but how could she obey on a morning like this? Surely Indians wouldn't come today if they hadn't come all winter or spring—and what was she supposed to do if they did come? Papa had taken the one good musket. Another hung on pegs over the fireplace, but it hadn't been fired in ages. "See to th' musket first thing I'm gone, lass," he'd ordered, but surely that too could wait.

But by the time she'd carried the heavy iron cauldron back and forth several times from nearby river to fireplace to barrel, she began to wonder if a warm bath was worth all the trouble. The water in the barrel cooled faster than she could heat another, and the barrel itself was no longer watertight. She plugged up a slight gap between two of the staves, but even then, water still seeped out slowly.

At least, it won't be as cold as riverwater, she thought, dipping in her hand and swirling the water around. She finally had enough so she could sit half submerged in the barrel.

Stripping off her soiled and spotted dress and what few undergarments she still possessed that weren't worn to shreds, she jumped up on a log to step into the barrel. My goodness! What would Mama have thought of her standing buck naked in a clearing in the middle of the forest? Crossing her hands over her breasts—creamy white in the dim green light—she cast a furtive glance around. From far off came the commanding gobble of a turkey calling his mate. Other than that, there was no sound—only the gentle creaking of the trees.

Without another moment's hesitation, she plunged into the barrel. Oh, the wonder of it, the luxury, the blissful feel of water and soap on bare skin! She rubbed the soap all over and closed her eyes the better to enjoy it. She dunked her head and lathered her hair and dunked again. Spluttering and laughing, she inhaled deeply of the elusive scent of the soap. Did it smell of roses or lily of the valley? It had probably come from England or France. Mama had brought it home to her after a visit to Philadelphia.

Philadelphia! It might as well be the moon. To think she might have been a powdered pretty lady living on a cobble-stoned street in a fine house! She could see herself curtsying to a ring of admirers and flirting behind a fan. Her hair would be half piled up on her head with the rest cascading down her back in red-gold ringlets. Her bosom would be daringly displayed in a low-cut gown of watered blue silk—accentuating the green of her eyes—and when she turned, she would allow for just the slightest sway of her crinolined skirts to reveal trim ankles and dainty feet in blue kid slippers. Oh, Mama had told her all about the beautifully dressed ladies of Philadelphia!

She imagined herself addressing the cultured, refined Secretary of State, Thomas Jefferson. "Why yes, Mr. Jefferson, I think it's lovely that you're building a new capital city on the shores of the Potomac—but whatever is wrong with Philadelphia?" Then she would flutter her lashes and apologize charmingly for intruding on the conversation of so learned a gentleman, but this gentleman being a *true* gentleman and not threatened by a lady's intelligence would encourage her to voice her opinions. He would listen to her, nodding gravely, and compliment her on the acuteness of her observations—unlike the country clods she'd thusfar met who only wanted to tumble her in a hayrick.

As Mama had once told her, in a revealing rare moment of dissatisfaction with her own lot in life, "A woman of education and gentle upbringing is more than just a child-bearer and a drudge. Remember that always, Rebecca, and do not waste yourself on a lout. Your father can't help it he's not a gentleman, but I want something more for you. Laboring like a fieldhand from dawn to dusk is no life for a *lady*."

And Rebecca, helplessly watching her mother's gentle charm fade slowly over the years, until she withered and died like a misplaced rose, knew she wanted more for herself as well. Were she in Aunt Margaret's parlor in Philadelphia, not only would she engage in conversation with men like Thomas Jefferson or Benjamin Franklin, but one day she would pause, look up, and find a handsome young man regarding her, a clean-smelling man, immaculately dressed. He would smile at her as if she were the only person in the room, step forward, and take her hand.

How long she sat there, her head against the barrel staves, her eyes closed in dreams, she had no idea—but somehow the scene in her head suddenly shifted. She was no longer in Aunt Margaret's parlor but in a bedroom. And her refined young gentleman was pulling her toward the bed. "Come, Rebecca," he whispered. "It's time you became a woman."

"No—I can't!" she gasped. "It isn't right!" And it *wasn't* right to be thinking or feeling the way she was. Her heart began to pound, her skin to flush. The man backed her up against the edge of the bed. She wanted to resist both the man *and* the dream, but a feeling of lassitude flowed through her. What would it be like to be possessed by a man? How would it feel to become a woman?

She slid down deeper into her bathwater, allowing the man in her dream to kiss her

26

ravenously, his tongue probing between her lips, his hands exploring down her bodice. The silk and lace of her imaginary dress slipped off her shoulders, and down, down, down onto the bed she fell—pulling him down on top of her. "Rebecca! Rebecca!" he groaned.

"Yes, oh yes," she answered, but part of her was still resisting. *Was* it wrong to feel like this? Was it wicked to desire a man's body? She wasn't even married! And there was no one she could ask. Even Mama had never discussed a woman's *deepest* thoughts and feelings: it simply wasn't done!

Scooping up the scented water, she allowed it to dribble down between her breasts. It felt almost like a caress. She sighed and sighed again, but could not recover the same intensity of emotion and physical longing she'd been feeling only moments before. This was the way her dreams always ended—over before they'd hardly begun!

Suddenly, her skin began to prickle. Intuitively, she realized she wasn't alone. Her eyes flew open. Not a foot from her face, another face looked back at her—a painted face. And a man's broad-shouldered painted body leaned over the barrel. Another vision jumped into her mind: Papa coming home to find her naked bleeding body, her scalp torn from her head! She sat straight up and began screaming.

Two strong relentless hands reached down and hauled her out of the water. She beat on the man's shoulders and chest, trying to wrench away. Wasn't she soapy? Wasn't she wet? That should give her some advantage! But the Indian had a lean wiry strength that made her blows glance off him like so many feeble slaps. He threw her over his shoulder where her blows fell on the curve of his near-naked buttocks. Then, as if she were merely a sack of oats or barley, he ran into the forest.

Branches and vines tore at her face, hair, and back like clawing fingers. She crossed her arms over her head and thought hysterically, this can't be happening! It can't be! But it was. She wriggled and screamed and kicked until cold realization hit her: what good would it do? There was no one to hear her, and the Indian's grip on her legs was strong as iron. Nor did her weight seem to bother him. She was not a tiny woman, being of medium height and build, but still, running as her abductor was, she thought he must surely be tiring—only it didn't seem like it.

The man ran with an easy lope as if he always took his exercise with a woman slung over his back. She tried clawing at him, digging her nails into his flesh. Her frantic gouging drew blood, but he seemed not to notice. On and on he raced through the forest. She was going to be sick if he didn't stop soon—but the jolting continued for what seemed like mile upon mile upon mile.

At last, he heaved her off him and slammed her into the ground. For a moment, she could only lie there, dizzy and nauseous, the scent of leaf mold full in her nostrils. She was lying on the forest floor on a bed of moldy leaves, and over her the tall figure of the Indian loomed against the trees. Her hands—like separate entities—fluttered up to cover her nakedness. She wanted to raise her head but she felt disembodied, like a sack of bones.

She saw herself as if still in a dream, white flesh gleaming against the rich black mold, damp hair streaming away from her in a wild red tangle. Her breasts were heaving, her thighs quivered. She could hardly draw breath. Terror sat on her chest like an ugly black vulture. What was the Indian waiting for? Why didn't he kill her—take her scalp and be done with it? Or was it something else he wanted first—some ugly vile thing?

She struggled to see him better. Her eyes focused first on his corded thighs, sheened with perspiration and sturdy as young trees; then her glance strayed to his breech clout which was richly embroidered and beaded, with a thick concealing fringe. Feeling herself flush, she quickly looked upward. From his waist-thong hung a feathered tomahawk, a sheathed knife, and a small beaded pouch. His belly was lean and hard, his chest sculpted with muscles. Slashes of blue and ochre stained his bronze skin. He wore a necklace of animal teeth—sharp as daggers, and his long black hair was pulled back and twined with a thong, from which protruded three white feathers.

She avoided his eyes, fixed on her with glowing intensity. His face was bathed in shadows—but the blue and ochre paint gave it a fearsome quality as though he were not quite human. "Stop staring at me!" she finally croaked. She'd be hanged if she'd just lay there and let him drink in her nakedness!

Maneuvering herself away from him, she crossed one arm over her breasts and the other over the flaming triangle of hair between her thighs. Never had she felt so vulnerable, so exposed—but at least she wasn't dead yet. Maybe if she didn't show fear or become hysterical, she had a better chance of remaining alive—of somehow escaping! If only she had something with which to cover herself!

The Indian's mouth quirked ever so slightly upwards, as if he enjoyed her discomfort. He reached down, grasped her forearm, and hauled her to her feet. She tried to jerk away. Without letting go of her arm, his other hand dropped to his waist thong. Eyes narrowing, he fingered his knife; then he said something—a single word she could not understand.

She didn't mean to defy him, but neither did she know what he'd said. So she simply stood there, panting, until he repeated the one word command. At the same time, he removed the knife from its sheath.

"But I don't understand you! Can't you see that?" Her voice caught on the question and spiraled upwards, like a child's.

The Indian wrenched her around roughly to face the forest then gave her a stinging little slap on her bare buttocks. Shamed by this familiarity and desperate to escape his knife, she nearly leapt down what she now saw was a narrow twisting path. So that was what he wanted her to do—walk ahead of him down the path! She'd have to concentrate to understand his wishes, but as soon as she could get that knife away from him, she'd plunge it into his chest or back!

The path they were on had to be a deer path for it seemed to follow no set direction. She could hardly tell where it went, and when she mistakenly blundered off it, he grabbed a handful of her hair and dragged her back on track. Finally, with his mouth set in a thin angry line, he tore down a trailing vine and looped it quickly around her wrists. The other end of the vine, he wound around his own waist. Now, she was forced to walk behind him, to watch that broad arrogant back. At least, she thought, this will be easier, but soon discovered it was not.

The Indian moved like some forest creature, swiftly and silently. His feet made no sound, not even the snapping of a twig. She stumbled along behind him, tripping over logs and vines and beginning to feel exhausted from the effort of trying to keep up. She was used to going barefoot, her shoes from home having long since fallen apart, but even now, when her feet were hardened, they rebelled at new discomforts. The leaf mold felt soft enough, but stray rocks and sharp sticks littered the path. In places, the underbrush was thorny. Her bare legs were constantly whiplashed and soon crisscrossed with welts and scratches. Where was he taking her anyway—to the ends of the earth?

Finally, she gasped, "Stop! Stop, please!" She knew she risked his anger, but he would be even more angry if she collapsed before they got where they were going. "I can't go any further," she pleaded. "Can't we stop and rest?"

The Indian wheeled around and cracked her smartly across the face. His eyes blazed. She cowered away from him, tasting blood. The man was truly a savage! Did it make him feel manly to strike a helpless naked woman? Even Will wouldn't do that! He barked another incomprehensible command, but when she opened her mouth to protest, his hand drew back to hit her again. Now, she understood. They must keep going, and she must resist the impulse to speak—but why? Who was there to hear them in the middle of the wilderness?

Jerking on the vine, he dragged her along behind him. Could it be white men he was afraid of—hunters or trappers? Maybe, it was soldiers! But the nearest soldiers were at the fort in Marietta, and Marietta lay a long way downriver, where the Muskingum emptied into the Ohio. Oh, why had

Papa struck out for a spot so far away from any settlement?

Papa, oh Papa, would she ever see him again? Even Will would look good if he came suddenly tramping through the forest. What was going to happen to her? If only she could sit down for awhile or have a drink of water!

On and on through the forest they went. Sunlight now dappled the greenery overhead, but she'd lost all sense of direction. Her arms, legs, and chest burned. Her whole body ached. Tangled hair hung across her eyes, obscuring her vision. The tightly tied vine cut off circulation in her hands. She tried wiggling her fingers but could not even feel them. Would they never stop? But what would he do to her when they did?

Suddenly, he stopped. She ran into the back of him. Quickly, he spun around, threw one arm around her waist and dragged her to him. His free hand found her mouth and closed over it—cutting off air. She struggled helplessly, pinioned to his chest, more terrified than ever. What was happening? What was he doing? Was this now the end?

He dragged her into the thick underbrush and shoved her down onto the ground. Her hair caught in the branches. The pain was swift and stinging as individual strands parted from her head. Then he knelt down, one knee on each side of her, his hand still clamped over her mouth and nose. And for the second time in twenty-four hours she gagged on a man's sweaty palm.

Then she saw the reason for her captor's behavior: three more Indians came loping soundlessly through the sun-speckled trees. Like her captor, these men were painted, but instead of blue and ochre, black and white slashed their faces and chests. One brave had divided himself in half—one side black, the other white. Tomahawks and knives hung from their waist-thongs, bows and arrows were slung over their shoulders, and all three carried muskets and powder horns. Ornaments of beaten silver dangled from their necks and ears. The savage who had divided himself in half wore a large silver ring in his nose. He gestured to his companions to stop. Cocking his head like some fierce bird of prey, he knelt and listened.

Her captor's hand tightened over her mouth. It gave her a curious feeling of power—to know that he too was frightened. It made him seem more human. She held herself so still, it seemed she was barely breathing. She couldn't cope with one savage let alone three more!

The ring-nosed Indian peered intently at the ground like a dog worrying a scent. Then it seemed he was looking directly at them, and her captor's body tensed. Her own muscles thwanged like wires. But the Indian looked away. Presently, he arose and gestured to his companions to follow. And they set off in a different direction.

Certain that it was safe now, she moved slightly, but her captor's hands and knees still held her down. For a long time, he made her lie there; then swiftly he stood up, dragged her up after him, and set off again. She was trembling with nerves and exhaustion. How can he know where he's going? she thought miserably. And how much longer before I drop?

It was late afternoon or early evening before he allowed her to stop again. The shadows were gathering among the trees, but by then, she barely knew or cared what time of day it was. Her feet felt like raw stumps, her mouth like wool, and there was a buzzing in her ears caused by light-headedness, thirst, and hunger.

She supposed she ought to be grateful it *had* turned out so warm, but she no longer cared about her nakedness. The only thing that mattered was to lie down and rest. But no sooner had she sat down when he dragged her up again, jerking his head to tell her something. More Indians? Well, if there were, she would just stay there and let them find her!

Once more, he picked her up and threw her over his shoulder, but this time, she didn't fight. Her arms and legs had turned to mush. He tromped a short distance, and before she realized what was happening, undid the vine at his waist, slid her off his shoulder, and heaved her into the air.

"Oh, God, no!" she cried, flailing the air with

35

her bound hands. She felt herself falling, falling—then she landed on her back with a splash in icy cold water. Her bottom scraped against stones and pebbles. Her spine jolted from the impact. Spitting and sputtering, she came to the surface.

The water was waist deep, and the Indian stood on the bank, arms folded, watching her with a faint look of amusement. So he'd been trying to tell her there was water nearby—well, how was she to know? Dear God, was this still the Muskingum or another river altogether?

The cold current tugged at her legs. Suddenly, she remembered how thirsty she was. Cupping her hands, she dipped water and furiously drank huge drafts of it. Nothing had ever tasted so refreshing and fine. Almost as if he scorned her greedy enjoyment, the Indian bent one hand only and dipped a mouthful for himself.

Well, she didn't care what he thought of her! The taste and feel of the water was heavenly on her bruised and beaten flesh. She scooped cold clear water on the scratches and welts across her face and breasts, while the Indian, never taking his eyes from her, moved a few paces downstream and gathered a handful of cattails. He came back and offered them to her, his face stern and commanding in the long-shadowed evening light. She stepped up onto the river bank, the air chilling her wet flesh. Now, what was she to do with cattails?

He took one of the cattails, snapped off the tuberous growth at the root end, and threw the rest of it away. Then, to her astonishment, he bit into it with strong white teeth, chewed, and swallowed; then offered the remainder to her. Hungry as she was, she had never dreamed of eating a cattail—but if she refused, would there be anything else offered?

Her stomach suddenly growled. She'd had nothing to eat since last evening when she'd fed Papa and Will. Trembling, she took the tuber and bit into it herself. It was slightly gritty but had a crunchy pleasant taste, almost like the vegetables from their garden back home. Less hesitant now, she broke off the tubers from the other cattails he gave her and ate them, grit and all.

Afterwards, she felt better. Perhaps, since he'd given her something to eat, he didn't mean to scalp her just yet—or perhaps, he was just conserving her strength for some other horrible purpose. The Indian, who'd been watching her and eating nothing himself, now made her sit on the bank. He tied the end of her vine to a nearby tree, tugging on it to make sure it was tight, then went down to the water.

Undoing his waist thong, he laid tomahawk, knife, and beaded pouch onto the grassy bank. Next, his breech clout came off. She knew she ought to look away, but somehow could not. He had watched *her* nakedness all day, now she would feast on his! But a slow steady flush began creeping across her body. She'd never really viewed a full-grown naked man before. Her breath caught

37

in her throat: his manhood was as large as a stallion's!

Completely disinterested in her reactions, as if it bothered him not at all to know she was watching, he dove into the river. His stroke was strong and smooth, propelling him effortlessly into deeper water. He was so at home, so comfortable, it made her own chilled flesh seem that much more of a personal weakness. She watched almost breathlessly as he alternately dove underwater and rubbed his face and chest. The war paint washed away—revealing a stunningly handsome man!

Then she grew angry at herself. What was she doing—admiring a savage's nakedness—while the opportunity to escape slipped through her fingers? Feverishly, she tried to undo the vine around her wrists. His unguarded weapons lay only a few feet away! She tugged and pulled and bit at the vine, but before she could loosen it, he came out of the river.

She shivered, looking up at his strong lean body. Without paint, glistening with water, he was all male animal. A strange feeling arose in her, warming her chilled flesh. He said something: another command. Her heart thumped against her rib cage.

He leaned down to untie the vine from the tree, his face only inches away from hers. He was, she could see clearly now, strong-jawed and clean-shaven. His nose was straight, his mouth firm, the planes of his cheeks and forehead looking as if they'd been sculpted from marble. His eye caught hers—and then, she noticed something. The discovery was heart-stopping. Shouldn't his eyes be black or brown? Weren't all Indians brown-eyed? But the bold eyes raking across her were as blue as her own Papa's!

"You're not an Indian, you're a white man!" she blurted.

Two

"You *are* a white man!" she repeated, with more certainty. Surely, she hadn't imagined that brief flicker of understanding in his deep blue eyes!

Now, his eyes were like ice chips, distant and cold, and his quick tug on the vine brought her scrambling to her feet. But her discovery had given her new courage and more than a little indignation. How dare he continue this pretense! How dare he break every rule of civilized behavior known to mankind—or at least to white men!

"You understand every word I'm saying—I know you do! Why do you pretend otherwise!" She had to tilt her head back to look at him, and for a moment, it seemed like she was back in Pennsylvania where men simply didn't go around stealing naked women out of their baths.

He turned abruptly on his heel and strode over to where he'd left his breech clout and weapons, tugging her along behind him, and she suddenly remembered where she was. Here, there were no rules, no standards for proper behavior. Hadn't she herself dared to bathe outside in a barrel? Hadn't she nearly lost her virginity to a man who claimed to be her father's friend?

"At least, you could tell me what you plan to do with me—where you're taking me. How long can I expect to remain like this—naked as a newborn babe?"

He put on his breech clout and weapons, his glance flickering over her appraisingly. Was he deciding whether she pleased him? Embarrassment flooded through her. It was so humiliating—so unfair to be caught in this compromising situation! A woman's nakedness should be a gift to the man she chooses, not a forced and frightening experience. How could he be so arrogant, so at ease, while her own heart hammered wildly every time he looked at her?

"I am taking you to a Delaware village on the Scioto," he said suddenly, his speech so plain and understandable and his tone so matter of fact, it took a moment before shock set in.

"You *do* understand! I knew it! You speak in my tongue! But why—"

His fingers pressed against her lips. "You talk too much, little Cat-Eyes. In the forest, it is always better to be silent—to listen instead of speak. Did I not try to teach you that lesson once today already?"

She remembered all too vividly the stinging slap across her mouth. Nevertheless, when he took his hand away, she spat indignantly, "My name is Rebecca McDuggan—not Cat-Eyes! And I will do much better understanding you from now on if you speak plainly in my language."

His eyes darkened to the shade of thunder-clouds. "Sometimes to speak is to die. Remember that, Cat-Eyes, and you may yet live to see the sunrise."

A chill ran through her bones. There was no mistaking the power nor the violence in this man. He would kill her as easily as he had thrown her over his shoulder and run off with her. Perhaps, instead of provoking him, she ought to turn her attention to how they might pass the night. Already, it was almost dark, and in the forest, night fell swiftly, like a blanket being tossed across a bedstead. The air probed her chilled flesh with icy fingers, and she could not help shivering.

"Come." He jerked on the vine. "You will make a place for us to sleep."

Was she supposed to collect pine branches and leaves—make some sort of pallet? She knew nothing whatever about the sleeping habits of Indians, and the stern set of his mouth did not invite questions. He dragged her into a stand of thick heavy trees of immense girth, then stood looking upwards until he found one that seemed to suit his purpose. The tree, about four feet in diameter, stood upright, but it was dead and hollowed out—containing a space big enough, she supposed, for one of them. He took his tomahawk and banged around inside the hollow, then untied her hands and motioned for her to start collecting leaves.

She rubbed her tingling wrists, considering. There could be no running away tonight; it was so dark now she could hardly see a hand's length in front of her. Besides, the Indian was scowling at her and waiting. She scooped up an armload of the ever-present leaves and dumped them inside the hollow, while he set about chopping brush with his tomahawk. When he had a large pile of it, he pushed it toward the hollow. "Get in," he ordered her.

"Where—where are *you* going to sleep?"

His eyes were unreadable in the darkness. "We will both sleep inside the tree, unless you prefer to be bound hand and foot and left to prowling animals."

"But we can't sleep in there together! It wouldn't be proper!"

"Do not test my patience. Get in!"

Shivering with apprehension, she obeyed, and he climbed in after her, crushing her against the cool inside bark of the tree. He pulled the brush across the opening, and they were encased in utter darkness, so close together that she knew when he breathed deeply before moving slightly away from her. She took a deep breath herself and smelled old rotted wood and damp musty leaves.

Then his hands, warm on her cold skin, found her waist. She jerked away and banged her head.

"Hold still, you little fool." She felt the coldness of the vine being drawn about her middle. He tugged and pulled on it to knot it. "Sit down. There is room," he told her.

She squatted down in the bottom of the tree, bumping knees with him. There *was* room, but barely, and the leaves made a soft cushioned resting place, if she could have rested. His hands touched her shoulders, sending a spasm of fear rippling through her. He turned her around so that her back was toward him, opened his knees and pulled her between them so that she found herself seated comfortably with ample space for her own legs. It would be even more comfortable if she could lean back against his chest. His arms remained around her, inviting her to do so, but she held herself rigidly, hardly daring to breathe.

"If you touch me," she whispered into the blackness, "I will find some way to kill you."

"I am already touching you." His hands moved across her shoulders in a lingering caress. "And your skin is very soft, little Cat-Eyes, softer than doeskin. What a pity you are not a gentler creature."

"Indeed! What a pity!" She pushed his hands away. "Doesn't it matter to you that I loathe and fear you—that I would not be here if I could get away from you?"

"Ah, but you cannot get away from me." His

hands came back again, moving down her arms to her waist, rubbing gently in a motion that made her skin tingle. "By daylight, we may be enemies, and if you do not obey me or try to escape, you will regret it—but there is no reason we cannot seek pleasure from one another in the darkness."

"I don't want your—your pleasure! And I think I would rather be outside, tied up, than inside with you!" She tried to get up and scraped her shoulder against the inside of the tree.

His hands tightened around her waist, pulling her back down. "The night air grows cold, little Cat-Eyes, and you are naked, remember?"

How could she forget! Frustration and anger brought tears to her eyes. "I would rather freeze to death than submit to a man I don't desire!"

He made a sound she could not identify, but it seemed suspiciously like a laugh. "Do you think I could take you here—where there is barely room to turn around or sit?"

"I don't know what a man like you could do! Anything you want, I suppose! You of all people could find a way!"

"Yes, I could find a way." His voice was suddenly husky. He pulled her back against him, holding her tightly, then his hand found her breast. His touch was light as a feather, tracing the curve of her fullness.

"No—I beg of you!" she whimpered.

"Be still, little one—does this not please you?" His lips nibbled her skin in the hollow of her neck, sending a tremor down her back. There was a throbbing in her groin, a sudden feeling of warmth and wetness.

"Don't do this!" she pleaded. "I—I belong to another! We're going to be married!"

"And this other—does he hold you like this?" His fingers played over her body, stroking softly. Her breasts tingled shamefully.

"*He* is not a savage!" she lied, thinking of Will who was a savage of another kind. "He would never take a woman who didn't want him!"

His hands suddenly stopped their roving. He pushed her away from him, shocking her with his quicksilver anger. "Nor do I take a woman who is made of wood, not flesh! Do all white women have bodies like painted gourds—beautiful but empty of feeling?"

"I am not empty of feeling!" she sputtered. "But—but white women choose their own men! Most of them," she amended. "They are very loving wives!"

"Pah! If they are all like you, they cannot be loving." Scorn edged his voice. "Your own nakedness shames you."

She was suddenly confused and hurt. What did he want? What did he expect? What did Indian women do—run around naked all the time, throwing themselves into any man's arms who looked at them? She heard him shift around, seeking a new position, but there was no better one than the one they'd already found. She edged away

47

from him as far as she could get. The Indian touched her again, coldly, impersonally. He pulled her back to the spot between his knees. "Do not be afraid, Cat-Eyes. I have lost my desire to enjoy your body. An empty gourd tempts me not at all."

"Nor do you tempt me!" she said furiously, sitting up straight as a stick. She was determined to hold the position all night if necessary. No matter how sleepy she became, she would not lean back against him!

But the moments crept by slowly, and there was nothing but the blackness and the silence and the smell of dead wood and leaves. Rebecca began to feel chilled. The Indian neither spoke nor moved; she might have been utterly alone. Indeed, she had never felt such a sense of abandonment and loneliness. She was also ashamed. What was wrong with her that her body should so respond to the caresses of a savage? Part of her had wanted him to go on even while she begged him to stop!

Something with many fast-moving little legs scurried across her foot. Choking back a scream, she slapped it away. How many other such scurrying creatures were sheltering in the tree with them? The blackness seemed to press in on her, weightier than a goose-tick quilt. A deep despair filled her. What would Papa think when he came home to the empty cabin? What awful thoughts would run through his mind when he found the barrel of water and her discarded clothes? Thank

God, he couldn't see her right now! But what if they never saw one another again?

She suddenly remembered an incident she'd heard about when she was only nine or ten years old. It had happened during the war when so many atrocities on both sides had been committed—but somehow the things the Indians did in company with the British seemed so much worse than anything done by the colonists. Awakening from a half-sleep, she had shivered with horror as Papa's voice—hard and angry and incredulous—drifted up through the rafters and reverberated in the loft. "They stripped 'im bare-assed naked and tied 'im to a stake and whut they done t' the poor bastard then with their fire an' knives an' pointed sticks ain't fit fer 'ee t' know, lass."

But then he'd gone ahead and told Mama what had happened anyhow to a certain Colonel William Crawford who'd been captured by the savages. Unknown to either of her parents, she'd nearly upchucked her dinner. Tears had streamed down her cheeks as she heard how the poor doomed colonel, at the height of his sufferings, had begged a nearby white man to put a musketball through his heart, but the white man, being part Indian himself and a traitor working for the British, had laughed in the colonel's face.

Simon Girty—that was the traitor's name! She'd almost forgotten it and forgotten too that Girty was said to still be living among the Indians and stirring up deviltry. Maybe the Indian between whose knees she now sat was one such as Simon Girty—a white man turned renegade traitor! *That* would explain his blue eyes. But then, if he'd gone over to them like Girty, why hadn't he wanted those Indians to find them today?

So many questions and so few answers! She shuddered from head to foot. And the Indian's arms tightened around her body. "Sleep now, little Cat-Eyes. A long journey lies ahead."

Yes, she thought bitterly, a long journey to where? To a death too awful to think about? Or to life in the arms of a traitor turned savage? If she couldn't get away from her captor, she'd have to— to kill herself! That was the only answer. She'd been brought up to believe in living a good and righteous life even if church-going wasn't exactly Papa's idea of Sunday recreation. But would God hold it against her if she did kill herself? Surely not when one considered the choices!

She fell asleep suddenly in the middle of a thought, not knowing that she did so. Once, she heard an owl hoot in the distant darkness and felt the Indian stir against her, but she was too wrapped up in warmth and drowsiness to move. So she merely stayed where she was, snuggled close to his broad warm chest. He had a clean woodsy smell, faintly musky, and not at all unpleasant. Tomorrow would be soon enough to escape— maybe even kill him, or failing that, kill herself. Now, she must sleep, sleep, sleep, let the blackness enfold her like a butterfly's wings.

The Indian awoke first and she had the sinking feeling of another opportunity lost. She might have seized one of his weapons or untied the vine and stolen away while he slept, but as it was, he pushed aside the brush to reveal the dim gray light of morning; then they crawled out of the hollow and stretched to relieve their cramped muscles.

The damp morning air was surprisingly warm on her naked flesh, but a pressing problem immediately confronted her. How was she to tend to personal needs right in front of him and without benefit of total darkness?

No such modesty deterred him; he went about tending to his own needs as if she were not present. Seeing him thus occupied with his back to her, she moved off to the end of her tether and hurriedly squatted down. Another humiliation and the day had not yet begun. Was she never again to know the blessedness of privacy? Even in a one room cabin, *some* proprieties were observed.

Breakfast that morning consisted of more cattails and some other bitter tasting roots the Indian pointed out to be dug up, but when he turned over a log and gestured to the squirming white grubs, she protested, "I can't eat *those!* They're ugly and slimy and—"

His blue eyes flashed. "They are the difference between living and dying. Pinch them between your thumb and finger—like so." He showed her how, then popped the grub into his mouth and

51

swallowed. "They are not so bad as they seem and will give you a strength that cannot be found in roots."

"I thought all Indians were hunters, but you—you're nothing but a grub-snatcher!" As soon as the words were out of her mouth she regretted them, but she needed decent food—red meat cooked over a good hot fire! She faced him defiantly, her back straight, her breasts heaving. "I won't eat grubs! If you want me to be strong, you must find some meat!"

Coldly furious, his eyes raked over her. "If a man brings a woman meat, he brings it as a gift. If he does not bring it, she feeds herself. From now on, you will find your own food as a proper squaw should."

"But—but—" If he didn't feed her she would soon die! She had no weapons, no way to hunt for herself, and it was too early in the growing season for nuts and berries.

"The wise squaw does not argue but looks for ways to please her man. Then and only then may she know the happiness of a full belly."

Oh, the arrogance of this tall bronze savage! So he was determined to turn her into the kind of woman he wanted! Well, she would remind him yet again that she was not here of her own choice! "I am not a squaw, and you are not my man!" she hissed between clenched teeth.

"That is true," he agreed, surprising her. "If you die on the trail, it matters little to me."

With that, he again bound her wrists with the vine and set off through the forest, and the morning passed much like the day before, with her tripping and stumbling behind him.

They stopped to rest only once—at noon, when sunlight briefly bathed the forest in golden radiance, long fingers of light probing the forest floor. A small dappled stream gurgled over rocks nearby, and she lay on her stomach in the ferns and drank greedily. She felt exhausted and slightly dizzy, while the Indian, dipping water slowly as though it might run out, looked fresh as he had that morning. Didn't he ever tire—or was he some sort of magical being with powers of which she could only dream? Her stomach knotted up like a fist. Thinking the cramps were from hunger, she pulled up a plant that looked like what they had eaten that morning, but he slapped her hands down before she could raise the tubers to her mouth.

"No! Do not eat."

She understood at once; the plant was poisonous. But her feeling of intense relief at not having bit into it was soon replaced with a sharp determination. This plant might be the very thing she needed if death was the only way out of her predicament!

She leaned forward. There were many such plants springing up around her, but on close inspection, they did not look at all like the plants whose roots she had eaten that morning. These

53

stems were simple, round, smooth, and erect, standing about knee high, and each one supported two smaller stems which in turn supported two deeply lobed leaves and a solitary white flower. The root of the plant she was still holding was dark brown, fibrous, and about half the size of a finger.

The Indian took the plant from her hands. "We call it *Ki-ta-ma-ni*. The flower becomes a yellow berry which is good to eat when ripe. And the root itself has many powers when picked in the right season. It is known to cure ailments of the liver, but at any other time—"

She suppressed a shudder. "When is the right season?"

"During the moon of the falling leaves, the shaman directs the women to gather it into small bundles which are then hung to dry in the lodges and saved until needed."

"The shaman?"

"He is our medicine man—our doctor, you would call him. He is very wise and knows the uses of every plant in the forest."

Watching him as they sat beside the stream, Rebecca wondered why he was treating her so civilly. She would have liked to ask him more. Her own mother had been fond of herbs and often used them medicinally. What she really wanted to ask, however, was how he had come to speak her language so well—to know terms like "doctor" and "ailments of the liver"—if he *wasn't* a renegade traitor!

But the Indian's face grew quickly stern again. The white feathers in his sleek black hair shook as if he were scolding himself. "But Indian ways would not interest you—a white woman. If you still wish to eat *Ki-ta-ma-ni*, go ahead. I shall not stop you."

Stung by his sarcasm, she shifted from a sitting to a kneeling position. "If you don't care what happens to me, why don't you let me go?" She waved her bound hands under his nose. "Go ahead! Cut the vine, and you'll be rid of me forever!"

His blue eyes darkened to a dangerous color that was fast becoming familiar. "What I have taken, I have taken." He stood up. "Come, we go now."

Again, it was nearly dark before they stopped for the night. He led her almost fainting from dizziness and hunger to the river and she wondered anew, was it still the Muskingum? Had it been there all along? Or was this now the Scioto where he'd said he was taking her?

She stumbled into the water, her stomach a hard ball of agony, and fell face forward into the shallows. The water embraced her with cold tugging arms. Choking and gasping, she drank deeply as though each drop meant survival.

Afterwards, much revived, she pulled cattails with a vengeance. The Indian stopped her as she straggled back up the bank, clutching a pile of them to her breasts. He stretched out his hand. "A wise squaw does not eat until after her man has eaten.''

"I am not a squaw, and you are not my man," she said tiredly, but she handed him the cattails and went back for more for herself.

That night, they slept inside a huge fallen log she'd found. Like the tree of the night before, it was completely hollow—only larger and far more comfortable, the discovery of which gave her enormous satisfaction. She would show that arrogant savage! She was smarter by far than any brown-skinned, brown-eyed, dumpy little squaw!

But then anxiety overcame her, what would he do tonight stretched out full length beside her? Before she crawled into the log, she stripped a large piece of bark from a shaggy tree and tied it around herself with a vine. At least now she wouldn't be skin to skin with him.

He noted her rough attire and grunted before crawling in himself, "An empty gourd is still an empty gourd no matter what covering it wears."

And again, she felt strangely hurt and insulted, though his lack of interest in her was exactly what she wanted. Taking care lest an arm or leg brush against him, she lay down in her half of the log. Her stomach churned and rumbled, demanding more sustenance than mere cattails. The tender skin of her breasts itched and burned from the rough bark covering. But when she finally fell asleep, it was once more with a sudden ferocity, like falling off a cliff.

*   *   *

A delicious savory smell soon tickled her nose, and a sizzling sound taunted her ears. Was she dreaming? Her mouth began to water. Woolly-headed, she opened her eyes, realizing suddenly that the Indian was no longer lying beside her, and the light at the log entrance, where the brush had been pulled away, was a soft misty gray. It took only a moment to wriggle out of the log.

A light mist was rising, and the Indian sat cross-legged nearby, coaxing a tiny fire in a small pit. Over the fire lay a thin slab of stone, and on the stone, so large their tails flopped over the edge, were two fileted fish. She knew better than to shout with delight, but all her senses came suddenly alive and began to clamor. The smell—the heavenly smell! Eagerly, she sat down across from him, wondering how soon they could eat.

He looked up from the fire, his blue eyes now gray—gray as the trees, the gray mist, and the gray river. "The fishing is good, Cat-Eyes, but I shall not wait long for a lazy squaw. If you wish to eat, you must hurry to catch your meal."

Catch it! But she'd never fished nor caught anything in her life! She had no hook, no line, no bait. How had he caught *two* fish—with his bare hands? She wanted to weep. If he refused her one of those fish, denied her even a small taste, she could not go on. Another day on the trail without solid food in her stomach, and she'd collapse before nightfall! She hurried down to the river and waded

57

in up to her knees but even with unbound hands—he'd not yet seemed to think of it—she knew it was hopeless. There were no fish to be seen.

Hollow as the gourd he accused her of being and on the verge of desperation, she ripped up more cattails. Coming out of the river, she nearly tripped over a small dead log in the high grasses. Grubs. There would be grubs underneath the log. Could she bring herself to eat them? Maybe if they were cooked, and she pretended she was eating meat? She moved the log and snatched up several fat ones before she could change her mind. They *were* meat—of a kind. An idea occurred to her. It probably wouldn't work, but what harm was there in trying?

Hurrying back to the fire, she smiled sweetly at the Indian and sat down beside him. "What a beautiful morning! Did you sleep well?"

The Indian glanced at her sidelong, maintaining a haughty silence. He poked at one of the fish to test its doneness. The skin was crisping—the meat white and flaky. She could hardly take her eyes from it. "I slept like a baby!" she continued, feeling foolish but determined. "And this morning, I am ready to try eating some grubs!"

She put down the cattails in one hand and opened the other, revealing the squirming white mass. With thumb and finger, she picked up one the way he had shown her the day before. "They look quite good actually—I took care to pick only the fat ones."

"Then what are you waiting for, Cat-Eyes?" Laughter suddenly twinkled in his eyes. "Eat! They will give you strength."

Nausea rose in her throat. "No—no! These—the very best ones—I brought for you. After you have eaten, I will get some for myself!"

She pinched the grub to spare it misery, recoiling as she did so, then popped it on the stone griddle next to the frying fish. Quickly, she did the same with the others, and next cleaned the cattails, separating the largest tubers from the puny ones. Again smiling sweetly, she offered the choice ones to him.

He was still watching her with amusement, the strong line of his jaw softening so that he appeared startlingly less fierce—almost boyish. "Since you have brought me *Wap-ki-mo-si-a,* grub worms, and tubers in the manner of a wise squaw, I will give you one of the fish."

"I accept the fish," she said demurely, concealing her triumph behind lowered lashes.

"But you must still learn to eat grubs, insects, toads—whatever the forest offers. And in time of danger, which is almost anytime, you must learn to eat them raw and be glad of it. Never scorn what the earth gives you, lest the gifts be withheld and you then starve."

Insects and toads—ugh! And how odd that he should speak of the earth and forest as though they were persons—alive and feeling! Only with difficulty did she somehow manage to keep a pleasant

59

expression on her face. "From now on, I scorn none of the earth's gifts," she promised, but she fervently hoped he wouldn't put her words to the test, especially now, when there was that beautiful fish waiting to be devoured!

Though it needed salt, the fish was the best she ever ate, and the price of her pride was a small thing to pay for it. Afterwards, following his lead, she washed and bathed in the river, taking care to keep her bark covering in place, and working the tangles out of her hair as best she could with her fingers. She'd never bathed this often before in her entire life, but admittedly, the cold water seemed to awaken new sources of energy in her body. She felt tingly and alive and vibrant. Obviously, the Indian felt the same.

Watching him as he swam out to where the water was deep, she thought he was in a strange different mood this morning. He hadn't yet bound her hands and seemed not so inclined to hurry. She looked toward the bank where his weapons and breech clout lay. Then, she looked back at him. When he dove underwater, she found herself scrambling for his knife and tomahawk.

Never once thinking of consequences, having surprised herself, she was soon crashing through the forest. His weapons were firmly in her hand and the hot food had made her strong again—now, at last she would be free! But was this the time to escape? In broad daylight, wouldn't he catch her easily?

She stopped running, listening breathlessly, and began looking for someplace to hide. There were no logs, no hollowed-out trees—and if there were, he would likely spot them and look there first. Where wouldn't he look for her?

A cool breeze sighed in the trees, stirring the branches. Yes! The branches of the trees! If she could somehow climb a tree, she would be safe until he gave up looking for her and went away! She grabbed hold of one of the vines snaking down from a big sycamore. It looked strong enough to hold her, but she'd have to put down the knife and tomahawk—hide them in the brush—in order to free her hands for climbing.

It took only a moment, then she was swinging on the vine and hoisting herself up hand over hand, bracing her feet against the trunk. Not a moment too soon. From only a short distance away, his voice surprised her. "Don't be a fool, Cat-Eyes. You cannot hide from me. I had thought you were wiser. You will die in the forest if I have to leave you here alone. Is that what you want—a slow death by starvation?"

She didn't move. Concealed by the foliage, she could see that the tree she'd chosen was on the edge of a small natural clearing. Oh, why hadn't she chosen a place where the growth was thicker? In a sea of swaying foliage, growing greener as the mist evaporated, no one would ever spot her—not even a man whose piercing gaze reminded her of an eagle's!

He spoke again softly, as if he knew she was nearby. "This is no time to play games, Cat-Eyes. It is more dangerous here than you know. I cannot wait for you if you do not come out now."

He must be almost right under her tree. She held her breath. If he looked directly upwards, her white flesh and red hair would jump out at him. Then suddenly, she heard a shout—a snapping of twigs and rustling of leaves. A loud thwump! sounded right underneath her, followed by a terrible curdling yell. She clung to the rough bark of the tree trunk: to change position or look and see what was happening might mean certain death!

A few moments of scuffling—thuds, grunts, and ground shakings—and it was over. Peering down through the leaves, she saw three black and white painted braves: the same Indians they'd evaded on the day she'd been carried off!

They were pinioning *her* Indian to the base of the sycamore, his head lolling forward, his shoulders slumped. His three proud white feathers, now dirty and bedraggled, stuck up awkwardly from the nape of his neck.

The black and white Indian with the ring in his nose shouted and shook him, but he was unable to answer. Ring-Nose struck him across the face then, snapping his head back so that for a moment she caught sight of blue eyes unable to focus and an ugly red gash staining his temple.

In spite of all he'd done, she felt a rush of pity. The man was hurt, and his captors seemed intent on hurting him further. But Ring-Nose suddenly let go of him, and he slid to the ground. The other two braves rapidly turned him over and bound his hands and feet behind him with two strips of rawhide. They stood over him then, conversing in short angry grunts, none of which she understood, except that Ring-Nose seemed furious.

His deep guttural voice rose and fell, punctuated by gestures, and once, he kicked at her captor with a savagery that confirmed his origins. Who *was* this fearful looking creature? What did he want? And what would happen if he suddenly looked up into the tree?

She dared not make even the smallest of sounds or movements. Right under the tree, their voices buzzed like argumentative bees. Their silver bangles jangled. One wore a red feather entwined in a single braid. She decided to call him Red Feather. The other wore a silver ornament on a thong around his neck. It reminded her of a twisted sliver of moon. Twisted Moon seemed a good name for him. And the third, of course, was Ring-Nose.

For her own captor, bound and trussed like a pig for slaughter, she had no name. How strange that she'd never asked him or wondered about it before! Now, she might never know it. It seemed almost a pity. He looked so defenseless lying face-down in the trampled grass, but she mustn't allow herself to feel sympathy for him. As soon as it was possible, she must get down from the tree and flee. She would follow the path of the river and pray it would take her home!

Ring-Nose suddenly put up his hand and made a slashing motion that quickly cut off discussion. Red Feather and Twisted Moon nodded, turned abruptly, and began picking up branches and pieces of wood.

Ring-Nose turned her captor over, took hold of his feet, and dragged him away from the big sycamore toward the center of the clearing. He barked an order to Red Feather. She almost fell out of the tree trying to see what would happen next. Together, Ring-Nose and Red Feather untied her captor and stretched out his arms and legs on the uneven ground. They sharpened stakes and pounded them into the earth with their toma-hawks—one for each hand, one for each foot. Then they retied his hands and feet to the stakes.

He groaned and opened his eyes as they finished securing him. Ring-Nose leaned over and asked a question, then struck him hard across the mouth when he didn't answer. He turned his head away, facing her. And through the screen of leaves, she saw a trickle of red on his lips that matched the red on his forehead. Twisted Moon, in the meantime, continued to bring more wood and to pile it nearby. Wood was plentiful in this little clearing —but why were they gathering it? Did they mean to make a fire?

An awful realization hit her. That's exactly what they were doing! And there could be only one reason they wanted a fire now—in the middle of the morning!

Horrorstricken, she watched Twisted Moon position the wood-pile carefully, while Red Feather sharpened sticks. Grunting in short guttural syllables, Ring-Nose unsheathed his knife from his waist thong and waved the blade over her captor's body. Those corded muscles she had so admired tightened almost imperceptibly. Ring-Nose asked a question or gave a command, she wasn't sure which, and her captor slowly shook his head no. Ring-Nose erupted in a blood-curdling yell that sent shivers down her spine. Then as if he were carving a piece of meat and not a body, he drew the blade of his knife across her Indian's chest and down his belly.

Sickened, she looked away, expecting to hear a scream of pain. But there was no sound, not even a gasp. Had they killed him so quickly then? She looked back. Her Indian lay looking up into the treetops, as if bored with the whole proceedings. A long crimson line ran down his middle. Ring-Nose yelled again and brandished the knife.

She closed her eyes and clung to the tree trunk. This was horrible! It was inhuman! She couldn't bear to watch it. Why didn't her Indian scream? But if he did, what would she do then—faint and fall out of the tree? To listen would be as bad as to watch!

Then Red Feather said something. Was it a protest? Or merely a question? She opened her eyes and bent down the leaves to see better. Ring-Nose stood up, knife still in hand. Twisted Moon stood up too, offering his opinion. Red Feather and Twisted Moon seemed to be in agreement, but Ring-Nose wanted to get back to the business at hand. His face an ugly mask of hatred, he kicked at her Indian's ribs.

Red Feather and Twisted Moon picked up their muskets and powder horns and waited. Finally, Ring-Nose wiped his knife blade on the grass and slid it back into its sheath. He too picked up his musket, and the three of them loped into the forest, leaving her captor stretched out between the stakes.

She was astounded by their sudden departure. Were they coming back to finish what they'd started? Of course, they'd come back! Now was the time to make her escape! She had only to grab hold of the vine and lower herself to the ground. She'd be gone before they knew she was missing—if indeed they knew about her at all!

But then, the naked out-stretched figure on the ground spoke to her, "Get down from the tree and run, little Cat-Eyes. Run to the river and hide in the shallows where your trail cannot be so easily followed."

How long had he been watching her? When had he discovered her hiding place? His eyes—blue as the sky, blue as morning—caught and held her. Like a sleepwalker, she got down from the tree.

Three

There was no reason on earth why she should help him. None whatsoever. He was a savage violent man who had come to a savage violent end. When those three braves returned, they would torture and kill him. Why endanger herself by remaining a single moment longer?

The blue eyes did not beg. They did not even seem to consider that it was in her power to free him. He did not expect it. He merely watched her, having told her what to do, and now waited to see if she would do it. And perhaps for that very reason she couldn't leave him to his fate.

Quickly, she found the tomahawk and knife in the brush then ran to cut the thongs that bound him.

"You don't have to do this," he whispered as she bent over him. "Now, when they return they will come after us both."

"Are you such a poor excuse for an Indian that you can't get us away?" she snapped.

He took no offense at her insult. "You are a brave woman, Cat-Eyes," was all he said.

"I am not brave! I am stupid to help a man who has meant me harm! I don't do this for you—only for myself. I am a Christian woman; I can't leave a man to die!"

He made the nearest sound to a laugh she had ever heard from him. "Ah, little Cat-Eyes, don't you know Christians can be the cruelest of us all?" Then he was on his feet before she could even ask him how badly he was hurt. Scrambling to her own feet, she saw that the wounds on his chest and stomach were only deep scratches, made to torment not kill, but his bloody temple was badly swollen. He swayed and nearly fell.

"Lean on me!" she urged him, and he put his hand on her shoulder, struggling to gain control.

"We must get to the river—find reeds to breathe through," he directed haltingly. "They will look for us there, but if we are careful and stay underwater, they will not find us."

Taking his arm, she led him back toward the river, and it was she who found and chopped down the reeds. He lay on the bank, still dizzy, and once, he turned over on his side and was sick in the grass.

"Come!" she tugged on his hand. "The water will make you feel better." She wanted to ask where the three braves had gone and how soon they might be back, but he looked so pale and weak she feared he might pass out. The distant sound of musketfire reverberated on the still air. "Hurry!" she begged. If the cold river didn't revive him, nothing could—and where would she be with a collapsed Indian on her hands?

He stumbled after her into the water and fell face forward, submerging himself. Relief flowered in her breast when he came up, shaking water like a puppy, and took a reed from her with some measure of his old authority to show her how to breathe through it.

She must be careful to suck in only through her mouth—not her nose, and she must keep herself as far down in the water as possible lest her bright hair attract attention. They would begin swimming downstream and use the reeds at the first sign of being followed.

This would have been a good plan had she been a better swimmer, but all she had ever done was splash around and float a bit in the creek back home, and even then, Mama had been scandalized. He took the knife and tomahawk from her, and she waded out into the river after him: to where the water was up to her neck and as cold as melted snow. Then she tried paddling but could not make any headway.

Three times he had to wait for her to catch up, and finally, he gave up swimming himself and walked beside her. The current tugged and pulled at them, seeming to go one way at the top and quite another at the bottom. It was slow going, and panic assailed her at every step.

They had not gotten very far when shouts and war whoops sounded from the bank behind them. Looking back, she saw not only the three Indians she expected but a score or more of others emerging from the woods. "They're gaining on us!" she choked. "What can we do?"

For answer, the Indian grabbed her elbow and dragged her unceremoniously into a canebreak.

Here, the water was shallower and the bottom mucky; she had trouble keeping her footing as clouds of mud swirled up from the uncertain icy depths. Her teeth chattered loudly, and he cautioned her in a whisper, "You must stay still as a rabbit when the hawk is flying. Breathe slowly and deeply. Do not shake the reed and do not raise your head out of the water until I lift you up."

He scooped up a handful of mud and rubbed it into her hair, then shoved her down below the surface, the bent reed between her teeth angling upwards into the air. At first, she got no air when she sucked in on the reed, then she got a mouthful of water. It took every ounce of courage she had to keep from thrashing around hysterically. Only the knowledge that a swarm of braves were searching the riverbank for them kept her under.

Who *were* all those Indians? she wondered. Where had they come from? She swallowed, breathed in again, and discovered that if she pinched her nose shut with one hand and held the reed in the other, it worked better. Now, her biggest problem was to fight her body's natural inclination to rise to the surface.

Time passed slowly: measured by the thuds of her heart. One, two, three, four—she counted thuds until she got to sixty, then started over again, pacing her breaths. On every tenth beat, she sucked in air, held it, then slowly let it out again. Her whole body felt numb and weightless. She shivered with cold. The murky water grew colder by gradations, the top feeling almost warm now, while the bottom was cold as ice.

One, two, three—how long could she go on like this? Her lungs began to burn. She felt curiously sleepy. It would be so easy to just let go of the reed and allow the water to carry her away.

The Indian's hand on her shoulder came as a shock or rude awakening. "They have gone upriver to search. Hurry! When they discover their mistake and come back again, they may guess what we are doing."

He led her, gasping, back out into deeper water. "But I c-can't swim! And the w-water is going too fast!"

"Let the water hold you and take my hand. I will do the swimming. When you need to breathe, lift your head."

She tried to do as he instructed but terror got the

better of her. The moment she felt the bottom drop away from her feet, she panicked and began struggling. He flipped her over on her back and caught her by the neck with the crook of his arm, holding her face upward. "Be still or I shall leave you! Now is not the time to be a silly witless female!"

His scorn cut into her like a knife. She lay still then, depending on him to keep her mouth and nose out of water, and was agreeably surprised at how easily she floated. The Indian began swimming, and now that they were no longer fighting the current, they made good progress down the river. Twice more they stopped and hid in the reeds when their pursuers came too close, and when at last, the river eddied into a swampy place, he pulled her after him into the oozy muck. "They will not find us in the swamp. I doubt they will even look. Here, we shall be safe."

But his idea of safety was not hers. The deeper into the swamp they waded, waist high in weeds and water, the less safe she felt. Water snakes unwound themselves from half submerged logs and glided past them. Beetles skated across the slimy surface, and swarms of mosquitoes rose up to catch in her hair, nose, and mouth. Nothing remained of her bark covering but the knotted vines which had held it in place—and the exposed half of her body drew the fierce insects like flies to honey. She was soon slapping and itching with a feeling close to madness. A bobcat or a panther screamed and snarled in the depths of the bog. Had she been journeying into hell, it couldn't have been much worse than this. The stink of decay and lingering death was everywhere around her.

"It is not much further," the Indian told her. "We are coming to a piece of solid ground nearly surrounded by swampland. We will hide there until dark."

Until dark! Panic closed her throat. She'd be dead of snake bite before then—if the mosquitoes didn't get her first! An enormously long glistening body, patterned in dark colors, glided past her. Recoiling in terror, she all but knocked the Indian down. He gripped her arm, "Move slowly. Do not excite yourself. You are a guest in the home of *Ka-na-pa-quah*, Brother Serpent. Behave with dignity, and he will behave the same."

A dozen screams fluttered in her chest, but she managed to obey. Anyone who called a snake brother could not be disobeyed! At last, they came to solid land. Not so solid as she had hoped but at least better than oozing slime. Soft and springy, the land welcomed her bruised feet, though she noticed that her footprints filled with water and disappeared almost as soon as she looked back at them. She wanted to stop and rest, scoop mud on her skin to deter the mosquitoes, but the Indian led her on, "Not yet, Cat-Eyes. We cannot stop yet."

Ahead, the forest thickened, and a green-gray

light bathed the trees and vines which were much larger and more lush than any she'd seen before. Enormous twisting roots erupted from the ground and disappeared again, endlessly tangled together in some ancient forgotten design. Then the land became slightly more firm, and the light grew darker, as though here, in this lush forest, sunlight never penetrated.

The Indian stopped and turned to her. "Now, we are safe. You can rest and look for night shelter. I will go look for food."

Rebecca looked back over her shoulder at the way they had come. All around her the forest seemed to pulsate with some dark unseen force. Her skin rippled with goosebumps. She didn't want to stay here where darkness must fall in late afternoon and sunrise barely come at all. "Are you sure they won't come after us?"

The Indian regarded her calmly, his eyes so dark and shadowed they appeared like smudges in his deeply grooved face. "They are Shawnee, and this land is Shawnee burial ground—sacred to their people. On this land, they neither hunt nor kill. It is the land of their ancestors and they will not profane it."

It wasn't hard to imagine old ghosts walking among these great black trees. She half expected they were watching—angry that she trespassed, she who was not even Indian. She wondered where their graves were. "Is there nowhere else we can go?"

He shook his head. "I have already told you. There is no need for fear."

"Are *your* people buried here too?" she flung at him challengingly. "In the middle of a swamp?" She was furious that her fear was so obvious—and even more furious that he seemed able to read her thoughts. Just because he'd gotten them out of immediate danger, was no reason for him to think he was so smart!

Were it not for him, she would still be back at the cabin—a palace compared to the places she'd lately been sleeping! Moreover, she was exhausted, dirty, and naked again, her hair such a filthy tangle she'd probably have to cut it off to get rid of the knots. Her legs began suddenly to quiver, and to keep from falling down she sat down quickly on a log.

"I am not Shawnee: I am Miami," he said calmly. "We have our own burial grounds further west though we consider this land to be our hunting grounds." He squatted down beside her and with a sweep of his hand indicated the whole forest. "Once all this land belonged to us—what you call the Northwest Territory. We were the chosen people of *Manitou*—the Great Spirit. He gave us this land for our children and our children's children."

"Really! Is that so?" She glanced away to show her disinterest, but *was* interested despite herself.

"But then the Six Nations of the Iroquois came raiding down from the north and stole our women and children. They killed our strongest braves and fled time and again back to their own country like thieves in the night. And after them, we fought the Shawnee, the Delaware, the Hurons, and the Wyandots. We fought the Ottawa and the French and even, for a time, the English. And now, the Long Knives come, and the land is once more being taken from its rightful owners, the Miamis."

"That's a very nice piece of history," she snapped. "But you've left out the most important and recent facts! This land belongs to the United States! We won it from the British! Surely you've heard of the great war between *our* peoples: the War of Independence? If you'd supported us instead of them the land might still belong to you!"

His glance was withering, his tone sarcastic. "I know of your great war. It had nothing to do with us or our lands. We traded peacefully with the British, and we would have traded peacefully with the Long Knives. But trade was not enough. Because you defeated the British, you think to defeat us and take what is ours."

"That's not true!" she exploded. "And your people did far more than trade with the British during the war! Surely, you remember the Hair-Buyer—Governor Hamilton at Fort Detroit—for whom *your* people *gladly* provided so many of *my* people's scalps! Even now, we constantly hear stories of how the tribes and the British are still plotting against us. You chose the losing side, but it seems you cannot stand to pay the price of your misplaced loyalties!''

She stopped abruptly. Whatever was she doing, ranting and raving, provoking him over something that had happened when both of them were children and which neither of them could do anything about? There were more important things to discuss right now, and the sooner they discussed them the better!

Summoning every ounce of boldness possible, she demanded, ''I want to be taken home! I saved your life back there, and you may repay me by taking me home!''

The Indian was unabashed. He touched his bruised swollen temple. ''Is not the life of a Miami warrior worth the life of one ignorant squaw? I have already paid my debt and more—but I shall leave you here if you wish.''

What was he talking about? What did he mean? ''I do not wish to be left here—I wish to be taken home!'' Hysteria crept into her voice regardless of her efforts to stop it.

He sighed and leaned back against a tree, closing his eyes as if his head ached. ''You are a most troublesome squaw—and one who has no manners. Those Shawnee were after you or whoever lived in your cabin. If I had not gotten to you first, you would be dead or worse by now."

"Dead! You mean—"

"Yes. I saved you." He opened his eyes and looked at her. "And because I did, warned you away as they think, the Shawnee believe I am a spy—a traitor to my people."

"Why—that's ridiculous. A spy!" She had never even imagined there were such things as Indian spies. Besides, if he *was* a traitor, it was certainly not to the savages!

The Indian grunted. "Your war chief, Anthony Wayne, has many such braves spying among the tribes. These spies, some of them half-breeds, live and act like tribesmen but their hearts belong to the Long Knives."

"Then that's what you are—a half-breed!"

He stiffened. "But I am not a spy. My mother was a full-blooded Miami who lived most of her life among the Delaware. The Miamis are my people now, and I would never betray them."

He could not have surprised her more by these revelations if he'd claimed he *was* a spy, one of Anthony Wayne's Indian scouts. "But—but why *did* you take me instead of leaving me to the Shawnee? What were you doing near our cabin? And where did all those other Indians back there come from? Who were they?"

His hand came up to stop her questions. "Those who came after the first three were also Shawnee. Did you not mark their war paint and ornaments?

Both parties have been raiding all up and down the river, and their meeting place was nearby. But one of my captors did not wish to interrupt his pleasure to go and meet his tribesmen—until the other two assured him there was no way I could escape and that his pleasure would be even greater for having been delayed."

At the mention of Ring-Nose, Rebecca shuddered. "But the musketfire! Why were they firing?"

"Mayhap it was a signal," he said tiredly. "Or one of them spotted game." He turned his head and looked at her in a way that didn't seem tired at all. "As for why I was near your cabin, I came to find a man—a great hairy bear of a man who is known to shoot my people in the back when they come to trade with him. Mayhap you know him: he wears a Shawnee necklace of severed fingers, and his cabin is somewhere near yours on the river."

Will! He had come after Will! She could hardly conceal her shock but knew what he accused Will of doing must be true. There was nothing Will liked better than to "rid the country of a few more stinkin' savages." But she mustn't let on she knew him! This Indian would never take her home or let her go if he knew Will and Papa might be coming after her.

The Indian was watching her closely. "This bear of a man—you are his woman? He is the one

81

you are to marry?"

"No! Oh, no! I—I could never be the woman of a man like that!" Her cheeks burned hot as fire, but she looked him squarely in the eye, hoping to convince him of her sincerity. "A man like that will come to his own bad end! It isn't necessary for you to punish him."

"He killed my brother," the Indian snapped. "I cannot rest until I take his scalp!"

Damn Will! she cursed him inwardly. Did he think he was doing his country some kind of a favor—shooting people in the back? She wondered how many other brothers, sons, and fathers of dead savages were roaming these woods searching for him or for other men who were just like him. And how many innocent settlers would unknowingly pay the price of revenge—then seek revenge themselves?

No wonder this was a violent savage land! She hated it all the more for the part her own people had in making it what it was. Timidly, she reminded him, "You still haven't told me why you took me away with you."

He suddenly smiled, unnerving her completely. "I came to find a great bear of a man with black hair covering his face and body. Instead, I found a naked woman with soft white skin and leaf-green eyes—cat-eyes. And hair the color of fire. Knowing the Shawnee would have wasted such beauty, tortured and killed her, there was nothing to do but take her. I myself was once Christian," he added in a faintly mocking tone of voice.

"You?" She couldn't at first believe it, but then she reconsidered: missionaries of many faiths had come to the wilderness to instruct the savages. They were not so plentiful now as before or during the war, but rivers and landmarks still bore the names they'd given them—Christian names, used by white men and Indians alike. "Were you baptized then? What faith were you taught?"

He glanced down at his hands, holding them out in front of him as if remembering something. His hands trembled. Quickly, he put them down, his eyes blazing when he looked at her. "I do not wish to speak of it! What does it matter? Your God is a false God, and your missionaries are false! My people live what they believe. Their gods are the earth, the rain, the sun, and the winds. Their true God is *Gitchi-Manitou*. They revere their gods and respect them, cherishing their gifts. Can you say the same thing of *your* God—your Jesus? Do your people respect Him and live His teachings?"

She was taken back. His accusations left no room for simple explanations about the good and bad in people. And it seemed absurd to be sitting here—naked—in a Shawnee burial ground arguing religious differences with a savage! But then everything that had happened to her since first she met him had been absurd. All her defenses, her pretenses, had been stripped away and she felt a

83

hundred years older—though hardly any wiser. "I try to live His teachings," she said quietly after a moment. "Though many times I fail. Do your people never fail?"

"Never! We are Miamis—the true people."

From anyone else in any other setting, such a statement would be absurd, she thought. But spoken here, in a place held so sacred by the savages that they abandoned their hostilities on entering it, she could almost believe it. How could anyone dare speak a falsehood where the souls of the dead could hear it?

"Please. Will you take me home?" she begged.

"I cannot," he answered.

"But you know I can't get back there by myself!"

"You will die if you go back, and I will likely die with you. Have you not seen for yourself? The woods are full of Shawnee raiding parties—and Delaware too, I suspect. I have friends among the Delaware, but the Shawnee believe the worst. Were we to be found together, what better proof could there be that I am a spy and a traitor?"

"You could explain—" she began and stopped. How *could* he? She could hardly explain it herself!

"I am surprised your cabin was not discovered long before this," he grunted. "The Shawnee chieftain, Blue Jacket, himself only a half-breed, has sworn that not a single pale face in any of the river valleys shall be spared the knife."

He stood up in a single swift and graceful

movement, startling her, for she never knew what to expect of him. "When I found you, it was in my mind to take you prisoner to Buckongahelas, the Delaware. The Delawares have lost many braves in our battles against the Long Knives—but there are those who would adopt you in place of their sons if you pass the test."

Pass the test! What sort of test? But she had no time to wonder for his next words spilled over her like icy cold water.

"Now, I do not know what to do with you. The Shawnee spoke of war—a gathering of the tribes along the Miami of the Lake. Your war chief has tired of building forts and is prepared at last to move against us." He shook his head and began pacing up and down. "I have been seeking revenge too long, and though I have not yet found my brother's murderer, I must go home to my own people."

He stopped and looked down at her. "I can leave you here or take you with me! The choice I leave to you."

She jumped to her feet. "What kind of choice is that? If you leave me, I will die of starvation, or else the Shawnee will find me!"

"Then it would seem the choice has been made." His blue eyes bored into hers. "But I warn you: the journey is long and difficult. If you cannot keep up, I will leave you behind. You must act and think like a squaw. A whining sharp-tongued woman is bad luck on a journey. She draws evil spirits who plot mischief.''

"But it isn't fair to make me go with you! It isn't fair to turn me into something I'm not! I'm a *white* woman—not a squaw! You have no right—'' She suddenly realized how ridiculous and futile her arguments sounded.

The little cabin in the clearing was two days journey away—upriver or down, she wasn't even sure which. The woods were full of savages sworn to kill her if hunger and exposure didn't kill her first. A war was brewing. Even if she made it somehow to the cabin, it would be more dangerous there than ever. Papa and Will might already be dead! The only place left to flee to was Fort Harmar in Marietta, a long way downriver— where the Muskingum emptied into the Ohio!

Nothing could be less fair. She was a naked woman, alone, without weapons, and the only one who could possibly help her—this tall arrogant savage—wouldn't, for whatever his reasons.

"You!" she cried. "It's all your fault! I despise you! I hate you!" Unable to stop herself, she flew at the Indian like a woman gone mad.

Caught off guard, the impact of her body carried them both to the ground. She was eye to dazzling blue eye with him, then he rolled her over and pinned her beneath him, his lean hard body arching above hers. Screams as primitive and wild as a panther's tore from her throat as she struggled to claw his eyes out. He smacked her once, hard. Then she was weeping and pulling him down on her as if he were the last human being on earth.

What did it matter what he did with her or she with him when the whole world was upside down and crazy and would never be right or safe again? There was only his body and her body—naked, dirty, bruised, and scratched. And she was filled with such desperate longing, such want and need, that nothing else seemed to matter.

"No, you do not want *this*—" he said gently, drawing back from her.

"Yes!" she sobbed. "Yes!" She clung to him and pulled him closer.

"Hush, now, be still . . ." he murmured, but now she could feel his heart racing as fast as her own. Her need became his need, and he took her first with his hands, exploring each curve and valley with a rough gentleness that shook her to the core.

He traced her throat, the swell of her breasts, and the soft white mound of her belly. His hands moved like feathers, teasing her flesh into quivering response. She could hardly bear it! All she'd ever wanted was soft words and whispering silk and flirtation, with maybe someday in the far off rosy future a man to love and cherish her and give her children in a safe and sheltered house! But what did she care for the future now? She may not *have* a future! All that mattered now was his touch, soothing away the hurt. Gentling her wildness.

Then he took her with his lips, and his gentleness proved a myth. He left a trail of fire along her flesh wherever he kissed her, and she thrust her body against his mouth as though he might somehow consume her in the flame of his own throbbing passion.

Then he took her with his body—hard and thrusting and animal-like. She cried out once in shock, then dug her fingernails into his back—trading him pain for pain and pleasure for pleasure. For after the pain, there *was* pleasure, and the pleasure mounted, blossomed inside her, flamed like a bonfire she couldn't put out!

She quivered and shook and shuddered against him and came slowly back down to earth—drifting—gently as a leaf carried on the wind. It came as a great surprise to feel the ground solid against her back, the moss cool and damp, and a sharp stick or rough stone digging deep into her shoulder blade.

Sighing, she held him against her, warm and strong and—but no, she must not think it: loving. There was no love here. There was only animal heat and passion. The sweet rippling sensations that still flowed through her were nothing but muscle spasms that even a dog or a cat might feel!

Tears welled in her eyes, spilled over, and rolled down her cheeks into her hair. The Indian stirred against her, "Cat-Eyes," he said softly,

"Little Cat-Eyes . . ."

But she was filled with a great self-loathing. Disgust nearly choked her. "I don't even know your name!"

He stroked back her hair with his fingertips. "I am called *Kin-di-wa*, the name of the great northern bird with golden feathers, the golden eagle."

And his eyes so reminded her of that proud fierce bird, she wondered how she hadn't guessed it. She heard herself beginning to laugh, teetering on the edge of hysteria. She might have plummeted downward again into some terrible abyss out of which there was no return—but those eyes bored into her, forcing her to a silence as vast as the forest itself.

"So. Kin-di-wa," she finally whispered, "I accept your—terms. But someday I'm going home! You can have your bloody land. I don't want it! I'm going back across the mountains to Pennsylvania—to Philadelphia! I will live my own life on my own terms and no one—*no one*—will interfere in my life again!"

Kin-di-wa, looking down at her, shook his head sadly. "It is all I have ever wanted—for your people to go back across the mountains—but it is too late now for that. You will never go back."

She didn't know whether he meant her or her people. "I promise you I shall!"

His eyes grew suddenly hard and cold—the

coldest blue she had ever seen. "No, you will not. For you will find that my land is beautiful, worth fighting for, worth dying for. It has always been so—the land will claim you. In time, you will feel as I do. In time, you will love this land." His eyes searched hers in the green-gray light. "It may be, if you are worthy, we will allow you to become one of us."

There it was again—the talk of tests and worthiness. "And if I am not worthy?"

"It will not matter; you will be dead."

She looked away from him, past his shoulder, and saw the silhouette of a white feather. One was still caught in his long black hair. And something cold and hard and sharp—his necklace of animal teeth—was digging into the tender flesh of her breasts.

"I am already dead," she whispered.

"No, Little Cat-Eyes, you are just coming alive."

His lips sought hers again, and his hands roved over her gently, persuasively. No—not again! she cried to herself, but her body would not obey. Her body was a willful pleasure-loving creature that wanted the gentle stroking, the caressing, to go on and on, even while a part of her kept insisting that she was no Indian woman—no squaw! She belonged to no one but herself! She would not be ruled by a savage nor possessed by a savage land!

But her body denied everything she told it. She opened to him like a flower, a luscious peachpetaled rose. One by one, the petals unfolded, and her resistance slipped away. He is all I will ever want, she exalted, all I will ever need!

Then there came to her ears a sudden crunching sound and a sharp click! And before she could even open her eyes to confirm her ears, the tensing of Kin-di-wa's muscles told her they were not alone.

Four

"Well, well, well—what in thunderation do we have here?" boomed a heavy male voice that was oddly familiar. "Git up, you ruttin' savage!"

Kin-di-wa's body leapt upwards and sideways, but in that same moment, there was a deafening roar, and an explosion of flame seared the air right above her. Her head thundered, her eyes stung, and the very earth seemed to rock and shake. She could see nothing but whirling fireballs and pin-pricks of light, smell nothing but smoke and ash.

Then the voice boomed again. "By God in heaven, a white woman—Becky!"

A great black bear of a man stood silhouetted against the powder haze, and even as she wheezed and coughed and rubbed her eyes, she could see his expression of shock. "Will!" she choked. "What are you doing here?"

But Will had no time to answer. "Son of a bitch!

He's gittin' away!" Swinging the musket around, he hurriedly began reloading, but couldn't ram powder and patched ball down the smoking muzzle fast enough. "Damn skittery bastard," he swore, "moves like lightnin'! But I got 'im! I know I did! Hell, I was too close not to!"

Kin-di-wa! He got Kin-di-wa! She tried to sit up, but the throbbing in her head and the dizziness made the forest spin around her. Then she remembered suddenly that where Will was, Papa should be. "Will! Where's Papa? Isn't Papa with you?"

Will seemed not to hear her. He bent over and thumbed a leaf poking out from the underbrush. "Hunh, no blood—damn his hide. But if I didn't git 'im solid, his backside sure must be burnin'!" The branch he'd finished examining flipped back with an angry snap. "If I hadna been so shocked t' see it wuz you, Becky, I'd 've got another crack at 'im. Does he got a shootin' piece—a musket or a long gun—hidden away somewheres?"

"No—no, only a tomahawk and a knife. Will, where's Papa?"

"Now, Becky . . ." He was suddenly solicitous and helped her to sit up, his meaty hand lingering over-long on her bare shoulders. "Jeezus, where's yur dress? Ain't you got nothin' to cover yurself with? This sure is a damn surprise findin' ya' like this."

Shrugging off his hand, she willed the earth to stop shaking. Her tongue felt raw and thick, as if it

94

didn't belong to her, and she could barely swallow. Maybe he hadn't understood her question about Pa after all. She tried again. "Please! Tell me where Papa is!"

"We—uh, we met up with some trouble, Becky. Seems our salt lick was also th' meetin' place for a bunch of Shawnee."

"Shawnee!" It could only be the same Shawnee who'd been after her and Kin-di-wa! "But—but you got away! You're here where it's safe! So where is my father?"

The big grizzly head jerked. The little pig-eyes glittered defensively. "How did *you* know it was safe here? This here is Shawnee burial ground— but ain't too many know about it but a few hunters and trappers like m'self. Even yur Pa don't know it—but if he has any smarts he'll keep a-comin' on through the swamp til he finds it."

"The swamp? You left him in the swamp?"

"Hell, don't look at me like that! We got separated! What else wuz I sposed t' do?"

A cold hard knot of anger formed itself in her stomach. All at once, she ceased to feel dizzy. "Was it you the Shawnee were firing at? I heard musketfire earlier."

His eyes avoided hers. "They did take a shot or two at us down by the salt lick."

"Papa! Was he hit? Is that why he isn't with you?"

"Now, Becky—don't go excitin' yurself. Them Shawnee couldn't hit a barn door at the distance we wuz away from 'em. They ain't such crack shots anyhow. All we got to do is set here an' wait, an' I spect yur Pa'll be along shortly.''

"You don't *know* what happened to him, do you?'' she scrambled to her knees. "You ran away and left him!''

His eyes narrowed. He gripped her arm. "Watch what yur sayin' there, Miz Becky. I ain't no coward! But y' can't always keep an eye out fer the other feller when y' git into a scrap. 'Sides, seems t' me, y' got a mite of explainin' t' do yurself!''

His glance fell on her naked body. It was a bold and knowing glance, and he ran his tongue over his thick lips as though he were suddenly hungry. "How's come you weren't a fightin' him? How's come you were just a-layin' there like you liked what he was doin' t' ya?''

Feeling the heat of his gaze, she was newly ashamed of her nakedness. In all the time she'd been naked before Kin-di-wa, he'd never once looked at her like that—as though she were a piece of meat waiting to be devoured. "Don't think I came away with—with that Indian willingly! I fought him as best I could!''

She hated the way she sounded so defensive, but she certainly didn't intend to tell him *everything* that had happened! "I never even saw him come up on me back at the cabin. I was bathing in the oaken barrel when suddenly, he reached down and grabbed me and carried me away! That's why I have no clothes,'' she finished lamely, "though I did try to make a covering for myself out of some bark. But I lost it in the swamp, getting away from the Shawnee.''

She scanned the trees around them, looking for that type of tree with the particularly shaggy bark. If she could find one, she'd strip off some bark and make another covering, but most of the trees looked smooth-barked, as if—irrationally—they had something to gain by thwarting her.

Will leaned toward her, chewing his lower lip. His familiar rank odor assaulted her like skunk fumes. "Why was you runnin' from the Shawnee?" he leered. "Did he want to keep you fer hisself?"

"No! No—that is, he's not a Shawnee, he's—he's something else!" And she knew immediately, she'd said too much. Will was squinting now, studying her, as he picked at his bristling beard. "An' jus' how do *you* know what he is or what he ain't—a little greenhorn like you?"

"Why—his war paint, of course! It was different from theirs. You needn't think me such a greenhorn, Will! I'm watching and learning every minute! Besides, the Shawnee would have found us the day before yesterday except we hid from them. Why would he have done that if he's a Shawnee himself?"

"I kin think of plenty o' reasons," Will leered again, then he looked furtively around. "But if he ain't Shawnee, he mightn't give a hoot that this is Shawnee burial ground. He might double back on us and try t' take ya back again. We best git movin' b'fore it gits dark.''

"No!" she cried. "What about Papa? You said we should sit here and wait—that maybe he'd find us!"

"Yur Pa can take care of hisself. If worst comes t' worst, he kin find his own way back t' th' cabin— unless," he eyed her speculatively, "you'd rather wait fer that red devil t' come back an' finish what he started."

"I just think we should wait," she said stiffly. "Papa could be hurt and not able to make it back by himself."

"I already done said—it ain't likely he's shot up. The only other reason he couldn't make it would be if the Shawnee caught up with him. And if they did, you an' me ain't never gonna see him again."

"I'd rather wait!" she insisted.

But Will's big hairy hand suddenly shot out and grabbed her breast. "Seems you is fergittin' somethin', miz high an' mighty Becky," he squeezed hard, bringing tears to her eyes. "Out here, all yur book learnin' an' yur sharp tongue don't amount to a hill o' beans. Out here, you is fair game fer any man that wants ya. An' I still wants ya—even if yur used goods, spoilt by some thievin' redskin."

"Stop it!" she gasped, trying to pry his hand away. "You're hurting me, Will!"

He chuckled into his beard and squeezed harder. "I ain't hurt ya half as much as I'm gonna. I'll learn you some manners yet, if it's th' last thing I ever do!"

Sparks danced before her eyes. The pain in her breast was terrible. "All right! I'll go with you!"

At that, he loosened his grip with one last nasty twist. Cradling her throbbing breast, she got to her feet. Once again, she had no choice but to do as she was bid. First, it was Kin-di-wa, and now, it was Will. Would she ever again be allowed to make a decision on her own—to choose where she would go, what she would do, and when she would do it? Even Papa had thought to rule her—to plan her present and future! But no more! She was through with being a weak and helpless woman. She'd get away from Will and find Papa if it was the last thing *she* ever did!

Darkness was closing in fast, her third night in the forest, but Will shoved her ahead of him through the great brooding trees with a vengeance. "I seed a big boulder back here aways—near t' the swamp yur Pa an' me come through. And whut looked like a cave half way up the side of it. If'n we kin find it, we'll be safe fer the night. Ain't no injun' gonna attack us there—Shawnee or no. There's graves all around an' bundles of bones up high in the trees."

"We're not going to sleep *there*, are we?" Only Will would consider lying down right beside dead men, she thought—or right under them.

"Better a bunch of dead injuns than one live one bent on killin' us," Will grunted.

99

Ah, but he would not kill me, she thought with some triumph. Worry knifed through her. Had Kin-di-wa truly been hit? Was he lying somewhere right near them, bleeding away his life—but stoic as ever? Would she ever see him again? And then she deliberately blocked him out of her mind. The only thing that mattered now was to save Papa!

They found the spot Will was looking for just in time. The great towering boulder and stone-covered mounds were barely visible in the failing light and heavy mist which coiled snakelike between the graves and across the hard rocky ground. A spring of some sort bubbled up out of the stones and made an eerie sound as it gurgled and hissed nearby, emiting a strange sulfurous odor and a cloud of steam.

Will went over to it, knelt down on one knee, and scooped up a palmful. "Phew! It stinks somethin' awful. Best t' not drink the stuff," he muttered. "It's unnatural warm. With all this decay around, it's probably pizened."

And she could smell it now—not just the sulfurous pool, but the stench of death and rot. The very air had a heavy quality, cloying and evil. She stared hard into the scattered, mist-shrouded trees but couldn't see any bundles of bones and was glad of it. And then she saw the skull, facing her at eye level.

"Will!" she screamed. "Look there!"

Stones went plinking into the pool as he scrambled up. "Tarnation, Becky, shut yur trap!

Y' want that devil t' hear us?"

He meant Kin-di-wa, of course, but for a moment, she thought he meant the grinning, gleaming horror with the broken teeth and pitted eye-sockets. All the waning light in the clearing seemed concentrated on the skull. "Do you see it?" she panted.

Will came striding over to her and peered into the blackness where she pointed. She heard his own sharp intake of breath, then he muttered, "Hell—ain't nothin' but a skull stuck on a post. I 'member seein' it b'fore when I come through here. See, there's feathers and charms and shells hangin' from the same post."

She did indeed see them now, but a sour taste was in her mouth, as if she'd tried to swallow vinegar and couldn't quite manage it. "It's meant to frighten us away, Will. I don't think we should stay here. Please—let's try to find a hollow log or a tree trunk. We'd be much safer there."

Will suddenly slipped his arms around her. "Feelin' scared, are ya?" His breath was hot on her shoulder. "Old Will'll take care of ya. That big rock ain't got a cave like I thought, but there's a nice long ledge we kin stretch ourselves out on sweet as ya please." His hands slipped down to cup her breasts. "Iffen ya be real nice t' me, I got a piece of jerky y' kin gnaw on. I bet it'll taste real good— when was th' last time y' et?"

"I'm not hungry! And get your hands off me!" She twisted away from him, thinking he must be mad to try and seduce her in a place like this.

But Will quickly spun her around, and grabbing her in a bear hug, pinioned her arms to her body. "Oh no, y' don't! Y'ain't gittin' away from me here. Y' spread yerself peaceful enuff for some damn redskin, an' b'fore this night's over, yer gonna do th' same fer me!"

Before she could protest, his thick lips came down over her open mouth. She struggled against him, gagging, as he thrust his tongue half way down her throat. The rude pushing and probing with that great wet organ made her think that soon he would be pushing and probing with another great organ. Was it also furred? she wondered half-hysterically. Wet and throbbing and *furred?* For that's what his tongue felt like, and she wondered if he could taste the bile rising up in her throat.

Then he stopped trying to kiss her, picked her up and threw her over his shoulder. "It's right over here—a nice comfy old ledge. T'night, little miss Becky, yur gonna find out what a real man is like."

She beat on his back, helpless as she'd been when Kin-di-wa carried her off with him. And she was even more angry, for Will was a white man who should have known better. "Don't do this, Will! It's wrong! When we get back home again, I'll—I'll—Papa will never forgive you!"

"Yur Pa ain't here t' pertect ya this time, miz high an' mighty Becky! An' even if he were, I'd tell 'im I'm doin' 'im a favor takin' a spoilt piece of goods offen his hands.''

"Oh, you're despicable! Loathsome! Let me go! Let me go!"

Will swung her off him then, onto a broad flat rock that jutted up against the smooth side of the boulder. It wasn't a cave, but the effect was the same, for a higher ledge overhung it. She felt something crunch beneath her and cut into her skin. There must be shells or pebbles on the ledge—remnants of some heathen ritual? Her fingers went questing for something she could use against him.

"Will," she begged, "I'll do anything you ask— even marry you when we get back home—but please don't take me like this in such an awful pagan place!"

He climbed up on the ledge and stood over her, black against black. By the sound of his movements in the pitch darkness he was tearing off his buckskins. "Quit yer squallin', Becky. I done told ya once, y'already b'long t' me. Ain't no sense t' fight it. Y' didn't fight that savage I found on top of ya!"

Her fingers scrabbled on the rock—searching— searching—and finding nothing. Then he fell on top of her, growling deep in his chest.

"No! I won't *let* you!" she cried, but her struggles only seemed to inflame him further. "Animal! *Animal!*" she screamed over and over, pummeling his shoulders, until he suddenly reared back and swatted her cheek with a blow that made her ears start ringing.

"I ain't no animal!" he roared. "I'm a man—go on, say it! Will Simpkin, you're a man!"

"Animal! You're an animal! A stinking abomination! You're worse than an animal—you're—you're—"

He swatted her face another ringing blow. But it didn't stop her, for the whole core of her being was bent on defying him—on denying what was happening to her. "You'll never be a man, Will Simpkin! You'll never make a woman desire the touch and the feel of you! All you'll ever be is a grunting, stinking animal—taking what you want!"

His hands found her breasts and twisted them cruelly, deliberately. She could not claw his hands away however much she tried. "I'll make ya call me a man!" he rasped. "I'll make ya! Y' think yur so high an' mighty! Y' dare t' go name-callin' the man who's gonna be yur own husband!"

"You'll never be my husband!" she gasped against the pain.

"You wait 'n see, little spit-fire! Y' belong t' me—only me! An' I'll kill any man that says ya don't!"

What happened after that, she would never forget, not even if she somehow survived the night and grew to be an old woman. It was like a nightmare—and yet at the same time so shockingly real it scorched her soul. After this night, she learned what it was to hate, to be consumed with hatred. He took away her dignity, her self-respect, and her womanhood—and in its place, left nothing but hate, seething hatred.

She clawed at his face, his cheeks, his eyes until he grabbed both her hands in his one huge paw and drew them back over her head, pinning them down to the rock. Then he kneed her legs apart and knelt between them, using his other hand to manipulate and explore her body. But whereas she'd been explored and manipulated once this day already, and she'd come to love and revel in it, this exploration by comparison was that much more bitter and painful. The Indian had teased and stimulated the tender flesh of her breasts, making her body respond almost against her will. The white man pinched and twisted them until she wept with pain.

The Indian stroked her skin and probed her hidden places with such a sure and knowing gentleness that the unexpected pleasure took her breath away. The white man alternately gouged and prodded—making her body quiver like a strung bow with painful anticipation. She was terrified at all the ways he could hurt her—and hurt her, he did.

When he tired of using his hand and fingers, he used his teeth instead. When he tired of his mouth and teeth, he used his great swollen organ. He didn't merely enter her, he rent her—and crushed her besides. The dead fingers of his necklace played about her face and neck as he rocked back and forth on top of her, grinding her into the rock the way a mill stone grinds flour. And by the time he stopped grinding and lay spent upon her, she felt herself to be half-dead—having long since lost the strength to struggle.

But he was not finished—far from it. He rose up on his knees again, pulled up her limp body and turned her over. "Kneel up," he commanded thickly, his hands once again reaching around her to tug and pull at her battered breasts. "Y' call me animal—I'll take ya like an animal."

And she had no inkling of his meaning, until he bent her over and spread her buttocks—and thrust into her with a lustful grunt. She knew then, in pain and shock and terror, that he *was* truly a man—not an animal. For no animal she knew would have done as he was doing.

He would not withdraw himself until she sobbed in agony. "Yes—yes! You are a man, Will Simpkin!" Then she fainted. And when at last she awoke again, he was stretched out sleeping beside her on the ledge, an arm and a leg thrown heavily across her as if he'd proven his ownership to the grinning skull who watched them.

It was the skull, shining in the moonlight, that gave her the idea. The brilliant sphere of a full moon was shining down directly on the impaled skull, the hissing pool, and the mist snaking over the graves. So many graves, she couldn't count them, but she could see them clearly now. Their stones gleamed silvery white, and some of them were marked with wooden stakes from which dangled the worn remnants of ceremonial feathers, shell necklaces, beads, and painted gourds.

"Will," she moaned softly, "Will, you've got to help me."

"What? What is it?" he stirred beside her, his great hairy arm knocking pebbles and broken shells off the ledge with a clatter.

"Will—I need water!" she quavered. "You've hurt me—torn me apart inside. I need water—and—and moss or something soft to stop the bleeding. Please, Will, you've got to help me or I'll die!"

"Hunh? But there ain't no water! Only that pizened pool." He got up on one elbow and leaned over her—took his leg off her body.

She lay there in a ball and moaned, feeling every bit as awful as she pretended. And there was something warm and sticky on her thighs, something oozing out from between her legs. "I don't care if it's poisoned or not—you've got to get me some! And some moss from the forest! Don't you see what you've done? I'm bleeding to death inside!"

"Aw, come on," he grunted. "I didn't hurt ya all that bad!"

But there was doubt in his voice, and hearing it, she began moaning even louder. "You were too big for me, Will! You've torn something vital! Oh, lord, the pain—I can't stand it! Water—please, Will—get me some water!"

It was enough to make him clamber over her and

107

off the ledge. "Hell, I'll git ya some water! But ya can't do more'en taste it, ya hear? An' wash yurself off with it. Ain't no tellin' whut it'll do t' ya!"

He turned his back on her—that great broad back that was covered with crinkly curling black hair. And the desire to wreak revenge on him gave her the strength she needed. She pulled herself up, all the while keeping an eye on him as he strode over to the pool.

"There's gourds over there on the graves, Will. You could scoop up the water in a gourd."

"Save yur strength, damn it! Lie still an' save yur strength. We gotta git outta here in th' mornin'!" Will stomped over to one of the graves and yanked off a small gourd affixed to a stake. "Too small t' be much good," he grumbled, but took it anyway to the pool.

While he was thus occupied, getting the gourd, she got down from the ledge. Her insides felt ready to drop out. Good lord, she thought, I am bleeding! The warm gush of liquid down her thighs could only be blood. He *had* injured her some way, but the thought strengthened rather than weakened her. Indeed, she felt curiously detached from her body, as though it were no longer a part of her. Unsteadily, she walked toward the skull. By this time, he was bending over, then kneeling down beside the pool.

The skull was heavier than she expected, not easy to remove. Its inside cavity was packed with hardened clay, a piece of which broke and crumbled as she wrenched the skull off the stake. But she was growing stronger now with each measured breath. Her body knew exactly what had to be done and did not flinch from its duty—no matter how much it hurt just to put one foot in front of the other. Holding the skull in front of her, she moved quietly back to Will. He was dipping up water—filling the gourd to the brim—and so intent on not spilling it that he never once glanced her way. She drew close to him, holding the skull up high as though it were a trophy.

"Becky! What in hell are y' doin'?" Still kneeling, he looked up at her in surprise, and she brought the skull crashing down into his face.

With a loud cry, he lost his balance and tumbled sideways into the pool. She didn't wait to see what happened next. Her legs began pumping of their own accord. Her feet ignored the sharp stones and pebbles and carried her away toward the shelter of the forest. Mindlessly running, she hardly even saw the stone-laden graves she darted around or the blanketed bundle on a wooden platform high up in the branches of a tree.

She heard someone gasping and didn't know it was herself. Thinking it might somehow be Will coming after her, she only ran the faster. But then, after she'd finally stumbled and fallen and dragged herself into a thorny thicket, she heard his howl of outrage, "Becky! Becky! Come back—damn you!"

A string of curses followed. The words bounced off the trees and reverberated through the forest.

"Y'll be sorry y' done this t' me, Becky! Y'll be sorry y' run away from me! By God in heaven, I'll kill y' fur this!"

What a pity she hadn't killed *him*, she thought. Crawling out of the thicket, she ran on through the endless forest. On and on and on—dodging trees, stumbling and falling, getting up again and going on. She didn't stop—couldn't stop. If she allowed herself to drop she'd never get up again. Long after his curses no longer carried to her ears, she kept running, until it seemed that the blackness of the night was running with her. It was part of her. She melted into it, was swallowed up, and no longer heard or saw anything.

Blackness was a warm blanket, a soft coverlet, shielding her from pain. Then it was a phantom river, smooth and flowing, and she swam through it effortlessly as she'd never been able to swim in water. She felt so peaceful—so safe and cozy! But then her eyes began to sting. The blackness became a cloud drifting away from her, floating out of her reach. No! she cried, don't go yet! But the blackness receded, and pain roared into her consciousness. Every muscle shrieked its discomfort. Her bones felt sharp as knives. A rustling sound beat on her eardrums, and a warm breath blew in her face.

She opened her eyes to another pair of eyes—large, round, limpid ones. A wet black nose touched her shoulder as strong white teeth tugged at the leaves of a plant sticking out from under her. She moved her elbow, and the creature stiffened in alarm. It's long ears flickered. They were white inside, edged with the same reddish brown as it's elongated face. The brown eyes blinked. Then the creature was gone, leaping away nimbly on tiny delicate hooves.

Rebecca moaned as she tried to sit up. Never had she felt so terrible—nor so hungry and thirsty and weak. She looked around. The early morning sun gilded the treetops, and a cool breeze shook the leaves. Squirrels chittered, turkeys gobbled, and birds called in the trees. Ahead of her, not far distant, the swamp steamed in a misty green haze.

Water. The nearest water was the swamp. Slimy and fetid it might be, but she hadn't the strength to go searching for better. Slipping and sliding on the spongy ground, she made her way down to it and waded in. It felt cool and healing. Ignoring the brackish taste, she drank deeply, then washed the caked blood from her body, noting with relief that she'd stopped bleeding. Even the mucky bottom felt good as she squished mud through her toes. Cattails abounded for the taking. She waded in among them—keeping a sharp lookout for snakes and battling at the mosquitoes disturbed by her passing. Then she heard a strange noise.

It seemed to be coming from further in among the reeds. Past the cattails, the end of a log protruded from behind a clump of densely growing reeds. The noise came again—a low groan of sheer misery. Her heart began thumping. It would be too incredible to be what she hoped it was, yet she had a flash of premonition that sent her crashing forward toward the sound. "Papa! Is it—is it you?"

It was. Draped over the log—so weak he couldn't answer—lay the collapsed figure of her father. His last remaining strength seemed to give out as she reached him. The bony knuckles slipped from the log, the log rolled over, and she had all she could do to keep his head out of water as he slid downward beneath it. With an arm under each of his armpits, she managed to hold him up till the log cleared them and floated away. His head lolled to the right, and she saw that one half of his face—the left half—had the aspect of raw bloody meat. His ear on that side was missing; only a jagged flap of flesh remained.

"Oh, Papa! What have they done to you?" she sobbed, but he was too far gone to answer. She half-dragged, half-floated him back to the bank. It took several harrowing minutes to get him up on solid ground. Only the fact that she refused to admit defeat gave her the strength to manage it. At last, he was stretched out on his back and she sat gasping beside him. Then she leaned over him, trying to discover the full extent of his injuries.

His buckskins were wet, torn, and dirty, but a quick exploration of his limbs and body with her fingertips revealed no broken bones or gunshot wounds. Only his head had been injured—but what a terrible injury it was! Aside from the missing ear and torn flesh, the line of his jaw was uneven and felt almost mushy to her touch, as did the bones on that side of his skull.

She smoothed back the wispy remnants of his reddish-colored hair—choking back sobs. His skin was like putty, clammy and gray. What could she do for him? How could she help him? She had nothing from which to fashion a bandage, nothing to ease his pain. He moaned through quivering lips, his eyes fluttering open.

"Papa! Can you hear me? It's me, Becky!" She lifted his head gently and cradled it in her arms.

A frown passed over his ruined face. His eyes tried to focus. "Becky?"

"Yes, Papa! I'm here with you. I got you out of the swamp!"

"Swamp?" His lips struggled to form the words. "Where's Mama? Have 'ee seen Mama?"

Mama! Her breath seared her throat. Where did he think he was? "Papa," she said softly, "you were with Will. Remember Will? You went with him to the salt lick."

"Will," he repeated, then more sharply, "Becky! 'Ee must tell Becky! She mustn't marry that damn scoundrel!"

"Yes, Papa, I know. I know all about him, and I promise you, I'll never marry him!"

"Tell Becky t' go—t' go back to Pennsylvania, to her Aunt's in—in Philadelphia!" His breath rattled with each word. "Becky—my little Becky, she deserves—somethin' better."

"Oh, Papa!" she wept. "Don't talk anymore. You must save your strength!"

But he spoke once more, with great effort, "Tell Becky—tell Becky—her Papa—loves her."

His breath stopped. His eyes stared. She knew he was gone. She sat and rocked him, awash with agony. Papa, oh Papa! Oh, yes, she had always loved him! But she had looked down on him too. He couldn't read, he couldn't cipher, he couldn't even write his own name! And she, who could do all those things, had wanted someone better for herself than he was. Bitterness and shame choked her.

She wondered if she had ever really bothered to know him. What had he wanted from life—but to be a pioneer in the wilderness? Papa had longed for one thing, and Mama had longed for another! Both had been disappointed. And now, both of them were gone. If only she had loved them more, appreciated them more, tried to understand them!

Bits and pieces of memory suddenly came back to her. Mama and Papa in bed together, laughing and sharing secrets. How she'd loved to waken and hear them in the dead of night! Papa taking out his kilt from the big chest of cedar, putting it on, and drawing a shriek of laughter from Mama for his bony knees! And the three of them coming in from the orchard with gunny sacks of fruit at harvest, or sitting down to shuck corn, or sharing a cool tankard of buttermilk.

And it came to her like a stab of lightning: despite their differences, Mama and Papa had been truly happy! She'd grown up to the sound of their shared laughter, their grumbles when the crop failed or the calf died, and their mourning when first a baby brother and later a sister had been stillborn. She'd been nourished and fed on their love. What did it matter really, that what they thought they wanted neither of them had ever had? The only thing that seemed to matter now was that once they had loved each other—and once, they had loved her.

She sat for a long time, rocking Papa and grieving. A raccoon crept past her down to the water. Waterfowl rose up from the swamp in a blaze of wings and feathers. Bees hummed in the dappled sunshine, and butterflies fluttered by. But she saw none of it. Now, I am alone, she thought, now I am completely alone.

But then a voice said softly, "Let him go, Cat-Eyes. The man is dead. You must let him go."

And looking up she saw Kin-di-wa.

Five

His lips were thin and drawn, his color less than healthy. Powder burns blackened the flesh of his shoulder, and probably also his back which she couldn't see, but it was truly Kin-di-wa. Tall and muscled and standing straight—unconquerable as an oak tree. "Let him go," Kin-di-wa repeated. "Let him go, and I will bury him."

"I cannot believe he is really dead," Rebecca whispered. "He was my father, and now, he is dead."

"Death comes to all of us," Kin-di-wa said. "Our last great adventure. You must not grieve too much: mayhap he has gone to a better place."

Doubtfully, she unwound her arms from around Papa's body. "Do you think it is really true? Do you think there is really a heaven or hell—or someplace else besides this one?"

"Your people and mine believe it. It is perhaps the one thing upon which they both agree—so who are we to question it?"

She seized the comfort his words offered. "I should like to think of him in a happier place—a place where there is no pain or ugliness. No deceit or treachery." She thought of Will who had so betrayed Papa's friendship. "But why do we have to die to find such a place?"

Kin-di-wa knelt down in front of her and gently closed her father's eyes with his fingertips. "I do not know, little Cat-Eyes. It is a question that has no answer. Come now, we will bury him, and then we must be on our way. The war drums have been sounding since sunrise. I must get back to my people."

"War drums?" And then she heard them. Slow and muffled and urgent. The sound emanated from the ground beneath her—more of a pulse than distinct separate thuds—as though the heart of the earth were beating. "But what do they mean?"

"They mean war, and every warrior who hears them will return now to his own people. From tribe to tribe, from village to village—across the whole of the Northwest Territory—the drums call everyone home. For a while, there will be no more raids along the rivers, no missions of revenge. Each tribe will make ready for war. Disputes among us will be forgotten. Enemies will become as brothers, and I shall probably fight beside the very Shawnee who tried to kill me."

This information made her shiver, and she found she had much to think about as she helped Kin-di-wa prepare a grave for her father. He scooped out a shallow hole in the spongy ground while she collected stones to weigh down the earth so no scavengers could disturb Papa's body. To find the stones, she had to go away from the swamp and search through the forest. Mindful of Will, she took care to move cautiously—quietly as a deer.

She came back with the last armload, dreading what was to come—this crude simple burial without even a plain wooden box—and found Kin-di-wa standing guard over the fresh mound which was already layered over with branches, then heaped high with stones. He held out Papa's buckskin shirt. "I have scrubbed it with sand and brushed it down with moss. It is a fine shirt. Put it on. He has less need of it now than you."

Setting down the stones, she took the shirt with trembling fingers and slipped it on over her head. It was indeed a fine shirt; she'd cut and sewn it herself, giving it a wide fringe on the bottom and at the ends of both sleeves. The mere feel of it, the pungent smell—damp leather and some kind of crushed herbs he'd rubbed against it—comforted and soothed her. Relief and gratefulness welled up

119

in her that Kin-di-wa had spared her the sight of mud splattering across Papa's face, of earth piling up on his naked chest. Papa's shirt brought back to mind the man he'd been, not the stiffening body he was now.

"We must say some words over my father. But—I can't seem to think of any."

"Then I will say them."

She went to stand beside the tall fierce-looking Indian, deeply shamed by her lapse of memory. Try as she might to think of one, no prayer, no psalm she'd ever memorized came to mind. She could not even think of the words to the Our Father. She hoped Papa wouldn't object to having his burial service conducted by a heathen savage.

"Great Spirit," Kin-di-wa began. He stopped, then began again, this time softly and more deliberately. "The Lord is my Chieftain; I shall not want. In green meadows he gives me rest. Beside still waters he leads me; he refreshes my soul. He guides me in right paths for his name's sake. Even though I walk in the valley of darkness I fear no evil; for he is at my side with his bow and his lance that give me courage."

Kin-di-wa paused and made a sign over the grave: one slash straight down and one across it—the Christian sign of the cross. "He spreads the ground before me in the sight of my enemies; he anoints my head with sweet water; my cup overflows. Only goodness and kindness follow me all the days of my life; and I shall dwell in the lodge of my Chieftain forever . . . Amen.''

Rebecca could not speak. The sound of war drums, louder now than before, filled the silence. She hugged herself, fighting back tears, and finally managed to push a question past the lump in her throat. ''Where did you learn that, Kin-di-wa? It is our 23rd Psalm.''

''It is the prayer that was said over the graves of my mother and ninety-three others who were herded into their little mission church and massacred by the Long Knives. I learned it at my mother's knee—after she had abandoned her Indian ways and tried to live as did the people of her husband. Her husband, my father—a *courrier du bois* or woods runner as he was called— deserted her before I was born, but she always believed he would come back, especially if she took up the ways of his people.''

''*Did* he ever come back?''

''Never. And the place where she died, waiting for him, is called *Gnadenhutten.* My brother and I ran away from it and found our true people after her death.'' He paused and turned a blue-eyed gaze on her that shook her to the depths of her soul. Such agony! Such pain! The equal to her own.

Then the shutters came down in his eyes again, and his gaze was once more distant and detached.

"I have not forgotten those words—nor have I forgotten that it was Long Knives, soldiers of the very people whose ways she had adopted, who slit her throat for nothing more than being Indian."

"Oh!" she gasped in strangled sympathy. It seemed incredible that white men could have done such a thing, but now she remembered having heard the tale once before in her youth. It had happened at a Moravian mission on the Tuscarawas River, and afterwards, the soldiers had claimed it was all a mistake.

What could she say to him in the face of something so awful? She wanted desperately to offer him the same comfort he had offered her—in the form of Papa's shirt and the gift of a prayer in her own tongue. But his wound was so old, so deep, it frightened her. She was only just beginning to understand how grief and outrage might twist one's life, one's whole being. Last night, and now, this morning, had taught her lessons she too would never forget. "I'm sorry, Kin-di-wa," she finally murmured, "for you and for myself. It is a terrible world we live in."

"To be sorry avails one nothing," he snapped. "To be stronger and wiser than one's enemies is all that counts."

Yes, she thought, that is all that counts. If she had killed Will the first time he laid hands on her, none of this would have happened. Not Papa's trip with him to the salt lick. Not what he'd done to her last night. Not his leaving Papa in the swamp to die. If only she had been stronger!

"Kin-di-wa, the man who found us and tried to kill you is the man who killed your brother. He came here with my father. Last night, he—he—" It was another thing too awful to discuss. "I ran away from him. He must still be somewhere nearby."

Kin-di-wa stiffened. His eyes burned like live coals. "So it is true then. After he wounded me, I ran until I fell, and then I dreamed that it was he. In my dream, I saw his necklace, and when I awoke, I thought mayhap I had looked back and truly seen his necklace, not merely dreamed it. But a great weakness had come over me, and I was unable to get up and go after him—and when I finally did go, I could not find him. Nor you." His glance impaled her. "Why did you not stay with him? He is one of your own people."

"I told you once, and I spoke the truth. I could never be the woman of a man like that! He—he left my father to die in the swamp!"

Kin-di-wa studied her intently. "I do not think that is the only reason, Cat-Eyes, though it is reason enough. What was it he did to you last night that so destroyed your feeling for him? Once, you would have had me believe that you never even knew him. Once, you lied to protect him. Why do you wish me to find and kill him now?''

"Isn't that what you're going to do? Find him and kill him?" she demanded. "He means nothing to me—he never did! And he deserves to die for killing your brother and deserting my father! What other reasons do you need?" Her hand accidently brushed his shoulder, causing him to jerk away involuntarily. Instantly, she was ashamed. "I'm sorry! I—I forgot you were hurt."

She saw now how blistered and raw his flesh was, both his shoulder and part of his back. Will's musket blast must have grazed him and all but knocked him unconscious. Remembering his head wound from the day before, she could only cringe at her own selfishness. His strength was something she had begun to take for granted. "Of course, you cannot go after him until your injuries heal."

He grunted scornfully. "They are only powder burns. They will heal soon enough. But tell me truly—what happened between you and this man?"

The look on his face startled her. It was worse than the look he'd borne when he spoke about his mother, for now his anger seemed fresh—almost as if it were directed at her. "He—he—did nothing! I've already told you! It's for my father's sake I want him dead!"

"You lie again, Cat-Eyes." His tone lashed her. "Do all white women speak with a false tongue? Answer me truly!"

Now, anger boiled up in her. What right had he to question her! How dare he keep insulting her race! "All right!" she fairly screamed at him. "I'll tell you what he did! He did what you and all men do whenever they get the chance! He raped and degraded me! He took me like an animal! He—he—" She *couldn't* say more. A single sob burst from her throat and hung tremulously in the air between them.

"Say no more, little Cat-Eyes," his voice was unexpectedly gentle. "You have said enough."

"No!" she cried. "I have not said the whole of it! If ever a man touches me again, I will kill him! I swear it! Do you hear me? On my father's memory, I swear it!" She backed away from him though he made no move to touch her.

"And would you kill a man who meant you no harm, a man who touched you with love?" he asked softly.

The question gave her pause, but then she remembered the feel of Will's hands on her body and the brutal way he'd thrust into her. She experienced anew the sense of loss and violation. "I would kill even you, Kin-di-wa. *Especially* you, for I—I don't know how else to fight you!"

The muscles in his jaw tightened. "Now I have three reasons to find the man who wears the

125

Shawnee necklace of fingers—my brother, your father, and you. But even if the reasons numbered more than the stars in the sky, I could not put all of them together ahead of my duty. We must return to my people. Revenge will keep until another day."

The thud of the war drums came louder still. The drums filled her ears with their incessant warnings. "I—I'm not coming with you. I have thought it over. If you could take me back across the swamp to the river, I can surely find my way back home."

He sighed. "No, little Cat-Eyes. I will take you nowhere but back to my people. You must come with me."

"You don't understand! I can look after myself! And I want to go home where people are civilized! I—I don't want any more of this!"

He made a move to draw her to him, then checked himself. "You must be strong, Cat-Eyes. Only the strong will survive. But you must not be foolish. I will give you my protection—and that is all I will give you until such time as you want more than that. We shall be as brother and sister on this journey, for as I have already told you, an empty gourd tempts me not at all."

She wanted to believe him—was desperate to believe him! The swamp and the forest and the difficulties of survival were still too much for her to handle alone. But neither could she handle any more assaults on her body and spirit. It mattered not at all that he had only taken her the first time because she had succumbed to a moment of weakness. She had meant what she said: if any man touched her again, she would kill him.

Something delicate and tender and vulnerable inside her had been snuffed out like a candle in a windstorm. She didn't know what it had been—so briefly had it flowered. But Will had destroyed it, and there seemed no chance now that it would ever reawaken. Not even this rare man, this man of iron tempered with gentleness, could erase last night's scalding memory. She had become what he said she was—an empty gourd.

"If—if you mean what you say, that we shall be as brother and sister, then I will come with you."

The blue eyes barely flickered. "I always mean what I say."

It took so long to reach Kin-di-wa's village she lost count of the days. He wanted to arrive there by the end of the Flower Blooming Moon—the month of June—or at the very latest by the beginning of the Lightning Moon—July. Were he going by himself, he told her, it would take only half that time. She resolved not to hold him back any more than necessary, but the resolve proved difficult to keep: she simply couldn't match his pace, no matter how hard she tried!

She couldn't even keep track of the days; they blurred into one another. On about the third or fourth day, she put four knots in a length of vine and tied it around her wrist. But by the evening of the sixth day, she couldn't even remember whether she'd knotted it for that day or not. Each day seemed incredibly long—spent as it was half-running through the endless woods. Each night was incredibly short, and she slept like a person drunk with fatigue and over-exertion.

Kin-di-wa stood by his promise to treat her as a brother treats a sister. Indeed, he took it very seriously. Only he was the big brother, the one who knew everything, the one who pushed and browbeat her each step of the way. Or so it seemed. He no longer allowed her to drink her fill at river or stream or to eat until she felt satisfied. "No, Cat-Eyes," he would say. "You will grow much stronger if you deny yourself. Your body needs only a little. All else you put in only slows you down."

And if she made too much noise stumbling along after him, he would stop and reprimand her—patiently but firmly. "Put your foot down like this, as though the ground is a duck's egg you hope to eat for breakfast. Watch where you are walking. Do you see that twig you snapped? That leaf you bent down? You are leaving a trail that even the tiniest squaw-child could follow."

Having no inclination to complain, she would

nod her head dumbly and try to do better. At least, her bare feet were now so hardened they scarcely felt a thing. Both her feet and her heart had grown calloused, and she plodded through each day like a sleepwalker.

Surely, this was all a strange dream from which she'd soon awaken. How else could there be so many trees—acres and acres of them? There was no end to the trees! But as long as she kept moving her feet, her bruised and aching body, she didn't have to think, to remember.

Whenever a vision of Papa's ruined face *did* jump into mind, and she stopped walking in sudden agony, Kin-di-wa was there to hurry her onward. If her body suddenly doubled up in a spasm of pain—a remnant of Will's rough handling of her—he was there to massage the cramps away, gently, in a brotherly manner. He fashioned an odd little container of bark— something he called a *"mocuck"*—which he made by heating a strip of bark and bending it, then lashing the sides together with basswood fiber.

"It is not so fine as a squaw could do, but it will serve," he told her. And in the mocuck, he brewed bitter-tasting herbal teas for her to drink and concocted herbal pastes to spread on his burned shoulder.

The first days were the worst, because she really didn't care what happened to her. As exhaustion piled on top of exhaustion, as her feet protested every step, she wouldn't have minded if he'd gone ahead and left her. Indeed, she often wished he would so she could lie down somewhere and never get up again. Papa was gone, Mama was gone, and the old Rebecca was gone too. Would it matter so very much if the empty shell of a girl she'd become simply laid down and died? All the fight had left her. She couldn't even conjure up a sense of protest when Kin-di-wa spoke to her as if she were a child.

"Look there," he would order her. And she'd dutifully look where he told her. "What do you see?" he'd ask.

"A tree," she'd say.

"What kind of tree?"

"I don't know—just a tree."

"Shagbark hickory, your people call it. We call it—" then he'd tell her some name she'd immediately forget. "Good for making strong bows. Ash and white oak are also good."

Actually, she knew the names of many trees. One could hardly grow up on a farm and be ignorant of such things! But she never admitted she knew one that he pointed out to her. What difference did it make? One part of this endless forest looked exactly like another. Trees, trees, and more trees. They came in every possible size and shape imaginable, but to her, they all looked the same.

"And what is that?" he'd ask, pointing to the ground.

She'd look and see nothing but last year's dead leaves.

"There!" he'd cry impatiently. "The scat of *a-ka-wit-ta*, Brother Porcupine!" Down on one knee he'd go. "He's been feeding on the buds and catkins of willows. Here is where his trail goes. The leaves have been stirred by his passing, and here is one of his quills. If we stalked him, we'd soon have quills to decorate our mocuck."

Gradually, under his relentless tutelage, her eyes and ears were opened. Despite her apathy, she began to notice things even before he pointed them out. Shriveled-up pieces of what looked like rotted gray-green cloth dangling from low-hanging tree branches were actually strips of skin from the antlers of male deer who'd been rubbing off their velvet. Trees, especially evergreens, that looked as though they'd been scraped clean of their bark from the ground up to their branches, told the story of deer who'd been hungry over the winter. Trees that held deep claw and tooth gouges had fed or entertained bears.

Kin-di-wa could identify almost any kind of track or animal dropping, and he knew which way the animal had gone and what it had been doing. He taught her to tell the difference between the small heart-shaped track of the white-tail deer, the

131

larger, more rounded shape of *wapiti* or elk, and the still larger track of the moose.

Once, he stopped mid-walk and whispered, "Listen!" And she heard a kind of long soft whistle. "Whiew-ew-ew," it sounded. And he told her, "Mother white-tail is warning her fawn of our passing."

This was Kin-di-wa's world, where the wind sighing in the trees carried messages only he could decipher. Where the language of birds and animals was as familiar to him as English or his own Miami tongue. Where food could be found at the tuberous end of a plant or underneath the ragged edged leaves that hid "hearts of my people," which she was amazed to discover were actually wild strawberries.

He delighted in showing her the wonders, the secrets of this dim green world, and his unconcealed enthusiasm for it made her begin to see it differently. The trees began to separate themselves into beech, white oak, chestnut, hickory, pine, sugar maple, and a hundred others. In the damp and swampy places grew swamp oak, gum, and sassafras. And everywhere, were frail white or purplish-tinged blossoms he called Wind Flowers, because when the wind blew, they looked as if they were floating.

She had always thought the forest was still and silent, but now, it seemed to come alive with clamoring voices—the bark of the fox, the yowl of the bobcat, the woof! of the foraging black bear. She heard them all but was never afraid, for Kin-di-wa's broad back and tomahawk stood between her and whatever threat might arise.

At night, she slept close beside him in whatever shelter they could devise or find ready-made, and often, she awoke to find his arm across her, protecting her even in sleep. Gradually, she became stronger. The ugly purplish marks Will had imprinted on her flesh faded to yellow and disappeared. Her body grew lean and hard muscled beneath the fringed buckskin shirt. Her long coppery hair swung in a braid down her back—tamed now through the aid of a crude comb Kin-di-wa had carved for her. She wore the comb on a thong round her neck where it dangled between her breasts, an ever-present reminder of his kindness and concern for her.

She had become, she reflected, half-Indian herself, and her interest in her surroundings blossomed, grew more avid everyday. The days spun into weeks, and full summer was upon them—lush and green and bountiful—filling her with a quiet contentment, almost a sense of peace. It seemed as though this journey might go on forever. Time had stopped. There was no past and no future. There was only the present—and Kin-di-wa.

"But how do you know which way to go?" she asked him one morning after a breakfast of roots and berries. "I can never tell which way is which."

She knew they'd been traveling in a roughly northwesterly direction, for he'd told her that his village lay west, then north from the swamplands along the Muskingum. They could have gone much faster by canoe down the various waterways and through the portages, but, lacking one, they'd had no choice but to follow Indian trails and deer paths cross-country through the forest and around the many bogs and wetlands. And in all this limitless vast stretch of wilderness, how did he know he wasn't going in circles?

Papa had told her that people always tended to go in circles in the forest—if they were lost, which Kin-di-wa certainly never was. Of course, one could tell by sun or stars, but what did one do when it was cloudy?

"I ask my friends," Kin-di-wa answered, and she thought for a moment he was poking fun at her, then, as he walked over to a huge old hickory tree, she saw that he was serious.

"If there is moss on the tree, it grows on the north side." He fingered the tree bark, but there was no moss growing on it.

"Yes, I know," she rebuked him. Did he think her totally ignorant? "I have heard that, but what do you do when there isn't any moss?"

"Then I let my friends tell me." He leaned against the tree, stretched his arm around it, and ran his fingers up and down the bark. Then he

134

stood up straight and looked down at her, his eyes twinkling mischievously. "My friend tells me north is that way." He pointed.

"You lie!" she cried. "That tree told you nothing!"

He began walking away from her, looking offended. She ran to catch up. "What? What did it tell you?"

He turned to face her, his lips quivering with silent laughter. "Oh, you!" she blurted. "You are impossible!" And she began beating on his chest with her fists until he caught her hands, threw back his head, and laughed heartily. "I thought—I thought maybe you really could speak to trees." She was chagrined. "You're able to do everything else!"

Abruptly, he turned serious. "Never believe what you cannot see, little Cat-Eyes. That is the first lesson of the forest. And what I have been trying to teach you is to use your eyes, your ears, your smell, your touch, your taste— so you can learn everything you need to know to survive. Come back to the tree and I will show you."

He led her back to the great hickory. "Feel here, on the south side of the tree."

She touched the rough flinty bark. It felt like tree bark—nothing different, nothing unusual. "Now feel here, on the north side of the tree." And she did so. "What do you notice?" he asked.

She hesitated, then stretched her arms around the tree as he had done and ran her fingers up and down the bark on both sides. The tree was so wide she could barely reach around it, and she had to concentrate to detect a difference from one side to the other. "I—I think the furrows in the bark are much deeper on the north side of the tree," she ventured.

Stepping back, she saw that he was pleased. "That is the message of all rough barked trees. The smoother ones tell the same story but it is a little harder to read." He took her hand and began walking. "There are other ways to tell north and south also. Do you see those trees that are always green?"

She looked ahead toward a stand of evergreens and pines hugging a slope that rose gently away from her on the right. "I see them."

"Look at their tips."

She had to tilt her head back and crane her neck to peer through the screen of foliage. "Why— they're all pointing slightly in one direction!"

"East," he told her. "They always look toward the rising place of the sun."

She was amazed. These signs had been here all the time, and she'd never even noticed them! Now Kin-di-wa dropped to his knees to examine a silvery spiderweb in the underbrush. He pulled her down beside him. "My friend, *Za-pi-kwa*, Brother Spider, spins his web whenever possible to face the gentle winds from the south. See—he has done it here!''

The web trembled in a breath of air. Exquisitely fashioned and delicate as a snowflake, it looked like the lace on a dress of some fine Philadelphia lady. Rebecca glanced up at Kin-di-wa with a feeling of awe. "But I never knew these things!" she breathed. "I cannot believe I have lived all this time and never really looked around me! We have trees and spider webs back home, you know, but I don't think I ever really saw them!"

"Ah, Cat-Eyes," he smiled down at her, his eyes holding a hint of deep sadness, "we never see what is closest to us—until we are about to lose it. Come. Now that we know how to find the direction we wish to go in, we must go more quickly."

Tripping after him, she felt a surge of purest joy. Now she would never again be so afraid of losing her way in the woods! Now, she would never be *completely* lost—without even a clue to follow! All her dread of this vast wilderness had centered on the fact that she knew nothing whatever about it—could never get out once she'd gotten in. She remembered how the trees had seemed to be pressing in on the little cabin in the clearing. She'd actually thought of them as some kind of monsters waiting to swallow her up in endless gloom. Whenever Papa went out, he used to blaze the trees so he could find his way back.

She wished she could share this woodlore with

Papa. He would have given much to learn these things—which was why he'd fallen into a friendship with Will. Will, having lived here much longer, had been teaching Papa everything he knew. Well, not quite everything.

Her happiness suddenly trickled away. It still hurt to think about Papa and Will. Her mind recoiled from it as from probing an ugly wound. But she knew now that she was healing. At least, she no longer thought about death as some sort of blissful escape. Perhaps, the old saying that time heals all wounds was true. She doubted it—but maybe time made the wounds more bearable.

That night, a sudden rain storm blew up. The wind awoke them as it whipped the branches of the trees into a frenzy. Lightning split the sky with streaks of jagged orange flame, the thunder boomed like a hundred cannons going off in all directions. Rebecca stumbled after Kin-di-wa in a panic as they searched for stronger shelter than the lean-to of pine branches in which they'd fallen asleep. There was no shelter to be found before the sky unleashed a torrent of stabbing rain that all but blinded them.

"Kin-di-wa!" she screamed as a lashing branch struck her full across the chest. His hand slipped from her grasp.

The air above her suddenly crackled. A white tongue of flame leapt down a tree trunk, and she heard a cracking, wrenching sound. The top half of the tree shivered, as if mortally wounded. Standing in front of it, looking up, she couldn't move. The lining inside her nose stung with an awful sulfurous odor.

"Cat-Eyes—run!" She thought she heard Kin-di-wa shouting, but the words blew past her on the wind. The tree creaked and swayed above her. It wants to fall down, she thought, but the other trees are holding it up.

The lightning was now so constant that the whole forest was lit up as if by daylight. Then she saw Kin-di-wa hurtling toward her, his body extended in a full leap. He crashed into her, rolled her over, and pulled her back out of the way of the falling tree.

The tree fell slowly, taking others with it. The air shook with groanings and creakings as enormous branches split and shuddered, pulling down more branches on every side. Rebecca clung to Kin-di-wa as limbs knocked together over them. The ground shook, and an avalanche of cold wet leaves rained down on top of them. Kin-di-wa shielded her with his body and dragged her back against the sturdy trunk of the nearest tree that was holding solid.

He wrapped his arms around her and hugged her. She was shivering uncontrollably. "It's falling on us!" she whimpered against his chest.

"No—it cannot reach us now." He spoke

directly into her ear.

And then they heard more creakings as the wounded tree slipped further downwards toward the ground, straining against the supporting arms of its fellow trees. But in the lightning flash, through the cavern of leaves, they saw it resting still high above them and to their left. For the moment, they were safe.

"Kin-di-wa! Kin-di-wa!" she wept.

"You are safe, little one, you are safe." He held her and rocked her, but still she trembled. The sheer violence of the storm had destroyed her blossoming self-confidence—the confidence she'd first lost when Will assaulted her in the Shawnee graveyard. Once again, she felt naked and vulnerable before a fury she could neither understand nor control. She had thought she was healing, but her body still remembered: her teeth chattered, her limbs shook, and her heart thudded like a beating drum.

The storm passed over quickly. Shielded as they were by the overhang of branches and leaves, the gentle rain that followed hardly touched them. But Rebecca couldn't overcome her terror—nor be rid of the tremors that flowed over her, wave after wave. Something inside her had shifted: she wondered if she were dying.

Then Kin-di-wa began chanting. In the stillness of the storm's aftermath, his voice rose pure and strong. She could not understand a word, but the ancient rhythms flowed over her as gently as the rain. She was soothed and comforted. Then his chant died down, and softly as the wings of a moth, something brushed her hair—had he kissed her?

No, she must have imagined it . . . and curled up in his arms, she finally slept.

The next day, they came to the river, on the other side of which lay his village, *Kekionga*.

Six

Rebecca stood at the edge of the river Kin-di-wa
called the Miami of the Lake and looked westward
toward it's headwaters at the juncture of two other
rivers, the St. Joseph's and the St. Mary's.

After the storm from the night before, the air had
a new-washed quality. Inhaling deeply, she mar-
veled at the vast stretch of brilliant blue sky, seen
clearly now for the first time in several weeks. A
flock of waterfowl rose up from the water and
filled the air with their keening cries. Their wings
flashed gracefully in the sunlight, and inter-
spersed among the darker bodies, were the gleaming, slender, white ones of the cranes after whom
the river and Kin-di-wa's people had been named.

The way Kin-di-wa said Miami sounded something like "Mommy" or "Maumee," and she
thought it very likely that most whites would
pronounce it "Maumee" without the subtle

distinctions between syllables he gave it.

"It is a very beautiful river," she acknowledged. "But tell me exactly where we *are*." She still felt somewhat disoriented, unable to pinpoint their whereabouts from the only landmarks she knew— the Muskingum River and the Allegheny Mountains, on the other side of which lay Pennsylvania.

Kin-di-wa unsheathed his knife and knelt down on the soft, damp riverbank. He cleared away some grass and twigs, revealing the rich dark earth beneath, then drew a long line. "This is the Miami of the Lake, the river before us. It flows to the east and a little to the north of here and empties into the great Lake of the Eries—a tribe whose people have long since disappeared." He placed a small stone far to the right and some distance below the line. "Here is your cabin along the Muskingum which runs north and south and empties into the great Ohio River."

"Yes," she traced the direction of the Muskingum with her finger. "I *know* where that is. To the east across the mountains lies Pennsylvania, and at the eastern edge of Pennsylvania," she reached and placed another small stone far to the right, "is my *real* home, near the big city of Philadelphia."

Kin-di-wa drew a line to show the mountains and another to show how the Ohio River ran, dropping south from its headwaters in Pennsylvania and following an irregular path to the west along the southern edge of the Ohio country.

"When you came past these mountains," he pointed to the Alleghenies, "you came onto the land of my people and all the tribes that make up our confederation. Your people call it the Northwest Territory, but it is really made up of three different lands: Ohio, Indiana, and the Illinois country."

He showed her the placement of these three areas spread out west of the Allegheny Mountains.

"Which one of these lands are we in now?" she asked. The headwaters of the Miami of the Lake lay past the line marking the end of the Ohio country.

"We are in the land the trappers call Indiana country—land of the Indians—but it is really the land of the Miamis, not of all Indians. East lies the Ohio Country, west lies the Illinois country with its great prairies, and north, very close to us, lies the land of the Potawatomis: Michigan, the land of the big sea waters."

"Yes, I see!" she cried. "And the Ohio River is way down south of here!"

"That is not all that lies south of here," he said grimly. He drew a point at the end of the line representing the Miami of the Lake, so that it looked like an arrow pointing west, and at the tip of the arrow point he drew an X.

"Kekionga, the main village of my people, is here where the three rivers come together: the St. Joseph's, the St. Mary's, and the Miami of the Lake. And here—" He drew another X below it and slightly to the east. "Here is Fort Recovery."

Just below that X he drew another. "Here is Fort Greenville. And here further south is Fort Jefferson. And again further south, Fort Hamilton. And yet again," his knife slashed an X on the Ohio River, "is Fort Washington."

His eyes burned with anger. He stabbed the knife into the X indicating Fort Greenville. "This is where *Chenoten* makes his plans to rob us of our lands."

"Chenoten? You mean Anthony Wayne?"

Kin-di-wa nodded curtly. "From here, he can come up the Wabash River," he drew another line west of Kekionga, "and come across its portage to the St. Mary's and Kekionga. Or he can come up the Auglaize," he drew a line south to intersect the Miami of the Lake further downriver, "and find other villages here."

"Yes, I see," Rebecca repeated with dwindled enthusiasm. She straightened up and looked at Kekionga, feeling a surge of sadness. In all the time they'd been together on this long journey, they had never once discussed what now lay ahead—her arrival among a people with whom her own people were soon going to war.

Her attention was now drawn to the place it had taken them so long to get to. "I—I never expected your village to be so developed."

At the juncture of three glistening rivers lay Kekionga, and even from where she stood as Kin-di-wa came up behind her, she could see the sturdily built lodges, like mounded beehives, a long low structure with walls made of logs, and a smattering of log cabins.

"Our council lodge is the large one there." Kin-di-wa pointed to the log-walled structure that was built like a cabin, only larger. "But we only gather there when the weather is wet or cold or we have important visitors—a chieftain or shaman from another village or tribe."

"And the cabins? Who lives in those?"

"Trappers or traders. Both the British and the French used to send them among us, but now only the British send them, and they do not stay as long as they once did. Some of the cabins have been taken over by my people; but most remain empty."

"Why empty? Surely your people don't object to a good sturdy cabin—especially in winter!"

Kin-di-wa grunted. "My people feel strongly about the cabins. For many, they are an ugly reminder of white men's ways, ways which are making us grow soft and weak and lazy."

Rebecca took silent exception to such a prejudiced idea but suspected that Kin-di-wa himself held this opinion: Indian ways are good, white men's ways are bad.

Her sadness deepened. The return of tension between them was like discovering a prickly nettle in a bed of soft leaves and pine needles. If only things could stay as they were—without the intrusion of anything ugly or hurtful! She glanced up to find him seriously studying her, as if he too sensed the change in their relationship.

"So—little Cat-Eyes. We come to the end of our journey."

What did she hear in his voice—a trace of the same sorrow she was feeling? Or did she merely imagine it? "Yes," she whispered. "You have come home."

Sorrow twisted like a knife in her bosom. Where was home for her? Would she ever get home again? She had no family left but Aunt Margaret, and she could hardly remember what the lady looked like! It had been four years or more—she was only thirteen or so at the time—since Aunt Margaret had come to visit Papa and Mama in far away Pennsylvania.

"Yes, I have come home." His hand came up to stroke her cheek. "And I have kept my promise— little sister."

And she knew she had not imagined it; there *was* a look of unhappiness in his eyes. But then his eyes darkened with some deeper feeling. The touch of his hand grew suddenly warmer, less gentle. Her cheeks began to burn as his fingers traced the curve of her jaw and her lips. What is happening between us? she wondered. What has *already* happened?

She backed away in confusion and looked about for some new—less dangerous—topic of conversation. Then she saw the long rows of well-sprouted young corn, delicately green but sturdy, that rimmed the banks of all three rivers as far away as the eye could see. "Oh, your corn has grown so high already! But—well, it *is* the second week of July. I guess our journey took longer than expected."

Kin-di-wa's hand dropped. "Yes," he said brusquely. "But as you see, my people are peace-loving. More interested in the growing of corn and squash, the gathering of fruit and nuts, and a good outcome to the fall hunt than making war. It is fortunate there was time to plant before this conflict came upon us."

The tone of his voice was cutting: Rebecca didn't know what to say to effect a return of his good humor. She noticed something strange. "But why is your village so still? Where are all the people? It—it almost looks abandoned."

His expression darkened even further. "I had thought to find Little Turtle still here, but I think we are too late. Everyone must have gone down-river to the council meeting place the Shawnee spoke of—the place called *Roche de Boeuf*."

"Roche de Boeuf?" To have come so far and to have further still to go was suddenly almost more than she could bear! She *did* want to go home! And the sooner they caught up with his people and got this battle over, the sooner she *could* go home!

"I should have gone there first," Kin-di-wa growled. "It would have been much closer."

Her exasperation was nearly equal to his. Did he mean they'd come a long way further than necessary—a long way further *west?* "Where exactly is this Roche de Boeuf?"

"It lies further east downriver," he snapped. "But I did not go there first because I thought Little Turtle would delay until the last moment possible—to see if Chenoten would come. Other Miami villages lie strung out along both these rivers, and Little Turtle would not have wanted to leave them all unprotected."

"Oh," Rebecca said in a small voice. "And the name—how did it get its name?"

"It is a French name given to a rock in the river that bears a face like a man's. On the banks is the Council Elm, and nearby is a trading post belonging to Alexander McKee. There is also a newly built British fort, Fort Miamis. McKee is spokesman to the tribes for the British, and doubtless, the tribe has gone there to remind him the time has come for the British to speak with actions not just with words."

So it is true! thought Rebecca. The British *are* conspiring with the Indians! Anger leapt in her chest. Was the war with Britain to be fought all over again? Had independence to be won again and again? Why couldn't the British keep out of this conflict? Perhaps, some new treaty with the Indians could prevent more bloodshed, but not if the British became involved!

"Who is this Little Turtle?" she demanded hotly. "I should like to know more about him, other than what I've heard from settlers who have good reason to hate him!"

In response to her haughty tone, Kin-di-wa turned on his heel and strode away. Stalking after him, she couldn't help noticing how well the powder burns on his back were healing. His skin was tender and pink as a baby's bottom, and there would probably be scars, but he carried himself as well as ever—proudly, and arrogantly—as he began searching the river bank for a canoe. Earlier, he had told her canoes were always kept hidden along the bank so homeward bound travelers could cross the river to Kekionga.

"Ah," he grunted, "there is a canoe, I think, hidden in that canebreak."

He waded into the water and freed a half-submerged canoe before bothering to answer her, then motioned for her to come and help him tip the water out. Only *after* he had the canoe righted and ready to use did he reply. "Little Turtle is our war chief—not just of all the Miamis—but of our whole confederation: Miamis and their lesser tribes, as well as Shawnees, Delawares, Ottawas, and others."

"But—what I meant to ask—is what sort of person is he?"

"He has no equal. There has been no one like him since the time of Pontiac." The canoe was pointing out into the river now, and he held it still for her so she could climb into the front end.

"The frost of winter is on his head, but the fire of wisdom lights his thinking. Only *he* has been able to make ancient enemies sit down together and

151

smoke the peace pipe. Only *he* has been able to fashion them into a single arrow to strike straight into the hearts of the Long Knives. Even the Iroquois, the confederation of the Six Nations, praise his courage and his wisdom. Because of *him*, we defeated two of your ablest generals—Arthur St. Clair and Josiah Harmar."

Kin-di-wa held up his hand and spread his fingers. "Once the tribes were separate, like this: now, we have become as one—like this." He made a fist.

Rebecca couldn't help but be impressed. She settled herself into the canoe, being careful not to tip it. "So many—and now joined together under one?"

Kin-di-wa climbed into the back end and unlashed the paddle from the side of the canoe. "So many," he repeated drily. "But not so many warriors as your Anthony Wayne has soldiers. The backbone of the Iroquois confederation was broken long ago; so the Iroquois are of little use to us. Even united in a new confederation, we are not two times a thousand, while your Anthony Wayne has three times a thousand or more."

Three thousand! She hadn't known Wayne had so many. The information heartened her. "But he is not *my* Anthony Wayne," she pointed out, dipping her fingers in the water while he stroked. "He is an old sick man who should never have been sent out here. Once, he was acclaimed a hero, but now it is said he is mad. He is known to be hot-headed and reckless—more concerned with the appearance of his troops than the safety of the settlers. But my father always liked him. He thought him a great man and a wonderful strategist.''

"He is Chenoten," Kin-di-wa informed her, "the whirlwind, the chief who never sleeps. Two winters he has been here, but in all that time, while he invaded our lands and built his forts, we have never been able to surprise him. His sentrys guard his forts and supply trains well. He has trained them so they pretend they are going to do one thing, then go and do another. And they do not retreat under attack like the soldiers of your other generals."

"You mean General St. Clair and General Harmar."

"Yes," Kin-di-wa nodded. "He is not like those who came like women into the woods—with their silver forks and white table coverings and dishes that shattered easily. Chenoten is a warrior—not so great as our war chief, Little Turtle, but still a true leader of men."

She was shocked. "Then you admire him!"

"No—but I respect him, as Little Turtle does. Do you not know that an old sick wolf is more to be feared than a young one in his prime? If he has not strength, he has cunning. Or so Little Turtle has always said."

Through the slap, slap, slap of the water against the gently rocking canoe, she heard the sarcasm in

153

his voice and resolved to keep her mouth closed about what she'd heard from anyone white. Even Papa. She was stung by Kin-di-wa's new attitude—his antagonism toward her—yet it gave her a surge of reckless hope to hear "the enemy" praise Anthony Wayne. Perhaps, the settlers had a stalwart defender after all! Perhaps, when it came to the clash of arms, it would be the Indians who were driven off—not the settlers!

But I must remember to guard my tongue, she thought. I'm in enemy territory now, among people who might just as well scalp as look at me!

And she began to wonder how far Kin-di-wa's protection would extend if she happened to say something really stupid and be understood by one of his people. Somehow, their easy sense of camaraderie had completely vanished! They weren't brother and sister after all. They weren't even lovers—at least not now. They were enemies, and she'd do well not to forget it.

"Kekionga," Kin-di-wa grunted, as the canoe glided into the village.

Rebecca started, and her first impression that it was abandoned grew even stronger. Then she saw a small bent figure come scurrying out of one of the lodges. The figure waved and headed toward them—an old woman with frizzled white hair and skin as leathery and dark as a dried hickory nut.

"Crow Woman. She is too old to travel but not too old to watch over the corn. They must have left her here."

Left her here! Rebecca thought. Well, what could one expect of savages?

The old woman tottered down the bank toward them, and Rebecca thought she had never seen such an ugly old crone. But the wide toothless mouth stretched itself into a grin, and the black beady eyes shone as bright as a bird's. A torrent of words poured out of her, to which Kin-di-wa responded in short clipped tones. The old woman was obviously glad to see him—or anyone it seemed. Now, she turned her attention to Rebecca as the canoe scraped the bank.

Rebecca stood up and climbed out, and instantly, the old woman's hands were on her—tugging at her braid, examining her buckskin shirt, poking and prodding as she cackled with glee. Rebecca turned to Kin-di-wa in alarm.

"Do not be afraid," he said. "She hasn't seen many white women before. You are a wonderment to her."

So Rebecca stood quietly for a moment while the old woman stomped all the way around her, looking her fill. Then she peered into Rebecca's eyes, and her mouth dropped open. Rebecca caught a nasty whiff of decay and saw blackened empty gums from which only a few broken stumps protruded. With a loud screech, the old woman pointed to Rebecca's eyes.

Kin-di-wa grinned. "She thinks you have eyes like the puma—the mountain cat."

But when the old woman took hold of Rebecca's

shirt and lifted it to peer underneath, Rebecca slapped her hands away. "Tell her that's enough! Tell her—tell her I will give her a strand of my hair if she leaves me alone now."

Kin-di-wa spoke rapidly, and, grieved and angry, the old woman backed away. But her eyes gleamed with anticipation as Rebecca took hold of a single strand of hair that had escaped from her braid and yanked it out. She handed it to the woman, and instantly, the old face was once again wreathed in smiles. Crow Woman held up the strand of hair so the sunlight glistened on it. She chattered delightedly, like a squirrel with a nut.

"She says your hair shines like the sun and is the color of flame. She says you are very beautiful, but your hips are too small. Only that is no matter, for surely the spirits smile on anyone with eyes the color of a mountain cat's or new leaves in the spring."

"Tell her I thank her for such kind words, only I am sorry my hips do not please her!"

"She wants us to go to her lodge and eat with her," Kin-di-wa translated. "It would be bad manners to refuse. Besides, she will speak of nothing serious until her curiosity about where I have been and where I found you is satisfied."

The old woman led the way to her lodge, and Rebecca had a chance to admire the sturdily built lodges as she and Kin-di-wa followed Crow Woman down a beaten path winding through the neatly laid-out village. The lodges were made of young saplings molded and lashed into circular forms, then molded and lashed crossways with more young saplings. Mats made of reeds and rushes covered over the skeletons of wood, leaving only single small holes at the top for smoke to escape. A long pole from which hung another mat leaned against the side of each lodge. Evidently, the mat could be adjusted to keep rain and wind from blowing down the hole.

Rebecca took note of everything, especially that some of the lodges had been stripped bare of their mats. She thought the inhabitants had probably taken them with them to Roche de Boeuf. Then her thoughts turned again to Crow Woman whose dirty buckskin smock did not bode well that her lodge would be any cleaner.

Rebecca was sidestepping three yellow mongrel dogs who had come sniffing at her legs, when Crow Woman suddenly stopped and turned into one of the lodges. Kin-di-wa went in after her, flipping aside a deerskin. Rebecca stepped in herself and was immediately encased in cool darkness. As her eyes adjusted to the gloom, she saw that, unlike its owner, the inside of the lodge was immaculate and strangely luxurious.

Mats and skins covered the walls and floor. Wolf, deer, rabbit, mink, and otter—even a gigantic bear skin on which the head and yawning jaws still remained intact—offered themselves up to be touched and felt. To Rebecca, whose feet had blistered, calloused, blistered and calloused yet

157

again on this long journey, to see so much comfort gathered together in one place seemed almost incredible, especially when she'd been expecting to find a rude hovel where the inhabitants lived hardly better than animals.

Sleeping platforms, covered over with skins and pine boughs, jutted out from the walls of the lodge. A ring of stones rimmed the low fire over which hung a small iron caldron, and bunches of dried herbs dangled from the rafters. Assorted baskets and embroidered pouches peeped out from beneath the platforms. Every inch of available space was used—filled with containers or hanging foodstuffs, but the effect was one of orderliness, neatness, and comfort, with everything in its place.

Crow Woman peered into her face again, gauging her reaction. Rebecca smiled and nodded—trying to show how impressed she was. Then Crow Woman took her arm and led her a few short steps to the center lodge pole. Her thin bird-like hand fluttered up to touch what was hanging from it, and Rebecca recoiled in horror at the string of dried scalps dangling right in front of her at eye level. Long black hair wound in a braid, a thatch of dirty blond, brown hair, gray hair, even a thatch of reddish-colored hair, made up the string.

Kin-di-wa spoke quietly behind her, "She does not mean to insult you. The scalps are a badge of honor to her family. She guards them and keeps them to tell of the bravery of her menfolk. Her husband died fighting the Long Knives in the battle against St. Clair. Two of her sons also died, and now, of all her family, she is the only one left.''

Crow Woman fingered the reddish-colored hair of one scalp, and, grasping Rebecca's braid, brought it closer so she could compare the colors. She said something, and Kin-di-wa explained, ''Crow Woman thinks your hair is much prettier— much softer than that of the flame-colored hair on the scalp.''

Rebecca felt sick to her stomach. She disengaged her braid with a determined tug of her head. Crow Woman regarded her with pleased delight. She held up the single strand of hair Rebecca had given her. *''Mi-shi,''* she chortled.

''Wonderful,'' Kin-di-wa repeated in English.

Crow Woman wound the strand of Rebecca's hair carefully around the strip of rawhide stringing the scalps together, while Kin-di-wa translated her rush of gibberish. ''She will keep it always—a gift from a new friend. And now she wishes you to be seated. Rest yourself. She thinks you must be tired from your long journey.''

Rebecca sat down uncertainly beside Kin-di-wa, crossing her legs as he did, Indian fashion. They sat on the mats beside the cook-fire, and she found it hard to keep her glance from straying upwards to the dangling scalps. With the gruesome reminders of so much death and bloodshed hanging over her head, she didn't know if she could eat. The scalps had been taken from white

159

people, and if she had not come to this lodge with Kin-di-wa, who knew but that this strange old woman might not want to add a whole new braid, not just a strand of hair, to her grisly collection?

The old woman now busied herself with ladling out gourds of steaming hominy from the iron pot. Before passing them to Rebecca and Kin-di-wa, she sweetened the hominy with generous dollops of a sticky brown syrup that Rebecca recognized as the boiled-down sap from the sugar maple. Such hearty hot fare set Rebecca's mouth to watering in spite of herself.

They ate hungrily and in silence, using their fingers to scoop up portions of the gooey delicious mass. Crow Woman waited to eat until Rebecca and Kin-di-wa had finished, and then only after all the remnants of the meal had been cleared away, did the old woman settle herself on the mats with an air of preparation: the time had now come to speak of things Kin-di-wa wanted to know.

A rapid conversation followed, of which Rebecca understood nothing except repeated references to Chenoten, the Indian name for Anthony Wayne. Crow Woman had many opinions which she didn't mind sharing, and Rebecca sensed that Kin-di-wa was gleaning every last shred of information from her that she was capable of giving.

Rebecca concealed a yawn. She longed to curl up for a nap on one of the skin-heaped sleeping platforms but didn't wish to be thought impolite.

It would be so pleasant to linger here a few days and enjoy the comfort of a roof over one's head and a soft place to sleep.

Finally, after what seemed like an interminably long time, Kin-di-wa arose and made as if to go. Rebecca scrambled to her feet, lest he leave without her, and nearly fell into the cookpot as a leg muscle cramped. Kin-di-wa caught her by the arm, his blue eyes glinting down into hers with an air of authority that warned her he was going to command her to do something—something she wouldn't like doing.

"I should like to leave you here," he said. "Here, with Crow Woman. She will look after you."

"What?" Rebecca croaked. "You can't go on to Roche de Boeuf without me!"

"There's no reason for you to come!" Kin-di-wa snapped. "Chenoten is preparing to leave Fort Greenville. My tribesmen have been attacking his supply wagons, and Crow Woman said there was talk of attacking Fort Recovery. No one knows with certainty what Chenoten will do, only that he must be mad enough by now to act as the hornet stirred up from its nest. You will be safer if you stay here. And if he comes here first, he will doubtless see that you get home safely."

"But I don't *want* to be left here!" she wailed. The tempting comfort of the lodge, excepting the scalps, of course, suddenly seemed like an enormous ironic joke, a joke at her expense. "I want to be where you are!"

And she hardly knew what she'd said until she saw the blue of his eyes grow suddenly warmer and the lines of his face soften. "I am going to Roche de Boeuf, little one, but if you wish it so much, knowing that you may lose your chance to get home sooner, I will take you with me."

Dear Lord! she wondered. What *had* she said— or at least implied?

"I—I—if there is no way of knowing what Anthony Wayne—Chenoten—will do, then I had rather go with you," she stammered. "Besides, I think he must go there first, or why else would Little Turtle have abandoned the village?"

The light went out of his eyes. "Then come with me, if you must," he growled. "But I warn you, what you find *there* may be far worse than if you had stayed *here!*"

He brushed past her and went out of the lodge. Crow Woman watched her avidly, licking her lips. The old woman knew something had occurred that would make juicy gossip if only she could have understood it and had someone to whom she could gossip. Rebecca wheeled around to go after him, but Crow Woman suddenly came hobbling after her with a speed alarming for one so old. Her bony hand plucked Rebecca's sleeve.

"I have to go! He's leaving!" Rebecca jerked away.

Crow Woman thrust something soft and beaded into her hands. She muttered and smiled her toothless grin, then stepped out of Rebecca's way.

Looking down, Rebecca saw that the old woman had given her a pair of soft sturdy moccasins decorated with blue and white beads and a pattern of red-dyed quills—porcupine quills?

"Thank you! Oh, thank you!" she cried, running after Kin-di-wa, who was striding purposefully toward river and waiting canoe.

He barely gave her time to get in before he shoved off and took up the paddle, his attitude such that she wondered if she ought not to have stayed behind after all. She had not even had time to properly thank Crow Woman for the beautiful moccasins! What must the old woman think?

She slipped on the velvety-feeling footwear and wondered at the perfection of the fit. And then as Kin-di-wa stroked furiously, driving the canoe in long swift glides down the Miami of the Lake toward Roche de Boeuf, she realized fully what she had said, *"I want to be where you are."*

Had she really meant that? Would his leaving her be such a loss? What if Anthony Wayne's forces did come first to Kekionga?

They would find nothing but an empty village and a shriveled old crone named Crow Woman. They wouldn't find Rebecca McDuggan, and she wouldn't soon be on her way home to Pennsylvania or at least to the safety of a fort until the upcoming clash was over. Oh, what a fool she was! To let her feelings get the best of her. To let her head and her heart become muddled.

The peaceful village in its verdant setting was

soon left far behind, and the afternoon shadows grew long on the river. The river was a glistening path snaking eastward through the close dark forest. Rebecca glanced back at Kin-di-wa and saw his profile as his eyes scanned the river bank. Outlined against the sinking sun, he appeared as if a sun-god. His bronzed body rippled with muscles. His straight fine nose had a noble tilt. The high cheekbones and firm strong mouth seemed carved of marble or some other precious stone she'd never seen but only read about in books.

Yes, he was magnificent, the most stunning man she had ever met, but did she love him? Or was she merely becoming attached to his presence, to the feeling of safety she had when near him?

With him beside her in the deep woods, she had no fear of snarling wolves or cougars, of grunting, woofing bears—she could even overcome her terror of lightning-struck trees! He made every danger seem smaller, every hardship easier.

When he spoke to her, patiently explaining or teaching something, his voice fell on her ears like a welcome caress—but what did all this *mean?* What had been the meaning of his look when his fingers roved down her cheek and across her lips?

For the first time since Will had so abused her, she remembered Kin-di-wa's love-making, and a tremor shook her from head to foot. The thought of that muscled chest pressing against her breasts, of his aroused manhood probing between her thighs, brought a flutter to her loins. She had to breathe deeply to breathe at all.

She longed to run her fingers once more down his body—to make him cry out his need for her. His dark head would bend to her breasts. His lips would rove where they would. His hands—those fine strong hands—would caress and stroke and demand her complete surrender. She would drown in the blue of his eyes, be lost in the surge of his passion.

But then she thought of Will—and shivered.

Kin-di-wa caught her still staring at him, and his eyes leapt with those icy blue sparks she dreaded. She knew even before he spoke that his words would somehow wound her. "When we get to Roche de Boeuf," he said, "you will stay in the lodge of Two Fires, the widow of my dead brother. She is not yet my woman, but soon, according to custom, we will marry. I will take the place of her husband and be father to her son."

And like an arrow piercing into her heart, came the lightning-quick certainty: she did love him!

And nothing he could have said would have wounded her more than this—that he should marry another. That he should be lost to her! That he should be father to another woman's son.

She turned her face away so he couldn't see what his words had done, as tears slid down her cheeks and fell soundlessly on her breast.

Seven

It took several days to reach Roche de Boeuf and the Council Elm. Half of the tribes had gathered where the Auglaize River intersected the Miami of the Lake, and half had gone further downstream to Roche de Boeuf. Since Little Turtle was at Roche de Boeuf, Kin-di-wa stopped only long enough at the Auglaize to gain information which he passed on to Rebecca with a disgusted snort.

"I cannot believe my tribesmen could be so foolish! Against Little Turtle's counsel and that of the British, they have attacked Fort Recovery. They were sent to cut off Chenoten's supplies, but instead, they stormed the fort. And were driven back from their efforts with nothing to show for it but three hundred horses. Chenoten was not even there! He hasn't yet left Fort Greenville."

Rebecca phrased her response with care lest he remember whose side she was on and grow even angrier. "I should think the horses would prove quite useful. You don't have many horses, do you?"

"It is not our way to fight from the back of a horse," he snapped. "Horses are useful, yes, but not worth the cost of defeat. We failed to take the fort, so we have lost honor in the eyes of the British and Chenoten himself. All because of the jealousy of a minor chieftain who had not the sense to recognize the wisdom of Little Turtle's counsel."

She did not ask who the chieftain was but sensed that the power of Little Turtle's leadership was perhaps not all that Kin-di-wa had earlier claimed it was. But then any man must find it difficult to hold together so many previously warring factions. "Why did the British and Little Turtle advise *against* attacking Fort Recovery?"

"Because the fort cannot be taken! We have not the warriors or arms to conduct a long siege. It has always been Little Turtle's strategy to lure the Long Knives *away* from their forts and supply lines. To bring them to a place where the advantage of our way of fighting can make up for our lesser numbers."

Rebecca remembered the story of how Arthur St. Clair had been defeated despite his enormous, well-equiped army. The Indians had been able to overcome their disadvantages by attacking at dawn on a snowy cold morning when they were least expected. Far from the protection of the nearest fort, Fort Jefferson, St. Clair had been totally surprised. And on top of the humiliation of a complete rout, four horses had been shot out from under him as he tried to make his escape.

"Has Little Turtle again chosen such a place?" she asked. "Where your style of fighting can count to advantage?"

Kin-di-wa shot her a suspicious glance, then shrugged his shoulders. "The place is well known already. You will soon learn of it from someone else if not from me. We call it Fallen Timbers. A great twisting wind storm once uprooted the trees there and knocked down a portion of the forest. We shall hide among the fallen trees and wait for Chenoten to come and find us. It is not easy for a man to enter the place—and it will be even less easy for one who doesn't know it to get out. Not even Chenoten will leave it alive!"

Fallen Timbers. Rebecca was struck with a feeling of dread. The very name conjured up the image of a dim shadowy place, much like the Shawnee burial ground, where the trees were bigger than anything she had seen before. Only these trees, with their huge round trunks and tangled limbs, would be lying like great dark monsters waiting to swallow up an army, to gorge themselves on blood. Fallen Timbers was a name, she was sure, that would find a place in history.

They came to Roche de Boeuf soon after that, and, as Kin-di-wa had said, it was a large rock in the middle of the river. Wind and water carved, its surface resembled a man's face. Kin-di-wa expertly skirted some rapids and beached the canoe on the north bank of the river near the great Council Elm. The elm stood in a grassy area which had been tramped down by the passing feet of hundreds of tribesmen who had met there over the years.

"Stay here," Kin-di-wa told her. "I will return for you after I find Little Turtle and the place where my people are settled."

Rebecca sat down in the shade of the giant tree. She saw no one nearby but could not escape the feeling that their arrival had been noted, and that hidden eyes were watching her from the trees beyond the clearing. She wondered where the new British Fort Miamis had been built—on American soil!—and how far Kin-di-wa would have to go to find Little Turtle. He'd said the fort, Colonel McKee's trading post, and the Indian camp were all close by, but in the wilderness that could mean anything—an hour, two hours, or a half day's journey away.

The day was warm, and it was now close to noon. The sun shone bright and hot. Grateful for the shade of the big old elm tree, Rebecca lay back in the grass to wait for Kin-di-wa's return and to speculate about this Two Fires, the woman Kin-di-wa was supposed to marry. It seemed a terrible custom—to have to marry the wife of your dead brother and to have to look after his children. But she supposed it was practical. A woman and a child needed a man to protect them and secure their meat, else they would soon die.

Besides, it was time she admitted it: Kin-di-wa did not belong to her. She had no claim whatsoever on him. Nor did she want any. What she felt for him was mere physical attraction, not love. And such attraction meant nothing to her—not after Will. She had only to remember the pain and humiliation Will had caused her, and any sense of desire for Kin-di-wa quickly fled.

The battle would be fought. The man they called Chenoten would win. She—Rebecca Mc-Duggan—would go back home to Pennsylvania. Her Aunt Margaret would take her in, give her fine clothes, introduce her to Philadelphia society, and she would meet a handsome educated man—preferably blond—fall in love, marry, and live happily ever after.

Kin-di-wa would be forgotten. The Ohio country would be forgotten. In time, even the memory of Will Simpkin would cease to haunt her! The name of Fallen Timbers, should the battle indeed be fought there, would lose its power to intimidate and frighten her. She would remember it only as a distant place where a few Indian tribes had been defeated. And those who were dumb enough to want to spend their whole lives chopping down trees and clearing fields for planting, could come to the Northwest Territory in peace—and the devil take them all!

This Two Fires was probably ugly as sin, short and dumpy in the manner of all squaw-women, and dumb as an ox. Kin-di-wa, if he survived this

171

battle, would breed hordes of children by her. They'd all be herded onto some reservation somewhere, like the eastern Indian tribes, and have to live there forever, a conquered beaten people. It would be what they deserved for all the trouble they'd caused good Christian people!

Papa—or was it Will?—had once told her that Indians were a backwards race, like Negroes in the South who were kept as slaves for their own good. All dark-skinned peoples were backwards, because they stubbornly refused to accept the advanced ways and teachings of the white man. They resisted attempts to convert them to true religions, they clung to ancient tribal customs concerning the planting and cultivating of the earth, and they engaged in secret heathen rituals. Will said they were dangerous and should all be enslaved, driven off, or murdered. Of course, who was Will to talk?

But still she wondered. Indian ways were so different. So hard to understand. Just when she thought she was beginning to understand Kin-di-wa, he would do or say something that shocked her—and act as though what he'd done was the most rational thing in the world. She'd been so foolish, so very gullible, to think he harbored any special feeling for her. He'd known when he made love to her that he belonged to another woman!

At least here at Roche de Boeuf, they would no longer be alone together. She needn't worry anymore that her defenses would once again slip. Her body was such a traitor to put such lusty and shameless ideas in her head. She ought to be grateful to Will! He'd taught her what she should have known by instinct: men are not to be trusted. Men cared nothing for a woman's feelings. A man would use a woman only to satisfy his passions, his animal urgings, then he'd leave her for another.

Well, she'd not make the mistake of putting her trust in a man again! From now on, her heart, head, and body would belong only to herself!

Soft feminine voices suddenly murmured right above her. Rebecca opened her eyes to find two women standing over her: one, a tall, willowy, young Indian maiden, and the other, a smaller woman, fine-boned as a child.

The small one took a step closer, and Rebecca sat up with a startled exclamation. Mischievous, black eyes flashing, the girl knelt down in front of her as if to show there was no necessity for being afraid or making a fuss.

"You—Cat-Eyes. Pretty Cat-Eyes," she said in a soft precise English. "I—*Wan-gan-o-pith*, Sweet Breeze, son of Little Turtle." She pointed to herself.

"Son?" Rebecca repeated.

The black eyes glinted with amusement. The delicate mouth curved upwards. "Not son? Maybe daughter then—I forget."

"Yes, daughter," said Rebecca. "You mean daughter of Little Turtle."

"And wife of *Apekonit*, he of the red hair—like

173

yours. Only not so pretty."

The girl's eyes were enormous and so expressive—like a fawn's eyes, only they crackled with vitality and good humor. Rebecca smiled into her pretty oval face. "No, I think you must be mistaken again. Your husband would have black hair—see? Like your braids."

The girl's hair hung in two neat, shiny, black braids down over her shoulders and across her childish breasts to her waist. An embroidered headband crossed her forehead, and her dress or smock, of finest soft doeskin had an embroidered bodice and was thickly fringed at sleeve and knee. Rebecca reached over and fingered a long black braid. "Black. Your hair is black. And your husband's must be black too—unless he's a white man."

"He *is* white man," Sweet Breeze said. Her slender eyebrows quirked upwards. "And Miami too! He is—adopted son of my father. Brought home when little boy."

Rebecca began to feel excited. Another white person nearby! No doubt, he too had been taken captive! "Your husband whose name is Ap— Ap—"

"Apekonit," the girl supplied.

"Can you take me to him? Maybe we know each other! Maybe we met when we were children!" This possibility wasn't really so far-fetched as it sounded, for she *had* known a boy named Clarence Tuttle who'd gone west and been stolen away by

Indians. His parents had come back to Pennsylvania broken-hearted, unable to go on living in a land that had dealt them so cruel a blow. She remembered him especially because he too had been cursed with bright red hair.

"No. Cannot take you to him. He gone." The girl's eyes became two large pools of sadness. "He gone to his own people—gone to Chenoten. Apekonit no can kill own people anymore. Go home to Chenoten. Kill own Miami people now everyone say, but I know better. Apekonit no traitor to Miami. He come back to true home one day—come home to lodge of Sweet Breeze—and we make big strong sons together."

Another deceitful man. Rebecca's heart went out to the slim young girl with her huge sorrowing eyes. "What was his English name? The one he had before he became Apekonit. Do you know it?"

"His name Wells, William Wells. He teach me say it—teach me speak white man's tongue plenty much good. Is not so? But I be needing practice. Apekonit make me practice everyday. His Miami name means color of root same color as hair. Your hair, his hair—red root color."

"Yes, you speak my language very well, and maybe I can help you practice now—while I am here." Rebecca smiled again, charmed by this guileless child. But she felt disappointed too. This William Wells wasn't her Clarence Tuttle after all. Then her glance fell on the second woman who'd been standing silently nearby.

This second girl was taller and even prettier than the one called Sweet Breeze, but with a strange haunting kind of beauty that had none of Sweet Breeze's warmth or charm. Her skin was pale bronze, her hair blue-black: long, shiny, and braided into one single heavy rope whose total length down her back Rebecca couldn't see. Her nose was straight and as noble as Kin-di-wa's, her lips full and naturally red.

Rebecca noticed how her doeskin smock, less intricately embroidered and beaded than Sweet Breeze's, clung seductively to full rounded breasts and hips. She is enough to make a man's heart beat wildly, Rebecca thought. She looked up into the girl's beautiful black eyes, full of mystery, and discovered an intense hostility.

She was taken back. "Hello, do you speak English too?"

"She not speak white man's tongue," Sweet Breeze explained. "That why I come with her to get you. Kin-di-wa say we bring you to lodge of Two Fires."

"Two Fires?" Rebecca's heart skipped a beat. Was this breathtaking creature Two Fires—the woman Kin-di-wa must marry?

"Two Fires pleased you come visit. She woman of *Ka-ta-mon-gli*, Black Loon, Kin-di-wa's brother. Soon be Kin-di-wa's woman." Sweet Breeze smiled at Two Fires, oblivious to Rebecca's discomfort. "Kin-di-wa fine strong warrior like Black Loon, breed good sons, bring home plenty meat and train Little Walks Tall be good hunter too. Two Fires lucky squaw.''

But Two Fires didn't look pleased with her luck or that Rebecca had come to visit. She looked mad enough to bite. Rebecca got to her feet, and Two Fire's glance swept over her from head to moccasin. Her nostrils flared. Sparks of anger leapt in her eyes. She said something which caused Sweet Breeze to color and look embarrassed.

"What did she say?" Rebecca demanded.

"Two Fires shame her lodge and Kin-di-wa's good name!" Sweet Breeze said indignantly.

"How? Why? What did she say?"

"She say white man's whore woman not good enough sleep in Two Fire's lodge. No matter that Kin-di-wa command it, she no want to take you there."

"Then I won't sleep in her lodge! I'll sleep somewhere else! Tell her that!" Rebecca drew herself up straight and returned Two Fires's glare. The girl was a fraction of an inch taller than she was, and her haughty attitude made Rebecca's blood begin to boil. "Tell her the lodge of *Kin-di-wa's* whore woman isn't good enough for *me!*"

Sweet Breeze clapped her hands to her face. "Oh, no! I not tell her that! Kin-di-wa be plenty mad already you two speak like spitting cats. I tell her that and she draw knife on you."

"A knife!" And it seemed to Rebecca that this jealous beauty was just waiting for such an excuse. The black eyes never blinked. Well, I won't give

177

her an excuse! Rebecca thought. But neither will I stand for threats!

"All right," Rebecca tried to keep her voice calm and even. "Tell her I'm sorry she's inconvenienced by my arrival, but I don't intend to stay here long. I am going back to my own people soon—at the very first opportunity. And tell her this: whatever else I may be, I'm not a whore. I don't have a knife but if she does not take that back, I shall have to prove it to her with my fists!" Rebecca raised her fists menacingly and scowled as hard as she could.

Sweet Breeze translated rapidly, and some of the animosity faded from Two Fires's eyes. The girl's voice—low and melodious—rose and fell in a long speech Rebecca hoped was conciliatory and apologetic.

"Two Fires say she sorry she call you whore, but she hear all white women be whores, taking away men who belong to others. You too beautiful to be good woman, and she worried you try take Kin-di-wa. If you no try take him, you welcome in her lodge. But if you give him come-hurry sign with great green cat eyes, she cut your throat, even though Kin-di-wa be plenty much mad at her."

Two Fires nodded as if to give weight to Sweet Breeze's words, and Rebecca fought a wild impulse to laugh. Here was this gorgeous creature, the loveliest girl she'd ever seen, accusing *her* of being too beautiful to be good! She put out her hand to Two Fires, "I promise you I will not try to take Kin-di-wa away from you. I understand he belongs to you.''

And her heart twisted against her unspoken thought: he doesn't want me anyway. How could he—when he has you?

Two Fires, hearing this translated, smiled a real smile then—one that reached her eyes, and took Rebecca's hand. She was all the more beautiful when she smiled, a radiant dark-eyed Indian goddess. Her tender red lips spoke a soft reply.

"Two Fires say welcome to the Miamis. Welcome to Roche de Boeuf." Sweet Breeze grinned. "And now she wishes you to go to her lodge and meet Walks Tall, son of the great warrior Black Loon, soon to be Kin-di-wa's son."

Two Fires's lodge stood somewhere in the midst of dozens of others that were crammed into a little clearing half way between Roche de Boeuf and Fallen Timbers. Here, Rebecca found the hustle and bustle that had been missing in Kekionga. Children darted between the make-shift lodges, and horses and dogs roamed freely—snorting or barking. Babies cried, outdoor cook-fires sputtered and sizzled, and a whole cacophony of chattering voices assaulted her ears. The smell of woodsmoke, leather, and cooking hung like a pungent haze over the clearing. And not far distant through the surrounding trees, the river glistened like a golden ribbon sewn onto a green and brown dress.

"We break camp soon, move other side of Fallen Timbers," Sweet Breeze told Rebecca as they threaded their way through the lodges. "Move nearer Fort Miami. Much safer there. *Saginwash* protect us when Chenoten come."

"Saginwash?" Rebecca asked.

"English. British. We call Saginwash. King's store at Fort Miami filled with plenty guns to fight Chenoten. And more Saginwash soldiers arrive only yesterday."

Rebecca stepped around an open-mouthed child who suddenly glanced up from a game involving two sticks and a handful of stones. The boy was completely naked, she noticed, as were most of the children darting between the lodges. He gaped at her incredulously, tossing his long black hair out of his eyes so he could see her better. "How many soldiers do the British—the Saginwash—have?" she asked.

"Three companies of Twenty-fourth Infantry, a detachment of Royal Artill—Artill—"

Rebecca came to her assistance. "Artillery?"

"Yes, artillery! The men who make the big guns thunder. And now, one hundred more soldiers come yesterday from Fort Detroit." Sweet Breeze grinned, not a little boastfully, "I work hard to learn big words like infantry and artillery."

Rebecca was too stunned to compliment her. This battle at Fallen Timbers could *easily* turn into another war with Great Britain! She tried to think of the British commander's name at Fort Detroit, but the only name she could remember was Governor John Graves Simcoe of Upper

Canada. Papa, of course, had known all their names. Like most veterans of the last war with the British, he had made it his business to keep track of such things.

"Big Saginwash Chief, Governor Simcoe himself, come to watch building of Fort Miami. He order other posts be built near big waters of Lake Erie too," Sweet Breeze further informed her.

"Governor Simcoe is *here?*" Rebecca stopped walking in dismay. Immediately, she was surrounded by children who stood quietly gaping up at her.

And past their curious dark-skinned faces, a number of women stopped poking at cook-fires and halted their chattering to stare at her. In their stares was something hostile and questioning. She was momentarily distracted from being upset that Governor Simcoe himself had come to Roche de Boeuf, for the women seemed to be muttering, "Who is this enemy white woman who has come among us?"

"Big Saginwash Chief not here now," Sweet Breeze said. "Go home to Canada Country but leave soldiers here with us." She too then noticed the interest they were drawing. "Hurry! Hurry! Do not lag!" she cried harshly. "Kin-di-wa no like new slave woman be lazy good-for-nothing squaw!"

Rebecca choked on her shock. "I'm not a slave woman!"

"Shhh . . ." Sweet Breeze whispered. "Go quick.

KATHARINE KINCAID

Follow Two Fires into lodge." She began to shout
in the native tongue, and suddenly, everyone
who'd been staring began to laugh heartily and
point to Rebecca. She caught the mention of Kin-
di-wa's name, and one of the children took hold of
her braid from behind and tugged on it cruelly.

Two Fires stood in front of a lodge entrance,
gesturing for her to enter. Her lovely lips curled
upwards in a smile of ill-concealed satisfaction.
Then she turned on her heel and went into the
lodge.

Rebecca hurried after her, feeling her face flush
as red as her hair. She waited only until Sweet
Breeze let drop the skin at the lodge entrance, then
turned on her indignantly. "Why did you tell them
I'm a slave? First, I'm called a whore—and now,
I'm called a slave! Is that the way you treat all your
visitors?"

Sweet Breeze looked apologetic. "Please no be
angry with me. But this is war time. Even in peace
time, no white woman come among us as friend
and visitor. She come only as slave or captive.
Maybe she come as warrior's woman—his whore.
Since you no Kin-di-wa's woman, then you must
be his slave. I tell them you pretty white woman
slave he bring home to serve Two Fires."

"But I'm not a slave or a whore! Can't I just be a
friend?"

Sweet Breeze dropped her eyes. "Better you be
slave. No need make explanation then when talk-
talk starts. How come Kin-di-wa friend of white

woman? How come Sweet Breeze friend of same? Kin-di-wa turning traitor? Sweet Breeze turning same? In war time, talk-talk everywhere. Must be careful.''

And Rebecca remembered how the Shawnee had accused Kin-di-wa of turning traitor. No one could be more loyal to the Miamis than Kin-di-wa, but his blue eyes and mixed blood made him suspect. And Sweet Breeze must also be suspect: she'd fallen in love with a white man who'd abandoned his Indian ways and gone back to his own people!

Rebecca's sympathy for the young girl deepened. "Then I will pretend to be a slave—but only for a little while. I want it to be clear, at least to both of you, that I am a guest here. I'm going back home, remember, as soon as this battle is over. When it's safe to travel." Rebecca glanced toward Two Fires. "Tell her that, will you? I want her to understand."

While Sweet Breeze translated, Rebecca looked around the lodge. It was almost identical to Crow Woman's, except there were no sleeping platforms nor so many luxurious furs. The lodge had obviously been built in haste—almost thrown together in a make-shift manner—but the same sense of neatness prevailed. Baskets, bundles, and cooking utensils had all been arranged in careful order, and over the stone-rimmed fire, a bubbling caldron hung.

Then, off to the side of the lodge in a heap of

skins, a movement caught Rebecca's eye. A pudgy little foot shot up, rapidly followed by a second one, and a small dimpled hand waved and caught hold of the first foot. Something cooed and hiccuped. Two Fires crossed the lodge and knelt down, murmuring low in her throat. Her eyes lit up like twin glowing candles as she lifted up her naked son.

"Walks-Tall," Sweet Breeze told Rebecca unnecessarily. "He wake up from nap."

Two Fires held the baby almost carelessly, balanced on her hip, while his fat dimpled hand went questing down the front of her laced-up smock. She pushed his hand away, speaking gruffly, but Rebecca could see that this plump little boy-child was Two Fires's pride and joy. Back his hand came again, plucking at her breast. The child grunted but didn't cry, and Two Fires sat down cross-legged on the mats and began to undo her dress.

Rebecca and Sweet Breeze sat down too. Rebecca didn't know much about babies, never having had a small brother or sister, but she guessed that little Walks-Tall must be little less than a year old. Certainly, he couldn't walk yet—though he looked quite capable of trying. What a funny name for him! Walks-Tall. Then a picture of Kin-di-wa jumped into her head. Kin-di-wa always walked tall, with a proud and arrogant posture, even when he was hurt. His brother must also have walked tall—so perhaps the name was indeed appropriate.

As soon as Two Fires freed one breast from the bodice of her dress, Walks-Tall gulped it into his mouth. He sucked loudly and noisily, an expression of bliss on his face. His free hand sought and found his mother's other breast, and he clung to it tightly as though it might somehow get away from him before he was ready for it. He was a beautiful, lusty man-child, with enormous black eyes, golden skin, and raven-black hair.

"You have husband? You have sons?" Sweet Breeze asked.

"No," Rebecca answered.

"Nor do I have sons." Sweet Breeze sounded wistful. "But I shall have them one day—when Apekonit comes back."

Rebecca thought of Kin-di-wa's mother who'd been abandoned by a white trapper. "What if he doesn't come back?" she asked directly. "You are the daughter of a chief. Surely, you could have any warrior you want."

Sweet Breeze plucked at the mat they sat on. "Apekonit come back. I know it. And I no want other warriors."

"But will your people allow him to return? Didn't you say he went to join Chenoten?"

"When he comes back, they will forget he served Chenoten. Apekonit great warrior. He slay one—two hundred soldiers during war with Chief Arthur St. Clair. His arm grow stiff from scalping. My people not forget *that*."

A prickly feeling ran up Rebecca's spine. She glanced upwards at the center lodge pole. Sure enough, there hung a long string of scalps. She wondered who they belonged to—Kin-di-wa or his brother. "If he fought so hard in that battle, why then did he leave you? Why did he join Chenoten?"

Sweet Breeze sighed. "Apekonit has evil spirits inside his head. They make him dream bad dreams. He dream he kill his brother. Is not so strange. Blue Jacket, the Shawnee chieftain, kill *his* brother in that battle. Blue Jacket once white man also."

"But dreams alone could not force him to go—could they?"

"Dreams can make a man do anything," Sweet Breeze disagreed. "After battle with Arthur St. Clair, dreams get worse. Apekonit no more talk, no more laugh. One day he take my father, Little Turtle, downriver to Council Elm and say, 'When sun reaches meridian, I go cross river. I go join Chenoten. If you meet me in battle, you must kill me, as I will then kill you.' Then Apekonit go away and join Chenoten."

Rebecca was sorry she'd asked. Sweet Breeze seemed not even to realize she'd been deserted—run out on by her husband, this Apekonit, this William Wells! Sweet Breeze turned to her with grave dignity, her eyes brimming with unshed tears. "But I know Apekonit come back. I am his heart. We are his people. He fight against us now because he must. When fighting ends, he will come back.''

You poor deluded girl! Rebecca thought. Tears welled up in her own eyes. She didn't know it was possible to love so much—as much as Sweet Breeze loved her Apekonit. If only there were no wars to tear lovers apart! If only people could learn to live together in trust and peace! For a single fleeting moment, Rebecca had a vision of a world where a love such as Sweet Breeze's could grow and flower—could one day bear fruit. If she and Kin-di-wa could only find such a place, their love too might stand a chance! But then she remembered the way the world was; Sweet Breeze—and she herself it seemed—had been doomed to bitter disappointment from the very day they were born.

Little Walks-Tall finished his meal with a gurgle of contentment. He struggled to get out of Two Fires's arms. She set him down on his feet, let go, and for a moment, he teetered there uncertainly. Excitement shone in his big black eyes. He took a step, laughed joyously, then fell down kerplunk! on his rounded bottom. His mouth curled downward, and Rebecca thought he was going to cry, but then he looked up and saw her. His eyes widened with curiosity.

''Come, little Walks-Tall, come and meet Cat-Eyes!'' Sweet Breeze held out her arms. He crawled toward her without hesitation, reaching Rebecca first. He blinked at her like a little owl, his face as round as a pumpkin's crowned with a thatch of straight black hair. Her throat constricted. Reaching out, she gathered him into her arms.

"How beautiful you are!" she cried. *"Mi-shi,"* she said over his head to his mother. "Wonderful."

Two Fires nodded, her eyes shining. *"Mi-shi."*

"But that very good!" Sweet Breeze exclaimed. "You learning Miami tongue!"

Rebecca was embarrassed. The word hadn't come out sounding much at all like the one Crow Woman first used to describe her hair. Perhaps, she just needed more practice getting her tongue around the strange sounding Indian words. Perhaps, Sweet Breeze would help her. Or Two Fires.

No, she wouldn't ask Two Fires! Just because Walks-Tall was such an adorable baby was no reason to make friends with his mother! Indeed, Rebecca reflected, she'd already become far more friendly with Two Fires than she ever intended— considering the circumstances under which they'd just met.

Still, she could not resist nuzzling the baby's soft smooth skin, and he reached up and grabbed her hair. As she was struggling to disengage his hand, Kin-di-wa strode into the lodge. Immediately, Two Fires jumped to her feet.

"Ah," said Kin-di-wa, "I see they found you."

Rebecca fought down the feeling of relief and happiness she experienced every time she saw him. She sat calmly, fondling Walks-Tall, as Kin-di-wa walked over to her and smiled down at the baby. Walks-Tall's fingers were firmly entwined in her braid, and he was endeavoring to eat the shiny red coil.

"I see you have met Walks-Tall too." Kin-di-wa spoke a few quick words in the nature of a command, and Walks-Tall, looking up at him, let go of the braid. Kin-di-wa's hand came down on the baby's head, and Rebecca almost winced at the look of pride in his eyes. The child might have been his own son, instead of his brother's! She put the baby down.

"He will make a fine strong warrior, will he not? If his mother does not spoil him." Kin-di-wa then turned to Two Fires and spoke again. Her lovely face blushed a rosy color, she nodded, and padded quietly out of the lodge.

"He send Two Fires to bring hunk of meat from kill of best friend, *Peshewa*," Sweet Breeze whispered in an aside. "Tonight big feast in lodge."

Kin-di-wa overheard her. "You come too, Sweet Breeze. I have already invited your father."

Sweet Breeze smiled shyly and rose to her feet. "You honor me, Kin-di-wa. Your friendship mean plenty much—especially now Apekonit gone. I go now and dress best doeskin and beads. We celebrate your return."

Kin-di-wa snorted. "It is not a good time for celebration. What I went away for, I did not achieve. Black Loon's murderer still wears his scalp."

"Not important, Kin-di-wa. You find him one day. More important you come home to fight

189

Chenoten." Sweet Breeze smiled at Rebecca. "I find new doeskin for Cat-Eyes too. Old buckskin shirt good covering for man—but not for pretty woman."

After Sweet Breeze had gone out, Kin-di-wa hunkered down in front of the bubbling caldron which exuded a warm savory aroma. He poked at its contents with one finger, burning himself— then shook the injured finger and blew on it. Rebecca thought he must either be very hungry to have done something so foolish, or else he had something else beside a hot caldron on his mind. He turned a piercing blue-eyed gaze on her. "So, little Cat-Eyes, you have met my brother's wife and son, who soon will become my wife and son. What think you?"

Rebecca averted her eyes to the baby who was now exploring among Two Fires's baskets. "Two Fires is very beautiful, and Walks-Tall—he would bring joy to any father."

Kin-di-wa licked his finger. "It is expected that we marry. A squaw cannot live alone, and Two Fires has no family—no brother or father to take her in."

"I understand," Rebecca murmured. Was Kin-di-wa trying to tell her something? He needn't offer any explanation; the lovely Two Fires was explanation enough. "When will the ceremony take place?"

Kin-di-wa suddenly took hold of her chin and brought her face around to look at him instead of

Walks-Tall. "Look at me when I speak to you, Cat-Eyes. Am I not still your brother?"

Tears pricked her eyelids. "We were never truly brother and sister. We were never *anything* together."

His blue eyes flickered. "That is not so. On the journey here, we were brother and sister. I protected you and brought you meat. You cooked my meat and prepared our beds. And once—before that—we were lovers."

"And now, I'm to be your slave!" she said bitterly. "The woman you brought home to serve Two Fires."

Kin-di-wa's hand dropped down to her shoulder. The warmth and weight of it burned through her buckskin. "Who told you such a thing, little Cat-Eyes? It was never in my mind to make you a slave. You are like the eagle—a wild, free thing. I would try to tame you, but never to enslave you."

"No, *you* are like the eagle. Isn't that your name? Golden Eagle? And it was Sweet Breeze who said I must act the slave. Among your people, there is no other choice it seems. I am either slave or kept woman. Whore is the better word for it. So if I must *act* the slave, then that is what I am. Since your people don't understand simple friendship, all that's left is to be your enemy!"

His hand caressed her shoulder. "It does not matter what my people think. It matters only what you think. You will be safer here if they think you a slave—though it would be even safer if you were

191

my kept woman. Then no one would insult you. And no other brave would dare look on you with lust.''

So *that's* where he's heading! Rebecca thought furiously. He wants both Two Fires *and* me! She brushed his hand off her shoulder. ''I will never be a savage's whore!'' she spat.

His mouth tightened. ''Someone should teach you, Cat-Eyes, to more closely guard your tongue.''

''You've taught me enough already!'' She would have gotten up then—gone anywhere to get away from him, but his hand slid suddenly around her waist. He pulled her to him.

''Cat-Eyes, little Cat-Eyes,'' he whispered, ''what fire *is* this you've set burning in my veins?''

''No, don't!'' she begged, but he tilted her head back and his lips came down upon hers. They set her mouth aflame. A warm liquid feeling gushed through her. She struggled helplessly for a moment, as the close shelter of the lodge spun away from her. Then neither lodge nor cook-fire nor little Walks-Tall seemed to exist. They simply floated away, and she floated with them. Soared above them. Suddenly, there was nothing to hem her in. She felt herself rising—rising to meet him in this flight of passion, this long burning kiss. Then his hand strayed down to her breast.

It ended instantly. She broke away from him and came back down to earth with a grinding thud. ''No! Don't touch me!'' she sobbed. It might have been Will himself whose hand had reached for her. Revulsion shook her.

"I am sorry, little Cat-Eyes. I have frightened you. I am sorry. It will not happen again."

Her breath was coming in great ragged gasps while she fought to keep her tears in check. Little Walks-Tall peered up at her in alarm. "I have frightened little Walks-Tall." She tried to make a joke of it, to still the tremor in her voice—without success.

"It is all right," Kin-di-wa whispered. He leaned forward and brushed her lips with a second kiss. A gentle, brotherly kiss. "It is all right."

"Nothing is all right!" she protested, and as if to prove her point, a slight sound near the lodge entrance suddenly demanded her attention.

Two Fires was standing there, eyes smoldering with rage and shock. She held a bloody slab of meat, and the blood dripped down her fingers, plopped to the mats, and formed an ugly spreading stain.

Now she will kill me, Rebecca thought. Now she will find some way to kill me.

Eight

"Ah, but you plenty much beautiful!" Sweet Breeze exclaimed to Rebecca. "Your hair like flame-colored waterfall." She fastened a beaten silver brooch to the newly braided rope of Rebecca's hair, then stood back to admire the effect in the flickering light of her lodge-fire.

The length of shining hair fell across Rebecca's right breast, and with her hair thus tamed and her body sheathed in soft tan doeskin, she suddenly felt nervous and fluttery—as if rediscovering a forgotten aspect of her shattered femininity. What would Kin-di-wa think when he saw her?

An embroidered band went round her forehead, and a thong decorated with small red-dyed feathers tied the end of her braid. The silver brooch and Crow Woman's moccasins completed her new wardrobe, and if her dress wasn't the blue watered silk she'd always longed for, it was at least far softer and more becoming than Papa's soiled buckskin shirt.

"It's very good of you to give me these things," she told Sweet Breeze. The young girl was looking quite lovely herself in an elaborately embroidered dress, shell beads, and braids wound through with feathers and silver ornaments. "But is it customary to dress a slave in such finery?"

"Not good worry too much about being slave. Slaves often given gifts—unless they bad slaves. Sometimes, they adopted into family. Well-dressed slave bring honor to Kin-di-wa. Show he value his property, value Two Fires. Besides," she grinned impishly, "no one tell Sweet Breeze no can give gifts. Sweet Breeze daughter of war chief. She do as she please."

Rebecca grinned back at her, wishing she need never go back to Two Fires's lodge. It had been such a relief when Sweet Breeze had come and gotten her to try on the dress. After that first awful moment when Two Fires's feelings had shown plainly on her face, the girl had come into the lodge with her meat and gone about her business as though she'd seen nothing that happened between Rebecca and Kin-di-wa.

Her face had quickly assumed a pleasant passive expression as she got out another iron pot, removed the first one from the fire, and carved the meat into chunks with a long sharp blade that set Rebecca's heart to hammering whenever she looked at it.

Kin-di-wa had acted perfectly natural too. Taking down a long curved bow fastened to the wall of the lodge, he occupied himself with demonstrating the finer points of bowstringing to little Walks-Tall.

Only Rebecca, it seemed, felt awkward and ashamed, spilling out a whole basket of dried berries as she tried to assist Two Fires in preparing the evening's feast. Then she'd further disgraced herself by blushing a furious red. Oh, how she wished she had the Indian gift for concealing her feelings!

But even Two Fires hadn't been able to hide that single look of savage jealousy. Rebecca shivered. Fair warning had been given; she must not intrude on the girl's relationship with Kin-di-wa. Or she risked having her throat slit!

"Cat-Eyes!" Sweet Breeze was standing there ready to go; then, suddenly, she appeared to think of something. "Cat-Eyes, wait! Must show you how pretty you look!"

Sweet Breeze darted away to rummage through a basket tucked in a corner of her tiny neat lodge. "No need big lodge," she had told Rebecca, "until Apekonit come home." She hurried back and thrust a glittering shard of glass into Rebecca's hand. "Peshewa bring me this. He say white women use look-see glass instead of river to see if pretty. He trade furs for it from trapper who come through river portage."

Rebecca took the piece of broken mirror with

197

fingers that suddenly shook. She hadn't seen a looking glass since she and Papa left Pennsylvania! Her own had been smashed into smithereens on the trail coming out. Holding the mirror up to her face, she was startled to see the changes brought about by nearly eight months in the wilderness.

Her skin still had a peachy color, but had darkened to a deeper shade of gold than she remembered, making her eyes leap out—shockingly green, against the blush of her cheeks. Her hair, parted down the middle, looked even redder than before. The sun had burnished it to a glorious coppery color that was streaked with russet highlights—the color of autumn leaves.

Her nose was still straight and small, tilted slightly upwards at the end, her cheekbones still high and prominent, her mouth still the same set of overlarge pouting lips. But despite all this, it was almost a stranger who looked back at her from the mirror.

Several damp curling tendrils of hair had already escaped from her braid, but the new embroidered headband otherwise did an admirable job of keeping the bulk of her unruly hair in place. It also made her look exotic—strange—as if she were a whole new person.

Or perhaps, what made her seem different was the shadowed haunted look in the depths of her eyes. She looked, she thought, much older. Where was the young girl who'd dreamed of one day riding in a fine carriage down cobblestoned streets? Where was the girl who hoped to capture a handsome gentleman with shy fluttering glances? The gaze looking back at her now was hardly innocent, hardly virginal.

A chill closed round her heart. Any gentleman who looked at her now would somehow know immediately that her body had been violated—plundered of all its secrets.

Yes, something has been lost, she thought, and what a fool I've been to think it wouldn't show!

She was deeply angered and filled with regret. Her eyes betrayed everything. She looked older because she *was* older—not in years—but in the experiences that shape one's whole being. The young girl was gone forever! Who *was* this brilliantly colored, unhappy-looking woman who stood there now?

Sweet Breeze's childish voice broke into her dark thoughts. "Why you sad, Cat-Eyes? I thought glass would please you—make you happy!"

Rebecca gave her back the mirror. "It—it's only that I didn't recognize myself dressed up like an Indian."

"But soft doeskin dress much better than buckskin shirt—is it not? And more comfortable with your legs free, than when you wear long skirts of your people."

"Oh, it's much better than the shirt!" Rebecca assured her. She remembered how her long, scratchy, homespun skirts had always been hot and uncomfortable. "But my people think a woman's legs and ankles should always be covered. Our men would be scandalized if we went around dressed like this—in a skirt that only comes down to one's knees!"

Sweet Breeze burst out laughing. "Why? Men no have legs and ankles too—like women?"

It did seem absurd then, and Rebecca began to laugh. "Yes, but—a woman isn't ladylike if she allows her extremities to be seen!"

"Oh, Cat-Eyes!" Sweet Breeze giggled. "I no understand your people. Your squaws wear dresses cut to here, sometimes, yes?" she indicated her nearly non-existent bosom. "Why then cover up knees? See here," she pushed her dress up to expose her thigh. "Indian squaw need good leg to roll basswood fibers, make good strong rope."

She made a rolling motion with the palm of her hand against her thigh to show the way fiber was rolled to make twine. "Big trouble do this with long skirt on."

"Yes, I should think so," Rebecca conceded. "When I go home, I'll have to tell my people to change their way of dressing, but I don't think they'll listen!"

"That is trouble with your people, no listen when hear good advice." Sweet Breeze put away the mirror. "Come now, we go to feast."

The sun that had shone so warmly earlier in the day had already set in a blaze of crimson, so Sweet Breeze took up a crudely made pitch pine torch and thrust the end of it into her lodge-fire where it sputtered into flame. The torch would light their way back to Two Fires's lodge.

As Rebecca followed Sweet Breeze through the maze of glowing huts, she noticed that the village had settled down from its chattering bustle to a sleepy murmur. Each lodge emitted a snug warm light as lodge-fires sent up spirals of gray mist through the smoke-holes. Shadowy figures moved between the dwellings or sat outside in front of entranceways. The fires which had been lit outdoors for cooking or other purposes had all but smoldered out, and Rebecca sensed that now was the time of day when families put aside work and gathered together to exchange gossip. She looked about with envy, remembering how it had been with her own family. Soft laughter and talk filled the air, but not a few voices fell silent and faces stared intently after them as they passed by.

As they neared Two Fires's lodge, the figure of a short squat woman joined them. "It is *Tecumwah*," Sweet Breeze whispered. "Peshewa's mother. We be eating her son's meat so it only right she come. She has no husband. Peshewa's father was commander of French Fort Vincennes. Tecumwah half-sister of my father. Between my father and Peshewa, Tecumwah plenty well looked after. She help Peshewa manage portage too—make many good trades for winter furs."

Rebecca planted the name firmly in her mind along with all the other new names she was

201

learning. She was going to be interested to meet this Peshewa too. Another half-breed. Would he too have blue eyes—like Kin-di-wa?

She stole a look at Tecumwah in the torch light: or would he be round-faced, stolid, and swarthy like his mother? Tecumwah's small black eyes swept over Rebecca with disinterest—as if to say, this is only Two Fires's slave, what does *she* matter?

When they arrived at Two Fires's lodge and entered, they found Kin-di-wa and Peshewa already seated on mats with their backs to them, engaged in earnest conversation. Two Fires was stirring a large caldron over the fire, and little Walks-Tall was nowhere to be seen. Then Rebecca spotted him bundled into some sort of contraption which hung from the side of the lodge.

It took her a moment to realize he was laced into a lavishly embroidered and decorated cradle-board—a kind of carrying device about which she'd heard much but never seen. Made of wood and hide, it had a small shelf at the bottom to support his feet, and a wooden bow projected from the top. A strip of hide could obviously be draped over the bow to protect him from the elements, but as it was not needed in the lodge, such a strip had been discarded. The cradleboard hung from a leather strap fastened to a lodge pole, and Walks-Tall looked quite comfortable, if a bit cramped.

He's getting too big, she thought, to be so confined, but it didn't seem to bother him. He yawned widely and looked sleepily about. Rebecca resisted the impulse to go over to him, lest he begin to whimper and cry to be let out.

Sweet Breeze beckoned to her to sit down in the shadows, away from the men, and she was only too happy to do so. She hoped no one would take much notice of her, but Kin-di-wa, sensing her presence, glanced up and favored her with a small shadow of a smile. He had changed to a ceremonial breech clout. At least, it looked ceremonial to her with its colorful designs and elaborate fringe. He also wore two spanking new white feathers in his hair which was tied back with a silver encrusted thong.

She tore her eyes away from him without smiling in return, and his voice came low and softly, "Come into the light from the fire, Cat-Eyes, so my friend and his mother may see you."

Sweet Breeze gave her a nudge, and she obeyed, kneeling down beside Tecumwah who'd taken her place nearer to the men. The man called Peshewa leaned forward, as if startled, and looked her slowly up and down. Chagrined by this careful inspection, she raised her eyes to stare back at him.

He looked every inch a savage, a man exactly like his mother. His features were blunt and plain, his eyes two small black beads—slanted slightly—above a crooked nose. His head had been plucked of all hair, except for a strip that stood on end and ran back the length of his head. This ridiculous shock of hair was made even more ridiculous by

KATHARINE KINCAID

the addition of blood-red quills that stuck straight up and made him look, she thought, like a rooster.

He was short, squat, and powerfully built, with arms that seemed too long for his body, and she couldn't tell what he was thinking as his beady eyes inspected her. He made her feel uncomfortable, so she amused herself by studying the tattoos running across his chest. Done in black and brown dye, they depicted the figure of a man in various exciting exploits—shooting down a bear at close range with bow and arrow, herding a band of horses, and reaching down to scalp a white man. Suddenly, she realized that the crudely drawn figures looked amazingly like the man himself.

"This is my friend, Peshewa," Kin-di-wa said. "His name means Wild Cat—for good reason. There is no other warrior I would rather have by my side in battle, unless it is Little Turtle himself, or Little Turtle's son, Apekonit."

He repeated this statement in the Miami tongue, and Peshewa's eyes glittered. He spoke haltingly, "Kin-di-wa—good friend. Peshewa stand by him always—same as stood by Apekonit."

So Peshewa and Apekonit and Kin-di-wa had *all* been friends, Rebecca thought. And this savage-looking Peshewa spoke English. She studied him more carefully, trying to see what Kin-di-wa saw in him. And he studied her with more than casual interest. Then Peshewa nodded toward her while addressing himself to Kin-di-wa. "If she slave, I buy her from you. If you no want, I take her."

Her insides did a somersault. He was talking about her! She felt the color rush into her cheeks, and Two Fires, catching her expression, stopped stirring the meat in the caldron. Even Tecumwah leaned forward, watching intently as a hawk, though Rebecca had no idea if she understood what had been said.

"Good Friend," Kin-di-wa began. "You do not want Cat-Eyes. She does not belong to me—or I would gladly give her to you. She goes home to her own people soon, when Chenoten is defeated."

"I want," argued Peshewa. "I keep little red-haired squaw in furs and meat. Make plenty happy. I no have wife. *She* be my wife. My chosen one choose another." His glance strayed past Rebecca to where Sweet Breeze sat in the shadows.

Intuitive certainty struck Rebecca: *It's Sweet Breeze he's in love with! But he knows he can never have her—so he's willing to settle for me!*

"Cat-Eyes is a very difficult squaw," Kin-di-wa pointed out. "You would not be happy with her."

Not be happy with her! Rebecca was outraged. How dare he talk about her as though she were absent! How dare he judge and criticize her!

"Pardon me, both of you," she cut in, and both Two Fires and Tecumwah glanced up in shock. Sweet Breeze stirred behind her, and even Peshewa and Kin-di-wa looked startled.

What's wrong, she wondered, don't Indian women ever speak up in front of men?

Her insides quavered, but, having begun, she stumbled on bravely. "Among my people, a woman is never merely given away. Among *civilized* people, a woman and a man choose one another, and since it's *my* future being discussed, I feel it's only right to tell you how I feel!"

She turned to Peshewa, whose red quills were quivering. "I thank you, sir, for your offer. Were I to choose a husband from among the Miamis, I would certainly consider you. You're a most attractive man, and I'm flattered by your interest. But I'm sorry to say my mind is already made up: as soon as possible, I'm going home—back to my own people—to look for a husband."

She sat back breathless, with a small sense of triumph. She'd show these Indian women what strong stuff she was made of! She'd show Kin-di-wa too! He had no right to treat her like some mindless squaw!

The effect was all she'd hoped for. Kin-di-wa's eyes grew stormy, while Peshewa sat up straighter, preening, like a cock before a hen.

"Did I not say she was a difficult squaw, my brother?" Kin-di-wa snorted. "Now you can see why you would not want her."

But Peshewa looked far from disappointed. He grinned at Rebecca, revealing square yellow teeth, which reminded her of a horse's. "My white man name *Sieur de Richardville*. Is good proud name. My blood half-white. I make good husband. No need you decide right now. I give you time.

Think on it, Little Cat-Eyes."

Kin-di-wa glowered. Two Fires, watching the men's faces, smirked. Tecumwah sat still as a stone, scrutinizing Rebecca with hostile eyes. Rebecca wondered what Sweet Breeze, behind her, was thinking. Had she done the right thing?

Marriage to this quill-bedecked savage wasn't even a distant possibility—she couldn't even imagine it! But maybe, just maybe, if she feigned an interest in him, Two Fires's jealousy would abate.

She smiled sweetly at Peshewa. "I will think on it, Peshewa."

A slight sound came from the entranceway. Kin-di-wa leapt to his feet. *"Michikinikwa!"* he cried.

And Rebecca twisted around and saw the man she'd heard so much about—the great war chief, Little Turtle. Suddenly awestruck, she scrambled to her feet with everyone else and backed into a corner beside Sweet Breeze.

The great man came into the lodge almost humbly, but his very presence filled it. Standing half a head taller than Kin-di-wa and a full head taller than Peshewa, he was less muscularly built than either of them, but he carried himself with a grace and pride that could only belong to a chief.

Rebecca studied his dress. His tattooed chest was bare, but he wore leggings in addition to his breech clout. A long headdress of feathers intertwined with silver medals hung down his back. Heavy silver earrings brushed his shoulders, and necklaces of silver and animals' teeth adorned his neck.

But it was his face and his eyes that awed her most. He had a broad intelligent forehead, a stern forbidding expression, and eyes that seemed to look right through her. His black hair was streaked with gray, but he hadn't a trace of weakness in him—no sign of age, no hint of any slowness of mind or body. His eyes saw everything.

He nodded his head to give them permission to be seated, and Two Fires nervously prepared a place for him. She spread out a blanket woven of hundreds of rabbit skins, and grunting his approval, he sat down on it and crossed his legs.

Kin-di-wa's eyes glowed, and he seemed to have forgotten Rebecca's impertinence. A flood of gutteral syllables burst from his lips. Rebecca felt a pang of acute disappointment. If they spoke in the Miami tongue, she wouldn't be able to understand *any*thing!

Then Sweet Breeze whispered in her ear. "Kin-di-wa say welcome to humble lodge of simple warrior. It long time since he entertain great war chief."

Little Turtle responded in a full rich voice which thundered and reverberated in every corner of the lodge. Rebecca was stunned by the power in his vocal cords: this man could obviously sway hundreds—thousands—when he chose to employ such remarkable tones!

Sweet Breeze grinned at her reaction. "My father

great orator," she whispered. "When he speak in council, braves come far to hear him. His voice like Manitou's, thundering in storm clouds."

"But what did he say?" Rebecca whispered back.

"He ask if Kin-di-wa safe and well. He say Kin-di-wa right arm to him, second only to lost son, Apekonit, and he miss him very much. Now, he ask about success of journey."

A look of shame crossed Kin-di-wa's face. He began speaking, but *his* voice—which she'd always thought manly and powerful—sounded weak and shallow in comparison to the majesty of Little Turtle's. And she guessed he must be explaining his failure to avenge his brother's death.

Her own emotions churned. Will Simpkin ought not to be alive! His scalp should be dangling right now from the lodge pole! Then a feeling of horror swept over her—what was she thinking? Was she—a Christian educated woman—no better than these savages?

Suddenly Little Turtle's eyes were on her. "You!" he commanded, pointing. "Come—here!"

"My father call you," Sweet Breeze whispered, and Rebecca was smitten with sudden weakness. She tried to get up, but her legs would not support her. This was the great Little Turtle singling her out—the man whose very name could strike terror into a settler's heart. Under this man's wily leadership two distinguished American generals had been defeated! And soon, another would face him in battle.

"Cat-Eyes!" Kin-di-wa barked. "Come here!"

She went. Little Turtle gestured for her to share his rabbit-fur blanket. She knelt down on it gingerly, afraid to look any of them in the eye. Her stomach fluttered with nausea.

"So, little white woman, name of Cat-Eyes." Little Turtle thundered. Struggling to breathe calmly, she raised her eyes to meet his. His eyes were large and black. They sparkled with a fine intelligence and wry good humor. He enjoyed intimidating her! "So. Kin-di-wa find you—bring you home. You know how to read and write?"

"What?" she asked stupidly.

"You understand bird tracks—written in white men's books."

"Of course!" The last thing she had expected from him was a question concerning the extent of her education.

"Ah!" he shook his head, eyes crinkling. "That good! Very smart squaw! My son, Apekonit, read and write. Kin-di-wa read some too—but no write very good. That so?" He turned to Kin-di-wa.

Kin-di-wa nodded. "When the missionaries tried to teach me how to write, I ran off into the woods to hunt instead."

"Ah yes," Little Turtle grunted. "Before boy turns to man, he often throw away good teaching. Is pity you no learn how to write. Skill much needed now."

And Rebecca was amazed to see her proud Kin-di-wa hang his head like a rebuked child. Up to now, she'd thought him totally confident. Impervious to criticism.

Peshewa now spoke up. "Apekonit no can be replaced, great Chieftain. When he go away, he take skills with him."

Little Turtle sighed. "This I know. He teach me speak white man's tongue. He teach you. He teach Sweet Breeze. But he no teach us read or make bird tracks. Kin-di-wa read message of Chenoten, but no can write message back. Is pity."

"I can write them for you!" Rebecca burst out.

Again, there was shocked silence, as Little Turtle's eyes sought hers and held them. "Why you help Miamis, little white woman? Is not betraying your own people?"

"I—I—" Confusion threatened to overcome her. "I would never betray my own people! I only thought to help!"

She cursed her inability to hold her tongue, but Little Turtle said nothing and his eyes were not unkind. Unlike Two Fires's or Tecumwah's— their eyes were openly hostile. Whether because of jealousy at the attention she was getting or because they understood what had been said, she didn't know.

"Perhaps, if you wrote to Chenoten—communicated with him—there might be peace," she said in a small voice. "I would do anything I could to help bring about peace."

"So would I, little white woman." Little

Turtle's stern forbidding face cracked and split into an amazingly impish grin, reminding her of Sweet Breeze. "Old tired chief and red-haired squaw find something to agree on. Is good—is it not?"

"It's *very* good," she repeated with relief. His sly knowing smile reminded her of someone: could it be Papa? Surely not, she thought. No two people she knew resembled one another less.

"Pah!" Peshewa spat, startling her. "Peace impossible!" His red quills shook. "Chenoten no understand peace talk. Only understand power! We make plenty talk at treaties. We make our marks. Then white men break treaties! No can trust Chenoten. No can trust *any* white man!"

Rebecca shivered. Peshewa's violent outburst frightened her. She glanced at Kin-di-wa to see what he was thinking: he sat very still and straight, studying his hands. His expression was unreadable.

Peshewa pounded his fist on the mats. "Next peace message Chenoten send, I take back to him myself! I deliver own message—a war club in his skull!"

Little Turtle raised his hand to calm Peshewa. "Enough! We eat now. Save talk of war for another time. This is night to celebrate. We celebrate return of our brother, Kin-di-wa. We celebrate capture of new slave he bring home to Two Fires."

Rebecca almost choked, but Little Turtle's

kindly eyes bored into her. "No, not slave, we know that. But better and safer she be known as such. And better she no more speak of peace between red man and Chenoten."

And Rebecca understood the warning. This great man, for reasons of his own, had decided to befriend her; but clearly she must guard her tongue. There were subtle undercurrents flowing here—things she didn't understand. Was Little Turtle *really* interested in making peace? But what about Peshewa and his other tribesmen? And why was Kin-di-wa so silent?

Peshewa's ill-contained hatred of whites was *shared* by Kin-di-wa, that she knew, but he now seemed strangely withdrawn and reluctant to express those feelings.

Her head began to ache from tension. The odor of cooking food circulated through the lodge as Two Fires ladled out the stew over which she'd been laboring these many hours. She dipped up chunks of meat and vegetables with a gourd and placed the steaming mixture in bowls made from maple burls, a wood whose tortuous grain Rebecca immediately recognized. The food was then passed first to the men, along with crude wooden spoons, then to the women, and lastly, to Rebecca.

Two Fires's fingers brushed hers, as Rebecca accepted her bowl. Two Fires shot her a placid look, betraying nothing, but Rebecca noticed that her bowl held a smaller portion than anyone else's.

And it was all vegetables—no meat. She took it without a word, resolving then and there, to overcome Two Fires's jealousy no matter *how* difficult that might prove to be. She might even befriend the girl: after all, her life depended on it!

The hot food was quickly devoured, though Rebecca found her beans and squash tasteless. It was still too early in the season to harvest fresh vegetables: these had obviously been dried and kept from the previous summer. However, the small sliver of meat in the bottom of the bowl that had somehow escaped Two Fires's notice was delicious. The bowls were passed back and forth for refills again and again, until the men's hunger finally waned. Tecumwah and Sweet Breeze also took seconds, but Rebecca determinedly desisted.

After the meal, water from an earthenware jar was dipped out, sweetened with maple syrup, and passed around in a large gourd. By the time it got to Rebecca, after Two Fires had drunk, the water was gone. Rebecca ignored her thirst and merely smiled at Two Fires.

This is nothing but a game, she told herself, and I am going to win it! Then a niggling thought occurred: merely by playing this game, she was giving up Kin-di-wa!

Two Fires shoved the dirty bowls in Rebecca's direction, while she herself got up to tend to the now fussing Walks-Tall. Rebecca rinsed each bowl with a small amount of water from the jar, then wiped them clean with large leaves she found stacked in a basket.

Sweet Breeze joined her in the task, showing her what to do, and where to put away the bowls, while the men kept up a continuous stream of talk and took long draughts on a stone pipe they passed back and forth between them. Tecumwah joined in on the conversation from time to time, and Rebecca experienced a deep frustration that she could understand nothing of what was said.

"Will you teach me your language, Sweet Breeze?" she whispered.

"Oh, yes!" Sweet Breeze responded happily. "You learn quick already."

"Then tell me first—what is the name of that awful stuff they are smoking!" Rebecca wrinkled her nose against the cloying smell of the pipe smoke.

"Is *kinickinick*," Sweet Breeze explained. "Made from willow bark, dogwood bark, and leaves of sumac. Also sometimes called *sam-pah*."

"Kinickinick. Sam-pah," Rebecca repeated. "It's terrible!"

"You get used to. Braves smoke plenty much."

Rebecca put away the last wooden spoon, then dipped up a gourdful of plain water and drank thirstily. "Sweet Breeze," she put down the gourd. "Do you think your father will really allow me to write his responses to Chenoten's messages? Does he have writing materials?"

"Yes," Sweet Breeze answered softly. "And I think he let you. But he anxious know you better first. He anxious speak more to you about white man's ways."

"I didn't think he would be so interested in my people's ways!"

"He more interested than you know, Cat-Eyes." Sweet Breeze knelt down with Rebecca in the rim of darkness outside the fire-glow. "He talk all time to Apekonit. What white man think? How he plant? How he fight? What he eat? Why cut down trees? My father want know everything about white man."

"But why? He makes war on white men!"

"That why," Sweet Breeze explained patiently. "No can defeat enemy no can understand."

Rebecca's awe of Little Turtle grew. Perhaps, Arthur St. Clair and Josiah Harmar had failed to defeat the Indians because they'd never bothered to understand them! Probably, they'd looked down on them—the way Will and her father had—a backward people. They'd dismissed them as savages!

And she was struck with a new thought: if it was necessary to understand a people in order to defeat them, perhaps it was also necessary to understand them to live with them in peace!

"Any question your father wants to ask me about my people, I will be happy to answer," she promised Sweet Breeze. "Please tell him for me, will you? I will answer as truthfully as I know how."

Sweet Breeze smiled. "I tell him. He be pleased. But you, Cat-Eyes, must no look for my father to love white man who steals his land. He love Apekonit only. He no love Chenoten. Chenoten he drive out or kill to save land for us, his people."

But this is all so wrong! Rebecca agonized. The threat of war and death and bloodshed was hanging over them like some ominous dark storm cloud. She could smell the coming rain, see the brilliant stabs of lightning, hear the thunder. And she could do nothing to stop it!

She glanced over at Two Fires whose lovely dark head was bent to her son. The baby was nursing again, one fat dimpled hand reaching up to pat his mother's cheek. And as much as Rebecca feared and despised Two Fires, she had to admit that this sight of mother and son together was beautiful—peaceful.

What would happen to little Walks-Tall and Two Fires if Anthony Wayne *did* win this battle at Fallen Timbers? What *usually* occurred when blood-crazed soldiers rampaged through Indian villages? It wasn't hard to guess. Even if Anthony Wayne was a decent man who would not want to see women ravished and children run through with long knives, how could he prevent it? Evil things would be done in an instant—never to be undone!

217

Rebecca felt sick with dread. Little Turtle himself seemed to be a good and decent man, but had he ever been able to prevent *white* babies from having their brains dashed out against trees or their tiny scalps torn from their heads? Had he ever *tried* to prevent such things? From all the stories she'd heard, she doubted it. And she couldn't really expect Anthony Wayne to do much better.

Little Walks-Tall suddenly grinned up at his mother, and her milk dribbled out of his mouth and ran down his chin. Two Fires whispered something and hugged him. The baby latched onto her breast again with a contented sigh, and a giant fist squeezed Rebecca's heart.

She looked at Sweet Breeze, kneeling beside her, and saw the envy and longing on the young girl's face, as she too watched Two Fires and her son.

I know exactly how she feels, Rebecca thought. I wish *I* were Kin-di-wa's wife, and little Walks-Tall were *my* son!

Long after the feast was over, and Two Fires, Kin-di-wa, and little Walks-Tall had gone to sleep, Rebecca lay sleeplessly on the mats and skins assigned to her by Two Fires and thought about this long day. It hardly seemed possible they'd arrived only that morning—or rather, that noon.

She'd made two friends today: Sweet Breeze and, hopefully, Little Turtle. But she'd made an enemy out of Two Fires. She'd wrongly encouraged Peshewa to court her, to the apparent dismay of his mother, and she'd made Kin-di-wa jealous! Not a very good record for her first day among the enemy. What would tomorrow bring?

Misery and loneliness flooded over her. Her position here was quite impossible! She ought to have stayed with Crow Woman. How could she bear to see Kin-di-wa everyday and know he belonged to someone else? When would his marriage to Two Fires take place? And when it did, where would she go then?

She could hardly stay in the same lodge with them. Going to bed this very night had been awkward enough! Privacy did not exist. Kin-di-wa had taken one side of the lodge, Two Fires had given her the other, and the space in between had gone to little Walks-Tall and Two Fires herself.

What had Kin-di-wa been thinking as he sprawled out on his skins? Did he wish she weren't there? A lovely desirable woman was his for the taking, and he'd had little of women lately. She of all people knew *exactly* how little! He was only a man after all—like all men. And his burning kiss told the story: that magnificent restraint of his was finally cracking!

The thought of Kin-di-wa and Two Fires *together* knotted her stomach. She closed her eyes against the image, but it would not go away. Two Fires: standing tall and graceful before Kin-di-wa

219

as he lay on his furs, watching and waiting. Two Fires: undoing her long black braid so her hair fell down her back like a shimmering cloud of blue-black silk, the color of a raven's wing. Two Fires: unlacing her smock and drawing it down over her shoulders to reveal her perfectly formed breasts.

Rebecca had already seen those magnificent breasts—so full and womanly, so soft and golden. A man would have to be made of stone not to desire her!

Two Fires would then step out of her smock and kick it carelessly aside. Kin-di-wa's eyes would be glowing like blue flames. He would reach up, take her hand, and draw her down on the furs with him, the shaft of his manhood already straining against his breech clout. Two Fires's hands would search and find him, drive him to a frenzy. Kin-di-wa's mouth would find her breasts. Rebecca could almost hear him moaning.

Her eyes flew open. She *did* hear moaning. And in the dim light of the dying lodge fire, she saw Two Fires kneeling beside Kin-di-wa, awakening him with a kiss and a moan of passion from deep within her throat.

The girl was naked, a pagan goddess: her head thrown back, her eyes closed, her hair streaming down her back. Her lips parted, and she moaned again, then took hold of Kin-di-wa's hand and brought it to her full ripe breasts.

For only a moment, a long moment in which

220

every muscle in Rebecca's body shrieked its anguish, Kin-di-wa seemed to resist. Then with a harsh intake of breath, he drew Two Fires down beside him.

And Rebecca looked away, shaking with silent protest.

Nine

Morning did not come soon enough for Rebecca, but when it did come, Two Fires had to shake her out of a deep sleep. Startled, she sat up quickly, and Two Fires thrust a large earthenware jug into her hands and jerked her head toward the lodge entrance, indicating she wanted Rebecca to go and fetch water.

Rebecca took the jar and scrambled to her feet, noticing, as she did so, that Kin-di-wa was gone from the lodge, and little Walks-Tall was standing in the corner, hanging onto a basket and piddling on the mats. Two Fires uttered a disgusted exclamation and stalked over to the baby. She scolded him soundly in a low voice and led him outside around the corner of the lodge, to show him, no doubt, where he ought to be doing his business.

Anger and hurt swept over Rebecca with

renewed ferocity as she viewed the large buffalo robe that still bore the imprint of Kin-di-wa's body. She could recall the exact moment when Two Fires had left his side and returned to her own skins beside little Walks-Tall. And she could recall every sound of intimacy she'd been forced to listen to and endure the night before—the quick heavy breathing of passion and Two Fires's throaty soft moans.

The whole thing had been over with very quickly, but Rebecca had suffered through most of the night, reliving every moment. At the height of her pleasure, Two Fires had cried out Kin-di-wa's name, and then her voice became muffled, as though someone put a hand over her mouth.

The woman has no shame at all, Rebecca reflected. Leaping into the arms of her husband's brother is hardly the proper way to mourn her husband! Fully awake now, she went stalking out of the lodge and almost ran into Two Fires, returning with little Walks-Tall.

For a moment, she and Two Fires glared at one another; then Two Fires smiled coolly and stepped aside. Her black eyes held a look of triumph, and Rebecca could have kicked herself. Must she always display her feelings so openly? Why give Two Fires the satisfaction of knowing that she was aware of what had gone on during the night? She could have just pretended she'd been sleeping the whole time!

Clasping the water jar to her chest, Rebecca

hurried in the direction of the river. The entire village was astir, and on this cool cloudy morning, it looked even larger than it had looked the day before. Indeed, in almost every direction, small groups of braves and squaws could be seen busily constructing new lodges. Rebecca counted twenty lodge poles set in a circle for one lodge, and several braves were just now bending the poles downward toward the center of the circle and lashing them together to form the outer framework for the lodge.

Another group was lashing saplings crossways around the circumference of an already half-completed frame—leaving a space at one point for a door. A handful of squaws sat nearby, sewing together mats made of cattail rushes. These mats, Rebecca knew, would serve as ceilings and walls for the new lodges.

Everyone had obviously been up for hours, though the morning dew still lay heavy on the ground, and Rebecca wondered how she'd slept through the feverish activity she saw about her. Had more people arrived during the night or perhaps in the still hour of the dawn?

On the fringes of the village, the forest loomed up darkly, but scattered between the trees, were many make-shift shelters: lean-tos of wood and branches, buffalo robes stretched between trees, and mats suspended between stakes. Well over two hundred families were camping in the vicinity this morning, when only yesterday she would have estimated the number as being closer to one hundred.

As Rebecca approached one lodge, a woman carrying a tiny clay pot came out and dumped its glowing contents onto the middle of a neat small stack of wood, then grunted her approval as the wood caught fire. She glanced up at Rebecca with curious eyes and muttered something, but Rebecca hurried past.

She didn't trust these dark-skinned, dark-eyed women with their long black braids and crude dresses of tanned leather and doeskin. Some of the women wore only skirts; their whole upper bodies were bare! And some of them had tattooed faces— their chins especially.

Naked children darted everywhere about, and Rebecca noticed she was beginning to draw a following as she wended her way through the lodges toward the river. Slender brown bodies trailed after her. Wide black eyes stared up at her. Rebecca didn't know whether to smile at the children or not. She didn't see a single smiling face among them; then, suddenly, a boy stood in front of her brandishing a long stick.

He was taller than the rest of the children, or at least taller than the the fifteen or twenty she could see darting in and out between the lodges. And unlike these others, this boy wore a breech clout with a tomahawk fastened at his belt. His hair had also been plucked, leaving only a single long strand, neatly braided, at the back.

CRIMSON DESIRE

He spoke to her loudly, in a commanding tone of voice, and pointed at her water jar.

"I'm sorry," Rebecca said, "I don't understand you."

He repeated his command and waved the stick at her threateningly. Irritated by his manner, Rebecca brushed by him and kept on walking. She heard something whistle through the air then, and felt a stinging thwack! on her shoulder. The boy had struck her!

She whipped around, ready to confront the young upstart and give him a piece of her mind—if not a taste of his own medicine, but pandemonium broke loose. Suddenly, all the children began shrieking and screaming and leaping on her. Instinctively, she threw up her arms to defend herself, and the water jar went crashing to the ground.

Children converged on her from everywhere—at least thirty or forty, and most of them had sticks with which they now began beating her. The greater number were boys, but here and there, a girl darted in close to her, and one jabbed her painfully in the breast with a stick on which the point had been sharpened.

Her first instinct was to fight back: but these were only children! She couldn't possibly fight children! And in the moment of her indecision, blows rained down on her back and shoulders, and several smaller children hunched down and began lashing at her legs with long sticks that seemed to

227

have come out of nowhere. It might have been a game of some sort except for the painfulness of the blows—and the bloodthirsty looks on their faces.

"Stop! What are you doing?" she cried. But at the sound of her voice, the children became even wilder. A stick lashed across her mouth, and she tasted the saltyness of her own blood. Panic-stricken, she looked around for help. Only everyone had suddenly vanished!

The squaw who only a few minutes ago had been lighting a fire with her potted embers was nowhere to be seen. The chatting group of women sewing mats had disappeared. In the distance, were other figures but they all had their backs to her—were walking away from what was happening! She bit back a scream. Obviously, no one intended to help her!

Children were now running toward her from every corner of the crowded village. They laughed and shouted while their elders drifted into their lodges or deliberately turned their faces away. The children snatched up sticks from woodpiles as they ran, and Rebecca, shaking with horror, leaned down and snatched up a stick herself from a handy woodpile beside the doorway of a nearby lodge.

She couldn't believe it: children, of all people! Attacking her as if she were a rabid dog, an enemy—or a slave of no account.

After the first flurry of blows, the children now hung back, enjoying the spectacle of her fear. They poked and jabbed at her with their sticks. She used her one stick to ward off the feints. A grinning little boy—not much bigger than Walks-Tall— broke away from the tight circle of bodies now surrounding her. He ran toward her—stick poised to issue a mighty whack. She took the blow on her arm, leaning forward to catch him lest he trip and fall on his own stick.

Something heavy, hard, and sharp missed the back of her head and thunked down on her back, bringing her down to her knees. At the same moment, a voice cried out, and Rebecca, reeling from the blow, searched desperately for the source of the cry.

Sweet Breeze was running toward her, shouting. Immediately, the children scattered—slipping into the shadows between the lodges. By the time Sweet Breeze reached Rebecca, not a child could be seen. But their sticks lay tossed on the ground, and a shaken Rebecca looked down to see a crudely made war club lying in the trampled grass.

She picked it up. A heavy blunt-edged rock had been lashed to the wooden handle, and the handle itself bore carvings and was decorated with several dyed feathers. No doubt this was the very instrument which caused the terrible ache she now felt in her back. Had it struck her head, she might now even be dead.

"They were trying to kill me!" she blurted to Sweet Breeze.

Sweet Breeze took the war club from her and turned it over, examining it closely. "No, they making sport of you, Cat-Eyes. That all. Not trying to kill you.''

"But—that tomahawk! It missed my head only because I bent down at just the right moment!"

Sweet Breeze hefted the tomahawk in her hand, feeling its weight. "Yes, this war club could kill. But that only one child—all the rest were making sport.''

Sport! Was that what Sweet Breeze called an attack by children armed with sticks? "It only needed one to strike a death blow," she said stiffly. "And he was more of a man than a child!"

"Yes, I saw him," Sweet Breeze tucked the tomahawk into her waist thong. "The tall one with breech clout. He Shawnee boy—not Miami. Big difference. No Miami try kill slave of great Miami warrior, Kin-di-wa. Only Shawnee who all the time stir up trouble."

"I don't care *what* he was—Shawnee, Miami, or whatever! He nearly killed me! And the rest of the children acted like—like savages!" Rebecca bent down to retrieve her water jar, which miraculously hadn't split in two. Its outer lip was chipped, but at least it would still carry water.

Water jar now in one arm, she attempted to brush off her dress with a shaking hand. Her arms and legs were crisscrossed with welts, and a spot between her shoulder blades ached with a nasty thudding feeling. "Where are the children's parents? Why didn't they do something? Everyone either disappeared or pretended they didn't notice anything happening!"

Rebecca knew she was shouting but was so angry she didn't care. Let the whole village know how she felt! If only they understood English, and she'd tell them right to their faces!

Sweet Breeze took her free arm and began steering her toward the river. "Hush, now, Cat-Eyes. Is not wise to make big fuss over so small a happening."

"Wise!" Rebecca pulled her arm away. "Your people have a strange sense of wisdom! Should I have allowed them to *kill* me? I thought you said I'd be safe if everyone thinks I'm a slave!"

"You *are* safe—see? Children all run away." Sweet Breeze gestured around them. "But if you make big fuss, my people think you not brave."

"I don't care *what* they think," Rebecca muttered, but she lowered her voice. "Don't they care what *I* think? My people would never allow their children to attack a guest!"

Sweet Breeze sighed. "Come walk with me to river. We get water for Two Fires, and I explain how my people think."

Grudgingly, still stunned and frightened, Rebecca trudged after Sweet Breeze. She could understand better if she'd been attacked by adults—someone who'd lost a relative in the many clashes between settlers and Indians. But to be attacked by children! No, she couldn't understand *that* at all.

Sweet Breeze slowed down so they walked side by side, then began speaking in a calm low voice.

231

"Do not blame children for beat on you with sticks. Shawnee boy stir them up. He young warrior not yet blooded. Too young to go in war party, but not too young to practice. He say, 'Hah! Enemy squaw come among us. Is good thing take revenge on her for bad deeds of her people. Make enemy squaw pay. Bring honor to Shawnee.'"

Rebecca found Sweet Breeze's imitation of the Shawnee child's voice almost amusing but, considering the circumstances, didn't feel like laughing. "How do *you* know what he said? Did you hear him?"

"No—but I know how he think. Is how all men think. From time little boy—like Walks-Tall, young braves taught must bring honor to tribe, must make war on enemies. Shawnee or Miami—taught all the same."

"But why didn't someone stop him? Tell him to leave me alone?"

Sweet Breeze shot her a startled glance. "We never tell children no can do something that bring honor to tribe. Almost never correct or scold them. Children learn from mistakes. If baby put hand in fire, he get burnt—but he never put hand in fire again."

Rebecca thought of little Walks-Tall. Walks-Tall never went near the fire, and Two Fires never seemed to worry that he might. But Two Fires *had* scolded the baby for piddling on the mats and shown him where to go outside, so maybe this rule only applied to some things. "You mean no one

232

ever scolds a child or tells him no?"

"*Almost* never," Sweet Breeze replied. "No one ever tell child not to make war on enemies especially. Is good to make war on enemies. Or else enemies take all you have and kill you. This we know from experience."

What a terrible way to bring up children! thought Rebecca. Filling them up with fear and encouraging them to fight! But then she remembered how little white boys often played at shooting and killing Indians—and no one ever told them to stop it either. "Will—will the children attack me again?" she faltered.

"No, I tell them you best-loved slave of Kin-di-wa, and Kin-di-wa be plenty much mad—take stick to them—if you be hurt. Kin-di-wa already make known to everyone you no run line like other slaves."

"Run line—what do you mean?" They were almost to the river now, but Rebecca turned to face Sweet Breeze on the narrow path leading through the trees and down to the riverbank. "I don't understand. What line are you talking about?"

Again, Sweet Breeze looked surprised at her ignorance. "If you plain ordinary captive—like most captives—then your bravery must be tested. You run down line with other captives. Since you woman, only women and children beat you, but if you man, then everybody beat you. You must get to end of line and touch post. If you brave and make it, then you be adopted into tribe. If you not brave, then you die by fire.''

Death by fire. That was how Colonel Crawford had died, and now she remembered having heard of this other practice—the gauntlet, a name bestowed on it by early French traders. *This* was the test Kin-di-wa had once mentioned: if he'd taken her to the Delawares as he originally planned, she'd have had to run the gauntlet! "But—what makes *me* different from all your other white captives?"

"Kin-di-wa say not necessary you run line. You prove bravery and earn place in tribe already."

"How?"

"You save his life. Is that not so?"

"Yes, but—"

Sweet Breeze shrugged her shoulders. "If Kin-di-wa say so, it good enough for me. Good enough for most everyone. But some still waiting to see if you brave for themselves. Until everyone thinks so, you only slave—or kept woman. Unless, mayhap you marry."

Rebecca's back and shoulders throbbed anew. She hated this insecurity about her position here. And she hated the three choices open to her: slavery, whoredom, or marriage.

They arrived at the river then, and Sweet Breeze beckoned her down the bank. Hugging her water jar and following, she wondered how she could possibly convince the other tribal members of her bravery. But why should she even *want* to convince them? She wasn't going to stay here long enough for it to matter!

Of course, until she was fully accepted into the tribe—by everyone—she'd have to watch out for unprovoked attacks like the one she'd experienced this morning. A slave in any culture must be prey to ridicule and scorn. A slave in this culture was obviously prey to even more than that: torture at the hands of children.

As she bent over and submerged her jar in the cold flowing water, Sweet Breeze's last comment pounded in her brain: *unless, mayhap you marry.*

She straightened up, and Sweet Breeze caught her eye. "Cat-Eyes, what think you of Peshewa?"

Rebecca coughed to hide her surprise. What was the girl doing—reading her mind? "He—seems nice enough." She hoisted the filled jar up onto her hip.

"I know Peshewa long time. He good man, Cat-Eyes. Make good husband." Sweet Breeze helped Rebecca balance the jar as they reclimbed the bank. "If you marry him, you no be slave anymore. You no be kept woman. You be proud Miami squaw and have own lodge and lodge-fire."

"Yes, but—" The water jar was heavy, even with Sweet Breeze's help, and Rebecca stopped walking to catch her breath. "But I don't love him, Sweet Breeze! How can I marry a man I don't love?"

"Maybe you learn to love him. Unless you already love someone else."

The image of Kin-di-wa's lean muscled body leapt into her mind, and Rebecca fought to keep from blushing. "There's no one else, Sweet Breeze."

But Sweet Breeze studied her with knowing eyes. "It much better for you—much safer—if you marry Peshewa, Cat-Eyes. Make Two Fires happy. Make Peshewa happy. Make me happy too—then we be good friends together always."

But what about *my* happiness? Rebecca thought. Sweet Breeze of all people ought to understand she couldn't possibly marry someone she didn't love!

They began walking back toward the village. "Look there!" Sweet Breeze suddenly cried. "Delaware come!"

And Rebecca saw a massive group of people at the far end of the village: men, women, and children milling about like a herd of buffalo. Some were on horseback but most were walking, carrying bundles under their arms or on their backs, supported by wide leather bands that crossed around their foreheads.

The women were especially loaded down, like beasts of burden, while the men moved freely and proudly, carrying only weapons of war—rifles, bows, and war clubs. Pack horses stomped and whinnied, dogs barked and snapped at the horses's heels, and children raced around the fringes of the group, drawing the attention of the villagers who had begun streaming out to greet these newcomers.

"My father be plenty happy they arrive," Sweet

Breeze told Rebecca. "Each day, more warriors come. Is good. Chenoten have three times a thousand soldiers, and we need every brave who can hold a war club."

Yes, three thousand. Rebecca remembered Kin-di-wa quoting that same number. But why was it necessary for the gathering Indians to bring along their children and their womenfolk? Wouldn't it be safer for them to stay at home in their own villages? Or did they fear the Long Knives too much to remain home without protection?

"I must go and welcome women of Buckonga-helas, chief of Delawares. Have not seen them for many moons. Must help them put up lodges too."

Sweet Breeze turned to Rebecca. "So many strangers among us, Cat-Eyes. Is another good reason for you to marry. Shawnee, Ottawa, Wyandot, Delaware, Miami—we be like many bears try to share same den. Braves play at war to prepare for battle with Chenoten. Sometimes get killed or injured. They gamble with game of straws—sometimes lose weapons, furs, horses, even women. Is dangerous time. Women need protection of husband. Is better you marry—yes?"

And Rebecca could see it might be better. The village was taking on an air of volatile excitement. She'd felt it yesterday when she first arrived, and again, this morning when she'd first gone out. No doubt, the children had been feeling it too. With so many people crowded into one place, *any*thing

237

could happen.

She nodded to Sweet Breeze. "I told Peshewa I would think about it, and so I will." But her stomach lurched as she bid goodbye to Sweet Breeze. How could she seriously consider marrying Peshewa—or anyone—when it was Kin-di-wa she loved?

Feeling as if she were crossing a deep ravine on a very narrow log, Rebecca approached Two Fires' lodge. Then a woman came hurrying out of it and nearly collided with her. It was Tecumwah, Peshewa's mother. The older woman straightened up, glanced furiously at Rebecca, and uttered a loud "Hmmmph!" and stalked away.

What now? Rebecca wondered. She went into the lodge feeling more apprehensive by the minute.

Two Fires looked up from a collection of iron pots, skins, and mats Rebecca had never seen before and smiled widely. Her mysterious black eyes lit up with childish pleasure, and she motioned to Rebecca to come kneel beside her. But a wave of suspicion washed over Rebecca. Why was this beautiful golden skinned girl—her rival for Kin-di-wa's affections—suddenly being so friendly?

Curiously, she knelt down. *"Mi-shi!"* Two Fires exclaimed, thrusting an iron pot into her hands. *"Mi-shi!"*

It was an ordinary iron pot. Rebecca couldn't see anything so wonderful about it. Then Two Fires picked up some wooden bowls and spoons and thrust these too into Rebecca's hands.

"*Mi-shi! Mi-shi!*" she cried.

Little Walks-Tall, standing up and hanging onto a lodge pole as though his life depended on it, chortled after her, "Mi—shi!"

Two Fires laughed delightedly, and to Rebecca's utter amazement suddenly hugged her, all the while crying, "*Mi-shi! Mi-shi!*"

Then she leaned back, gathered up pots, bowls, skins, and mats and loaded them all into Rebecca's lap. Rebecca was dumb-founded. Did Two Fires mean these things were for her? But why? Where had they come from? And why was Two Fires so happy?

Two Fires pointed to the loot, then pointed to the doorway. "Te-cum-wah," she said slowly. "Te-cum-wah."

And Rebecca understood: Tecumwah had brought the gifts. But why would someone who didn't even like her bring presents? It didn't make sense!

Two Fires got up and obligingly cleared a place for the gifts near Rebecca's bed of skins. She helped arrange the articles neatly, stopping now and then to flash a brilliant smile and to repeat the word, *mi-shi,* which was beginning to sound like a chant.

Little Walks-Tall, meanwhile, groped his way around the lodge, repeating in garbled baby fashion, "Mi—shi, mi—shi."

Not until Sweet Breeze stopped by the lodge late that afternoon, did Rebecca have an opportunity to learn the meaning of the gifts. She was sitting outside with Two Fires, trying to learn how to do quill embroidery on a piece of buckskin, when Sweet Breeze suddenly came up to them and whispered a greeting in the Miami tongue.

Two Fires smiled and showed her the intricately patterned embroidery, almost like a snakeskin, that she was making to decorate a pair of moccasins. She had been holding a few quills in her mouth to soften and flatten them and had to remove them before she could phrase a soft-spoken welcoming reply.

Rebecca too had a mouthful. And Sweet Breeze leaned over and grinned. "How you like quill-work, Cat-Eyes?"

"I wish porcupines were born with fur—or anything else—besides quills. Then maybe I wouldn't have to chew them. Ugh!" Thusfar, the only thing Rebecca had become adept at was flattening the long, hollow, brown-tipped quills with her teeth.

"Is good you learn quillwork," Sweet Breeze scolded. "Squaw who do good quillwork is much appreciated wife."

"Then I'm afraid I won't *be* much appreciated when I get married," Rebecca said darkly.

Two Fires invited Sweet Breeze to come into the lodge, and before Rebecca could inquire about the meaning of the presents, Two Fires was showing

Sweet Breeze everything and exclaiming over each one.

Rebecca finally got a word in edgewise. "Why did Tecumwah bring me these? I tried to ask Two Fires but she didn't understand. Whatever the reason, the least I can do is thank Tecumwah."

"No thank her!" Sweet Breeze shook her head. "Is not our way. Besides, gifts come from Peshewa, not his mother."

"Peshewa?" The meaning of the gifts—and of Tecumwah's hostile attitude—began to come clear. "But why didn't Peshewa bring me the gifts himself?"

"Is not our way," Sweet Breeze explained again. She ran her fingers lightly over a particularly fine piece of doeskin. "Mother or sister always bring gifts to intended wife. If girl like brave, want to marry him, she keep gifts. If not, she return them."

Rebecca's stomach flip-flopped. So that's why Two Fires had been so happy. She knew a marriage proposal when she saw one—and she'd been overjoyed at the knowledge that the problem of Rebecca's presence in the lodge was so soon to be resolved. "Why, I must return them immediately then! If I had known that's what they meant, I would have sent Tecumwah back with them right away!"

She pointed to the gifts and then to the door. "You'd better take them back, Two Fires! I don't want these presents!"

Two Fires's eyes flashed with furious understanding. She spoke rapidly, and Sweet Breeze translated. "Two Fires say she no want to take presents back to Tecumwah. She already accept them in your place. She tell Tecumwah you be happy marry Peshewa."

"What?" Rebecca gasped. "She had no right! I wouldn't marry Peshewa if he were the last man in the whole Northwest Territory!"

Sweet Breeze shook her head. "Must be reasonable, Cat-Eyes. Must not shout or insult Peshewa. Two Fires no do something so awful. You not here. Presents waiting. This is lodge of Two Fires. She may accept or not accept as she pleases."

"But she can't take it upon herself to decide my future for me! I'm *not* her slave!"

Two Fires was standing rigidly now, eyes blazing. Fury, jealousy, and something else— fear—flitted across the girl's face. Rebecca struggled to control her own wildly surging emotions. "Please tell her I'm sorry, but I cannot accept these gifts. I will take them back myself if she refuses. But they *will* go back!"

Sweet Breeze spoke calmly, taking a longer time to translate than Rebecca thought necessary. But then Two Fires suddenly bent down, gathered together the gifts, picked them up, and swept out of the lodge without saying a word. Rebecca couldn't believe it—she had won!

"Sit down, Cat-Eyes." Sweet Breeze sighed and knelt down on the mats. Rebecca sat down beside her. Little Walks-Tall dropped to his knees and crawled over to the entranceway—looking after his mother.

Sweet Breeze called him back, then turned to Rebecca. "This not end of it, Cat-Eyes. Courtship just beginning. I explain same to Two Fires, and when she remember old customs, she forget her anger."

"What do you mean? I sent the gifts back. Two Fires took them. *That* should be an end to it."

"No. Tomorrow, next week, whenever he wish, Peshewa send more presents. Better presents next time. He try wear you down like water wear down rock. He kill buck—he send meat. He trade for looking glass—he give to you. No use be stubborn. Peshewa be more stubborn. When married, you get everything he have. Might as well take now. Put an end to carrying presents back and forth."

"This is ridiculous!" Rebecca wailed. "Isn't there anything I can say to him to put an end to it? I can't marry him! I don't love him! Why won't he accept that?"

"Only one way to put end to it." Sweet Breeze gathered Walks-Tall into her lap. "Only one way make Peshewa know rock cannot be worn down."

"How? Tell me how, and whatever it is, I'll do it!"

Sweet Breeze shot her a solemn look. "Become woman or wife of another brave. Become Kin-di-wa's woman. Peshewa leave you alone once he know you belong to friend."

And, hearing it spoken, Rebecca suddenly

realized that the idea of being "Kin-di-wa's woman" was not new to her; it had been lingering just below the surface of her consciousness for quite some time. But acknowledging it, she was deeply shocked.

Her culture would never condone such an "arrangement" with the enemy. It didn't condone any kind of relationship outside marriage, although, of course, such relationships did occur—but not among God-fearing women. Why, she'd be ostracized forever from the company of "proper" women—and condemned to hell-fire for all eternity!

Yet, the idea persisted—refused to go away. Among these savages, might it not be a reasonable thing to trade her pride and the use of her body for Kin-di-wa's protection? For his assurance that she would indeed get home? If she could ever get over her revulsion at being touched, she might even enjoy being Kin-di-wa's woman. For a time. And after she got home, who would ever know?

But then her mind closed firmly against the idea; she might get pregnant living so promiscuously. And—there was something else. Something even more important than fear of getting pregnant. A certainty had begun to grow in her, a resolution about her future. She wanted something more from a man than merely to share his bed. She wanted—to be loved. To be cherished for her own sake. And she wanted to love and cherish in return.

What would be wrong, she wondered, with having the same depth of feeling between her and whoever her man—her husband—might be, that Sweet Breeze seemed to have for her absent Apekonit?

Maybe the girl *was* filled with foolish illusions, but Rebecca had come to admire Sweet Breeze's steadfast loyalty: though far apart from her loved one, she still loved. She honored a bond of trust. And wasn't that the very core of loving? Once you loved, you didn't go lusting after another. Your entire life and happiness depended on being with your beloved.

No, Rebecca promised herself. She wouldn't willingly settle for less. With every breath of life she drew, she'd fight to gain such a love—she'd keep searching until she found it!

"What say you, Cat-Eyes, you want be Kin-di-wa's woman?" Sweet Breeze's gentle voice startled her. "You very beautiful. I no think Kin-di-wa say no."

Rebecca lowered her eyes so Sweet Breeze couldn't see how brimful of tears they'd suddenly become. Oh, yes! She wanted to be Kin-di-wa's woman, but she wanted even more to be his *wife*—the woman for whom he would willingly sacrifice everything: his pride, his people, his personal safety. As she would willingly give up everything for him, even her life, if it was somehow necessary.

But to be his wife was impossible—a foolish daydream. She ought not to waste her time

KATHARINE KINCAID

imagining it. Kin-di-wa had responsibilities. He
had Two Fires and Walks-Tall to think about. A
ready-made family. Why should he even want
her—she who jumped at his very touch—when he
had Two Fires who came willingly into his bed?

"No," she whispered. "I can't be Kin-di-wa's
woman. I'm going back home, remember? Back to
my own people—as soon as I can. And until then,
I'll just have to make the best of things as they are."

Two Fires came back into the lodge just then, no
longer carrying presents. Instead, her hands were
full of soil-blackened tubers, freshly picked.
Rebecca wondered if she'd picked them herself at
the fringes of the forest or whether Tecumwah had
given them to her. Two Fires's eyes were still
stormy and dark with disappointment. She busied
herself in the task of cleaning the tubers, saying
nothing to Sweet Breeze or Rebecca.

But Sweet Breeze was undaunted. She plunged
into a conversation, and the girl nodded but kept
on working.

"I tell her I must go now," Sweet Breeze
explained. "I only came to say she must not look
for Kin-di-wa until very late tonight. No," she put
up her hand to forestall any questions. "He not
send me. Braves never think to send messages to
save work of preparing meal. But I come anyway.
Save Two Fires work and worry."

"Where *is* Kin-di-wa?" Rebecca asked. She
hadn't seen him since the night before. Clearly—
after last night—he no longer concerned himself

246

with her whereabouts or safety.

"Kin-di-wa in big pow-wow with my father and other chiefs who now are here: Buckongahelas, Blue Jacket, and Tarhee, the Crane. More chiefs come tomorrow. Tribes moving down from Auglaize River now. Come to Roche de Boeuf like Delaware who come this morning. Chenoten leaving Fort Greenville. That what Buckongahelas say. Battle coming soon. Cannot be more than a moon away now."

Battle. War. Rebecca was ashamed to be so engrossed in her personal problems that she could forget what was going on around her. What were the chiefs discussing? Strategies for defeating Anthony Wayne? She said goodbye to Sweet Breeze with a heavy heart, then picked up her abandoned quillwork which was lying beside her on the mats.

At least, she had new tasks to occupy her hands and mind. New things to learn, a new language to master, new friendships to be made. She stole a glance at Two Fires who was rinsing some tubers in a gourd. This was *one* friend she wouldn't be making. Not after she'd rejected Peshewa.

The girl looked up and called Walks-Tall to her, then gave him a tuber to munch on. He grinned his nearly toothless grin and began gnawing at it happily. Then Two Fires tossed a handful of the still uncleaned plants across the mats to Rebecca. Her black eyes flashed, as if to say, "Here is your dinner. Clean it yourself if you want it!"

Rebecca put down the quillwork in as calm a manner as possible. I will not lose my temper again in front of her! she told herself. I will not let her know how much she annoys me!

Smiling with stiffened lips, Rebecca picked up the tubers. If they were to be her dinner, she'd eat every last one and be grateful. She'd dined before on tubers, she remembered, and they hadn't been all that bad!

These, she saw, were a common variety, a kind she'd eaten often. Except for one. She separated the strange one from the others and held it up to the fading light of the late afternoon.

The plant looked vaguely familiar. The tuberous end was dark brown in color, fibrous, jointed, and about half the size of her finger. Under the two deeply-lobed, wilting leaves, hung a large fleshy berry—greenish in color, but ripening to yellow.

She plucked the berry and lifted it to her mouth, catching a whiff of its tart odor. About to pop it onto her tongue, she heard Kin-di-wa's voice as clearly as if he'd been beside her. "No! Do not eat."

And slowly, she lowered her hand. The plant was *Ki-ta-ma-ni*. What was it he'd warned her about it? The only time any part of the plant could be eaten was in late autumn. Any other time, like now in almost mid-summer, the leaves, root, and berry were deadly. To eat any part of it was to die.

A wave of horror broke over her. Two Fires had *meant* for her to be poisoned. She looked up to find the silent girl watching her—her lovely face composed into an expressionless mask. Only her eyes betrayed her. They were enormous black pools of jealous hatred, implacable as death itself.

And Rebecca couldn't bear it any longer. She threw down the plant, scrambled to her feet, and dashed out of the lodge.

Ten

It was Kin-di-wa who found her. Afternoon had slid into early evening, evening into night, and a half moon was rising—fighting its way through a layer of clouds scudding across the sky. A silver path of moonlight lay across the waters of the river beside which Rebecca sat. Arms around knees, she studied the shifting shadows and wondered how she would ever survive in this terrible place—until the time came that she could go home.

Kin-di-wa slipped quietly up behind her, knelt down, and she felt his breath warm on her shoulder. "It seems I am forever running after you, Cat-Eyes—finding the places where you hide. Do you always run away from problems? Do you never stay and fight?"

"It seems problems will find me no matter what I do! I cannot get away from *them* anymore than I can get away from *you*. And as for fighting,

251

fighting is *your* way, not mine. I want only to be left in peace.''

"Cat-Eyes," his hand brushed her shoulder. "I am sorry for what happened. Two Fires told me she gave you *Ki-ta-ma-ni* to eat—by accident.''

"It was no accident! She gave it to me on purpose, and I would have eaten it, except I remembered what you taught me!''

"However it happened, I have punished her for it. She will not try to harm you again.''

Rebecca turned around to look at him in the pale glow of moonlight. *"How* did you punish her?''

"I told her of my displeasure and threatened to send her away. I made my voice thunder like Little Turtle's so others could hear and she would be disgraced. She pleaded and wept—and swore by Manitou that no more harm will ever come to you. There will be no more accidents.''

It must have been quite a scene, Rebecca thought bitterly, like the one she herself had created dashing headlong through the village to the river. What a shame to have missed the sight of the proud Two Fires begging and weeping! But was Two Fires totally to blame? No! It was Kin-di-wa she was angry with—Kin-di-wa who had brought her here *knowing* what might happen.

Kin-di-wa's hand now touched her arm. "You must not fear Two Fires. She understands I mean what I say. Come back to the lodge now. It is not safe for you to be here alone.''

She jerked away from him. "Nothing is safe here! Even children cannot be trusted!"

Perhaps he'd already heard about the morning's incident, for he said stiffly, "Do not say I didn't warn you, Cat-Eyes. I wanted you to stay with Crow Woman, remember? You should have stayed: Chenoten has left Fort Greenville, and our scouts believe he is heading for Kekionga."

Yes, she should have stayed with Crow Woman. Hadn't she herself come to that conclusion? How many foolish mistakes could she make? First, she allowed herself to fall in love with a man who didn't love her, and then she stupidly threw away an opportunity for a more speedy reunion with her own people!

"What will Chenoten do when he gets to Kekionga and finds no one there but Crow Woman?"

"He will come here—after burning Kekionga and our other unprotected villages and after destroying our corn crop."

Rebecca cringed. "But what will happen to Crow Woman?"

Kin-di-wa hunkered down on the bank beside her. "Little Turtle has already sent a party of braves to fetch her. I do not think Chenoten will harm her, but she will die if the village and the crops are destroyed. We can only hope he doesn't find our buried stores of grain—or it will be a long hungry winter, even if we *win* this battle."

Rebecca hadn't thought of the possibility of a

food shortage. "But you can always hunt! Haven't you always said the forest is full of food for anyone who knows where to look for it?"

Kin-di-wa grunted. "That is true—most of the time. But have you not noted how many hungry mouths are crowding in among us? The land can support only so many, and game is already being driven off. The deer, moose, and small bands of buffalo that roam these woods know when men have gathered in great numbers; they flee north to save their hides."

"I saw the Delawares who came today," Rebecca admitted. "And Sweet Breeze told me others will surely come tomorrow—moving down from the Auglaize. Just how many people will there be altogether?"

"If everyone comes who has promised to come, along with their women and children, there could well be over five thousand hungry bodies. A new camp has already been set up across the river at Presque Isle, where the Miami of the Lake flows into the great Lake of the Eries. Soon, this camp we now occupy will be moved down closer to Fort Miamis, and other new ones will be opened as well."

Rebecca was astounded. She remembered Sweet Breeze telling her the same thing: the camp would soon be moved. But she'd had no idea how many Indians were actually gathering in the area! Of course, food supplies would be strained! She began to worry. Would Anthony Wayne *really* destroy the corn crop? If he did, whole tribes—women and children—would suffer, not just warriors.

Something hooted in the darkness, startling her, and Kin-di-wa sat up straighter, watching and listening. A dark body, wings outspread, soared across the river, seeking prey on the other side. Since it was only an owl, Rebecca couldn't understand Kin-di-wa's uneasiness. "What is it?" she asked.

He made an effort to relax, leaning back on one elbow to look at her. His face was splashed with moonlight, and she saw that his eyes looked disturbed—almost frightened. "Among my people, *Meen-de-gaw*, Brother Owl, is said to carry warnings. His cry is a bad omen, but he does not tell me anything I do not know already."

"What is it?" she asked again, moving closer to him. In all the time she'd known him, he had never once shown fear, only caution, as when the Shawnee had been searching for them in the woods and river.

He paused a moment, plucking at the grass. "I am afraid about the outcome of this battle."

"You mean—afraid to die?"

He shook his head. "No, not afraid of death. To die is the destiny of every warrior—and every man or woman who is born. I am afraid of—losing. Afraid for the future of my people."

She was struck with a sense of foreboding herself then, to hear this strong proud man admit to the possibility of defeat. "But surely—this is only one battle! You have fought so many! And your people have survived every one. They will surely survive this one too."

"No, Cat-Eyes. This is our final battle. I feel it. Little Turtle feels it. This battle will decide everything."

"Then why do you insist on going through with it? Why don't you meet with Anthony Wayne and come to terms? There must be *some* way you can compromise—some way our people can both live in peace!"

He lay back on the grass and stared up at the moon, his mouth set in such a grim stark line she wanted to reach out and stroke it with her fingertips—to smooth away the pain. He lay without speaking, lost in thought, and she couldn't stand it any longer.

"Kin-di-wa, you're a fool! Little Turtle's a fool! You have only to ask for peace—demand it—and you can avoid this defeat and suffering! My people are not so unreasonable! We only want to come here and settle in peace. To farm the land and raise our families."

Warming to her subject, she got up on her knees to face him. "You don't know our history, the things we've fought for—peace and freedom and justice for everyone! If you could only read our Declaration of Independence, the document written by Thomas Jefferson that made our whole people revolt from tyranny, you would see—"

Lightning sparked in his eyes. "I have read your Declaration. A very noble document, but to whom does it apply? To red men? To black men? No! Only to white men!" He sat up. "It does not now— nor will it ever—apply to my people. You and Apekonit are both the same! You chase after words—the writing of bird tracks—as the clouds chase after the moon. You think to find meaning there and purpose, when the only real things that exist are those that can be seen! The *actions* of men—not their thoughts or their dreams—are what they must be judged by!"

"No, Kin-di-wa, you are wrong!" She reached out to him pleadingly. "We all fail! We don't live up to our dreams! We're weak! But we *must* have dreams! If we have no dreams, we're nothing but— but animals!"

She leaned toward him, and his hands grasped hers. He would not allow her to pull away. Instead, he drew her to him, his eyes blazing in the moonlight. "And what are *your* dreams, little Cat-Eyes?"

You are my dream, she almost cried, but her throat was so tight she couldn't speak. She could only stare up into his face—that beloved hand-some face. He hesitated a moment, bent down closer, and then his lips sought hers.

Tentatively, she kissed him back. Tasted the sweetness of his mouth, the probing question of his tongue. He gathered her into his arms, bent back her head, and ravished her mouth with his kisses. His lips were hot. Demanding. Unrelenting.

Teetering between desire and fear, Rebecca tried to push him away. She felt him shudder and draw back, as if coming to his senses. Then she molded her body against his. What was the use of fighting it? She wanted him! He belonged to *her!* Not to Two Fires. Not to the Miamis! Not even to this hate-torn land! He belonged to her and her alone. And she would prove it to him! She returned his kisses with ardor, sliding her arms about his neck.

He kissed her until she was breathless and felt herself soaring, soaring upwards—like the eagle soars to the sun. And she knew only a moment of terror, of sudden rigidity, as his hands found her breasts. "I will not hurt you," he moaned, "I swear by Manitou, I want only to love you."

"Yes," she whispered. "Love me—love me, my beloved savage!"

He lay her down in the cool sweet-smelling grass, and gently drew up her doeskin. She could not help flinching, as the doeskin came free of her body, and the moonlight splashed down on her naked breasts and thighs. But his touch was so gentle, so reassuring, she was able to lie still and conquer her misgivings.

He undid her hair from its long braid and smoothed out the tresses. Her hair lay about her like a sea of flame. He buried his face in it, nibbled her ear through it. "Cat-Eyes, little Cat-Eyes." His tongue stroked the lobe of her ear, and a liquid feeling flowed through her, like a river of molten fire—wildfire! "You are one moment, woman, and the next moment, child. As timid as a fawn. What *are* you, Cat-Eyes, child or woman?"

"I don't know, Kin-di-wa! I don't know!" She shivered with something close to dread. "Tell me—tell me who I am!"

His lips moved down her neck, roved over her face. He kissed her forehead, her eyelids, the tip of her nose. He thrust his tongue gently between her lips, and she was smitten with such a sense of weakness, of lassitude, she could hardly move.

"You are woman," he murmured. "Here . . ." He kissed the hollow of her neck. "And here . . ." His mouth moved down to the valley between her breasts. "And here . . ." His tongue darted over her nipples, teasing them into taut peaks. "And even more so, you are woman here . . ." His mouth trailed down her belly and nuzzled the triangle of curly hair between her thighs.

"No!" The cry exploded from her. She tried to sit up, but his arm and half his body held her down. Gently, he stroked her quivering flesh—her legs, her thighs, her belly. And his hand strayed down to the forbidden place. His fingers slid into her. "Do not deny me, Cat-Eyes. A man must know his woman. He must know the touch of her, the feel of her, even the smell and taste of her. Do not deny me."

His fingers slid in and out gently—exploring, teasing, rubbing in a circular motion that made her quiver and throb with anticipation, with desperate need. "Your woman place is beautiful, Cat-Eyes. It is warm and giving. Does this not please you?"

A low moan escaped from her throat, embarrassing her. But she could not ask him to stop—she could not say anything! His fingers seemed to know exactly what pleased her. Without stopping these intimate caresses that so unnerved and aroused her, his free hand roamed up to her breasts. Light as a feather, he traced her fullness, teased her nipples, pulled on them gently. And now, her body was no longer her own. She was floating up, up—soaring into the face of the moon.

Then he was moving over her, bending his head down, and his tongue entered her secret womanplace. Lightning raced through her body as he kissed her deeply, reverently. Her back arched as she strained against his mouth. She began to shake from head to foot.

And then he stopped. "Not yet, little one, not yet. Wait for me. We will climb together—up to the moon and stars. Up to Manitou. Wait for me!"

She opened her eyes and saw him poised over her. Saw him tear away his breech clout. His naked manhood strained toward her in all its fierce beauty and power. She opened her thighs to him, drew him downward, and guided him into her.

And they climbed together. Above the clouds. Past the moon. Through a veil of shimmering stars. They rode the winds of the heavens. And they were one—man and woman together in the ancient mystery of love.

Yes—I am woman! I am *Kin-di-wa!* Rebecca exaulted. Her body exploded in shattering pleasure. She held Kin-di-wa and rocked against him, driving him onwards, until she knew by his abandoned thrusting, by the shudder of his body, that he too had found the miracle: the complete loss of self in herself that she had found in him.

They lay together, limp and spent, savoring the inexpressible sweetness of their joining.

"Kin-di-wa, Kin-di-wa, my—love." She had almost said husband.

He kissed her breasts, first one, then the other, with great tenderness. There was a dampness on her cheeks that she brushed away awkwardly with one hand. He lay his head down on her heart. "I would have shown you once it could be like this, little one. Only we were interrupted."

"Yes," she whispered, but the memory of Will no longer seemed to have the power to hurt her. What Will had done, and what she and Kin-di-wa had just done, had nothing in common. They were two acts so very different she could not even remember why she'd been so afraid! She'd put off this moment far too long. "I didn't know how wonderful it could be! I didn't *want* it to be like this!"

Kin-di-wa lifted his head and stroked back her hair. "Why did you not *want* it to be like this?"

"Because—this happiness should only come to husband and wife, to those who belong to one another."

"Cat-Eyes, Cat-Eyes," he murmured, shaking his head. He rolled away from her, stood up, and put on his breech clout. Then he reached down to take her hand. "Come here. I want to show you something."

She got to her feet unsteadily and scooped up her doeskin. Her body didn't seem to want to move from the crushed grass of the river bank. But he led her down the bank to the water's edge, where the cold water tickled her toes and drove away the languor that had fallen over her.

The clouds had all but fled by now, and only the low-hanging half moon remained. Stars winked above the shadow of the trees on the opposite side of the river, and the river itself flowed past calmly: in no great hurry to get to the Lake of the Eries.

The night air was cool on her bare skin, and Rebecca moved closer to Kin-di-wa. He put his arms around her. "What do you see, Cat-Eyes?" he whispered in her ear.

She smiled to herself, remembering how often he'd asked that same question on their journey. "I see a world made for lovers. A world far away from war or arguments that divide people and set them against one another."

His arms tightened. "Do you not feel the presence of Manitou?"

She looked up at the sweep of moonlit sky,

studded with brilliant pin-pricks of light. "Yes, I can feel His presence. And I think He must be very angry with us."

"Why?"

"Because—of what we just did."

Kin-di-wa was silent for a moment, considering this. "No, Cat-Eyes. If He is angry, it is because we have hatred in our hearts for our brothers, not because we have love for one another."

She pulled away from him, suffused with guilt, then turned to face him accusingly. "But we aren't married, Kin-di-wa! And we never can be! Have you forgotten the woman you lay with last night?"

His face lost its gentle dreamy look and hardened into the face she knew better, the harsh and angry one. "So you were awake and saw us. I did not mean for that to happen—especially in front of you. But what passes between Two Fires and myself has nothing to do with us . . . What is it you *want*—a ceremony by one of your missionaries? What can a ceremony do that we have not done already?"

Rebecca backed further away from him. So he didn't mean to have made love to Two Fires! Perhaps, he hadn't meant for *their* love-making to have happened either! "Just what *is* it we've done already?" she flung at him.

"Back there," he pointed up the bank to where they'd made love under the trees. "Back there we became as man and wife. You gave me your body. I gave you mine." He made a gesture to include the

263

whole of the sky. "Our love was witnessed by Manitou. By all that He has fashioned! What need have we of ceremonies?"

"Kin-di-wa," she protested. "It isn't meant to happen like this! We—we aren't animals! We're supposed to make promises to one another! To have holy words said over us! What we did back there was—weakness!"

He shook his head. "The first time I took you was weakness. This second time was not. I have wanted to plant my seed in you—to make you my woman—for a long time. It only needed for you to be willing, to be ready."

He stepped closer and took her face in his hands. "I will give you words if you desire, little one. I will make promises. I make them now—where Manitou can hear me."

He threw back his head, closed his eyes, and raised his voice in a chant. "Great Spirit! It is Kin-di-wa who speaks to you! Do you hear me? I take this woman—this Cat-Eyes—to be my wife. I will protect and cherish her. I will bring her meat. And I will warm myself at her lodge fire all the days of my life!"

He looked down at her again, half-smiling, half-serious, and kissed her gently on the lips. Then his voice was completely serious. "I want you to bear my son, Cat-Eyes. I want to fill you again and again. I want our children to be the best of both our worlds. I want our *own* world together. Is that not what you want?"

Her heart was hammering in her chest. Yes! *Yes!* she wanted to cry. And the idea of marrying out here under the moon almost made her laugh, made her want to throw back her head and shout her own promises to the moon—or to the Great Spirit, if he was indeed listening.

But the image of Two Fires stood before her. Two Fires: the beautiful Indian girl with her jealous smoldering eyes. "But what about Two Fires? Where will you send her?"

His hands dropped down to her shoulders. "I can send her nowhere, little one. After last night, she is my *first* wife. After tonight, you are my *second*. You will learn to get along together. You will be as sisters. She has promised me this. Now, you must promise me too."

She was horrified. "Your—your *second* wife!"

"Among my people, it is not uncommon. Many braves have more than one wife."

She began shivering uncontrollably then, as if she'd been thrust suddenly into winter. How could she have forgotten—yet *again!*—how very different were their customs, their beliefs! "N-no, Kin-di-wa! I—I can't do it! I had rather marry Peshewa than share you with another!"

"Peshewa!" He stepped back from her. His eyes narrowed. "Then I shall tell him to send back his gifts. If you do not want me now, Cat-Eyes, when I have offered the best I can give you, then you do not want me at all." He stood there glaring at her for a moment, then turned and began

265

to stalk away.

"Kin-di-wa! Wait!" She went running after him. He turned to her, scowling. "Please. Give me some time! I—I have to think about this."

"You shall have your time," he snapped. "Until Chenoten comes. In the morning, I shall be gone from here, and I shall not return until the battle. Then, if I am still alive, you can tell me what you have decided."

"Gone! But where are you going? Is it dangerous?"

"It is better you know nothing about it. Now, put on your doeskin. Or Two Fires will be offended."

In the morning when she awoke, he was gone, and a gentle rain was falling. It plopped on the mats covering the lodge like giant tears. Everything was gloom. She sat up to find Two Fires sitting cross-legged and regarding her silently while little Walks-Tall nursed. The girl looked strangely passive, her dark eyes expressionless, as though she'd resigned herself to Rebecca's presence.

But how can she *not* resent me? Rebecca wondered. If I were she, *I* certainly would!

She got up, smoothed down her doeskin, and scooped up water in a gourd. The water jar needed filling. She drank only a little and splashed some on her face, then took up the jar. Rain or not, she didn't intend to stay here in the lodge with Two

Fires. The girl's passive scrutiny was more than she could handle this morning.

Thank heavens, Two Fires had been asleep last night when she and Kin-di-wa came in! At least, she'd pretended to be sleeping. Rebecca started for the entranceway, and Two Fires said something to her. Rebecca stopped and turned.

"*Pe-tal-onwa*," Two Fires said. She waggled the fingers of one hand and made a downward motion as if to demonstrate falling rain.

"What?" Rebecca said. The girl repeated the motion. "Oh! *Rain*. Yes, it's raining. *Pe-tal-onwa*."

Two Fires pointed to a heap of skins. She pantomimed picking up a skin and draping it over her head.

"Oh! A covering to keep the rain off!" Rebecca selected a large buckskin and drew it over her head and shoulders. "Thank you."

"*Wi-nik*," Two Fires said.

"*Wi-nik?*" Rebecca was uncertain as to the word's meaning.

"*Wi-nik*. Thank—you." Two Fires furrowed her brow in an effort to say it properly. "Thank—you."

Was Two Fires trying to speak her language? Rebecca couldn't believe it. She whirled around to study the girl more closely. Two Fires smiled shyly and waggled her fingers again in a downward falling motion. "*Pe-tal-onwa*. Rain," she said in a soft voice.

"Yes, rain! And I'm going out in it. Down to the river to fetch water. Do you understand?"

Two Fires nodded. Little Walks-Tall detached himself from his mother's breast, and struggled to sit up. "Rain. Thank—you," Two Fires said to him, and he blinked at her, like a little owl.

Stunned and disbelieving, Rebecca hurried out into the gray wet morning. Was Two Fires the same girl who'd tried to poison her only last evening? It didn't seem possible! Of course, Kin-di-wa had ordered Two Fires to get along with her, but she'd never imagined this would mean a complete change of heart!

Then another thought occurred to her; could the girl be bluffing? Pretending to extend her friendship until such time as she found a new and better way to get rid of her rival?

It was very puzzling. Two Fires seemed too proud a woman to pretend something she didn't feel. And why would she go to the trouble of trying to learn a whole new language when she really didn't need to? Rebecca herself, being the intruder, should be the one making the greatest effort to communicate! Rebecca could come to no conclusions about the girl's behavior: it was impossible to understand these people!

She hurried through the village, noticing how the rain had dampened the villagers' enthusiasm for work. Here and there, lodges were still under construction, and a woman was determinedly trying to light a fire under a lean-to of mats. But other than that, the village seemed curiously silent and subdued. Then, as she came to the stand of trees rimming the river, she saw a large group of people gathered further downstream in a clearing.

Her curiosity stirred, she set down her water jar in a grove of young sycamores, pulled her skin closer about head and shoulders, and slipped through the trees to investigate.

At least fifty or sixty braves stood on the inside of a circle, but the object of their attention was hidden from her view. Squaws and children, oblivious to the soft steady rain, pressed in on the fringes. Rebecca heard someone speaking—a man. Then another man's voice added something. They were speaking in the Miami tongue, but their voices sounded halting, awkward, the way hers sounded when she tried to get her tongue around the strange Miami syllables.

She moved closer to the edge of the group, sliding her skin forward to form a flap overhanging her face. She didn't want anyone to recognize and point her out: Kin-di-wa's red-haired slave! Another woman, also covered with a skin, came up to stand beside her. Rebecca stood on tiptoe trying to see the speakers. The crowd shifted in front of her, stirred up by what the men were saying, and Rebecca caught sight of a tall man dressed in buckskins—a white man!

He wore a furry coonskin cap, the bushy tail of which hung to one side of his face and almost obscured his bushy furry beard. His hair and beard were coppery-colored, much darker than her own hair, but close to Pa's in shading. And his beard bobbed up and down when he spoke in a powerful gruff voice, with many gesticulations, as if he were afraid he might not be understood.

Then the tall man stopped talking, hawked, and spat a long stream of dark-colored liquid, which steamed when it hit the wet ground. A shorter man stepped forward, also dressed in buckskins—another white man!

Lean and wiry, moving almost like a bobcat, he harangued the crowd with far more assurance than the first. His hair and beard were a dark dirty brown, streaked with gray, and his forehead was badly scarred. He thumped on his barrel chest, threw back his head, and shouted—daring his audience to contradict him.

A brave called out from the sidelines. Every head turned to see who was speaking, and Rebecca forgot herself and jostled closer. She saw the brave first in profile, his hawkish nose looking oddly familiar. The man turned, and a silver ring inserted through one nostril glinted with a metallic light. Rebecca took in the rest of his appearance with a thudding heart. The silver earrings and necklaces were missing. The black and white war paint had washed away, but she didn't need anything else to identify him: it was Ring-Nose, the leader of the three Shawnees who'd chased her and Kin-di-wa into the swamp!

She'd seen and heard enough. Not that she'd

understood anything that had been said, but she wanted to get away from there, back to the safety of the lodge. The feel of danger was close around her, like a mist rising up from the ground. Were all of these people Shawnee? If they were, how would they feel about a captive white woman—a slave—spying on them?

She turned around and bumped into the other woman who wore a skin over her head and shoulders. The woman's skin slipped back, and Rebecca recognized Sweet Breeze. Quickly, Sweet Breeze drew the skin back into place, took Rebecca's arm, and began dragging her away from the group. Rebecca needed no urging.

They walked hurriedly and silently away from the group, clutching their skins around them, and the weather cooperated in their escape by beginning to rain a little harder. Rebecca's moccasins squelched in the wet grass and mud of the river bank as they reached the screen of trees. "Wait!" she gasped. "I've got to get my water jar!"

"Leave it," Sweet Breeze whispered. "You come get later. Come with me to lodge."

So Rebecca followed Sweet Breeze to her lodge on the other side of the village from Two Fires's lodge. On entering, she took off her buckskin covering and shook it out, wrinkling her nose against its damp pungent smell. Sweet Breeze did the same, then bent and stirred up her lodge-fire, adding a few small pieces of wood before sitting down cross-legged on the mats.

They both removed their moccasins and set them on stones close to the tiny warm fire, and Sweet Breeze took a handful of dried leaves from a nearby basket, and crushed them into an iron pot. She poured water over them from a filled gourd, hung the pot from a wooden tripod over the glowing flames, then sat back and regarded Rebecca with an accusing frown.

"You no should have gone there, Cat-Eyes, with McKee stirring up bad feeling against Long Knives."

"McKee? You mean Alexander McKee, the man who runs the trading post?"

"Tall man who chew kinickinick. Yes, he own trading post. He spokesman for Saginwash, British."

"Kin-di-wa told me about him," Rebecca recalled. "Is that what he was doing? Stirring up bad feelings? I should think he wouldn't need to bother; there are bad feelings enough already, aren't there?"

"Always bad feelings, yes. But when time of battle approach, there always be some who need reminding why we do this—why battle so important. Squaws especially lose heart. No want to lose their husbands and sons! And when squaws lose heart, braves begin losing heart also."

"So that's what they were up to!" Rebecca resented anew the intrusion of the British and their sympathizers. Alexander McKee was no doubt just trying to protect his fur trade! At whatever cost in blood. "Who was that other white man?" she asked.

"He Simon Girty—one time Long Knife. One of *your* people, but now, no longer. He live among tribesmen now, and speak plenty much bad about Long Knives."

"Simon Girty!" Rebecca could not conceal her horror. Simon Girty—here! Back into her head came the memory of Pa's voice drifting up through the rafters. "They stripped 'im bare-assed naked and tied 'im to a stake and whut they done t' the poor bastard then with their fire an' knives an' pointed sticks ain't fit fer 'ee t' know, lass."

Simon Girty had taken part in the butchery and burning of Colonel Crawford! He'd stood by and watched—refused to even put the poor man out of his misery! "Simon Girty!" she exclaimed again.

"Where else he go but here? He always come for battles. Like vulture or traitor-dog, he always thirst for blood. Want make *sure* battle take place, and he even more pursuasive than Alexander McKee!" The embroidered bodice of Sweet Breeze's doeskin heaved with sudden anger, surprising Rebecca. She hadn't realized Sweet Breeze shared her sentiments about war and battles.

"But—is there really a chance the battle *won't* take place?" Rebecca suddenly remembered what Kin-di-wa had said to her only last night, something about Apekonit, Sweet Breeze's husband, chasing after dreams. Intuitively, she burst out, "Sweet Breeze, where is Kin-di-wa? Has he gone to Apekonit to try and stop the battle?"

Sweet Breeze sighed and looked away.

"*Tell* me, Sweet Breeze, where has Kin-di-wa gone?"

"Is best you know nothing," Sweet Breeze protested.

"I will tell no one, I swear to—to Manitou!"

"All right. I tell you." Sweet Breeze caved in. "But if anyone ask, Peshewa especially, you must say you know nothing. Kin-di-wa no tell you where he go?"

"That much is true," Rebecca assured her.

"But is long story. Must tell from beginning. Is good you understand how Kin-di-wa's mission come about."

"I'm listening. Go *on!*"

Sweet Breeze settled herself more comfortably on the mats, like a child making ready to share secrets. "Kin-di-wa and Apekonit blood brothers," she confided. "They close as man and wife. Peshewa blood brother too, but not so close anymore. Peshewa never understand why Apekonit leave Miamis. But Kin-di-wa, he understand."

"He did?" Rebecca would never have guessed it; indeed, she'd assumed the opposite—that Kin-di-wa, despite his affection for Apekonit, condemned him for switching sides.

"Kin-di-wa have white blood too, you know," Sweet Breeze reminded her. "Like Apekonit, he often feel pull of his other people. Not so much as Apekonit, maybe, but he feel it."

"I—I didn't realize that either," Rebecca admitted. "I thought his loyalty was only to the Miamis."

"Oh, yes! He plenty much loyal to Miamis!" Sweet Breeze exclaimed. "In battles with General Harmar and General St. Clair, Kin-di-wa and Apekonit fight side by side." Her eyes glowed with pride. "No one braver than they! In battle against St. Clair, they kill all soldiers who man big guns—cannon—then steal cannon away and hide it. They reason we win that battle, for without big guns, the Long Knives lose courage and run away."

Sweet Breeze's eyes then saddened. "Many tribesmen slain that day. Even more Long Knives slain. And afterwards, scalping and torture begin. It very bad, Cat-Eyes. White women who followed after troops suffer terribly. They raped and burnt and scalped while still alive. No prisoners taken. Tribesmen run too wild for that."

And Rebecca could just imagine how terrible it must have been. She wondered if Simon Girty had taken part in that carnage. More importantly, had Kin-di-wa?

"My father try, but no could stop it. Even Apekonit run wild—like maddened dog. Apekonit, Kin-di-wa, Peshewa—everybody. They run wild remembering terrible things Long Knives do to us. And afterwards, Kin-di-wa and Apekonit be sick at heart. Apekonit want go join Chenoten. He say killing must stop. Long Knives not all bad men. He remember stirring words from talking paper—tell about justice and peace for all."

"The Declaration of Independence," Rebecca interjected sadly.

"Yes." Sweet Breeze tossed her long braids back over her shoulder. "Apekonit say it reveal true intentions of Long Knives. He say Long Knives fight British, and many die to defend meaning of talking paper. He go join Chenoten to make meaning of paper come true."

"But Kin-di-wa could not go with him?"

"No. Kin-di-wa think on it, but decide he cannot go. He say talking paper only that—talking paper. He believe Long Knives's good intentions when he see them. Not before." Sweet Breeze suddenly stopped talking and peered into the caldron. The water was starting to bubble. She took a gourd, dipped it in, and passed it to Rebecca, but Rebecca shook her head no. She had no heart to drink tea, while listening to this unhappy tale.

"Kin-di-wa could not go," Sweet Breeze repeated. She held the steaming gourd between two slender hands and blew into it, waiting for the tea to cool. "But since that time, he never take part in raids against settlers. Others go—but not Kin-di-wa. They call him coward behind back. Not to face—for Kin-di-wa strong warrior, and they no wish to stir up his temper. But behind back, they call him old woman."

"Old woman!" Rebecca exclaimed.

"Yes," Sweet Breeze nodded. "And I think Kin-di-wa know it, but not care anymore what people think. Besides, it true: he no more have stomach for killing and scalping. He very quiet. No speak up in council. No take woman for wife. He sit and brood in Tecumwah's lodge. He go hunt alone, and be gone for many moons."

"And then his brother was killed by a white man." Rebecca leapt ahead of Sweet Breeze's story. She understood immediately what had brought about a resurgence of Kin-di-wa's hatred of the Long Knives—and a painful recollection of his mother's death.

"Yes, Ka-ta-mon-gli, Black Loon, shot while selling furs to white trader. He turn his back, and trader shoot him, then steal furs. Trader shoot other tribesman too, but he survive. Come home to tell story. Then, Kin-di-wa swear vengeance. Like Blue Jacket, Shawnee Chieftain, he say he no rest until Long Knives driven out forever, and he go in search of Black Loon's murderer. My people rejoice to see Kin-di-wa's courage return."

Rebecca sighed. *She* did not rejoice. Were it not for Will Simpkin's treachery, Kin-di-wa might never again have taken up the war club. Eventually, with continued encouragement, he might have gone over to the Long Knives! Might have become one of her own people and made something of himself, instead of remaining just—a savage.

She was seized by a startling insight. "But he

saved me! He knew the Shawnee were on their way to our cabin, and he didn't—he *couldn't* let them kill us! He took me away with him to save me!"

Sweet Breeze sipped her tea and shot Rebecca a puzzled glance. "You no realize how beautiful you are, Cat-Eyes. Any brave who find you unprotected likely take you away with him. If not to keep for himself, he sell you to another—except maybe Shawnee who rather scalp you."

"But—but—" Tears rushed to Rebecca's eyes. "Don't you see? He's *not* a savage, after all! He's a decent human being who regrets the wrongs he's done!"

She turned excitedly to her friend. "Oh, Sweet Breeze, Kin-di-wa and I are not as different from one another as I thought! Despite everything that's happened to him, the teachings of the missionaries got through to him after all!"

But Sweet Breeze had lowered the gourd and was staring down at it, an offended look on her pretty face. "None of us be savages. Not even the worst of us. We—many of us—think *you* the ones who are savages."

Too late, Rebecca was contrite. "Oh, Sweet Breeze, I didn't mean—I wasn't implying—I never thought *you* were a savage!"

Sweet Breeze straightened her back. Pride flashed in her great dark eyes. "I know what I am, Cat-Eyes. I am Miami. I am one of true people. My heart belongs to white man, name of William Wells, but I am still myself. I will live and die among my people. I never leave them, never betray them—even if my heart die because Apekonit not come home to me one day."

Rebecca was racked with shame. This slender girl's commitment to something outside of herself made Rebecca's own uncertainty about who she was and where she was going seem that much more unbearable. Sweet Breeze was truly noble, a rare and fine human being, while she herself was—weak, selfish, small-minded, even petty.

"This William Wells, your Apekonit, he *will* come back, Sweet Breeze! Knowing you, he couldn't help but love you! Your love must reach out to him wherever he is: such love cannot be denied!"

Sweet Breeze suddenly smiled, her eyes lighting up with a dazzling radiance. "I think so too. Apekonit come back. I know it." She touched her hand to her breast. "I tell my heart, 'no need for you to die, heart! Be patient! One day, happiness come again!'"

She laughed at her own foolishness in talking so to herself. "And now, I tell you where Kin-di-wa go—but you no must tell *any*one, Cat-Eyes."

"You *know* I will not!"

"You already guess it: Kin-di-wa go to Apekonit. Try make peace one more time before battle. My father send him. If anyone change course of Chenoten, Apekonit do it." Pride sparkled anew in her eyes.

"Apekonit chief scout for Chenoten. Chenoten

trust him plenty much. And Little Turtle trust Apekonit do best he can to stop this battle. He trust Kin-di-wa go find Apekonit—not get killed, even though it plenty dangerous crawl past enemy lookouts.''

Was Kin-di-wa's mission to contact Apekonit *secretly?* Rebecca shivered. No wonder he hadn't wanted her to know where he was going: on a dangerous mission whose success he didn't even believe in!

''Now, you see why big trouble happen if anyone find out,'' Sweet Breeze warned. ''Shawnee, Ottawa, most Miamis no want peace now. Think victory certain. Think Chenoten be like St. Clair and Harmar—easy to beat. But Little Turtle know better. Chenoten not like Harmar and St. Clair.''

Rebecca remembered Kin-di-wa telling her this too. What had he called Anthony Wayne? The Chief Who Never Sleeps. The Whirlwind. Oh, if only Kin-di-wa's mission *could* be successful! The more she heard of Anthony Wayne, the more certain she became: Wayne was, indeed, like a great driving windstorm. And if the mission failed, he'd destroy whole tribes and scatter them, the way the wind destroyed and scattered great trees! ''Do—do you think Apekonit *can* persuade Chenoten to come to terms with Little Turtle?''

Sweet Breeze bowed her head and shrugged. ''I hope so, but my father no be making great compromises, Cat-Eyes. Is Chenoten who must compromise. All tribes want one thing only: white settlers must not cross mountains and river—Ohio River—and come onto our lands. If settlers who now here go back across river and mountains, we make peace. No more make raids. River and mountains must be boundary."

"You mean the Allegheny Mountains?"

"Yes—Alleghenies. And Ohio River. They must not come west of Alleghenies or north of Ohio River."

Rebecca's heart sank. Anthony Wayne would never agree to that! Again and again, these boundaries had been disputed—to no avail. Too many settlers were already here. Veterans of the Revolutionary War had been promised homesteads on these lands! The Land Ordinance of 1787 had provided for their orderly settlement and governing, and, eventually, new states would be formed from them and admitted into the Federal Union of the United States of America!

"Oh, Sweet Breeze!" she wailed. "Can't Little Turtle compromise just a little? Couldn't the boundaries be reconsidered? Perhaps, he could at least allow those who have already settled here to stay!"

"No!" Sweet Breeze insisted vehemently. "These are *our* lands, do not forget. It is Chenoten who must compromise."

And Rebecca, trying for once to see things from someone else's point of view, was forced to agree.

Eleven

The Lightning Moon, the month of July, drew to a close in a blaze of shimmering heat. Early morning fogs shrouded the river and surrounding forest, but by noon of each day, the fog had burned off, leaving a smothering blanket of warmth. Mosquitoes swarmed everywhere, and cases of fever began to crop up among the close-packed Indians.

Watching a well-muscled brave go into tremors and grasp hold of a tree for support, Rebecca could only be grateful for her own robust good health. Her only experience with physical weakness or illness had occurred during the time of recovery from Will's abuse. But while the prospect of fever was frightening, she strongly resisted the preventive measures taken by Two Fires so that she and little Walks-Tall would not come down with it: the wearing of foul-smelling amulets and the drinking of noxious brews.

Each morning, Two Fires determinedly set out to find various plants and roots. A portion of these she carefully dried and stored, and the rest she made into tea. In the evenings, little Walks-Tall was subjected to decoctions made from ripening corn silk, wild ginger, dandelion roots, or the bark of a species of sumach. Rebecca occasionally partook of these teas—a small taste so as not to give offense—and found them abominable. But they must have been effective for Walks-Tall remained plump and healthy, a joy to watch as he teetered from basket to lodge pole or back and forth between Rebecca and Two Fires.

Those who did come down with fever were likewise treated with charms and herbal remedies, along with incantations by a shaman, and they managed to overcome the disorder far more rapidly than Rebecca had known white men to do. Since her own mother had died of fever, she was much impressed and began to pay close attention to the lore of plants and herbs that Two Fires seemed quite willing to teach her. The charms and incantations, however, she politely ignored.

Often, she and Two Fires trudged into the forest, taking turns carrying Walks-Tall who was bound into his cradleboard for such trips. Other times, she stayed in the village with Sweet Breeze. Two Fires continued to make attempts at friendship, though she had lost interest in learning Rebecca's language, and instead, Rebecca tried to learn as many words of the Miami language as she could.

Sometimes, she found the girl studying her from beneath long black lashes as if wondering if they shared the same concern: when Kin-di-wa returned home again, exactly what would be their relationship—to Kin-di-wa and to each other?

It was a strange unsettling time. Rebecca imagined herself sharing a lodge and a husband with Two Fires for the rest of her life and shivered with revulsion. But she also noticed that many lodges contained two, sometimes three squaws, a passle of children, and only one brave. By custom, Miami braves often took the sisters, nieces, or aunts of their chosen mate for additional wives; providing the man was an accomplished hunter, the arrangement seemed to please everyone involved.

One problem kept Rebecca from being able to get used to the idea of husband-sharing: when Kin-di-wa invited her to lie down with him on his buffalo robe, would Two Fires stand around and watch—and vice versa? Or would all three of them share his buffalo robe together?

Never! Rebecca vowed. But never would there be any privacy, especially in the dead of winter. And never would Rebecca totally possess Kin-di-wa in the manner she so much desired.

During the long hot nights, she tossed and turned on her skins, aching with indecision and unfulfilled desire. She longed for the feel of his mouth on hers, the sensation of his hands roving over her trembling flesh. She would close her eyes and imagine him bending over her, parting her thighs, entering her with fingers, tongue, and finally—his glorious pulsating manhood.

At such moments, she actually hated Two Fires. Were it not for her, Rebecca could gladly give up her old ambitions and dreams and freely embrace this new life, this wonderful love she'd found.

To make matters even more complicated, there was the continuing problem of Peshewa. Twice, he sent more gifts to the lodge. Twice, Rebecca sent them back. Tecumwah tramped into the lodge and out again—so loaded down she looked like a pack horse. But Rebecca refused to allow the gifts to remain in her presence for even so long as a minute. Peshewa must not be encouraged, not even at the risk of insulting his mother who would grunt and shake her head angrily, disliking Rebecca more with each visit.

Then, when no more gifts arrived for several days and Rebecca began to relax in the belief that Peshewa had given up, Sweet Breeze told her that he'd been sent north by Little Turtle to rally the Potawatomi. But before he left, he put it about that when he returned, he intended to press his suit even further. He'd vowed to his mother—who'd been trying mightily to dissuade him from chasing after a foreigner—that he would bash in the head of any brave who sought to win Rebecca in his absence. There was only one man he'd step aside for: Kin-di-wa, should he decide to keep Rebecca for himself.

Rebecca began to be grateful that at least the upcoming battle provided distraction from her personal problems. Hunting parties came and went, mock battles were staged away from the camp sites, and the camp sites themselves were continually being expanded—though as yet, the main one at Roche de Boeuf had not been moved any closer to Fort Miamis.

The Indians on the Auglaize delayed their arrival for more than a week from the time Sweet Breeze said they would come. Then they began to trickle into Roche de Boeuf as though they had all the time in the world. Sweet Breeze said they had been waiting to see if Chenoten would, indeed, go to Kekionga.

"That Chenoten!" Sweet Breeze complained. "He can no be trusted to do anything!"

"What do you mean?" Rebecca questioned. "Kin-di-wa told me he's left Fort Greenville, on his way to Kekionga."

"No," Sweet Breeze tossed her head. "He no leave after all. He tricking us again."

"But for what purpose?"

"Soldiers! He waiting for more soldiers. We think he have three thousand—but now we hear he has only two."

"Only two! But that's wonderful—isn't it?"

Then, Little Turtle's scouts brought news that another fifteen hundred Kentucky Long Rifles, under the command of General Winfield Scott, had arrived at Fort Greenville, swelling the enemy numbers to more than thirty-five hundred.

"These—changes in information. Do they mean Kin-di-wa is there at Fort Greenville? Sending home *better* information?" Rebecca paused from scraping flesh off the inside of a stinking hide someone had given Sweet Breeze.

Sweet Breeze shrugged. "*Some*one giving information to scouts. Or else they see this all for themselves." She straightened up from working on her side of the hide. "It not easy to know what be true and what be untrue."

She then went on to tell Rebecca how, after failing to take Fort Recovery, some of the disappointed tribesmen had drifted away and gone back to their own villages. Others fell under the influence of the French. Two French traders, Antoine and Jacques Lasselle, were trying to lure the tribes away from the influence of the British— telling them falsehoods—evidently hoping to regain a foothold in the fur trade.

Rebecca was aware that only the year before, in February of 1793, France had declared war on Great Britain, but since her and Papa's arrival in the wilderness last autumn, she'd had no further news. Now, in the midst of *this* conflict, it was particularly distressing to discover that the two countries were still at war and didn't mind using whatever means they could to further their own interests.

Intrigue was swirling through the woods,

thicker than the morning fogs, and Rebecca wondered dismally what was happening in far-away Washington. Did the President *know* he was being drawn into another war with Britain—maybe even into a war with France? Did he know the Indians were being pulled first one way, then another, with only the wisdom of Little Turtle to stand between them and certain destruction?

How she'd love to confront Alexander McKee, chief instigator of so much of this trouble, to tell him what she thought of him. The tall British loyalist, often in the company of the traitor, Simon Girty, never seemed to miss an opportunity to harangue whoever would stand still long enough to listen—but Rebecca could not figure out exactly what level of authority McKee had in representing the British.

One sultry hot afternoon in early August, the Moon of New Corn, as she and Sweet Breeze took refuge in the cool interior of Sweet Breeze's lodge, she asked her friend to enlighten her.

"Alexander McKee be colonel in Saginwash army," Sweet Breeze explained. "He good friends with Governor Simcoe who come here to build fort—but now fort still not finished. And we no see rest of promises kept that Saginwash make to us either."

"*What* promises did they make to you?" Rebecca yanked a quill through a piece of buckskin on which she was still trying to learn the art of quillwork.

"McKee say Saginwash give us blankets, guns, rifles, ball, flints, knives, tobacco, and war paint—give us food too. But we no see any yet, except some guns which blow up in tribesmen's faces."

"Then maybe he doesn't have as much influence as everyone thinks he has!" Rebecca couldn't keep the triumph out of her voice.

"Maybe not," Sweet Breeze conceded. She set down her own quillwork on the mats beside her. "But Tarhee, the Crane, Chief of Wyandots, go to Fort Detroit to make certain Saginwash give their support. He take old rusty hatchet given to him by Hamilton, the Hair-Buyer, during your people's war with Saginwash, and say he no return until Saginwash clean off rust—make hatchet like new."

"Oh." Rebecca was disappointed. Doubtless, direct supplication would succeed where Colonel McKee had failed, and weapons would soon come pouring in to further incite the Indians.

"Soldiers at Fort Miamis all be sick too," Sweet Breeze added. "All have fever. Not know secrets of herbs to cure themselves, and not trust our shamans to treat them."

"Oh!" Rebecca exclaimed more happily.

Sweet Breeze toyed with a quill, then stabbed it absent-mindedly into her discarded embroidery. "If we must fight, Cat-Eyes, if Kin-di-wa and Apekonit fail, we need all help we can get from Saginwash."

"Yes—of course, we will!" Rebecca's heart twisted painfully—as it had so often lately. She was not really a part of the "we" to whom Sweet Breeze was referring. But if the battle couldn't be averted, which side did she hope would win? More and more, she was leaning toward the "savages." But did that make her a traitor like Simon Girty?

Mid-week of the second sweltering week of August, a canoe-load of panic-stricken braves and squaws came ashore at Roche de Boeuf, and word spread through the camps like wildfire: Chenoten was on the march.

Chenoten! Chenoten! Rebecca heard Wayne's name on every tongue, but not until Sweet Breeze found her in a mass of people milling around near the Council Elm, did she know exactly what was happening.

"Chenoten be at Auglaize. He trick us once again—make everyone think he going to Kekionga then come up Auglaize instead!" Sweet Breeze was furious. "He burn all crops and destroy all villages there, and even now be building fort."

"A fort!" Rebecca recalled the crude map Kindi-wa had drawn for her in the soft earth of the riverbank. A fort where the Auglaize intersected the Miami of the Lake would be one more link in Wayne's carefully devised line of defense. Now, he had a string of forts snaking across the wilderness from Fort Washington on the Ohio to the very heart of the Miami Confederacy. Clearly, Anthony Wayne knew exactly what he was doing. "Is—is

291

there any other news?'' Rebecca faltered.

Sweet Breeze shook her head. "Those who fail to leave the Auglaize before, be coming now—running in terror. Still no word from Kin-di-wa."

"Are we going to move camp down closer to Fort Miamis now?"

Sweet Breeze nodded toward the towering elm. "My father come to tell us this. We break camp—move today."

Then Rebecca saw Little Turtle, in full regalia—silver earrings, medals, feathers, and war paint—standing under the tree. He lifted his arms to silence the people thronging about him. Then his magnificent voice rolled out over the crowd like thunder. Rebecca forgot the broiling sun beating down into the clearing and concentrated as hard as she could. A few random words jumped out at her: Chenoten, Auglaize, camp, and several others.

When Little Turtle finished speaking, McKee came up, accompanied by Simon Girty. He too gave a speech, which Sweet Breeze summed up for Rebecca. "McKee say more Saginwash soldiers come soon from Fort Detroit. Supplies coming also. He say Saginwash keep promise to protect Indians from Chenoten. Say Chenoten no have right to come onto these lands. These lands belong to Indians. Saginwash help Indians keep land."

"He speaks to you as though you were children!" Rebecca huffed.

Sweet Breeze shrugged. "All white men speak to

us as though we be children.''

On sudden impulse, Rebecca broke away from Sweet Breeze and jostled her way through the crowd to Little Turtle. Breathless, she stood before him, ignoring the surprised stares of the two white men beside him. Little Turtle's warm brown eyes sought hers. "Little white woman—I had forgotten you. I am ashamed we no have time to visit. No have time for you to teach me meaning of white men's bird tracks.''

"I am sorry too,'' Rebecca panted. She was having second thoughts about the wisdom of letting her presence become known to McKee and Girty. Girty was staring at her with an avid expression that reminded her somehow of Will. "I—I only wanted to let you know—if you need my services for anything—such as we spoke of that night we first met in Two Fires's lodge—I'm ready whenever you need me.''

"And what kind of services would the great Chief Little Turtle be needing from a red-haired squaw-woman?'' Simon Girty cut in rudely.

Startled, Rebecca returned the man's challenging stare, noting his small piglike eyes. The ragged ugly scar cutting across his forehead emphasized his expression of cruelty and cunning, making her feel trapped and cornered, as if he could see inside her head and read what she was thinking: that if she wrote a letter to Anthony Wayne from Little Turtle she might upset his plans.

"Why—it's none of your business, Mr. Girty!" she snapped in what she hoped was a firm no-nonsense tone.

"Know my name, do you?" Simon Girty grinned wolfishly. "Reckon there ain't too many folks this side of the Alleghenies—or even beyond—whut ain't heard of ol' Simon Girty an' his brothers!"

Brothers! Rebecca hadn't known there was more than one viper to come out of the Girty nest. She was about to voice that opinion, when Little Turtle stepped forward, positioning himself neatly between her and the two men. "My daughter must be looking for you, little white woman. Two Fires also. Mayhap, you did not understand my words; we break camp today and move closer to Fort Miamis. Saginwash look after us all, is that not so, Colonel McKee?"

He half-turned to the tall man with the copper-colored hair and beard. McKee nodded and cleared his mouth of a stream of tobacco juice. His cold gray-blue eyes were studying Rebecca like a snake's. "I never spoke nothin' but the gospel-truth, *Michikinikwa*." He used Little Turtle's Miami name. "And if this here little lady wants to help us in any way, we'd be mighty obliged to let her. Ma'am, Colonel Alexander McKee, at your service." He bowed low at the waist and tipped his coonskin cap.

An angry flush spread upwards from Rebecca's chest to her cheeks—the gall of these men! But the hint of warning in Little Turtle's eyes kept her from saying what was on her mind. "My offer was to help Little Turtle regarding a matter we—we spoke of some time ago. As for you gentlemen, I'd rather not have anything to do with you!"

She whirled away and went stalking back toward Sweet Breeze. The crowd parted to let her through, curious hostile glances following her as usual.

"Hell's fire an' damnation!" she heard Simon Girty swear. "If'n that pretty little red-haired piece don't already belong to some big buck—an' if ya don't fancy her yourself, Chief—I'd be obliged to take her offen yur hands! How'd she get so far away from her own folks, anyway, with a battle comin' on an' all?"

Little Turtle's reply was lost to her as she broke into a half-run, having spotted Sweet Breeze coming toward her.

The remainder of that long hot day was spent in moving. Two Fires gathered together everything she and Rebecca could carry and arranged it in neat sturdy bundles. There was no room for everything, and Rebecca wondered at Two Fires's stoic resignation at having to leave behind some of her meticulously designed baskets, woven fur rugs, and most of her mats. But then Two Fires shoved aside some mats covering the floor of the lodge and revealed a hidden storage place.

She clawed aside wood and dirt to reveal a well shored-up cellar, about three feet long and three feet deep, lined with pine boughs. Into this secret hiding place, Two Fires lowered her treasures; then filled the rest of the space with more branches and dirt. By the time she had finished, no one would have guessed anything was hidden there.

This silent beautiful girl constantly amazed Rebecca. Two Fires seemed to know exactly how to meet every contingency. Her choice of items to take with them was based on the barest essentials of survival and comfort: one sturdy cook-pot, several gourds, wooden bowls and spoons, all the weapons and dried foodstuffs, a careful selection of herbs, and only enough skins and mats to make a temporary shelter.

Two Fires showed Rebecca how to hoist her bundles onto her back and how to best support them by means of a plaited tumpline passed around her forehead. Rebecca, weighted down as she was, wondered how she'd even move, let alone march the unknown distance to Fort Miamis. At least, she didn't have Walks-Tall in his cradle-board strapped to her back as well!

Two Fires, almost unrecognizable under her bundles, led the way through the rapidly clearing village, whose stripped lodges looked especially bleak and forbidding. What a shame there'd been no time to dismantle the wooden skeletons and take them along! Rebecca was going to miss the security of having a roof over her head and walls around her. Miami lodges were as comfortable as log cabins, though she'd have to spend a winter in one before she'd admit it openly.

She and Two Fires joined the stream of squaws and children trudging east along the river. Those who were fortunate enough to have pack horses took everything they owned. Those who didn't were laden down as heavily as she and Two Fires. Few braves could be seen in the throng, and Rebecca concluded that breaking camp was squaw work. The braves evidently had better things to do—like planning new strategies for dealing with Anthony Wayne.

Several miles downriver, they neared the foot of some rapids, and through the sweat pouring down her forehead into her eyes, Rebecca noticed that the forest was becoming thicker. They had been walking through thinly timbered low-lands— almost prairielike in their grasses and vegetation, but now the trees grew more closely together and were greater in size and girth. The land sloped upwards and away from the river, and as Rebecca labored to the top of a rise, she saw a strange and frightening sight.

A stand of young timber, the saplings as thick as her wrist, had been sheared off at shoulder height by some strange and powerful force, and what was left standing formed a natural barricade to their progress. Two Fires paused a moment before deciding which approach would serve them better, then she determinedly set out to wend her way through the nearly impassable undergrowth.

On the other side of the stand of sheared off

saplings, they found even more forbidding obstacles. Huge oak trees lay in an impossible tangle, roots torn up and branches interlocking—one felled upon another—as though a giant had come along and played with them as a child might play with kindling.

Fallen Timbers! Rebecca thought with a clutching of her stomach. This was Fallen Timbers—the site where the battle was supposed to take place.

And she could understand why Little Turtle had chosen it. The entire area was clogged with enormous unearthed roots, huge felled trees, and a tangle of competing undergrowth. The devastation appeared to stretch for some distance along the length of the river and could not be easily avoided. One would almost *have* to pass through it on the way to the Fort—and once having entered it, could one get out? Not if every log hid a savage armed with musket or tomahawk.

After climbing over and under a half dozen logs in succession while balancing her heavy load, Rebecca called to Two Fires and motioned her over to a large rock. "Rest," she panted.

Two Fires came trudging up to her, sweat running in rivulets down her face, and a damp stain spreading across the front of her doeskin between her breasts. She slung down her bundles and inquired, *"Na-pa-pon?"*

Rebecca eased the tumpline off her forehead. "Yes, very tired," she responded in answer to the question. She lowered her burden to the ground then leaned back against the big rock.

Walks-Tall began fussing, and Two Fires slid the cradleboard from her shoulders. She unlaced the baby, took him out, and set him down on his feet. Walks-Tall crowed delightedly, wiggled his toes, and piddled on the forest floor. He took several hesitant steps, dropped to his knees, and began exploring.

Both Two Fires and Rebecca were too exhausted to do much more than lean gratefully against the rock, stretching their sore neck muscles. Then Two Fires noticed that the moss inside the cradleboard was soiled. She plucked it out with her fingers and threw it away. *"An-zan-zi,"* she said to Rebecca and pointed out into the maze of fallen trees. *"An-zan-zi."*

It took a moment before Rebecca could recall the meaning of the word—moss. Two Fires was going to look for fresh moss to line the cradleboard. She nodded and summoned up several words to let Two Fires know she would keep an eye on Walks-Tall. Two Fires grunted, climbed over a fallen log, and was quickly swallowed up in the trees.

Rebecca climbed on top of the rock, from which vantage point she could easily see Walks-Tall rummaging around in the underbrush on all fours. The baby was chortling in his own private language. He disturbed a striped-backed chipmunk who leapt away scolding in a high-pitched chatter, then he lifted one pudgy hand to examine the moats of debris floating in a sunbeam.

To him, this is all a wonderful adventure, she thought. How can he know that soon the very ground he crawls on may well be stained with blood?

Rebecca hugged her knees and looked more fully around her. Sunlight slashed the forest in various places, but the overall effect was still one of dim green gloom, as she had pictured it in her mind the time Kin-di-wa first described it to her. The windstorm that knocked down these enormous trees must have occurred a long time ago, for other trees had since sprung up around and between them, creating a nearly impenetrable barrier on the path to Fort Miamis.

She breathed deeply and tried to imagine what it would be like to march into battle here. Every tree and log could hide a waiting warrior. If Anthony Wayne fought this battle advancing forward—British-style—in straight rows, his soldiers would be mowed down like a herd of buffalo. Plenty of cover existed; but would his soldiers know enough to use it? They'd have to fight like Indians themselves in order to survive.

She realized she was unconsciously taking the part of Anthony Wayne—wondering what he would do—when lately, she'd begun to think of this battle only from the standpoint of Little Turtle and Kin-di-wa. Perhaps, this was a sign that she hadn't totally forgotten her origins. Or perhaps, she was merely doing like Little Turtle did, trying to think like "the enemy."

Sighing, she slid down from the rock. She hated this place and wanted to be out of it. It was full of evil and dark forboding. Perhaps, God had exercised his wrath here in anticipation of what was to come. If so, she wished He had destroyed it completely, wiped it off the face of the earth.

She glanced around for Walks-Tall and didn't at first see him. Panic rose in her throat as she called his name, then discovered him peeking out from underneath the rock where there was a deep indentation or cavity not easily visible to someone standing upright. "Why, you little rascal—hiding from me!"

She had to get down on her knees to haul him out.

His fat round cheeks dimpled with glee, as if he'd done something quite admirable, and impulsively, she hugged and kissed him, then smoothed back his blue-black hair. He was really a darling boy, and she was growing more attached to him everyday. If—*when*—the day came she had to leave him, it would be hard to say goodbye. He wouldn't understand why or where she was going. Already, in the short time she'd known him, he'd begun to act as if she were his second mother. Second mother. *Second wife.*

Trembling, she set him down again and gathered together their bundles. No sooner had she finished when Two Fires was back with two handfuls of soft downy moss. She relined the cradleboard, laced a protesting Walks-Tall into it,

301

and they resumed their tedious passage through Fallen Timbers.

Several more miles downriver, they came within sight of Fort Miamis, but the first thing that caught Rebecca's attention was not the fort itself—she'd seen forts before—but the bustling signs of white habitation apparent on both sides of the river. Cabins, corn fields, and vegetable gardens dotted patches of cleared land. And canoes, *pirogues,* and other small boats were pulled up on the river bank in easy proximity to the fort. One of the log structures, she was certain, had to be Alexander McKee's trading post, but she didn't know whether his post lay on this side of the river or the other. Even a small island in the river had been planted with corn and flowering vines—probably squash.

The fort itself was a four-bastioned affair, made of crudely cut logs and surrounded by a ditch and a wall of posts. The ramparts—or banks of earth—inside the stockade housed the soldiers' barracks which Rebecca noticed were roofed with logs at least a foot thick.

She stared shiveringly at the cannon protruding from slits in the bastions. The large lethal guns could be trained in any direction, and great attention had been paid to the protection of the waterfront. The river side of the fort was particularly elevated, with openings between the beams through which gunfire could be concentrated.

But for all this seeming might and power,

Rebecca thought Sweet Breeze was right: the fort itself wasn't properly finished. The barracks were in a state of half-construction with building materials laying about carelessly, as if awaiting a tidying hand. There were still too many trees in the vicinity as well—trees that could conceal invaders sneaking up on the fort. In her limited experience, the area around a fort was always perfectly cleared to provide the best vigilance possible. Except for the *abatis,* of course: layers of brush and sharpened sticks which were sometimes thrown up to provide additional protection from attack.

Inside the stockade, several soldiers moved about. Half-hoping for signs of fever, Rebecca stole several glances at them as she and Two Fires were carried forward in the tide of humanity emerging from the woods and flowing past the fort. They were not going to camp right beside the fort, after all, it seemed, but must keep on going to some further spot on the river.

Despite her fatigue and curiosity, Rebecca was glad. She had no desire whatever to rub shoulders with the despised "Saginwash," nor did she wish to stir *their* curiosity.

When at last she was finally able to divest herself of her bundles, it was very late in the day, and she was then so hungry, thirsty, and tired she could hardly stand upright. She helped Two Fires throw up a makeshift lean-to, gobbled down a handful of parched corn, and fell asleep almost immediately, pausing only long enough to wonder where Kin-di-wa slept this night. Was he with Apekonit? Was he safe? Had he too arrived at the Auglaize? When—oh *when* would she see him again?

The next several days were spent in trekking even further downriver and setting up camp beside a creek called Swan Creek which emptied into the Miami of the Lake. Rebecca did not think the site of the new camp was a particularly healthy one: it was rimmed by marshes and obviously a favorite breeding ground for mosquitoes. But Sweet Breeze assured her that here, so much closer to the mouth of the river, the women and children would be safe. British reinforcements need only come down the Lake of the Eries from Fort Detroit or from the British settlements on the River Raisin.

Rebecca and Two Fires, not knowing how long they would have to stay, thus set about building a more sturdy lean-to to keep off rain and wind. Made of cut saplings and branches, with mats tied down over the framework, the lean-to proved to be almost as good as a lodge. And with a fire at the side facing into the marsh, even the mosquitoes didn't seem so bad. The proximity of the marshes was at least helpful in that food could be easily obtained there—both cattails and several species of tubers, waterfowl and other game.

Then, at almost the middle of August, Sweet Breeze hurried to their lean-to to bring them the latest news. "More Saginwash come! Fifty soldiers from Twenty-fourth Regiment, eight artil—artil—"

"Artillerymen," Rebecca promted gloomily.

"And a detachment of Queen's Rangers from Fort Detroit! They come on big gunship, *Chippewa*, and bring ten times ten men from Canada Country to help build up fort and clear more trees!"

"Is that all?" Rebecca asked. She bent down over her quillwork with a less than civil attitude, not pleased one bit by the news.

"No! I save best part for last!" Sweet Breeze bubbled. "Saginwash bring three times one hundred barrels of presents—arms, powder, blankets, and food—plus fifty more!"

Rebecca was appalled. Three hundred and fifty barrels, each one an additional reason for the Indians to side with the British.

The *Chippewa* did not even sail back to Fort Detroit but remained anchored out in the bay off an island known as Turtle Island. On disembarking, Major William Campbell took command of Fort Miamis and had additional nine-pounder cannons from the British stores at Turtle Island hauled up the river after him.

To Rebecca, this seemed positive proof that another Revolutionary War was in the making. But depressed as she was over these developments, two things gave her hope: one of the French traders, Antoine Lasselle, who'd been accused of trying to steer Indian loyalty away from the British toward the "Old French Father," had accompanied the unarmed Canadians with seven or eight of his *"engages."*

He'd come, he said, to clear his name and show his good faith to the Indians and to the British. Did this mean that the possibility of French intervention in the battle had faded?

The second thing to lift her spirits was that the British garrison continued to be decimated by fever. The pale white soldiers in their heavy uniforms were no match for the mosquitoes and the heat. They took to liberally cutting their water with rum in hopes of avoiding the disease, while the Indians, including Sweet Breeze, laughed at them for their foolishness.

Rebecca could almost pity the poor redcoats, except she wanted so much for them to give up and go home. She herself now drank herbal teas with relish, not knowing if they helped or not, but unwilling to take chances.

So the days dragged by, while she worried, sweated, and looked after Walks-Tall when Two Fires went foraging in the marsh. She made good progress both in her quillwork and in learning the language, but could not put off the feeling she was living in some kind of dream: soon, the peaceful placid days must pass, bringing violence, bloodshed and—hard decisions.

Then one evening, as she was just dozing off in the heavy darkness, Sweet Breeze came to her lean-to and quietly whispered her name. "Cat-Eyes, come quickly! Little Turtle wishes to see you."

Rebecca fairly leapt off her mat and skins and followed Sweet Breeze through the slumbering camp to Little Turtle's lodge, which had been brought down piece by piece from Roche de Boeuf and rebuilt by the river.

On entering it, she half-expected to see Kin-di-wa, but the tall white man dressed like an Indian was someone she'd never seen before. She stilled her fluttering heart with an effort and knelt down between Little Turtle and the stranger, hoping she wouldn't be kept in suspense too long. Sweet Breeze knelt down too—but in the shadows, away from the soft glow of the lodge-fire.

Little Turtle wasted no time in telling her why he'd sent for her. "This man Christopher Miller. He bring letter from Chenoten."

Little Turtle held in his strong brown hands a long scroll of parchment. "I want you read it, little white woman. This Christopher Miller read it already, but I want make certain he no speak with forked tongue."

Rebecca took the parchment with trembling hands. She unrolled it and held it up to the light. There, down at the bottom, the signature of Anthony Wayne leapt out at her, and underneath it was the date and place where the letter had been written: Grand Glaize, 13th August, 1794.

Her fingers shook, and she could hardly find her voice, but Little Turtle was waiting, so she began reading as slowly and carefully as she could. *"To the Delawares, Shawnees, Miamis, and Wyandots,*

307

and to each and every one of them, and to all other Indians northwest of the Ohio, to whom it may concern:"

She cleared her throat and Little Turtle nodded. In the greeting at least, Christopher Miller had properly relayed the message. She continued: *"I, Anthony Wayne, Major General and Commander in Chief of the Federal army now at Grand Glaize, and Commander Plenipotentiary of the United States of America; for settling the terms upon which a permanent and lasting peace shall be made with each and every hostile tribe or nation of Indians northwest of the Ohio, and of the said United States; actuated by the purest principles of humanity, and urged by pity for the errors into which bad and designing men have led you; from the head of the army now in possession of your abandoned villages and settlements: do hereby once more extend the hand of peace toward you, and do invite each and every one of the hostile tribes of Indians to appoint deputies to meet me and my army without delay, between this place and Roche de Boeuf, in order to settle the preliminaries of a lasting peace, which may eventually and soon restore to you—the Delawares, Miamis, Shawnees, and all other tribes and nations lately settled at this place and on the margins of the Miami and Auglaize Rivers—your late grounds and possessions; and to preserve you and your distressed and helpless women and children from danger and famine, during the present fall and ensuing winter."*

Rebecca paused for breath and to allow the flowery language to sink in. Since it was difficult and confusing to read, it must have been even more difficult for those listening to understand.

Little Turtle grunted and nodded to the silent Christopher Miller, who sat with head bowed, listening, so that Rebecca could not see his face. "Is good," Little Turtle acknowledged. "So far this Christopher Miller no speak with forked tongue. Is also good Chenoten wish to meet with us. Go on, little white woman, read more of letter."

Rebecca read on: *"The arm of the United States is strong and powerful, but we love mercy and kindness more than war and desolation; and to remove any doubts or apprehensions of danger, to the persons of the deputies whom you may appoint to meet this army, I hereby pledge my sacred honor for their safety and return; and send Christopher Miller, an adopted Shawnee and a Shawnee warrior, whom I took prisoner two days ago, as a flag, who will advance in their front to meet me."*

So Christopher Miller had been raised by the Shawnee. Rebecca stole a quick glance at him. She hadn't been wrong in guessing that he was a "white Indian," one of those taken captive as a boy and reared like Apekonit and Kin-di-wa to become fierce warriors.

The tall lean man wore breech clout and leggings, kept his hair in the Indian manner— long and braided—but could not, despite brown eyes and hair, deny his white blood. Instead of high cheekbones and angular facial lines, his face was rounded, almost boyish. Freckles dusted his skin.

His brown eyes lifted to hers, and flustered that he'd caught her staring, she continued, *"Mr. Miller was taken prisoner by a party of my warriors six months since, and can testify to you the kindness I have shown to your people, my prisoners, that is, five warriors and two women, who are now all safe and well at Greenville. But should this invitation be disregarded, and my flag, Mr. Miller, be detained or injured, I will immediately order all those prisoners to be put to death, without distinction, and some of them are known to belong to the first families of your nations."*

At this, Rebecca gasped. Would Anthony Wayne really deal so harshly with his prisoners— especially two women?

Hurriedly, she read the rest. *"Brothers, be no longer deceived or led astray by false promises and language of the bad white men at the foot of the rapids; they have neither the power nor inclination to protect you. No longer shut your eyes to your true interest and happiness, nor your ears to this last overture of peace; but in pity to your innocent women and children, come and prevent the further effusion of your blood; let them experience the kindness and friendship of the United States of America, and the invaluable blessings of peace and tranquility. Signed, Anthony Wayne,"* she finished in a whisper.

Little Turtle stirred. "Well, then, Brother," he said to Christopher Miller. "You no longer need fear my war club sinking into your head. Pardon an old man's caution, but only in old days could a stranger's word be trusted."

Christopher Miller sat up straighter. "Michikinikwa, your wisdom is known the length and breadth of this land. But if you *had* trusted me, I should have doubted that wisdom."

Little Turtle leaned forward. "Now, tell me, have you met my adopted son—Apekonit?" There was a slight tremor in his deep rich voice.

"He was the one who captured me, the one they call Captain William Wells."

Rebecca heard Sweet Breeze's quick intake of breath. "So," Little Turtle murmured. "He now a captain. Is good. Apekonit never one to follow others. He good leader of men."

"Yes, and he is well, Michikinikwa, though only a few days past, he was shot in the wrist escaping from a Delaware camp."

"A Delaware camp? But Delaware have all come here."

"It was near here. He came with several other scouts—all dressed as Indians. They scouted Fort Miamis, then returned to Chenoten. On the way back to Chenoten, he stopped at a Delaware camp,

311

and a Delaware squaw recognized one of his scouts. Captain Wells was shot in the wrist, and another scout, Robert McClellan, was shot in the shoulder."

Poor Sweet Breeze! Rebecca sympathized, to hear that her own husband had been shot and wounded—that he'd actually been as close as Fort Miamis scouting for the enemy—and to know that he hadn't come to see her!

"My brother, Nicholas Miller, was with them too, as was William May, Dodson Thorp, and someone new among them—a half-breed they called by his Indian name, Kin-di-wa."

Now, it was Rebecca's turn to catch her breath. Kin-di-wa! Kin-di-wa had been with Apekonit as near to her as Fort Miamis! But—what did this mean? Was Kin-di-wa now posing as one of Anthony Wayne's scouts?

"This Kin-di-wa," Little Turtle remarked with studied disinterest. "You say he new among Chenoten's scouts. What tribe he come from?"

Christopher Miller looked puzzled. "Why, Miami, I think. Do you know him? You must if he is truly Miami."

"No." Little Turtle shook his head. "Mayhap, he come from some other tribe down Wabash River. Yes, I think so—must come from tribe far distant."

"Michikinikwa." A frown passed over Miller's boyish face. "What answer to his letter am I to take back to Chenoten?"

Little Turtle sighed deeply. "It not in my power alone to give you answer. If it were, I give you answer tonight. But I must confer with other chiefs, must hold big council. And council cannot be held until all chiefs have come from distant places. Most here now—but we still wait on Potawatomies."

Miller's frown deepened, making him look much older. "Chenoten is not a patient man. How long must he wait?"

"Ten days," Little Turtle promised. "Ten risings and settings of the sun. Is not so long to wait to see if peace is possible."

"Then I must go back and tell him. But it's not the answer he wants to hear. I cannot promise Chenoten will be patient."

"I understand," said Little Turtle. His glance fell on Rebecca. "Little white woman, I thank you for making sense of bird tracks, but what you read and hear this night must not be spoken of—you understand? Or many lives be sacrificed, especially one of which you know."

"Yes, I know," Rebecca nodded. Kin-di-wa's! If anyone found out that Kin-di-wa had been scouting for Anthony Wayne, his life among his own people wouldn't be worth a handful of parched corn. Oh, what on earth was he doing? Why hadn't he yet returned?

If indeed he *was* scouting for Anthony Wayne, as Christopher Miller said, then his life was doubly jeopardized: he'd be killed immediately if anyone besides Apekonit discovered where his true loyalties lay.

Sweet Breeze arose and came to her, signaling the time had come to return to her lean-to. Rebecca stood up, bowed respectfully to Little Turtle and Christopher Miller, then followed Rebecca out into the dark night.

They moved swiftly and quietly back through the camp to Two Fires's lean-to, but before Sweet Breeze could slip away, Rebecca plucked at her arm. "Sweet Breeze," she whispered. "Wait!"

"It not safe to speak now," Sweet Breeze whispered back. "Trees, lean-tos—even shadows—have ears. Many understand your tongue even if no can speak it."

"But I must know something! The letter from Chenoten—did it mean that Kin-di-wa's mission was successful?"

"Mayhap," Sweet Breeze answered. "Who can say but Chenoten himself?"

"But—will the other chiefs your father spoke of be willing to meet and make peace?"

"No can say, Cat-Eyes. Must wait till council meeting. Then we know."

An owl hooted somewhere in the black depths of the marsh. Rebecca was seized with a violent sense of terror and foreboding. She remembered when she and Kin-di-wa had last heard an owl. "Oh, Sweet Breeze! I'm so afraid!" She suddenly broke down.

"Shhhh . . ." Sweet Breeze cautioned, her own

voice trembling. "No matter what happens, you be safe."

"It's not for myself that I'm afraid!" Rebecca protested. "It's for your people and mine! For Apekonit—most of all, for Kin-di-wa!"

Sweet Breeze found Rebecca's hand in the darkness and squeezed it, surprising Rebecca with her strength. "Cat-Eyes, I know how you feel, but no use to waste your tears! Your people and mine will choose own course, no matter what we do, no matter what we say. Our men will do same thing. We can love them, give them counsel, but no can stop them. Is wise to let them go. We only women, remember, our destiny be to wait, and when this all be over, to pick up pieces and go on."

"No!" Rebecca cried. Every fiber of her being revolted against such a destiny for herself. "I—I'm not as strong as you, Sweet Breeze, but I swear to you, if there is anything I can do to stop this madness sweeping down on us, I will do it!"

Sweet Breeze let go of Rebecca's hand. Her barely visible braids swung in agreement with her denial. "There nothing you can do, Cat-Eyes. Listen to me—*nothing!*"

But Rebecca wondered.

Later, she tossed and turned and twisted again on her mat in the thick darkness. Over and over in her tired brain the haunting certainty pounded: something. There must be something she could do. And whatever it was, she would find it.

Twelve

It seemed Rebecca had barely fallen asleep when Sweet Breeze was once again shaking her. "Cat-Eyes! Wake up, Cat-Eyes!"

Rebecca opened her eyes groggily, took one look at Sweet Breeze's distraught face, and was instantly awake and alarmed. "What *is* it?" she cried. "Where's Two Fires?" Neither Two Fires nor Walks-Tall was in the lean-to, but the slant of light outside the shelter told her it was well past sunrise. They'd probably gone off to the marsh in search of breakfast, leaving her to sleep.

"She not here! I already look for her. Get up, Cat-Eyes, hurry!"

Rebecca scrambled to her feet and followed Sweet Breeze out of the lean-to. She'd never seen her friend so distressed. Sweet Breeze took her hand and almost dragged her to the side of a brown and white pony patiently cropping grass nearby. In one swift easy movement, she hiked up her doeskin and leapt astride, then patted the pony's rump behind her. "He good strong pony. Carry us both. Hurry!"

Rebecca hadn't ridden horseback in a long time, but she noted how Sweet Breeze held on with clenched knees, then clambered aboard the pony herself. Being a much smaller animal than the old farm horse Papa had owned, she found him less difficult to mount than she imagined, and once astride, the memory of how she used to sneak into the pasture to ride Old Pete returned.

Her knees automatically gripped tightly as Sweet Breeze kneed the pony into a trot, then into a canter along the river bank. In between gasps, as she thumped up and down on the animal's rump and hung onto Sweet Breeze's slender waist to keep her seat, she pressed her friend for an explanation. "Where are we going? What's happened?"

But Sweet Breeze would not respond until they were far away from the camp heading in the direction of Fort Miamis, then she allowed the pony to slow his pace. He blew through his nostrils, sides heaving from the exertion of carrying two people, and Sweet Breeze slid off his back, indicating Rebecca should do likewise.

"He rest then run some more." Sweet Breeze took the reins of the pony's rawhide halter. Her black eyes suddenly sparkled with tears, and Rebecca felt breathless and afraid.

"Now, I tell you where we be going," Sweet

Breeze said. "Word come from Roche de Boeuf: that one of Chenoten's scouts be captured."

"One of his scouts!" Rebecca cried. "You—you mean . . ."

"Yes, Cat-Eyes, I think same thing as you. Could be Apekonit. Could be Kin-di-wa. Runner who bring news not know his name, but say Shawnee and Ottawa took him. He was scouting Fallen Timbers or maybe waiting for Christopher Miller. Runner not know which one. Only know scout be taken, and Shawnee say he be put to death this morning."

"But—surely your father could save him!" The image of Kin-di-wa lying stretched out on the ground awaiting torture and death by knives and fire flashed through her mind. "Your father is the *Chief!* He has only to order it, and whoever the man is, he'll be spared!"

Sweet Breeze shook her head, tears spilling down her cheeks. She continued walking, dragging the tired pony after her. "No. Whenever enemy be taken, he belong to those who took him. Shawnee and Ottawa very fierce. Always hating Long Knives—especially Chenoten's scouts. They wait long time to catch one; now they make him pay for times when Chenoten make tribesmen look plenty foolish."

"But surely your father doesn't approve of torturing and burning!"

"I already tell you—is not my father's doing! Is not his captive. Only Shawnee or Ottawa chieftains, Blue Jacket or Turkey Foot, could stop it."

Rebecca was aghast. "Couldn't he ask *them* to stop it?"

Again, Sweet Breeze shook her head. "Is matter of honor. No chief interferes with matters belonging to another—especially so small a matter as this."

"Sweet Breeze!" Rebecca stopped walking. "I'd hardly call a man's life a small matter! Where are we going then—if not to try and stop this?"

The black eyes churned with pain. "We go find out who is to die," Sweet Breeze whispered. "If it be Apekonit, I must know it."

"Is that why you wanted me to come along?" Rebecca heard herself shriek. "So that if it *isn't* Apekonit, if it's Kin-di-wa instead—I'll be forced to watch *him* die?"

Sweet Breeze's eyes bored into hers. "Would you no want to know, Cat-Eyes? Would you no want to be there when it happened? The presence of a warrior's woman gives him strength to bear what must be. We give him great honor if we witness his death chant, heap ashes on our heads, and weep and wail when he is gone. Two Fires be most unhappy *she* didn't get to come! Mayhap, I should have waited and asked her to come instead of you."

A shudder ran through Rebecca from head to foot. What manner of people *were* these Miamis? How could *any* woman bear to watch her husband suffer and die so needlessly?

Then a worse thought occurred to her: if it *was*

Kin-di-wa, how could she turn away at the very moment when he might need her most? *She* was the one who should be there—not Two Fires!

"Let's hurry then, to wherever it is we're going." She flung herself onto the back of the pony and offered Sweet Breeze her hand. The slender girl climbed on in front of her, and once again they pushed the pony to a canter along the riverbank.

"We going back to Roche de Boeuf," Sweet Breeze said over her shoulder. "But I no be knowing if we can get there in time."

It took them several hours to get past Fort Miamis and pick their way through Fallen Timbers. It was well past noon and breathlessly hot by the time they rode into the clearing at the Council Elm as fast as the heaving pony could go. But the clearing was deserted—except for one lone figure, lashed tightly to the Council Elm. The man's head hung motionless. His body sagged unmoving against its bonds. Flies droned and swarmed over his bloody wounds—so many wounds as to render the body unrecognizable at a slight distance.

Sweet Breeze slid off the horse and approached the tree, her back and shoulders as rigid as a lance. Rebecca dismounted and hung back. She suddenly didn't want to know—couldn't bear to discover if this broken scrap of tortured humanity was her own beloved Kin-di-wa. The man had been scalped as well as riddled with arrows and musketballs, so it was impossible to guess his identity without going closer. Evidently, he'd been tied up and used for target practice.

She watched Sweet Breeze lift the man's chin to study his bloodied face. The man had been tall and well proportioned. He wore buckskin leggings and a breech clout—typical Indian dress. Sweet Breeze allowed the man's head to fall down again, turned and walked back to the heaving pony.

"It no be Apekonit or Kin-di-wa," she told Rebecca without expression.

Rebecca felt her legs go weak, and the ground swam up to meet her. A moment later, or perhaps it was several moments, she was lying on the river bank and Sweet Breeze was scooping water over her. She tried to sit up, her eyes searching for the Council Elm, but not finding it.

"Lean over," Sweet Breeze directed. "Put head between knees—yes, like so."

Rebecca obediently followed instructions as wave after wave of nausea flowed over her. "Wh— where are we?" she gasped.

"I put you over horse. We move downstream. It be better now, Cat-Eyes." Concern filled Sweet Breeze's voice. "This sickness you feel—it because you growing baby inside your belly?"

"No!" Rebecca exclaimed. At least as far as she knew, she wasn't pregnant. But Sweet Breeze was right to be concerned. Never could she remember a reaction such as this; it simply wasn't her nature to be faint or squeamish. Not even Papa's hideous wound had made her feel like this.

"Just give me a moment, I'll be all right." She leaned far over and was sick to her stomach in the long grass; then, indeed, she did feel better. And resentful of Sweet Breeze's composure.

How had Sweet Breeze managed *not* to get sick—not to lose her very sanity—examining that gruesome corpse to see if it was her own husband? How had she managed to sling Rebecca over the pony? Rebecca pressed her fingers to her throbbing temples, disgusted with what she'd seen and even more disgusted with herself. "Did you recognize him?" she asked. "Did—did he look anything like Christopher Miller? He said he had a brother among the scouts, someone named Nicholas."

"I never see him before, Cat-Eyes. He no look like Miller, and anyway, Miller started back to Chenoten at first light. He not expecting his brother or *any* of Chenoten's scouts. Now, maybe we never know who dead man be, but at least he not suffer much—and others all get away."

"Yes," Rebecca whispered, struggling to her feet. "The others got away."

Silently, she and Sweet Breeze started back toward camp, each wrapped in her own grim thoughts. As they led the pony through Fallen Timbers—for it was impossible to ride him there—they heard the sound of drums, a low roll of muted thunder sweeping up and down the river.

Sweet Breeze stopped to listen, and Rebecca nervously stroked the pony's withers. "The last time I heard the drums, they meant every warrior was to go home and prepare for war. What do they mean now?''

"The drums call warriors to council this night. Mayhap, Potawatomies have come. It for them my father be waiting. Or mayhap he think it best to go ahead with council anyway, whether they come or not.''

"Tonight? Tonight the chiefs will decide whether to accept Chenoten's offer of a treaty council?''

Sweet Breeze nodded. "Or else they decide if battle be fought—here, at Fallen Timbers." She appeared deep in thought for a moment, then began to turn the pony around. "It better we not go all way back to camp, Cat-Eyes. Council be held at Council Elm. Better we go back there.''

"Oh, no! Not back to the elm!''

Sweet Breeze shot her a level glance. "They cut him down now, Cat-Eyes. Take his body out in woods and leave for wolves. We not so savage to allow dead man attend our council.''

Yes, but you're savage enough to throw him to the wolves instead of burying him, Rebecca thought.

She still felt resentful toward her friend. Now that Sweet Breeze knew the scout wasn't Apekonit or Kin-di-wa, it appeared she took no further interest in him. Obviously, she didn't want to waste her pity on someone she didn't even know. But Rebecca pictured a woman somewhere, a white woman in a long homespun skirt with children clinging to it. She'd be waiting and wondering, watching for her man to come home. And one day, she'd hear how he'd died—lashed to a tree and riddled with musketballs and arrows.

Going back toward Roche de Boeuf and the Council Elm, they again passed the rock she'd sat and rested on while she waited for Two Fires to find moss for Walks-Tall's cradleboard. It stood almost in the very middle of the tangle of Fallen Timbers, and she remembered Walks-Tall crawling under the large boulder and hiding from her.

A shaft of sunlight penetrating to the forest floor further reminded her of the way the baby had lifted up his hand and tried to capture a sunbeam.

Tonight, for little Walks-Tall more than for anyone, the future would be decided. Indeed, he *was* the future, and she could only hope Little Turtle and the rest of the chiefs would put aside their desires for vengeance and victory—and remember the *children* whose best interests were served by peace.

Throughout the rest of that long hot day, the drums continued to spread the message: Come! Come to the Council Elm! The moment of decision is at hand!

The body of Chenoten's unknown scout was cut down and dragged away without ceremony. Rebecca did not see it but heard about it later from Two Fires who had come down from camp in the afternoon with Walks-Tall. She'd gone straight to the Council Elm, along with everyone else from camp, and seen the whole thing.

Now, it was evening, and Rebecca and Sweet Breeze joined the people thronging into the clearing. Two Fires and another squaw were with them, chattering gleefully about the death of one of Chenoten's hated scouts. Rebecca wondered at the girl's callousness. Of course, Two Fires didn't know the dead man might have been Kin-di-wa, but had she also forgotten that Sweet Breeze's husband was one of Chenoten's scouts?

Uncharitably, Rebecca wondered whether Two Fires wouldn't express the same satisfaction if it *had* been Kin-di-wa or Apekonit.

What lay behind the girl's beautiful black eyes could only be termed a mystery. The barrier of speech was fast disappearing as Rebecca made headway with the Miami language, but the barrier of culture loomed higher than ever. And the unresolved problem of Kin-di-wa stood highest of all.

Rebecca sighed. The drums reminded her that the hour of her own decision was drawing near: could she agree to accept Kin-di-wa on the only terms he could offer—sharing him with Two Fires? Or would she soon be on her way back home to Aunt Margaret in Pennsylvania?

Stiff with tension, she stood silently watching the enormous crowd of braves flocking to the Council Elm. Kin-di-wa ought to be here for this important occasion. Hadn't he said he'd come home when Chenoten came? Just how much closer did Chenoten have to get?

Rebecca didn't see Kin-di-wa anywhere among the bands of warriors who were settling themselves in a ring around a huge stack of firewood. The stack grew higher by the minute as a party of squaws filed past it dumping on more wood, and slowly, her tension solidified into fear.

Why hadn't Kin-di-wa returned yet? Anthony Wayne had made a peace gesture—either on his own or because Kin-di-wa's mission had been successful. Now, it remained only for the tribes to accept or reject his offer. What further good could be accomplished by Kin-di-wa continuing to place himself in great danger? Was that why he wasn't here—because someone had found him out?

Darkness was closing in rapidly. Nearly two thousand braves were jammed into the clearing, and soon, she wouldn't be able to see any faces except for those closest to the waiting-to-be-kindled fire. The braves sat cross-legged on mats and blankets, looking exceptionally serious. They talked and bantered little. If Kin-di-wa did come, where would he go?

The chiefs and their counselors held the most honored places nearest the front, and in the second row, off to Rebecca's left, sat Alexander McKee, Simon Girty, and another white man whom Sweet Breeze informed her was Matthew Elliot, a trapper and British sympathizer. Dressed in buckskins, the three white men sat on blankets alongside a handful of British officers from Fort Miamis.

The officers, resplendently dressed in scarlet uniforms with polished brass buttons and plenty of gold braid, stood out like peacocks in a clutch of hens, and directly behind them, Rebecca suddenly saw Ring-Nose. The fierce-looking Shawnee was sitting with a large party of his tribesmen, among whom she recognized the other two braves from whom she'd rescued Kin-di-wa when they would have tortured and killed him—as they'd probably helped to kill the hapless scout that very morning.

To still her thumping heart, she looked away from Ring-Nose and studied the opposite side of the clearing, and there, unexpectedly saw Peshewa seated in a large party of Potawatomies. Red quills quivering, he was speaking to someone beside him. Then he looked up, and glanced in her direction. Quickly, she looked away.

So the Potawatomies had made it to Council after all. And she could now expect to be receiving more unwanted gifts. If present and future events didn't interfere with Peshewa's courtship of her, she'd *have* to think of some way to discourage him completely. The mere sight of him set her teeth on edge.

Hunching her shoulders slightly, Rebecca tried to disappear between Two Fires and Sweet Breeze. She hoped Peshewa hadn't seen her. Of course, even if he missed seeing her and saw only her companions, he might guess she'd be sitting exactly where she was. Sweet Breeze sat on her right, Two Fires on her left. Two Fires was nursing Walks-Tall to sleep, and on the other side of Two Fires sat Tecumwah, Peshewa's mother.

Around them, squeezed together like beans in a fist, other squaws and children sat waiting patiently for the council to begin, apparently not minding that they were assigned the most inferior places, behind the braves.

Then, from somewhere behind Rebecca, a querulous female voice rang out, "Get up, now! Get out of my way!"

The voice sounded familiar. Shocked that she'd understood it clearly, Rebecca turned around in the failing light and saw an old woman jostling toward her, stepping on people, and prodding them out of her way with a staff. It was Crow Woman—the old crone she'd first met at Kekionga with Kin-di-wa!

"Make room!" Crow Woman shrilled. "Show respect for your elders!"

Catching sight of Rebecca, the old woman's weathered face split into a wide toothless grin. "So—Cat-Eyes!"

Rebecca nodded and grinned, pleased that she could understand, for the first and only time she'd met Crow Woman, everything the old woman had said sounded more like a gibberish than human conversation. But now Crow Woman launched into a rapid stream of language that was too fast for Rebecca to follow.

Disappointedly, Rebecca moved closer to Sweet Breeze, making room so the old woman could sit down. Two Fires had thoughtfully brought along a mat, and Crow Woman settled her old bones on it gleefully, never stopping to draw breath. She rummaged through a pouch dangling from around her neck and uttered a sharp cry which drew the attention of everyone around them. Withdrawing the strand of hair Rebecca had given to her, she held it up, nodding and exclaiming.

Rebecca shrank away, embarrassed to be singled out, and Sweet Breeze leaned over and whispered in her ear. "She telling everyone how she met you and how you give her your hair. She say your hair be strong medicine! Only yesterday, she use it to break child's fever. She be plenty busy curing fevers since she came downriver from Kekionga, and she want thank you again for giving her your hair."

Oh, no! Rebecca thought.

Having wondered and worried about Crow Woman, she was glad to see the old woman had been safely evacuated from Kekionga. But she fervently hoped Crow Woman's enthusiasm for her hair wouldn't spread to others!

Already, Two Fires and Tecumwah were eyeing her long red braid with thoughtful expressions, as if discovering, right in their midst, possibilities they hadn't before noticed.

To Rebecca's intense relief, a sudden rapid thumping on water drums drew everyone's attention.

Little Turtle stepped forward out of the shadows and walked to the stacked wood in the center of the clearing. Holding a brightly burning torch which illuminated his regal face and made his silver ornaments sparkle, he signaled the council meeting was about to begin.

A hush fell over the gathering, and Rebecca felt an absurd thrill of pride and expectancy. The hated British officers, including the Commandant, Major William Campbell, had not outdone the great war chief of the Miami Confederacy.

His silver earrings, medals, brooches and necklaces put their gold braid to shame. The white feathers entwined in his hair outdid their tricornered hats and plumes, and as if to mock their scarlet-coated, white-breasted uniforms, every inch of his leggings and breech clout boasted beautiful meticulous embroidery which Rebecca surmised Sweet Breeze must have had a hand in making.

And now, as dignified as a king, Little Turtle stretched out the brand and ignited the bonfire.

It took a few moments to catch. He tossed the brand on top of the wood, stepped back, and folded his arms. Then he threw back his head and began chanting in a beautiful ancient rhythm Rebecca could not understand but found very impressive—

so impressive she made an effort to push into the back of her mind her anxiety about Kin-di-wa so as to concentrate more fully on what was happening.

Whitish-colored smoke curled up from the fire, snaking upwards toward the rapidly darkening sky. Leaning closer, Sweet Breeze whispered, "Smoke carrying my father's chant to Manitou. That reason fire be lit, even though night is warm. Fire be kept going now till council meeting over, so Manitou hear everything spoken this night."

Then Little Turtle made a motion, and all the chiefs—easily recognizable by their many ornaments, embroidered clothing, luxurious furs and feathers—got up and moved in closer to the fire. Sweet Breeze identified them one by one, and Rebecca tried to peg them in her mind. The first, Tarhee, the Crane, was easy. A tall, slender, angular-looking man who moved with an easy grace, he reminded her of a crane.

"Tarhee, chief of Wyandots," Sweet Breeze whispered. "His people live along Sandusky River, mostly at Crane Town, which be named after him."

The second was also easy, because Rebecca had seen him before—Buckongahelas, the Delaware. She remembered the day he'd come, the day she'd been attacked by the children.

"His name mean Breaker-To-Bits," Sweet Breeze said. She pointed out his enormous meaty hands, which did indeed look as though they could break anything to bits. Shorter than Tarhee, Buckonga-helas nevertheless conveyed a sense of great personal power and strength. His shoulders and chest rippled with muscles, but his face, atop a short thick neck, looked somewhat bashed in, as if his nose had once been broken in a fight.

Next came Blue Jacket, the Shawnee, about whom Rebecca had already heard a great deal. He would have been recognizable even without Sweet Breeze's comments, for he wore a blue hunting jacket left over from the Revolutionary War, had a red bandana tied about his forehead, and stood fully six feet tall. Handsome and fierce-looking, he carried himself with great arrogance and pride, as if he thought being a Shawnee was to be better than anyone else.

Rebecca found herself resenting him: did he think he was even better than Little Turtle? Did he think *he* ought to be the war chief of the confederacy? His haughty bearing seemed to say so.

The next chief was one Rebecca didn't know: Turkey Foot, of the Ottawas. Small and wiry, strutting like a turkey, Turkey Foot appeared to be as arrogant as Blue Jacket. He walked twice around the council fire, as if ascertaining whether it met his standards, then sat down beside Blue Jacket—his small head jerking turkeylike from one chief to another.

Red Pole, Black Hoof, New Corn, Leather Lips,

and one with an extremely difficult long name—
Mash-i-pi-nash-i-wish then took their places.
Rebecca had been determined to keep track of
them all, but she now began to realize this would
be impossible. There were too many tribes repre-
sented: Miamis, Delawares, Ottawas, Hurons,
Senecas, Shawnees, Chippewas, and Potawatomies, plus all their sub-tribes.

And each tribe and sub-tribe not only had a war
chief of their own but many minor chiefs as well.
She counted nearly eighty who sat down among
the decision-makers in the ring closest to the fire,
and decided to keep close watch on the most
important ones—Tarhee, Blue Jacket, Turkey
Foot, Buckongahelas, and of course, the most
important of all, Little Turtle.

First, the chiefs passed the feathered calumet
among themselves, exhaling long thin plumes of
smoke. Then, as the pipe completed its rounds,
Little Turtle began to address them. His magnificent voice flowed out softly at first, then swelled
with might and power.

Rebecca struggled to understand and was greatly
relieved when Sweet Breeze quietly began translat-
ing: "My father say Great Spirit be good to his red
children. Manitou give them beautiful country of
prairie and forest. He fill it with deer, elk, bear
and otter for food and clothing. He give them large
rivers of rapid waters to float their canoes, and he
fill rivers and lakes with more food. The young

men be swift of foot; their arms be strong and their eyes see everything. When they follow war path, they return with scalps of enemies. They defeat Long Knives many, many times, and many scalps hang drying in their lodges. But the trail be long and bloody; it has no end.''

Yes, but this could be the end, Rebecca thought hopefully. Little Turtle's speech was making a good impression. The faces of the assembled chiefs in the flickering light from the bonfire glowed with approval. The chiefs nodded among themselves, as if agreeing to every word. Elated, she bent to catch the continuing flow of Sweet Breeze's translation.

''The pale faces come from where the sun rises, and they be many. They be like leaves of the trees: when frost comes they fall and be blown away, but when sunshine comes again, they come back more plentiful than ever before.''

The crowd now grunted their approval, and in her elation, Rebecca almost forgot that *she* was one of the pale faces of whom Little Turtle was speaking. She was totally caught up in the response of the people around her, completely agreeing: the pale faces *were* like the leaves of the trees—persistent and far too numerous.

''The Great Father Washington . . .'' Little Turtle continued—*President* Washington! Rebecca thought, ''. . . send his war chief, Chenoten, with a great many braves to fight his red children.

But first, he send the painted quill, and ask them to smoke and talk in his lodge to see if battle can be avoided. He desires part of our country and will give blankets, guns, knives, and tomahawks with powder and lead for our young men, bright colored cloth and trinkets for our women. He say he be our friend and buy our furs and skins.''

Little Turtle looked out over the crowd, and his voice suddenly swelled with emotion. ''Brothers! We must consider Chenoten's offer, for I say to you the Long Knives also be children of Manitou! They be half-brothers of his red children! Manitou no want to see bloody tomahawk among his children—he hide his face in cloud if they refuse to talk to white chief!''

And in response to this, Rebecca felt as well as heard the sudden silence which fell like a cloak on the gathering. The women ceased to stir behind her, and the faces of the chiefs, she saw, began hardening into stone.

''My people, hear me well,'' Little Turtle pleaded. ''There is something in the wind which whispers to me we cannot defeat Chenoten. He *earn* names by which we call him—Whirlwind, Black Snake, Chief Who Never Sleeps. Never have we surprised him, and I think we no surprise him now.'' He cocked his head sadly, aware of the crowd's disapproval. ''But my ears be open. I will listen to great chiefs of the Ottawas, Potawatomies, Shawnee, and Wyandots. I have done.''

336

The silence now was ominous. Rebecca glanced around uneasily. The resonance of Little Turtle's voice hung in the air like an echo, but the stillness of the crowd, after their earlier enthusiasm, did not bode well.

He made no concessions of land, she thought defensively. All he did was suggest going to council to discuss the matter.

But the silence was so great she could hear the fire crackle as a log fell. She could even hear a cool night wind sighing through the surrounding trees. Even Sweet Breeze said nothing.

Then, abruptly, Turkey Foot, the Ottawa chieftain, leapt to his feet. He pointed to his ears with both hands in an impatient irritated gesture and began shouting, his thin high voice a mockery compared to Little Turtle's.

Rebecca elbowed Sweet Breeze who jumped as though she'd been pinched. "Turkey Foot say, 'My ears be open too. I hear words of Little Turtle, great chief of the Miamis. His head be sprinkled with frosts of many winters, but I no understand his wisdom. He say great Manitou be good to his red children, give us great country filled with elk, deer, otter and beaver for our support. He say our young men be swift of foot and strong of arm, and the scalps of our enemies hang drying in our lodges. He say Chenoten want part of our land and give us blankets, guns, knives and tomahawks for it—but why we need Chenoten?''

337

Turkey Foot pointed to Major William Campbell. "Saginwash give us these things too—and more! Saginwash buy our furs in country where snow falls before summer be done! Saginwash trade for cloths and trinkets—and Saginwash no take our land, no cut down trees, no drive off game and no destroy burial grounds!"

Now, Turkey Foot pointed to Little Turtle. "Why does great chief Little Turtle wish to smoke in lodges of our enemies? Why he wish to give away hunting grounds and sacred burial places? Why he want sit down with enemy we already defeat before and now have chance to defeat again? Is it because his own adopted son now sits in lodge with Long Knives? Is it because he no longer have strong heart and stomach—he grow weak like wolf who govern pack too long?"

The accusations had the effect of arrows zinging into flesh. Many onlookers began to hurl questions themselves, and Little Turtle stood with folded arms, patiently awaiting the proper moment to respond.

But Turkey Foot, sensing triumph, wouldn't give him the opportunity. Throwing back his head in a final challenging gesture, he cried, "Manitou give this country to us—not to Long Knives! He bids us bloody the trail of our enemies! Manitou is great! He is good! Will braves of his red children fight? Will they defend their council fire and protect the graves of their fathers?"

He swung around and pointed slowly to the different tribes and to their leaders—excepting only the Miamis, who like everyone else, were leaning forward intently, drinking in every word that Rebecca was hearing second-hand from Sweet Breeze.

"The Ottawas, Potawatomies, and Shawnees will follow war path of Long Knives!" Turkey Foot bowed dramatically to the west, stood up straight, and folded his arms like Little Turtle. "When sun sleeps again our enemies' scalps will hang from our belts! Chenoten will walk in bloody path toward sunrise. He will learn that medicine of red man be too strong for him, and he will go home and not come again!"

Pandemonium then broke loose as braves, squaws, and children shouted their approval, stamped their feet, and waved their arms. Chilling war cries, which Rebecca recognized as those the warriors hooted to put fear into their enemies' hearts, erupted on every side. Even Crow Woman and Two Fires began shouting, startling the sleeping Walks-Tall, who awoke and joined the tumult with angry wails.

Rebecca grasped Sweet Breeze's arm, but her friend shrank back from her, her face pale and damp, her eyes glued to her father who stood alone against the will of his people.

Rebecca was stunned—and momentarily confused. Sweet Breeze had told her earlier that all the chiefs would make speeches, then cast their votes in the traditional manner by means of offering belts to Little Turtle—white for peace, black or purple for war. But such formality hardly seemed necessary now. Were the chiefs not even going to give Little Turtle a chance for rebuttal?

Blue Jacket now leapt to his feet and began haranguing the crowd. Sweet Breeze forgot to translate, and Rebecca didn't bother to remind her. What was the use? She already knew what he was saying.

Mimicking his predecessor, the Shawnee war chief pointed to the red-coated British officers, Alexander McKee, and Simon Girty, and Rebecca knew Blue Jacket was only repeating what had already been said: the Saginwash will help the tribesmen drive off Chenoten and be victorious once again. The Saginwash will supply the necessary guns, ammunition, blankets, and food. The Saginwash will buy their furs and skins and give them trinkets for their women. The Saginwash! The Saginwash! How Rebecca wished she'd never even heard of them!

Glancing over at the British contingency, she saw Major William Campbell sitting stiffly, a pale young man obviously able to understand what was being said even less than she did. A small nervous smile quirked his lips as he nodded and watched the proceedings, uncertain how to react to being singled out by the impressive Blue Jacket.

But Alexander McKee and Simon Girty knew what was happening. Heads together with the newcomer, Matthew Elliot, they sat brazenly grinning and talking among themselves—pleased with the evening's outcome. And Rebecca was suddenly overcome with such a feeling of violent hatred she could barely contain herself.

Leaping to her feet, she stumbled across the bodies seated in front of her, drawing angry exclamations, but not caring whom she stepped on. A half dozen rows to the front, she stumbled into the clearing, and from there it was only a short distance to Major Campbell, Alexander McKee, and Simon Girty.

"You!" she cried, pointing at Colonel McKee. "You—you bastard! You traitor! You're the reason the tribes will not make peace! Don't you see what you've done? If it weren't for you, Little Turtle could pursuade them—save them from needless bloodshed!"

Alexander McKee stared at her open-mouthed, caught completely off-guard. The young British major blinked as if he'd seen a ghost.

Only Simon Girty had the presence of mind to protest. "Now, wait just a gol' durn minute, little lady, you keep on a shoutin' like that and you're like to wind up killed! Don't you see what *you're* doin'? You're interruptin' these proceedin's—an' takin' the wrong side to boot!"

"Don't you say anything to me, you—you

murderer! You scum!'' Rebecca was past caring what anyone thought of her. She was dimly aware that a hush had fallen over the crowd—that everyone was staring—but all she felt now was a seething hot anger demanding immediate release.

"I know *you*, Simon Girty!" she hissed. "I know what you've done—how you stood by and watched one of your own people be tortured and burned! You wouldn't lift a finger to help him, not even when he begged you! Remember his name? Colonel William Crawford! Even if *you* don't remember, *I* haven't forgotten it, and neither will history! Long after you're dead and burning in hell, people will remember what you did—how you laughed while he suffered and died . . .''

Simon Girty's face went ashen, as if all his blood had been drained. The scar on his forehead formed a high white ridge. Rebecca was pleased to note the effect of her words, but then a figure stood up behind him, and her throat closed in a paroxysm of fear.

It was Ring-Nose, the Shawnee. Whether because he understood what she'd been saying or whether because she'd interrupted the council, it was impossible to know, but his eyes glinted with fury. And moving in slow deliberate motion, his right hand deftly released the war club dangling at his waist.

Rooted to the spot, Rebecca could only watch as he lifted it, took careful aim, and drew back his arm to let it fly.

So this is how I'm going to die, she thought . . . Oh God, don't let it hurt!

But her last thought wasn't for herself, but for Kin-di-wa. Now, when he came back, he'd *never* know her answer. She'd never have a chance to tell him. She loved him! She adored him! She . . .

Thirteen

Rebecca closed her eyes, faint with fear, but strong arms suddenly encircled her and kept her from falling. She was picked up, tossed over someone's shoulder, and carried at a dead run around the bonfire, across the clearing, and into the shadows beneath the Council Elm.

Down the riverbank, her rescuer ran, then she felt herself being dumped into a canoe as if she were a doll made of corncobs or rags. A tall figure leapt in behind her, and within moments, the canoe was out on the river, bathed in shadows and protected from view by heavy clouds obscuring moon and stars.

No one followed, and Rebecca could only surmise that the whole thing had happened so quickly, no one had had time to think, let alone take action—except for Ring-Nose and her rescuer.

Hardly daring to draw breath, she lay still in the canoe as it shot forward down the river. Her arms and legs prickled; she couldn't move them. And she was appalled by what she'd done. What on earth had driven her to the folly of publicly attacking McKee and Girty—of interrupting the council meeting? It was a wonder she *hadn't* been killed! How many other braves had stood up and drawn out their war clubs? Surely others had been as riled as Ring-Nose by the sight of a red-haired white woman ranting and raving at their wonderful Saginwash!

Her rescuer's voice cut across her like a whip. "What did you think you were doing, Cat-Eyes? Giving my people a reason to kill you—or merely pursuading them to peace?"

She struggled to sit up, only that moment realizing who had saved her. "Kin-di-wa!"

"Little fool!" he hissed. "Have you gone crazy? I ought to have stripped you naked and beaten you in front of everyone! No squaw has ever spoken so in council to honored guests!"

"Honored guests! Is that what you call those vipers? It's you who are a fool then!" She suddenly remembered her self-recrimination of only moments before and was newly ashamed of her behavior. "I—I only wanted to help! I wanted to expose them for what they are: a bunch of troublemakers! If it weren't for them, Little Turtle's speech might have been better accepted!"

"What did you expect? One can always depend

on white men to stir up trouble—and white women! As for why Little Turtle's words were not accepted, it is because Chenoten will never compromise—and my people know it! Another council, another treaty would mean nothing! Except to put off what we know must come in the end anyway."

"But Little Turtle said . . ."

"Little Turtle knows this too! Only—like you and Apekonit—he still finds it necessary to go on trying! He would give the Long Knives one more chance to prove the truth of their talking paper—the one you call the Declaration of Independence that tells of their devotion to justice. But Little Turtle at least knows better than to hurl insults and get himself killed!"

"Kin-di-wa, I . . ." Words failed her. She was so glad to see him, so relieved he was still alive, but how furious he was! How he resented her interference! His anger echoed in his voice, shown in the set of his shoulders, and flashed in the depths of his eyes. Even in the darkness, it was unmistakable.

And her inability to frame an apology or thank him for rescuing her seemed to enflame him even further. He sent the canoe leaping forward so fast she almost toppled backward. "It was only good fortune, I got there when I did!" he growled.

"When did you come? I didn't see you!" She grasped onto the sides for support.

"I heard Little Turtle speak from the water, and

then Turkey Foot and Blue Jacket, but I had only beached my canoe and drawn close to the elm when I saw *you*—shaming me before my people! Do you not know you are *my* responsibility, *my* property, and what you do is the same as if I had done the thing myself?"

"Kin-di-wa, I didn't know!" she protested, but anger now welled up in her. "Is that your greatest concern—not my safety—but that I *shamed* you? I am *not* your property!"

"Indeed," he snarled. "You have made that very clear!"

"Oh, please!" She begged. "If you heard everything, then you can surely understand why I did it! I simply forgot myself! Don't *you* ever do anything foolish or stupid?"

He suddenly brought the canoe to a shuddering halt in the water, holding the paddle firm against the current. *"Yes!"* he whispered, and she was shaken by the depth of raw emotion emanating from him.

He paused, then he spoke again in a cold hard voice. "It is all over, Cat-Eyes. Chenoten will be here at Roche de Boeuf tomorrow or the day after."

"Yes, I—I know. After tonight, I guess we have to expect it."

"Do we?" he asked bitterly. "Must we always expect the worst?"

"Kin-di-wa . . ." She'd never seen him quite like this. "Tell me what happened!"

"I stayed with Apekonit as long as I could! I

even played at being a scout myself! Together, Apekonit and I convinced Chenoten to make one more offer of peace—to send an invitation to council. He said it would do no good, said it would be rejected, but Apekonit and I—we pursuaded him . . ."

He made a swift motion with the paddle in the darkness. Rebecca heard a loud snap. He'd broken it across his knee!

"It isn't your fault!" she exclaimed. "You did the best you could—even when you didn't believe in it!"

He tossed the pieces of the broken paddle into the river with a despairing gesture. "I knew this morning: when they lashed William May to the Council Elm and spent their fury firing muskets and wasting shot—long past what was needful to kill him. I knew then there wasn't a chance! But somehow I too had begun to hope . . ."

"You—you saw it?"

"Of course, I saw it! I was the one they were after—the one they *should* have caught!"

"Oh, Kin-di-wa . . ." She thought of him hiding somewhere and watching—knowing he could do nothing to stop it. No matter what he said or what he did—no matter what he even *thought*—his inclination was to peace. And what danger he'd placed himself in to achieve it! "But you *mustn't* blame yourself!" she consoled him.

"Pah! I *am* to blame! It was I who insisted we stay near Roche de Boeuf until Christopher Miller got safely back to Chenoten. I trusted Little Turtle to give him safe passage, but I did not trust the Shawnee! They could easily have arranged for an 'accident' to befall him, which would plunge us instantly into battle! We hid in Fallen Timbers waiting for him—William May and I. There were only two of us—Apekonit had stayed at the Auglaize with Chenoten. But William May did not want to stay; he thought it too dangerous. I called him 'old woman' and 'yellow dog,' and so he stayed. Then the Shawnee discovered us, and it was William May they captured—William May who paid for my bad judgment."

Rebecca inched closer to him in the canoe. "You didn't know what would happen! It could just as easily have been you! Sweet Breeze and I—we were afraid it *was* you—or her husband, Apekonit—who'd been caught!"

"You *knew* I was with the scouts?" He sounded shocked.

"Christopher Miller told us last night when I read Wayne's letter to Little Turtle. Afterwards, Little Turtle asked him about Apekonit, and he mentioned that you too were one of Wayne's scouts—but no one else knows it but Sweet Breeze! Little Turtle told Christopher Miller he'd never even heard of you!"

Kin-di-wa grunted, either from relief or scorn at the news, she couldn't tell. She placed her hand gently on his knee, offering consolation and seeking it herself. "I was so afraid, Kin-di-wa! We didn't know who'd been captured, and we went to the Council Elm and saw the man already dead and so mutilated, we couldn't even tell who he was!"

His arms came around her suddenly then, and his body slid forward beside her. "Ah, Cat-Eyes, my little Cat-Eyes . . . Did seeing this man and wondering who he was, tell you what was in your heart toward me?"

"What do you mean?" His face was now so close she could feel his breath. His changing mood made her shiver.

"You know my meaning! But how little you know yourself, Cat-Eyes! How much you fight yourself! What did your heart tell you when you saw him?"

Suddenly, he was leaning her back onto the narrow floor of the canoe. Startled, she pressed her hands against his muscled chest and turned her face away to avoid his lips. "It was terrible! Frightening!" she gasped. "I grew faint and sick to my stomach!"

How could he be doing this *now*, she wondered, in the midst of discussing a dead man whose gruesome image danced before her eyes?

But in truth there was no image, no matter how hard she tried to conjure it—no matter how guilty she felt that she couldn't. There was only Kin-di-wa pressing her down into the bottom of the canoe with the sweet weight of his body. There was only his nearness, his masculine scent, and the delicious feel of his hand sliding across her hip and up to her breast.

"Cat-Eyes," he pleaded in her ear. "Do not push me away! Do not deny me! I have died again and again these past few weeks. I have lived with death every moment—knowing I might be discovered by one side or the other, my people or yours! And nothing I could say would make any difference once they caught me! Despair was in my heart, Cat-Eyes—despair and a great loneliness that only *you* could take away! For it was only you I wanted, only *this* I could think of!" His lips found the hollow between her shoulder and neck, sending a spasm of desire rippling through her.

But with the desire came something else: a thousand doubts and fears. Now was the moment to tell him of her decision—the answer that had come to her when she thought she might be killed by Ring-Nose's tomahawk. She wanted to say yes! She *wanted* to with every fiber of her being! But the words stuck in her throat.

"Kin-di-wa!" She struggled against him. "I—I haven't yet made up my mind! To share you with another—to know you belong to someone else—"

His lips clamped over hers, shutting off her protests. His hand slid under her doeskin and up her naked thigh. He grasped her buttocks and thrust her body against his so she felt his manhood, hard and swollen and ready for her. His tongue probed her throat with violent urgency, and she nearly suffocated under the onslaught.

Oh, what was wrong with her that she could think of nothing but mating like some animal—a prowling she-cat?

Deep within her own body, a desperate heat was rising. Desire answered desire. She found herself clawing at his breech clout with one hand and anxiously pulling up her doeskin with the other so his mouth could find her breasts.

She pulled his head down to her body, inviting him to suckle her, to lick her, to take her nipples between his lips and pull on them. And when he did so, she reveled in the exquisite feeling that raced through her body down into her loins.

Then once again her conscience asserted itself. She pulled away. "Kin-di-wa! I love you! I want you! But God help us, we mustn't do this! It's not right!"

"Give in to it," he murmured huskily. "It is meant to be, Cat-Eyes. There is nothing more right than this! Manitou himself decreed that man and woman should serve one another with their bodies—should love and cherish each other . . ."

"But I cannot!" she moaned. His fingers slid into her woman place and stroked and petted and rubbed and made her throb with pleasure. "I *cannot!*" she cried again, even as she pulled him closer and gave herself up to him. "Kin-di-wa! Oh, my beloved!"

"You are mine," he whispered. "Mine! My woman, my wife, my child! I am your husband, your very heart. You cannot deny me!"

And she could not. When his mouth and hands were on her body, she would do anything he wanted! Anything he asked! He drew her hand down to his manhood. She stroked and fondled, seeking to give him the pleasure he gave her. A sleek wetness filled her palm as his manseed began to spill out.

Gasping, she withdrew her fingers, not wanting to waste a single drop of this precious seed from which her body would make sons and daughters—new life fashioned out of old!

He paused a moment, then pushed her hand back down. "It is all right. Hold me, Cat-Eyes, hold me!"

And he took her hand and taught her what gave him pleasure, what aroused him to such heights of passion he was at last unable to bear it any longer. He slid off her body, turned on his side, and lay back against the floor of the canoe. Then he lifted her atop him—thrusting into her from below.

She lay astride him, shocked at the boldness of this new position. Had she become a wanton woman? Would a *married* woman do this—ride astride her husband as if he was a horse? Then she discovered a sense of unexpected freedom of movement. No longer was she the passive one, the one to whom the thing was done—now, she would be the doer! Now, she could truly give to him, and in the giving—receive!

Trembling with her new found power, she began to move against him. His hands clasped her buttocks, and thus locked to one another, they moved together—rising, rising, rising—and breaking free of all that held them, all that bound them to the earth!

Once again, they soared to the heights and tumbled through star-strewn meadows on mountaintops seen only in dreams. They spun through mist-filled waterfalls and bathed themselves in tears of joy. Kin-di-wa filled her and she filled him. Never would there be another moment so precious—another time so dear!

She forgot she was in a canoe, and only when its frantic rocking almost spilled them into the water, did he clasp her close and whisper, "Enough now, little one, enough!"

But by then, the thing was finished, and her whole body quivered with pleasure in unison with his. He held her against him and stroked her tenderly. "Never has there been a woman who loves as you love—never!"

"Never has there been a man like *you*," she returned, but his remark reminded her of Two Fires.

Slowly, she slid to one side of him, removed her body from his. Then she drew down her doeskin, which had been absurdly bunched up around her shoulders. The moment she'd been dreading had come. How had she thought to avoid this heartbreak? How had she believed, however briefly, that things could work out between them?

Somehow, their love-making—so beautiful, so

bittersweet—only served to remind her: his body was not hers alone. Nor was his spirit. Somehow, she must find the strength she'd been sorely lacking—the strength to leave him and not look back. She was a white woman after all. Remember that, she told herself fiercely. *Remember* it!

"Kin-di-wa, it is because of this—miracle we share together, that I cannot bear to even *think* of you with another!"

He stirred in the bottom of the canoe, reached up to draw her back down on him. She almost lost her nerve then, but forced herself to continue. "This must be the last time! You belong to Two Fires! Not to me! And every time we love, I know my pleasure is stolen! I can't *live* like this, Kin-di-wa! I—I've made my decision. No matter what happens—I'm going home!"

His response was shocking. Teeth glinting in the darkness, lips curling wolfishly, his hand closed over her breast—that traitorous breast!—which responded immediately to his touch. "You know this will happen again, Cat-Eyes, and you know you may *never* get home. In a day, two days, three at most, we may all be dead, and I do not plan to die without enjoying my wife's sweet body again!"

"And will you love Two Fires also—take her—as you take me?" she choked. "Will she lay on one side of your buffalo robe and I on the other? Will you teach *her* what you've taught me—how to behave like a common whore?"

At that, Kin-di-wa let go of her and sat up, reaching for his breech clout. His anger blossomed between them like some awful poisonous flower. "So, my foolish little Cat-Eyes. You've made your choice! You stubbornly refuse to consider living in any way but the way of your people!"

"I'm *not* stubborn or foolish! I *could* adjust to your people's ways! I have already—except for the matter of—of—"

"Of a brave taking more than one woman to wife—and of a woman *behaving* like a woman."

His last remark cut to the quick. "I'm sorry," she whispered. "The part about the whore—I didn't mean that."

"Pah!" He moved away from her. "You mean you've *adjusted* to being a woman finally? To enjoying the body Manitou gave you?" He laughed a short cruel laugh. "And have you also adjusted to the fact of my people's enmity toward your people? What a stupid squaw you are! To be so concerned over the matter of how we shall love, when the matter of how we shall survive is the only matter that counts!"

"I *am* concerned over how we shall survive! All I've wanted, hoped, and prayed for is that peace can be achieved!"

"Peace at whose cost, Cat-Eyes, your people's or mine?"

"Why—my people's cost, of course!"

"Then you *do* think your people should depart our lands. They should abandon their homesteads and go back across the Allegheny Mountains and the Ohio River and never again cross our boundaries.''

"I didn't say that!" Oh, lord! He knew exactly how to confuse her—in argument over land rights as well as morals. And in a moment he'd ask her what she meant, what the boundaries *should* be and how far the tribes ought to go to protect their hunting and burial grounds.

But she didn't know the answers to *any* of these questions. Boundaries and land rights and strategies for peace were all beyond her. Maybe he was right: she *was* stupid and foolish. But she hadn't let her emotions run away with her *this* time! And she didn't intend they ever would again!

"I—I want to go back to the Council Elm!" she blurted.

"Back to the scene of your disgrace?" Sarcasm punctuated his surprise. "Ah, then you wish to give that Shawnee dog another chance to kill you!"

"I want to find out what is happening! Maybe Little Turtle has won them around to his viewpoint."

This silenced him—but not for long. "You cannot leave a thing alone, can you, Cat-Eyes?" His tone grew bitter. "No matter what danger the path might hold, you must go rushing ahead!"

"We don't even have to get out of the canoe!" she argued. "You said yourself you heard everything from the water! We only need to listen awhile!"

"We have no paddle."

Rebecca felt along the inside wall of the canoe and came across a spare paddle kept lashed there for just such emergencies as losing or breaking one's paddle. Unlashing it, she held it out to him. "Please. Little Turtle is such a great orator! Don't you want to know if maybe—maybe—"

It took a moment before he accepted it. "All right, I shall take you back. But you must know, Cat-Eyes. There is no use to go on hoping."

"One can always have hope," she insisted. "At least, until one is dead!"

Kin-di-wa began dipping in the river, turning the canoe around. "Then at least until I die in battle, I may have hope you will come to realize to whom you belong!"

It was too dark to see his face, but Rebecca wondered what message she would have found there: was he being sarcastic again? Having the last word as always?

The distance between them in the canoe was so short—but longer than any distance she'd ever traveled. Oh, how could she live without him? But how could she live *with* him?

"I belong to no one but myself," she said with soft determination, surprising herself, for she hadn't meant to voice her thought aloud.

Then his voice too came softly, but filled with bitter resolve: "Then after tonight you shall see me no more, Cat-Eyes, until the battle is over and I can take you home."

*   *   *

They hid in the shadows a short distance downriver from the Council Elm and found they could hear everything. Little Turtle was speaking, and his full-bodied voice carried easily to their ears.

Rebecca concentrated with every muscle in her body, unwilling to ask Kin-di-wa to translate, and because Little Turtle spoke slowly, defeat and sorrow weighting down each word, she was able to understand everything.

"I have heard the words of the great chiefs of the Ottawas, Potawatomies, Wyandots, and Shawnees. They are wise men. They are great warriors. They are young men, and their arms are strong. They are swift on the war path. They have driven the enemies of our people from our hunting grounds, and their scalps hang drying in our lodges . . . The chief of the Miamis is old. His limbs are no more like the elk. The snow of many winters covers his head. He is waiting for the Great Spirit to come, and when he calls, Little Turtle will answer, I am ready."

Moved by his eloquence, Rebecca broke down sobbing.

"Hush!" Kin-di-wa warned her, but she noticed through her tears that something glistened on his cheeks as well.

But Little Turtle's voice betrayed not a tremor. "The great chief of the Ottawas with the name of the bird that is so swift when it runs and speaks so

360

loud when it calls its mate, shall tell our young men where to hide to strike the enemy when he comes, to strike him when the moon is out of sight. He is a great chief and will lead our young men on the war path, and the chief of the Miamis will follow. This is the will of my people. I am finished. I have done."

Rebecca put her head down on her knees to stifle her sobs. To think of the great wise Little Turtle following that strutting turkey—Turkey Foot! To think of every hope for peace now dashed! To think that the only voice of reason—the single man of courage who stood alone against such madness—must step aside for a lesser one! She couldn't believe it was happening!

Kin-di-wa's hand fell on her shoulder. "You have heard what you came to hear, Cat-Eyes. I will take you downriver now to the camp."

Two days later, Chenoten arrived at Roche de Boeuf, and the drums beat out the new message: he is here! The enemy is here! The time for vengeance has come!

Since everyone had been expecting it, Chenoten's arrival was hardly alarming—except to Rebecca. Startled, she looked up from tidying the lean-to and paused to listen, noticing that Two Fires's hands never once stopped what they were doing.

Two Fires obviously had great confidence that everything was in readiness: the painted warriors had all gathered at Fallen Timbers, the women and children were safely settled out of harm's way at the camps downriver, and the shamans and medicine men had held a great dance the previous evening—to hasten a victory.

But Rebecca's stomach was knotted with anxiety, and to further add to her distress, Tecumwah once again came straggling into their presence, burdened down with an armload of gifts from Peshewa.

Amazed that either Peshewa or his mother could still have courtship on their minds at a time like this, Rebecca firmly shook her head no and pointed in the direction from which the woman had just come. But Tecumwah refused to be dismissed so hurriedly.

She set down the gifts and began speaking in her low guttural voice, accompanied by many grunts and gestures, and Rebecca was able to decipher at least the gist of her conversation.

Since Chenoten had now come, this was the last time Rebecca would be receiving gifts. She must accept them now or never—though why Peshewa should want such a contentious, poorly behaved wife was beyond Tecumwah's understanding. Rebecca ought to feel lucky Peshewa still wanted her, especially after the incident at the council meeting. And if she were so foolish as to refuse this time, she might never again have another chance. Chenoten had, after all, brought three thousand warriors with him and an enormous quantity of weapons, stores and ammunition.

Since Tecumwah seemed so well informed, Rebecca tried to ask questions but could discover only a little more: Wayne was hurriedly throwing up yet another fort—a place in which to keep his vast supplies, and the tribesmen, expecting battle momentarily, were now refraining from eating, according to ancient custom.

No, Tecumwah hadn't seen Little Turtle or Sweet Breeze. Yes, she'd heard this news from a source who could be trusted—Alexander McKee, the man at whom Rebecca had no business pointing her fingers the other night.

Satisfied Tecumwah had told her all there was to know, Rebecca again demanded that Tecumwah take back Peshewa's gifts.

But before she left, Tecumwah tried once more to warn her; there'd be no more opportunity to find herself a husband before the battle. Fallen Timbers would soon echo with the sound of musketfire and the cries of dying men. Many warriors might be killed and potential husbands become scarce. What was a woman without a husband? Better to be a widow than never to have married at all.

Rebecca shuddered: what typical Miami logic! Oh, *why* couldn't she think of anything to stop this looming battle? *Was* she slow-witted? Actually dumb? Or even worse yet, was she somehow becoming as passive as a squaw? White women, at the very least, would be wringing their hands and wailing—maybe even rolling bandages.

After Tecumwah departed the lean-to, grumbling at every step, Rebecca finished tidying the lodge. She then tried to play with Walks-Tall while Two Fires continued to grind corn. She tickled the baby's plump tummy, walked him around hanging onto one of her fingers, and attempted to teach him a song she knew in English. He laughed and giggled charmingly, but his sunny presence failed for once to make her feel any better.

How could Two Fires work so placidly? she wondered angrily. How did she manage to maintain such a smooth calm expression—as though nothing she could do would be any more important than making cornmeal?

Using dried pre-cooked corn, the girl placed a handful on a stone, then pounded it into a fine meal with another stone. The first stone was placed on a piece of bark to catch the meal, which she then poured into a *mocuck* for future use.

Rebecca was reminded that soon, the new corn at Kekionga ought to be ripening, but how would anyone get back upriver past Anthony Wayne to harvest it?

She gathered Walks-Tall into her arms and attempted to rock him, but the baby wasn't sleepy. He wriggled out of her arms and toddled over to Kin-di-wa's spare bow which hung from the side of the lean-to.

The bow's curving wood was carved and stained

with dye, and Walks-Tall patted and poked at it, as if anxious to try it out. Rebecca didn't like him playing with a weapon and moved it out of his reach. Immediately, he began wailing.

Two Fires looked up and motioned for Rebecca to give the bow back to him. *"We-lah."* Two Fires pointed to Walks-Tall. *"We-lah."*

The word meant man-child, and Rebecca understood. It was right for a man-child to play with a bow—and probably arrows too. Folly would perpetuate folly. The child would grow to be a man and follow precisely in the footsteps of his father and his uncle.

One day, he too would probably find himself hiding and waiting in ambush for white soldiers or settlers. Where would this madness stop?

"Well!" Rebecca cried to the startled Two Fires. "You can put murder weapons in your son's own hands if you want to, but I won't do it!"

She stalked away from the lean-to, intending to go down by the river, where, hopefully, it might be cooler. The day was cloudy, but the air was oppressively heavy and humid, as one might expect on the eighteenth day of August. But to Rebecca, it seemed a bad omen. If Anthony Wayne's soldiers were wearing the heavy blue-coated uniforms of the Army of the United States, they'd die of heat stroke!

Not so the Indians, but she worried about Kin-di-wa and his tribesmen too. The tradition of not eating prior to battle was clearly ridiculous. How would the warriors keep up their strength? What if Anthony Wayne delayed a day or two more? They'd be so weak from hunger, any advantage they had in going around half-naked in the heat would surely be overcome.

Thinking of Kin-di-wa made her flesh grow even hotter. True as ever to his word, she hadn't seen him since he let her out of the canoe at the camp. They hadn't spoken. She hadn't even begged him to be careful.

And now, pacing up and down the riverbank to which she'd come easily, without thinking, she faced some questions she'd been avoiding. Had she been wrong to let him go off to battle without the comfort her love could give him? *After* the battle would have been soon enough to tell him she couldn't be his wife. What if something happened to him? What if—?

She *wouldn't* think of him dying. So she thought instead of their last meeting. Kin-di-wa had shared his anguish with her. Admitted how afraid he'd been. He'd actually swallowed his damnable pride and arrogance and told her how much he needed her. And what had she done in response? Given him her body, but denied him her heart and soul.

Yes, she'd done the worst thing to a man that a woman could do: she'd sent him off to die without the knowledge that she loved him, that she accepted him as he was—without conditions or impossible demands. He'd pleaded for a shield of strength and security to take with him into battle. She'd given him—nothing but her own doubts, fear, and weakness.

She was so agitated, so unhappy with herself, she hardly saw the man stepping out from behind a tree—until he stood in front of her. Then she could only stare at him dumbfounded, wondering where he'd come from.

The scar on the man's forehead stood up in a high ridge as he snarled at her. "So here you are, little red-haired squaw-woman, comin' right out to th' river t' meet my canoe!"

"Mr. G—Girty! You startled me!" She saw the canoe he spoke of pulled up on the riverbank.

Simon Girty's lips curled upwards, revealing yellowed stumps for teeth. "You don't look so brave an' scrappy now as you did th' other evenin'! Whatsamatter, little squaw-woman, didn't you think Simon Girty would live up to his rep'tation an' come after ya?"

Rebecca took a step backward. She glanced around wildly for someone to call to, but the riverbank was deserted beneath the hot gray sky. "I—I apologize for calling you names! I guess I chose a poor time to express my feelings over some of your actions! Please forgive me!"

The man's eyes glinted coldly. His lips twitched with angry mirth. Unlike Will, who'd softened when she pleaded with him, this man showed no signs of being moved by weakness. If anything, her fear and trembling excited him. He stepped forward and took hold of her wrist in an iron-hard grip. "Y' called me murderer an' scum! Y' said my name would go down in history as the name of someone wicked and evil!"

"But I didn't mean that—honestly!" Rebecca's knees shook. "I was just upset because Little Turtle was urging the tribes to make peace with Anthony Wayne, and no one would listen! You've made so many promises to the Indians, they feel certain they can win! But any fool can plainly see they haven't got a chance! Why, they're outnumbered three to two!"

"Hah! That ain't the reason!" He twisted her wrist so hard tears leapt into her eyes. "You was mad 'cause you think I laughed when Colonel Crawford got whut was comin' to 'im! Well, I did! An' I don't feel one bit sorry about it! An' neither would you if you was raised up by the Injuns an' saw whut awful things your own people was capable of doin' to 'em!"

Rebecca twisted her body to keep her wrist from snapping. "What awful things do you mean? Why—why *didn't* you help Crawford then?"

Simon Girty loosened his grip and she snatched her hand away and rubbed her wrist, wondering if he had broken it—so great was the pain. "Colonel Crawford got what was comin' to 'im! He may not have killed them Injuns at Gnadenhutten hisself, but he was ridin' with the varmint that was responsible! There wasn't nothin' I coulda done t' help 'im even if I wanted to—which I didn't!"

"At Gnadenhutten did you say? Are you talking about the massacre of those poor Indians at the Moravian mission, Gnadenhutten?" Rebecca rubbed her wrist distractedly. Kin-di-wa's mother had been murdered at Gnadenhutten! But she hadn't known Colonel Crawford's death and torture had occurred in response to *that*.

Simon Girty cocked his head at her. "I guess you is too young t' 'member them things as they was happenin'." He took another step toward her, looking her slowly up and down. "But you ain't too young t' have had a cock between yur legs yet, are ya?"

Horrified, Rebecca backed away. "I belong to Kin-di-wa—a Miami warrior! He took me captive, but he—he plans to marry me! If you touch me, he'll find out and come after you!"

His response to this was to grab hold of the front of her doeskin and tug it downward. The doeskin itself held firm, but the bodice, which had been stitched to the dress with sinew, tore away with a loud riiiip! Rebecca's breasts spilled out, gleaming whitely before Simon Girty's bugged eyes.

"Now, if that ain't a purty sight! I ain't had nothin' t' git my hands on but brown an' white titties fer so long, I plumb fergot how pink an' white an' purty a white woman's could be!"

Rebecca struggled to hold together the torn pieces of her bodice. "I mean it—you'll die a death as terrible as Colonel Crawford's if you touch me!"

Simon Girty laughed then—a low and evil

sound, echoing with cruelty and malice. "Whut ever makes you think your fine an' dandy warrior will live to walk out of Fallen Timbers?"

"He'll live! I *know* it! But why aren't you there with him? Surely, someone who's done so much to cause this battle would hate to miss it!"

Simon Girty's eyes narrowed in an angry frown. "'Cause I gots my orders, that's how come! An' even a renegade outlaw like me obeys orders when he gets 'em!"

"Orders!" Rebecca exclaimed. "What kind of orders—from whom?"

Girty took hold of her arm and dragged her to him. "Now, wouldn't you like t' know?" He reached around behind her and tugged on her braid, jerking back her head so her lips were raised to meet his. His dirty brown beard brushed across her mouth before he bent down to kiss her.

"Stop it!" Hysteria shot through her. This couldn't be happening again! If she were taken by force once more, something inside her would snap! "I know why you're not at Fallen Timbers! Because you're a *coward*, that's why! You don't have any orders not to go there! Considering all the promises you've made to the Indians on behalf of the British, that wouldn't make much sense, would it?"

His attention was momentarily drawn away from her heaving breasts so she plunged on bravely. "That's why you can't tell me anything about your mysterious orders! You haven't got any—have you?"

"What I got or ain't got is no concern of yours!" he growled. "But I can't see as how it would hurt t' tell ya' since you ain't gonna have no chance t' spread it around anyway."

"Then tell me!" Rebecca hissed defiantly. "But I warn you, if you harm me in any way, you're as good as dead!"

Again, he laughed that same cruel laugh. "I didn't come t' harm ya'! I come t' take ya' t' the fort! I only got the idea t' have a bit of fun with ya' when I saw you was alone!"

Rebecca was stunned. "Why would I want to go to the fort?"

"It ain't what *you* want; it's what that pasty-faced little major wants. Yur little outburst th' other evenin' made him take an interest in ya. He don't want ya' goin' around stirrin' up bad feelin' against us—'cause we're gonna have bad feelin' enough as soon as this battle gits heated up!"

"What do you mean!"

"I mean yur gonna get yur way after all, little squaw-woman. We ain't gonna help the injuns at all—not one damn little bit!"

"Not help them! But what about all the supplies and ammunition you've given them! What about the soldiers, the cannon, the *Chippewa*—that big ship of yours off Turtle Island?"

"We ain't gonna help 'em any more than whut we done already!" Girty snarled. "I don't see the logic of it any more'n you—'specially since it'll all but wipe out our fur trade an' maybe even git us killed! But the major has got *his* orders that come by runner this mornin'. We ain't t' interfere! Them stupid jack-ass politicians over in England are settlin' up with the United States, an' none of 'em gives a hoot in hell whut it'll do t' the fur trade and Injun relations with Canada!''

"Oh, dear God! But if you *don't* help them, they'll be massacred unless—unless someone tells them your support has been withdrawn!''

"Oh no, you don't, little squaw-woman!'' He grabbed her arms with both hands. "You ain't tellin' nobody nothin'! That's why I come t' git ya! The major thinks it'd be much safer all around, if you spend the next few days in the blockhouse at the fort!''

Rebecca squirmed and struggled. "You're sending the Indians knowingly to their deaths! Let go—I've got to tell them!''

He held her firmly, glaring into her face. "An' if you did—whut do you think would happen?''

"I don't know! I don't care!'' Rebecca screamed. "I would hope they'd go to Anthony Wayne and make peace!''

"Exactly! *After* they shoot an' scalp everyone of us who betrayed 'em by makin' false promises!''

"And you'd deserve it—all of you—especially you and Colonel McKee!'' Rebecca suddenly managed to wrench lose from him, but couldn't turn around and run away fast enough. He came after her, arms encircling her in a bear hug across her naked chest. "Let go!" she gasped. "I can't breathe!"

His strength belied his small wiry figure. Rebecca felt the air being squeezed from her lungs. Her rib cage threatened to crack, but her frantic struggles only caused him to draw one arm up slightly higher. And suddenly, her throat was caught in the crook of his elbow. "P-please!" she gasped, but he only squeezed harder, and a blackness came flooding over her.

And the last thing she heard before she lost consciousness was Simon Girty laughing, "That's it, little squaw-woman, go on an' pass out! I'll have my way with ya' now, nice an' easy—an' no one'll ever be the wiser!"

Fourteen

Rebecca awoke to pitch blackness and the smell of moldy straw. She knew she was still alive because it hurt her chest and sides to breathe. But she didn't know where she was or whether it was night or day. She felt around in the straw and her hand came to a wall of logs.

Groaning, she sat up. Her head throbbed like a war drum, particularly in one spot on the back, just up from the twist of her braid. Feeling the spot, she discovered a lump. In addition to being almost squeezed to death, had she been hit on the back of the head?

Tentatively, she took stock of all her discomforts. Besides the tightness in her throat, chest, and sides, and the aching in her head, there was a rawness in her loins, as if she'd been roughly used in love-making. She moved her hips to sit more comfortably, and something wet and sticky dribbled out of her. Since it wasn't the time for her monthly flux, she knew exactly what had happened—Simon Girty had raped her.

She drew up her knees and rested her head on them to still her trembling and control her nausea. Thank God, she'd been out cold and hadn't felt a thing. The mere thought of that awful man pawing and grunting over her gave rise to a feeling of madness. What a bastard! What an animal! To rape a woman who'd not only lost consciousness —but for all he knew might already have been dead.

Was that why he'd found it necessary to strike her over the head? So she wouldn't wake up and struggle before he was finished? Or had she struck her head when he threw her down to rape her? Monster! Devil! The Great Spirit—God—must have a special place in hell reserved for men like him.

And then she remembered what he'd told her on the riverbank: the British did not intend to help the Indians after all—and neither did they intend to tell them this before the battle. A lightning bolt of fear flashed through her. The Indians *must* be told. She had to get to Little Turtle or Kin-di-wa. And they could then tell Turkey Foot and Blue Jacket. Once the war chiefs knew no help would be forthcoming from the Saginwash, surely they'd call off the battle and go out to meet Chenoten bearing a flag of truce.

But how was she to get out of this black prison

in time to tell them? Taking a deep breath, she got to her feet and stood there, swaying in the darkness. Then she began feeling her way along the log wall. There had to be a door somewhere, but very likely, it was bolted or guarded. She hoped it was the latter. A soldier would be easier to get around than a heavy wooden obstruction.

Dear God, she prayed, help me to be wise and canny—to use my wits for once instead of my impulses.

Down the wall she went, blindly feeling her way. A few short steps and she came to a second wall. The blockhouse couldn't be very big, for several steps down that wall, she met another corner, and then discovered the door. It too was made of logs, narrower ones than those of the walls, and the logs stood upright, rather than sideways. She put her ear to the door and listened, but couldn't hear a thing. Then she leaned against it. It gave not an inch. Finally, she began pounding.

"Let me out! Who's out there? Is anybody there?"

Something or someone stirred, then spoke in a low muffled voice. "You be quiet in there, you hear? I don't want no trouble while I'm on duty!"

"But—I'm thirsty! And I'm not feeling well—I may be sick or coming down with fever!"

"Don't make no difference to me," the voice said. "I got my orders! This door ain't gettin' opened till morning. Then who's ever on duty'll likely get you some grub 'n water!''

"Until morning!" Rebecca cried. "What time is it now?"

"Past midnight. So you might as well be quiet and get some sleep."

Past midnight. Rebecca reeled away from the door. She'd been unconscious for such a long time. And time was running out. Would the battle be fought this very day—after sunup? Back she stumbled to the door. "Uh, sir? Sir, listen to me! I really do feel sick. Couldn't you open the door just a crack so I could get some fresh air and talk to you?"

Silence. Nothing but silence. "Please?" she wheedled. "I'm too sick to run away, and even if I did, you'd just shoot me down with your musket! Please! Just open the door a crack!"

No one answered. Perhaps, the guard had gone away and left her to rot till morning. "Oh, damn!" she cried. "I'll never get out in time!"

Plunking down in the straw, she stared into the blackness. Her stomach heaved and rolled. It wasn't a lie to claim she was sick. Knowing she might feel better if she lay down, she curled up cat-like in the straw.

She didn't intend to sleep, but the next thing she knew she was awakened by a loud thud on the outside of the door. Then the door itself creaked open. A soldier in plain uniform, minus his scarlet coat, set a pail of water and a bowl of gruel inside, then began to close the door again.

"Wait!" Rebecca cried. Scrambling to her feet, she was swept with a bout of dizziness, and down she fell again, upsetting the bowl of gruel.

"Lordy—a white woman!" the soldier exclaimed. "A drunked-up white woman!"

"Not drunk—sick." Rebecca mumbled through parched lips.

"Easy there, I'll help you!"

His voice sounded different from the one last night: younger and kinder. And the easy drawl of the common man, one who had likely been born in Canada or the United States, was even more pronounced. On her hands and knees, Rebecca looked up and tried to see his face in the dim gray light of early morning. He reached down and took her by the arm. "Easy does it now, ma'am. You stood up too fast is all."

With his support, she was able to get up again on her own two feet, and gradually, the walls of her prison and the figure of the young soldier swam into focus. "Th—thank you!" she managed to gasp, then remembering the state of her dress, she pulled its torn edges together.

The young soldier averted his gaze from her still partially exposed bosom. He bent down and retrieved the bowl. "Looks like you'll need another bite of breakfast! It ain't much, but it's the best I can offer! I'll just go an' get you some."

"Wait!" Rebecca begged. "I—I think I'd better have a drink of water."

"Sure! Comin' right up!" He leaned over the

pail of water. "Don't seem to be a dipper here."

"I'll use my hands."

The young soldier picked up the pail and held it up to her while she formed a cup and drank from her hands. Discreetly, he looked away. In letting go of her torn bodice, her breasts had once again spilled out. Hurriedly, she concealed them as soon as she'd finished drinking. "Thank you so much. I've been so thirsty!"

"Think nothing of it, ma'am. Now, I'll just go and get you more gruel."

Rebecca studied him as he set down the bucket and picked up the bowl. Why, he's hardly more than a boy, she thought, but he's obviously been taught his manners.

His shirt was sweat-stained and soiled, but tucked in neatly, and his boots bore evidence of polishing. He grinned shyly at her from underneath the beaded moisture on his upper lip. "Won't take but a minute an' I'll be back—bet you're hungry too."

Rebecca nodded. "Is—is there any chance I could—you know—step outside for a moment?"

His hazel eyes widened. He shook his head. "'Fraid not, ma'am. I don't know why they put you in the blockhouse—didn't even know you were a woman! But I got orders that once a body's been put in here, it ain't supposed to leave!"

"I wasn't talking about leaving. I only wanted to—go out behind a tree." For once, she was glad she blushed so easily. It helped to conceal her true intentions.

"Oh!" The young soldier also blushed. "Well, I don't know—isn't there another bucket in here you could use?" He craned his neck to see behind her.

"Nothing," she pointed out.

"Well!" His forehead crinkled, and Rebecca grew hopeful. "I'll just have to find one for you then—I'm plumb sorry, ma'am, but a soldier has got to obey his orders."

"Yes, I can see that." Her disappointment tasted like ashes. "But—could you do something else for me then?"

"If I can, I sure will!"

"Could you ask Major Campbell if I might see him? Tell him—tell him it's a matter of great importance. A matter of life and death!"

"The major? You want to see the major?" The young soldier blinked.

Rebecca moved closer to him and plucked his sleeve. One half of her torn dress fell open. Gazing up at him with an expression she hoped was both helpless and appealing, she even succeeded in getting her eyes to water. "If I don't see Major Campbell this very morning, something terrible's going to happen!"

"Yes, ma'am!" The soldier breathed. "I'll tell him certain—exactly what you said."

"Oh, you're such a kind person!" Rebecca closed her bodice and fluttered her lashes gratefully. "I don't know how to thank you. Maybe someday we'll meet again, and I can tell you how I came to be in this—unfortunate position! I'm really not a criminal, you know—or an Indian either."

"Hell, I know that!" The soldier shuffled his feet awkwardly. "I can't understand what possessed the major to lock up a pretty little thing like you!"

"It's all a mistake, of course—that's why I have to see him! I do so hope he'll give me a chance to explain. If he doesn't—I know he's going to regret it!"

She sniffed and dabbed at her eyes, finding it incredibly easy to play on the young man's sympathies. It was almost as if a part of her had grown cold and calculating overnight.

"Now, don't you go a cryin'! I'll get you in to see the major somehow—an' he's not such a terrible sort, once you get to know him!"

Rebecca smiled through her tears. "I'm sure you will."

The young soldier went out and rebolted the door then, leaving Rebecca in dimly lit darkness. It was another gray and humid day, and the only light in the blockhouse was what filtered in through the chinks between the logs. She sat down on the straw to await the soldier's return. And to plan what she'd say to the major.

Not long thereafter, the soldier was back again with more gruel, but he had no real hope to offer her on the subject of seeing the major. "I can't say whether he'll talk to you or not, ma'am! He seems t'be mighty busy what with Anthony Wayne movin' closer every minute!"

"But that's what I have to speak to him about! I have news about Wayne—*important* news I can only divulge to him!"

The soldier regarded her doubtfully. "Well, I'll try it again for you, but I can't promise nothin'. With a battle brewin'—today or tomorra'—the major's got a lot on his mind."

"Please try one more time!" Rebecca begged.

But it was early evening and getting dark before Major Campbell sent for her. The young soldier escorted her through the enclosed fort to the major's quarters in a small cabinlike structure. Then he knocked on the door and opened it. "Prisoner here to see you, sir!"

Rebecca entered and saw the major, looking every bit as young and inexperienced as the soldier, seated at a rough hewn desk. His scarlet, gold-braided coat and the wilted mass of white lace at his throat made him look as though he were play-acting, a child masquerading as a man. He glanced up at her wearily. "Well?"

She drew close to his desk so he could see her better. Close enough so the light from his oil lamp revealed her state of near undress. "Major, my name is Rebecca McDuggan. I'm a citizen of the United States of America, and I haven't done anything wrong! So you have no right to keep me here: a prisoner in a British fort!"

The major leaned back, a look of surprise lighting up his tired, worried eyes. He took in the details of her rumpled doeskin and torn bodice with a tiny curl of his aristocratic lips. "Are whores considered to be citizens now in your barely civilized country?"

His accent was pure British upper class, and Rebecca knew then why he'd been made a major despite his young age. The British always promoted the aristocracy faster than the common man. "I am not a whore, Major, though Simon Girty chose to treat me like one."

"Oh?" One slender eyebrow arched. "That is not what Mr. Girty said. He told me you tore your—your bodice yourself, expressly so you could make trouble. That's the sort of woman you are—a troublemaker."

Rebecca bit back a retort. *She* certainly wasn't the troublemaker around here, *he* was. But her only hope to influence this man lay in her ability to keep her wits about her. "It's not I, but Simon Girty who's a troublemaker. I'm amazed you haven't yet discovered that for yourself."

The major leaned forward. "Let's not play games, madam. What is this news you have about Anthony Wayne?"

Rebecca stood up straighter, hoping she could remember the speech she'd rehearsed in the blockhouse. "I am not what you think I am, Major. It's true I was taken captive by the Miamis. But they would have let me go because I helped save the life of one of their warriors. Only I didn't want to go. My 'capture' was arranged, you see. I am actually a spy for General Wayne. I send back information concerning tribal politics to him—so he may know how to proceed.''

"*You?* A spy?" The major sat back in his chair and laughed heartily—almost without control. Rebecca felt herself flushing with anger, but dug her nails into her palms to keep control.

"That's exactly what General Wayne *hoped* you and the tribal leaders would think: a female spy is too ridiculous to imagine, let alone believe!"

The major ceased laughing and stared at her. "You honestly think I could believe that a tiny scrap of a half-naked woman—one who appears before me with her dress torn and her face smudged—is a spy for Anthony Wayne?"

Rebecca hadn't known her face was smudged. She wiped her hand across her cheeks and forehead, then glared at him defiantly. "Who would make a better spy? I am one, and I can prove it!"

The major's lips curled. "How? Do spies run around interrupting tribal meetings? Screaming at honored guests? If you were truly a spy, you'd have been dead long before this. In my experience, spies behave with decorum!"

"Well, I haven't been a spy for very long!" Rebecca admitted. "And I simply lost my temper the other night—but I can still prove the truth of what I'm saying!"

"Prove it then," the major smirked.

"On the day before the tribal meeting, a man named Christopher Miller arrived here with a letter from General Wayne. I can tell you exactly what's in that letter."

The major smirked again. "I already know the contents of the letter. Who does not know them? The letter was an invitation to council."

"Yes, but I could recite the letter to you precisely as it was written! And how could I do that—a mere captive squaw-woman!—if I were *not* a spy? As you are no doubt well aware most women out here in the wilderness can't even read!"

The major studied her thoughtfully, perspiration beading on his forehead. Rebecca began reciting, hoping to convince him further. "To the Delawares, Shawnees, Miamis, and Wyandots, and to each and every one of them, and to all other Indians northwest of the Ohio, to whom it may concern: I, Anthony Wayne, Major General and Commander in Chief of the Federal Army now at Grand Glaize, and Commander Plenipotentiary of the United States of America; for settling the terms upon which a permanent and lasting peace shall be made with each and every hostile tribe . . ."

"Enough!" the major snapped, and Rebecca concealed her relief. She didn't know how much more of the exact wording of the letter she could remember.

"The letter was signed, Anthony Wayne, 13th August, 1794," she risked adding.

"I *know* how it was signed! I saw the letter myself! But the question is: how could *you*—an insignificant, dirty-faced, squaw-woman—have managed to see it?"

Rebecca smiled. "You know the answer—I'm a spy. General Wayne made certain I knew the contents *before* he even sent it."

Clearly agitated now, the major tapped the desk top with a slender manicured finger. Then an expression of triumph lit his aristocratic features. "If indeed you are a spy, what is to prevent me from turning you over to the savages? I was afraid you might stir them up against us—as you tried to do the other night—but now I needn't worry! If I turn you over to them now, you won't live long enough to do any more damage!"

Rebecca gulped. "What I had in mind, Major, is that you might turn me loose so I can find my way back to General Wayne."

"And *why* would I wish to do that?"

"Because I can help you! I can tell General Wayne about your orders—that you will *not* take part in the battle! If he doesn't know, he'll likely attack the fort, and you'll be drawn into battle whether you want to be or not!"

The major's lips curled upwards in a contemptuous smile. "But that is what I hope he does! Do you think I wanted those orders? No! I only came to this God-forsaken outpost because it was a chance to establish my name— Major William Campbell, the man who defeated

General Wayne!"

"But—you can't disobey your orders!"

"Ah . . . what you don't know, my devious little spy, is that my orders say I may not initiate firing, but I am free to return it! I cannot help the savages, but if Anthony Wayne fires on the fort, by God in heaven I shall return his fire!"

"Return it!"

"Yes, return it," the major gloated. "Though by the time *that* happens, it will doubtless be too late to help the bloody savages."

Rebecca wondered how she'd ever thought this man to be so young and inexperienced. In his lust for glory and fame, he looked years older. And she almost felt too dispirited to go on with her deception.

But then she remembered the tribesmen waiting so unknowingly at Fallen Timbers. If only she could get to them, she might still avert this tragedy!

"Then why *don't* you give me to the Indians? I'd rather take my chances with them than rot away in your suffocating blockhouse!"

The major shook his head. "No, little spy. You know too much. Do you take me for a fool? Evans! Get in here!"

The door opened, and the young soldier bolted through it. "Yes, Major!" He snapped his heels together smartly.

"Take this woman back to the blockhouse. And be sure you inform the next guard that on no condition is she to be let out again until I personally *order* it!"

"Yes *sir!*" the soldier said.

On the way back to the blockhouse, Rebecca had to watch her step. It had already grown dark— the air so smothering and thick, she could have cut it with a knife. The soldier carried a pitch pine torch to light the way, but even so, Rebecca tripped and stumbled on the root from a cleared away tree. The soldier grasped her arm, then let go as she tugged it away.

"I'm sorry, ma'am. Guess the major wasn't too understandin', was he?"

"No, he wasn't." Rebecca said shortly. Instead of gawking around the fort, she ought to pay more attention to where she was walking! Not much could be seen in the darkness anyway, except eerie shadows and walls. The blockhouse lay straight ahead—the gate to freedom behind her.

She saw another root looming ahead of them, but instead of side-stepping it, tripped and fell deliberately. Then, she started wailing. "Oh, my ankle—I mean my leg! I think it's broken!"

"Broken? Naw, it probably just twisted or somethin'!" The soldier leaned down to help her up.

Rebecca clutched the ground. "Oh, lord, don't move me! You'd better get help! I know I heard it snap!"

"Hell, I was walkin' right b'hind you! I didn't

hear anythin'! Are you sure?"

Rebecca began to sob as convincingly as she could, taking care not to move around too much. "Oh, it hurts! It hurts! I need a doctor!"

Concern crept into the young soldier's voice. "Now, just a minute—you wait right here! Hey!" he shouted. "Hey, somebody!"

He held up the torch to look around. A figure standing guard on the parapet turned to look. Another came out of a bastion.

"Oh, give me the torch!" Rebecca twisted around and held out her hand. "Let me see how bad it is!"

The soldier gave it to her, and as soon as it was in her hand, she thrust the burning end of it into his shirt front. "Hey! What . . . ?" He gave a piercing scream and fell backward, and Rebecca scrambled to her feet.

"I'm sorry! I *had* to do it!" she called over her shoulder as she raced toward the gate. Out of the corner of her eye, she saw more figures on the parapet, and now the figures were running toward a ladder made of logs tied crossways.

"Oh, dear God, help me! Help me!" she panted. Out of the gate she ran and into the blackness, cries and commotion sounding behind her.

"Get her! *Get* her!" someone shouted.

Down she stumbled into a ditch, and hurriedly clambered out again. Then she ran straight into the *abatis*, a wall-like mound of debris and pointed sticks. But thankfully, the sticks were pointed away from her, and in a moment of frantic clawing, she got through the obstruction.

Now, a wide space dotted with twisted stumps and roots stood between her and the line of the forest. If she could only get across it and lose herself in the trees, she'd be safe. Once hidden in the brush and undergrowth, no one could find her—except perhaps Kin-di-wa. Only this time, it was she who was going to find him.

"There! There she is!" a man called out.

Faster and faster she ran, dodging barely seen stumps and roots. To fall now would mean capture—and possibly a real broken leg. If only she could see.

And no sooner had she made that wish when the air around her began to explode with streaks of color and light. The soldiers were firing their muskets—boom! Boom! Something whizzed past her head.

"Oh, God, please!" she begged. A tree loomed up in front of her. She twisted in mid-flight. The tree trunk shook and shuddered with the impact of a musketball, as Rebecca dodged behind it.

"I made it! I made it!" she sobbed. And running onward, she felt the trees close ranks behind her like a row of stalwart soldiers, shielding her from harm.

When at last she stopped running, she could see nothing ahead or behind her but inky darkness shrouding tree after tree. She could hear nothing but her own thudding heart. Gulping the heavy air, she leaned against a tree. It was incredible that she had escaped! But of course she would not have done so if she hadn't thrust the burning torch into the chest of that nice young soldier.

How badly had he been burned? What must he think of her? Despite the heat of her exertion and the warmth of the close dark night, she shivered violently. It was one thing to deliberately hurt someone who had hurt you—and quite another to hurt someone who never had.

As long as she lived, she'd never forget his look of shock and pain. It was another horrible memory to add to her collection. Another deep regret.

But there was no use fretting over it; what was done was done. The important thing now was to get to Fallen Timbers—a near impossibility in the darkness and in her present state of exhaustion. She slumped down to the ground. The spot she'd reached seemed as good as any to pass the night.

A soft layer of moss and last year's leaves cushioned the earth beneath her, and the trees were thick enough to afford concealment. British soldiers would surely have more sense than to try to find her in the forest at night. But if they did come, she knew they'd have difficulty locating her and their torches would warn her from far off.

Sighing deeply, she leaned back against the tree. She'd only close her eyes a minute to rest—then try to stay awake and keep watch. Never had it been so comforting to be safely hidden in the forest. The trees, the moss-covered ground, an insect whirring past—these were her friends, and if she could not be near Kin-di-wa, the next best thing was to be here. She might have gone mad remaining locked up in the blockhouse.

Now, when it didn't matter any more, she understood Kin-di-wa's love for the forest. In the forest, one could be free. One could be safe. Unlike the settlements of men, the forest was predictable. A tree behaved like a tree. A bear like a bear. An owl like an owl. Once you knew the forest's secrets, you need never be afraid. And with that comforting thought, Rebecca fell into a deep and dreamless sleep.

The gentle kiss of rain awoke her. She opened her eyes to discover morning—wearing a wet gray cloak. The entire world seemed bathed in dreary, humid half-darkness—as if God Himself were weeping. And arising, Rebecca remembered Little Turtle's warning at the council meeting: "Manitou will hide his face in a cloud if his children refuse to talk with Chenoten."

Indeed, it seemed he had done just that. But without the rain, she might have slept hours longer, and perhaps such inhospitable weather might delay the battle. Using the wood lore Kin-di-wa had taught her, Rebecca determined which way was north and began hurrying toward Fallen Timbers. As she remembered it, the site lay roughly two miles upriver on a rise or bluff. Could she have followed the river itself, she knew she'd soon come to it—but might also be more easily spotted.

Resigning herself to fighting the thick forest growth, she walked as fast as she could, but hadn't gone more than half a mile, when she heard the sound of distant musketfire. This spurred her into a run. Could the battle be beginning? Was Anthony Wayne approaching Fallen Timbers from the opposite direction?

The musketfire continued sporadically over the next half hour, then stopped abruptly. By this time, she was breathing hard and soaked to the skin. She shoved back several long red strands of hair which had come undone from her braid and kept on running.

Her braid thumped between her shoulder blades—a single heavy wet rope. She clambered over a fallen log, came to another and leapt it like a deer. But now, the going got rougher. More fallen logs. More saplings competing for every inch of forest floor. It took several moments before she realized that she was now running uphill too. And then, it dawned on her: this had to be the outskirts of Fallen Timbers.

Ahead of her, several muskets popped in unison, reminding her of a village celebration she'd once attended on the Fourth of July. Something bright red caught her eye. Something moved between the trees. Soldiers? Tribesmen? She had no choice but to find out.

Slowing down to a dog trot, she weaved among

the broken trees. Her panting sounded absurdly loud in the sudden silence. Then a man stood up with his back to her and fired a musket straight ahead. She almost ran into him. The bright red quills on his scalp lock shivered and shook, as she clapped him on the shoulder. "P-Peshewa!"

He wheeled around and yanked his war club out of his waist thong. His eyes gleamed whitely in his painted face. She ducked his upswung arm. "Peshewa, don't! It's me!"

The tomahawk sliced the air beside her. Peshewa shuddered, regaining control. "I almost kill you! What *you* be doing here? Go back! Go back!" He made a gesture for her to go back in the direction from which she had come. "Go to fort! Saginwash protect you!"

"Peshewa, wait! I've got to find Kin-di-wa! Do you know where he is?"

"Kin-di-wa! Why you want Kin-di-wa?" Hurt and jealousy leapt into his eyes. His glance fell on her exposed bosom. "Kin-di-wa no want to see you now! No time for squaw troubles! Go back!"

"You don't understand! I've got to find him or Little—" The sound of muskets and long guns, closer now than before, blew away the rest of her question.

Peshewa whirled back to the business at hand, but not before she saw his expression: lips drawn back like a snarling fox, eyes glinting like a mad man's. In the lust for battle, he'd already forgotten her.

She watched him a moment as he shoved his war club back into his waist thong and began reloading his musket. A short distance to the right and to the left of him, other braves leapt out of hiding and aimed for the unseen enemy.

How do they know where to fire? she wondered. A sharp acrid smell assaulted her nostrils. Even in the rain, a powder haze was curling insidiously through the woods, thicker than smoke from a council fire.

Rebecca began running down the ragged line of Indians. Kin-di-wa had to be here somewhere! She stumbled over a tree root and a musketball whizzed over her head. A pair of leather leggings ran past her, darting forward from tree to tree.

She jumped up and kept on going—being more careful now to duck and dodge. Ten or fifteen feet to her left, another line appeared. The half-naked painted figures worked in a curious stilted rhythm —fire and load, fire and load. But she knew by the sound of things, the soldiers were drawing closer.

Boom! Boom! Boom! The musketfire had grown constant. And through the puffy haze, Rebecca made out yet a third line.

Where would Kin-di-wa and Little Turtle be? In the line closest to the enemy of course. Rebecca veered sharply to her left, crawled under a log too big to climb over, and raced toward the front line. Braves were firing all around her now, heedless of the rain. Any moment now, she expected to see soldiers come charging through their defenses.

Huge puffs of smoke and sharp reports warned of their advancing presence.

"Kin-di-wa! Kin-di-wa!" Rebecca screamed. She thought she saw his tall lithe form stretched out on a log and firing.

Racing toward him, something struck her shoulder with a searing impact and sent her spinning to the ground. For a moment she forgot where she was. Too stunned to do more than sit up, she examined her wound and saw an ugly black welt where a musketball had creased her flesh. Then, the inner edges of the welt began to exude blood.

Lacking anything with which to bind it, she clapped her hand over it and got to her feet. Kin-di-wa! Where was Kin-di-wa? She saw the brave again—collapsed on the log. And the top of his head was gone.

"No! Oh, no!" Forgetting to duck and dodge, she stumbled up to the body. It took both hands and all her strength to turn him over, but the man was not Kin-di-wa.

Streaks of black and white paint on his face and the distinctive quill design on his breech clout identified him as Shawnee. He stared at her with sightless eyes, then toppled off the log. Horrified, she turned and ran.

"Kin-di-wa! Kin-di-wa! Where are you?"

Directly in her path, a brave was bending over another fallen warrior.

"Kin-di-wa! Have you seen Kin-di-wa?" She

forgot he couldn't understand her language. And she could no longer remember a single word of his.

He looked at her blankly and shook his head, and impatiently, she jostled him aside to see the fallen man. His ornaments and feathers marked him as a chieftain—a dead one now. But at least he wasn't Little Turtle or anyone else she recognized.

The brave said something and tugged at her arm, but she slapped his hand away and kept on going. Over logs. Under them. She slithered between saplings and crashed through brush. And whenever she spotted a brave with the same height and build as Kin-di-wa, her stomach leapt into her throat.

But she did not find him, and now, she had reached the rock in the very heart of Fallen Timbers.

The rock was something familiar, something stable, the very place where she'd rested and watched little Walks-Tall reach for a sunbeam. It offered protection from whizzing balls and exploding shells, and crouching near it, she realized she might stand a better chance of catching sight of Kin-di-wa or Little Turtle if she stayed in one place and waited for them to pass by her.

But no sooner had she crept in closer to the rock, when a brightly painted warrior leapt up on top of it, brandishing a tomahawk. Rebecca recognized Turkey Foot, the Ottawa chieftain, who had so persuasively opposed Little Turtle at the council meeting.

"Brothers!" she heard him cry. "Stand fast! They are coming!" Turkey Foot broke into a rallying war cry, followed by additional exhortations.

Pressed against the rock, Rebecca peered through the powder haze at the shadowy figures of Turkey Foot's followers. They seemed to be falling back. The front line was breaking up! Then Rebecca heard a dull thud whose impact shook the very air around her. Something hot, wet, and red splattered over her in a shower. And glancing up at Turkey Foot, she saw that he'd been hit: from the middle of his chest now gushed a bubbling red fountain.

For a moment he poised there, held fast by some unseen force, then he toppled and fell. A terrible rending cry arose, as every brave who saw him fall leapt out of hiding and converged on the rock. But this cry was quickly drowned out by a greater cry. Hundreds of voices, their owners as yet unseen, rushed toward them like a great wind out of the sky.

Rebecca was struck with terror. What was it? Only the Indians used war cries. But this sounded like an attack by demons.

And through the haze and slanting rain, she saw Chenoten's soldiers coming: blue coats faced with red, leather caps and plumes jauntily defying the rain, metal long knives gleaming, they charged forward with perfect discipline.

To her left and to her right, they came on

horseback, swinging their sabers and leaping their charges over the fallen timbers. In the center, they came on foot—row after row of glittering long knives.

Bayonets and sabers alike slashed into brush and thickets, routing the hidden Indians like so many startled rabbits. Metal clashed against knife and tomahawk. Painted bodies and uniformed ones struggled hand to hand. A soldier came rushing toward Rebecca, bayonet extended to impale her against the rock. She leapt aside and heard the loud whang! as metal and rock connected.

Before the soldier could turn and try again, she darted around the rock, stumbled across Turkey Foot's body, and remembered the niche where Walks-Tall had hidden from her.

Down on her hands and knees she dropped, clawing her way into the cavity. It wasn't big enough to go in head first. Twisting around, she backed in. And enough small branches lay within easy reach to provide for almost perfect conceal-ment. But no sooner had she secreted herself, when another whang! sounded against the rock.

The soldier was poking around the base. She pressed herself deeper into the cavity, crouching like a four-footed animal—the rock above, the wet ground beneath. The point of the bayonet struck between her splayed fingers; then it sliced past her cheek. "Dear God!" she prayed silently, holding her breath. "If only you spare me this time, I promise you—I'll never do wrong again!"

A vision of Kin-di-wa's face flashed before her. She'd already given him up! What *more* did God want from her?

But before she could bargain further with the Almighty, a scuffle sounded on the other side of the brush. There was an unearthly scream, a gurgling moan, and someone fell against the rock. A man's outflung hand, extending from a blue sleeve, flopped down through the branches, caught and held. Rebecca didn't dare push the branches aside to see what had happened to the rest of him.

All around her flowed the sounds of furious battle. Men screamed and cried and shouted. Horses whinnied. Muskets thundered. Again and again, someone brushed or fell against the branches concealing the mouth of her hiding place. The smell of burning powder vied with the thick sweet odor of fresh blood—so sweet it turned her stomach.

She buried her head in her arms and prayed she might keep both her life and her sanity. So this was war. How could anyone who knew what it was like permit it?

Nearby, someone groaned. Over and over, in an almost rhythmic fashion, there came a sound more animal than human. It tore at Rebecca's heart. Then the groan turned into a gurgle. The man choked and gasped. He groaned again. His ragged breathing—each breath a fight for life—demanded her attention.

401

KATHARINE KINCAID

Keep going! Don't stop! she begged, whenever his breathing faltered. And so the moments passed, one breath at a time, while the sound of fighting ebbed and flowed, like a vengeful storm crossing over. Then it seemed to diminish—moving rapidly away in the direction of Fort Miamis.

By the time Rebecca thought it safe to crawl from under the rocky overhang, it seemed as if hours and hours had passed. But she guessed the battle had gone on only an hour or two at most. She shoved aside the brush, dislodged the flopping arm and hand, and crawled out. The scene was worse than any she could have imagined. Around the perimeter of the rock, a pile of bodies lay heaped, red men and white, all grotesquely mangled.

One was sliced almost in half. Another had been beheaded. The leg of a third was smashed. The soldier who'd tried to bayonet her—the one whose hand had hung in the brush—had been stabbed repeatedly about the face. One of his eyeballs hung by tendrils to its socket. The rock itself had been stained such a darkening red that even the continuing gentle rain could not cleanse it.

Rebecca became violently ill. What little was in her stomach erupted with the first heave, and when nothing else would come, she continued heaving. Crouched over and holding her stomach, she retched and retched. Then dizziness swept over her. But there was no place to sit—no place to look that didn't reveal some awful new horror.

Then she remembered the man who'd been groaning. Was he still alive? Which body was his? What right had she to be sick when someone needed help?

With an enormous effort of will, Rebecca pulled herself together. She must set about examining the bodies to see if there were any signs of life. She counted eleven strewn in reckless abandon near the rock. One *had* to be the man who'd kept on groaning—but which one?

Six she discounted immediately as being too badly injured to remain alive. Three more were equally doubtful. To make up her mind about the other two, she pressed her palm to their chests. Both were Indians, and neither had a heartbeat. Indeed, of the total eleven, only two had been soldiers. Rebecca thought it a telling number: could there be any doubt as to who had lost the battle?

They're all dead! she agonized. Eleven strong brave men—and God alone knew how many more. Please Lord! she begged. Don't let one of them be Kin-di-wa.

Then, from a body she'd discounted completely, there came a slight sound. And even as she heard it, she became aware of other sounds. From behind trees and under logs, from out of bushes and clumps of greenery, from ten, twenty, fifty feet away—the groans of the injured and dying rose.

"Ni-pi! Ni-pi!" someone begged.

Water! The man wanted water! Rebecca whirled

around to see who it was. Someone else began a death chant. She didn't know where to start first. Rushing to the brave whose groan had first caught her attention, she recognized Turkey Foot, the Ottawa chieftain. How was it possible he still lived? Two other bodies pinned him down, and she herself had seen his chest torn open by a musketball.

As she struggled vainly to free him, two shaking hands suddenly reached down to help, and she was amazed to see it was Little Turtle. But what a change had come over him. His once proud shoulders were stooped in defeat. From feathered headdress to moccasins, he was smeared with paint, dirt, and blood. His eyes were shadowed smudges in a face as cadaverous as any dead man's. Even his hair—which she remembered being streaked with gray—seemed grayer than before, almost as if it had whitened during the course of the battle.

And when he spoke, his voice had lost the greater portion of its grandeur. "Others are coming, little white woman. We will see to him and help him sing his death chant. Go and help some lesser brave whose dying no one will notice."

"Little Turtle! Have you seen Kin-di-wa? Was he near you? I came here to try and stop this battle! To tell you the British have betrayed you!"

Little Turtle swayed like a broken reed in the wind. He closed his eyes, then opened them again to reveal a bottomless pit of pain. "Now, I know why the sound I have been awaiting I have not heard. Not a single cannon has thundered. Not a single redcoat joined us! Our warriors began fleeing to Fort Miamis as soon as they saw we could not turn back the Long Knives, and all this time, I have waited—but the Saginwash guns have been silent."

"They—received orders yesterday morning. I tried to find you or Kin-di-wa to *tell* you!"

"Kin-di-wa . . ." Little Turtle repeated. He seemed almost in a daze. "You ask me the whereabouts of a single man—Kin-di-wa. I sent him back to Fort Miamis to plead for the help they promised us, the help that did not come!"

"And—you haven't seen him since? He didn't return?"

"My people have been crushed, little white woman! If you would find Kin-di-wa, go look for him among the dead!"

"No! No!" Rebecca screamed. "He can't be dead!"

"Look around you," Little Turtle rasped. "How many living do you see?" Then, more gently, "But the sins of your people do not belong to you. Go and look for him. Mayhap, I am wrong, and he—of all our hundreds dead and hundreds more dying—is still alive."

And Rebecca arose from beside the dying Turkey Foot and ran back toward Fort Miamis.

Fifteen

Rebecca broke free of the woods bordering the clearing in front of Fort Miamis and stumbled and fell to the ground. She had run almost the entire distance from Fallen Timbers, stopping only to examine the bodies of dead and dying Indians she found scattered throughout the woods. She hadn't yet found Kin-di-wa, but she'd seen enough blood, gore, and suffering to bring about total collapse—could she have allowed herself to collapse.

What kept her going, kept her running heartlessly past those who still lived and needed help, was the thought that the next victim she stumbled across might be Kin-di-wa—dying alone and unaided. All others were painted strangers who must lie and wait for their squaws to search them out, as she was searching for Kin-di-wa. She'd met several Indian women in the woods, looking as anxious and distraught as she felt, and they too seemed bent on finding the one lone man whose life they treasured above all others.

Now, she lurched to her feet and surveyed the scene before her. It had stopped raining, and the clearing was littered with broken bodies—mostly of the defeated Indians. A heavy concentration of corpses near the walls of the fort gave silent evidence that the Indians had been banging on them, begging admission, but even now, when it was all over, the gates of Fort Miamis remained tightly closed.

From high up on the battlements, British soldiers watched dispassionately, as if the tragedy had nothing whatever to do with them.

Damn you! Damn all of you to hell! Rebecca cursed them inwardly. The least the British could do was to help gather up the wounded. But perhaps their *orders* prevented them—and perhaps, they feared Anthony Wayne's army.

Everywhere she looked, Rebecca saw blue-coated soldiers filtering through the trees. A large detachment of mounted soldiers had gathered close to the river, and at their head sat a man whose uniform sported gold epaulets and whose hair was carefully arranged and powdered beneath his tri-cornered hat. He sat stiffly and uncomfortably in the saddle, as if he might be injured, but his back was straight as a spear, and he snapped orders right and left in a brusque no-nonsense manner.

Rebecca was too far away to hear what he said,

but the man's underlings moved quickly to do his bidding. Then he spurred his horse to a canter and brought it to a halt beneath the very guns of the fort.

There, he sat and watched as his soldiers sped in every direction. Soon, lighted torches appeared in their hands, and they set about methodically firing every wood structure in the near vicinity— excepting only the fort itself. A half dozen soldiers took several canoes and set out for the island in the river. Another ten or twelve began paddling across to the other side.

Rebecca had no doubt they'd been sent to fire more buildings—one of which was Colonel McKee's trading post. She wasn't sorry to see Colonel McKee receive his just deserts, but oh, the arrogance of this conquering general! The British could easily blow him out of the saddle, but he showed no fear whatsoever.

The British, in the meantime, paced up and down their battlements, cannon ready and muskets primed. But Rebecca knew they could not fire unless Anthony Wayne fired first, and Wayne obviously knew it too. The straight proud man with the barrel chest seemed to take perverse delight in flaunting himself—daring them to fire, when clearly, they could not.

Then a shot rang out from the ring of trees. A soldier who had come up beside Anthony Wayne jerked and fell off his horse. General Wayne's horse half-reared. Other cavalry leapt forward to

form a tight blockade around their commander.
Wayne barked an order, and another half-dozen
soldiers spurred their horses to a gallop and raced
in the direction from which the single shot had
issued.

God help the brave who fired, Rebecca thought.
He cannot escape six men on horseback. And a few
moments later, the booming of muskets told her
the brave had not escaped.

Now, Anthony Wayne appeared ready to draw
back from the fort and permit the Indians and
Rebecca to enter the clearing and collect their dead
and wounded. The sodden log structures were
burning furiously with the aid of pine branches
heaped on top of them. The resinous oily mixture
given off by the branches emitted a sharp pungent
odor and caused the flames to leap and crackle
until the buildings themselves became roaring
sheets of fire.

Rebecca's nose stung. She was filled with
unreasoning anger, but there was nothing anyone
could do but helplessly stand by and watch the
destruction. She wished Wayne would hurry and
leave, but before the doughty general rode out of
the clearing, he ordered the infantry to trample
and uproot the vegetable patches scattered across
the clearing and up and down the river.

It was a last gesture of defiant warning, and only
when everything about the fort lay in utter
devastation, and the British flag itself was obscured in thick black smoke, did he raise his hand

to signal he was satisfied. Then the blue-coated soldiers began to file back into the shadowed woods, taking their own wounded with them.

Rebecca waited only a moment longer, then rushed forward. Other squaws and children rushed forward also, and here and there, small bands of old men—warriors too crippled or infirm to fight—began separating the injured from the dead.

Loud cries and lamentations sounded in Rebecca's ears as families located their loved ones. Death chants rose in agonized chorus as wives and relatives sought to ease their dying husbands, brothers, and fathers into the hereafter. Rebecca dashed from one group to another, from body to body, hunting for Kin-di-wa.

The bodies of the dead, she saw, were being carried to one side of the fort, wrapped in skins, and laid end to end in long rows. The bodies of the injured were loaded onto make-shift pallets made of skins and sturdy saplings. The pallets were then lined up on the other side of the fort, awaiting transport downriver to one of the camps.

Not a single recumbent form escaped Rebecca's attention. She pawed through the dead men first, hurriedly unwrapping their faces and gagging uncontrollably when some grotesque new horror was revealed. But after examining the fourteenth or fifteenth body, she hardly felt a thing. Only the odor bothered her: in the damp muggy heat, the newly dead were already beginning to smell, and

411

flies were defying the wetness to swarm over the unprotesting forms.

It was more difficult to search through the rows of injured. Men whose eyes were glazed with pain gazed up at her with great shame and sorrow. They had lost. They had lost to the Long Knives, and the agony of defeat was far worse than any wound they'd suffered.

Still not finding Kin-di-wa, Rebecca grew more frantic by the minute. She passed down the rows of injured a second time, and when again she didn't find him, turned back to the rows of dead men who now numbered in the hundreds.

Had she missed him because his face was destroyed? There were several head and facial injuries severe enough to render their victims unidentifiable.

Hesitantly, she bent over one faceless body whose height and build looked familiar.

"Oh, Kin-di-wa, Kin-di-wa . . ." she moaned over and over, hardly realizing that she did so. Then a voice came from behind her.

"I am not yet among the dead, Cat-Eyes. I am still alive—but barely."

Wheeling around, Rebecca was just in time to catch Kin-di-wa as he swayed and collapsed in her arms.

Down to the ground they fell, scarcely missing a tightly wrapped cocoon of skins. Quickly, she rolled Kin-di-wa off her, then knelt over him. "Oh, dear God!" she cried, as she drank in every detail of his appearance.

His face and lips were ashen—drained completely of color, beneath his blue and ochre war paint. Lines of suffering and determination were chiseled around his mouth, and his body bore so many wounds she couldn't at first count them or determine their severity.

But the wound that appeared to be taking the greatest toll was the one below his rib cage. With every broken breath he took, thick crimson blood poured through a ragged opening near his stomach.

How had he managed to stay on his feet long enough to find her? Not knowing what to do first, Rebecca scanned the figures moving to and fro around her. If only she could spot Sweet Breeze, Two Fires—or even Tecumwah! Then she did see someone she knew: Crow Woman was tottering past the rows of dead on her way to the injured with a gourdful of water.

Leaving Kin-di-wa where he lay, Rebecca dashed after the old woman. And soon it was down Kin-di-wa's throat they were forcing water.

"Enough! Enough!" the old woman scolded. "You want to choke him? Wounds in the stomach should be fed little water—but tea is good. And tea made from Birth Root, Horse Tail, or Five Finger Grass is even better."

"But where are we to find those?" Even after all Kin-di-wa's teaching, Rebecca had never heard of these herbs.

"I find them," Crow Woman promised. "But first we try to slow bleeding. Here, give me that."

The old woman tugged at Rebecca's torn bodice until the rest of the stitches gave way. She muttered something unintelligible about Rebecca's exposed breasts, but only when Crow Woman spoke slowly and used simple words, could Rebecca understand her.

But how lucky she'd come along! Rebecca thought. The old crone's manner was deftly efficient as she pressed down on Kin-di-wa's stomach to staunch the bleeding. Then, using the torn piece of doeskin to form a pad, Crow Woman untied Kin-di-wa's waist thong and retied it over the wound to hold the pad tightly in place.

"Now, we see what else wrong—then we must get him back to camp, and I go look for herbs. Ah, see here!" Kin-di-wa stirred as the old woman probed an ugly wound in his upper left shoulder. "Musketball enter here. If he does not die from bleeding stomach, he die of this. We must get ball out!"

Rebecca cringed. *"Is* he going to die? Can't you save him?"

Crow Woman shrugged her skinny shoulders. "His wounds very bad. Manitou must decide if he lives or dies."

Her clawlike hands dropped to a slash on Kin-di-wa's right arm. Beneath a flap of bloody skin and flesh, Kin-di-wa's pinkish-white muscle was exposed.

"This we sew up." She tapped it lightly. "The musketball we dig out. And this—" She felt along his lowest rib where a bayonet had likely struck before it slanted off into his abdomen. "This broken rib we bind tightly. The bleeding stomach must heal itself with the help of herbs and dressings. And if his wounds don't rot, then maybe he live. But maybe not."

Maybe. Maybe not. It was so little to give one hope. Rebecca smoothed back Kin-di-wa's tangled hair. Once again, he'd lost his white feathers. Sweat, paint, and blood ran together on his face. A bloody lump was turning black and blue on his forehead. But he was still alive. And knowing how close she was to losing him, she knew one thing more: if he lived through this, she'd *never* leave him.

"Wait here. My pouch down by river. I go get. Mayhap we need it." Crow Woman got to her feet and tottered away, while Rebecca sought to make Kin-di-wa more comfortable. She cradled his head in her lap, murmuring words of comfort and endearment.

"I'm here, Kin-di-wa, and I'll take care of you. Do you understand—can you hear me? I'll never leave you, *never*. I swear to Manitou!"

She traced the line of his jaw with her fingertips. It was almost the only part of him that wasn't bruised and bleeding. Such a strong stubborn jaw. "My husband," she whispered. And saying it for the first time, she knew it was true. They *were*

415

husband and wife: bound to one another forever—
or at least until death.

"Oh, Kin-di-wa! Why did it take *this* to teach me
what I should have known from the very first. Why
did I fight so hard against it? . . . You tried to tell
me but I wouldn't listen . . . Well, you were right
Kin-di-wa, you were right! Nothing in life makes
any difference—nothing matters—except how
much we love each other."

She bent over him, sobbing. "Don't die, Kin-di-
wa. Now that I've found you, please don't die!"

Crow Woman tapped her on her powder-burned
shoulder. "No use to weep. Go. Go get someone to
help us move him. We take him back to camp
now."

Rebecca gently dislodged herself and scrambled
to her feet. A fine help she was. Kin-di-wa could
die while she wallowed in her emotions.

Into the milling throng she went, searching for
someone she knew. And suddenly, there was Sweet
Breeze helping to move the body of a brave from
the ranks of the injured into the ranks of the dead.

"Sweet Breeze! Thank God I found you."

Her friend looked terrible: her smock was soiled
and blood-stained, her braid disheveled, and
fatigue and tension lined her face. So must I look,
Rebecca thought. She took hold of Sweet Breeze's
end of the makeshift pallet to assist her and
another squaw in carrying their grizzly burden
while she explained her problem. "Kin-di-wa is
badly hurt, and Crow Woman sent me to get

someone to help us move him downriver to the camp."

Sweet Breeze's grim expression darkened as they trudged along. "Many be badly hurt. I no can leave here to help you, Cat-Eyes, but I give you pallet—as soon as we finished with it."

"But I don't think Crow Woman and I can carry him all that way by ourselves!"

"I sorry, Cat-Eyes, but I no can help you. Daughter of Little Turtle must stay here and organize care and moving of *all* our wounded."

They lowered the pallet to the ground near the rows of dead and added their burden to the other victims. "Have you seen your father, Sweet Breeze? I know he's still alive and not wounded because I saw him."

Sweet Breeze shook her head. "I no see him—but I think he rather be dead than live to see all this. And so would I."

"Oh, Sweet Breeze! You can't mean that!"

But Rebecca saw now how deeply the defeat had affected her friend. Sweet Breeze's eyes were different, as if all hope and happiness had gone from them forever. No longer did she look as though she knew a wonderful secret: that Apekonit loved her and she loved him, no matter how great the obstacles between them.

Sweet Breeze folded the pallet in half and gave it to Rebecca. "Here. Take it now. Mayhap Peshewa and his mother help you carry Kin-di-wa back to camp. They here someplace."

"Thank you, I'll try to find them." Rebecca hurried away.

A nearby burning cabin suddenly collapsed in a shower of sparks and flame, and through the smoke, Rebecca caught sight of a brave with a distinctive red-quill headdress: Peshewa!

She ran around the fiery obstruction and came up to him where he knelt on the ground beside a fallen brave. He was singing a death chant with another Miami warrior whose injuries were so grotesque, Rebecca kept her eyes averted. She waited until he finished, leaned over, and closed the brave's eyes with the tips of his fingers. Then he looked up and saw her.

"Peshewa, can you come and help me move Kin-di-wa downriver to the camp? He's been terribly wounded, but Crow Woman says he might still live . . . Sweet Breeze gave me this pallet to carry him." She held it out to show him. "But she cannot take time to help me, and Crow Woman isn't strong enough."

Peshewa stood up. He too was covered with soot, paint, blood, and grime, and his red quills shook with impatience. "Where is Two Fires?" he snapped. "*She* is squaw who should see to Kin-di-wa's care—not you."

Rebecca was shocked and indignant. "I thought you were Kin-di-wa's friend. Do you want him to die? Is that it—to clear a path for yourself? Well, it makes no difference, Peshewa. Even if he does die, I'll never marry you."

Peshewa's jaw twitched. Emotions raced across his plain blunt features in rapid succession—jealousy, bitterness, and love for his friend. "Where?" he finally asked. "Take me to him."

Rebecca led the way, and they found Crow Woman chanting over Kin-di-wa and touching a long red strand of hair to his wounds. "Stop that!" Rebecca cried. "It's only a piece of hair!"

Crow Woman's eyes glinted in the nest of her ancient wrinkles. "Is strong medicine—stronger still, if you love him. Do you?"

Rebecca could feel as well as see the flush beginning in her naked breast, and she knew Peshewa saw it too. "Yes," she whispered proudly. "I love him more than my own life."

Crow Woman's head bobbed up and down. Once again, she trailed the single strand of Rebecca's hair across Kin-di-wa's wounds, chanting her mysterious gibberish.

"Please!" Rebecca begged. "Could we get him back to camp now—into some sort of shelter?"

"You take him," Crow Woman cackled. "I go look for herbs, then I come to camp myself."

So it was Rebecca and Peshewa who joined the trek of mourners carrying their wounded back to the shelter of the camp on Swan Creek. It took them all afternoon, and by the time they got there, the darkness of night was closing in. But it wasn't too dark to see what had happened: the entire camp was destroyed. Chenoten's soldiers had gotten there ahead of them and fired every lodge, torn down every lean-to, and trampled every square inch of ground.

"How? How could they do this?" Rebecca cried in anguish. "They're monsters! Murderers! Beasts!"

And Peshewa made her turn and look back west in the direction from which they had come. A dull orange glow lit the sky on both sides of the river. It looked as though every lodge and corn patch from Fort Miamis to Kekionga was burning.

But of course, not even Anthony Wayne could have done all that in one day. It would take many days and many groves of pine trees, rich in turpentine, to burn so much, but Rebecca suddenly realized what it meant to lose a battle. The suffering of the defeated Indians was just beginning.

She knelt down beside Kin-di-wa's pallet and took his cool clammy hand. He was still unconscious, as he'd been the entire journey from Fort Miamis, but his breathing sounded irregular, as if his chest was filling up with fluids. And the pad of doeskin bound to his stomach was saturated with blood.

She lifted his hand to her cheek where her tears washed over his fingers, pleading silently. *Don't die, Kin-di-wa. Please don't die!*

Looking up at Peshewa, she was hardly able to see him through her tears. "We have to build a new lean-to—and make a fire to keep the mosquitoes away."

Peshewa shook his head. "No lean-to. Lodge—we must build lodge. If he lives, it be many moons before his strength come back. By then, cold winds blow down upon us."

Cold winds. Winter! How would they survive—with no food and no shelter?

I won't worry now, Rebecca told herself, I'll worry when it happens. The only thing that mattered now was that Kin-di-wa should live through the night. I'll *make* him live, she swore. He won't die because I won't let him.

"Tomorrow, we will build a lodge," she said. "But tonight we need a fire—and a shelter of pine branches or skins in case it rains again. See what you can find, Peshewa, please."

And Peshewa went off without a word, returning minutes later with a surprise: he'd found Two Fires and little Walks-Tall. Two Fires came up silently in the darkness, looking as calm and unruffled as ever. Walks-Tall was fast asleep in his cradleboard on her back.

She bent over Kin-di-wa in the failing light, saw the extent of his wounds, and immediately broke into the Miami lamentation for the dead. Rebecca's skin crawled. "Don't!" she snapped. "He isn't dead yet!"

The eerie sound died away. But Rebecca noticed that Two Fires's eyes were dilated with fear and wildness, though, as yet, she shed no tears. Nor did she seem truly grieved. Rather, it was as though she were looking inward at some greater terror.

Was she reliving her first husband's death—the man whose son she'd borne and whom she'd *chosen* for a husband? Where had she been all this time while other squaws were searching for their dead and wounded?

"Shelter." Rebecca said slowly in the Miami tongue. "We must find him shelter."

Two Fires nodded. Gesturing for them to follow her, she led them around the still smoldering remains of the camp and into the marsh. Trying not to jiggle Kin-di-wa unnecessarily, Rebecca grew increasingly alarmed as the footing became uncertain. The ground was soft and mushy under her moccasins, and it had become so dark she could hardly see where they were going.

Then, ahead in the darkness, she saw a soft glow. The ground grew firm again. Two Fires led them straight to a brand new lean-to that had all the comforts of her old one—including a small cheery fire—and bore no signs whatever of the day's devastation.

Rebecca and Peshewa set down Kin-di-wa's pallet, and Rebecca turned to the beautiful silent girl. Gratitude flowed through her: she felt like hugging and kissing Two Fires. "How did you know to move the lean-to? You managed to save everything."

Two Fires gave a short rapid explanation. She had known what was coming, what always came after battle, and she was afraid for little Walks-Tall. So she'd moved camp that morning and stayed hidden all day in the marsh. She was sorry she hadn't come sooner to look for Kin-di-wa, but she wanted to make certain it was safe.

"But I'm so glad you stayed!" Rebecca exclaimed. "If you hadn't—" She bit back a sob, then remembered something else. "But Crow Woman won't be able to find us. She was going to look for herbs to dress Kin-di-wa's wounds."

"I find her," Peshewa said. "I get torch and go back along trail."

"Oh, hurry, Peshewa, please hurry! Crow Woman said the herbs would stop his bleeding."

Peshewa disappeared into the blackness of the marsh, and Rebecca knelt down beside Kin-di-wa. She bent over the wound in his stomach. The lower half of his body and the pallet was drenched with blood. But was it old blood or new? She couldn't tell.

The blood smell was thick and hot in her nostrils, and he lay so still he might have been dead. She held her fingers under his nose and felt the barest whisper of breath as he exhaled. His eyes looked so sunken. And there was a rim of white around his mouth.

Two Fires nudged her arm and handed her a gourd of water. "No! No water, Crow Woman said. Only tea. Don't we have some herbs to make tea?"

Two Fires shook her head no, and Rebecca understood that whatever herbs Two Fires had, they weren't the right ones to deal with this kind of catastrophe.

The girl set down the gourd and eased the cradleboard off her shoulders. She unlaced the sleeping baby and gathered him into her arms— holding him close and rocking him. Since Walks-Tall was already sleeping, Rebecca felt a stab of resentment. Why was she comforting the baby when he didn't need it? Or was she the one who needed comfort?

Kin-di-wa suddenly stirred and groaned.

"I'm here, Kin-di-wa, I'm here." Rebecca took his hand and began rubbing it feverishly, but Kin-di-wa lapsed back into unconsciousness, never knowing she was there. "There's *got* to be something we can do for him! Don't you know anything about treating wounds?"

Two Fires stared at her calmly, never ceasing her rocking.

She's waiting for him to die! Rebecca thought wildly. She doesn't think he'll make it. What's more, she doesn't care. All she cares about is her baby.

Back and forth, back and forth, Two Fires rocked. Her eyes stared at Rebecca, but her thoughts seemed far away. Rebecca couldn't stand it any longer. She seized the gourd of water, looked around for something with which to begin mopping up Kin-di-wa's blood, and set about cleaning him as best she could.

Two Fires was clearly crazy; she ought to have known *that* when the girl tried to kill her. Still,

Rebecca remembered, if it hadn't been for Two Fires, at this very moment she'd be trying to build a lean-to in the dark.

A long time later, when Rebecca had begun to despair that Kin-di-wa *would* survive the night, Peshewa arrived with Crow Woman. A single torch moved toward them through the marsh, and in its arc of light, Rebecca saw the old woman waving her hand triumphantly. "Horse tail! Good for tea and good for poultice."

She tottered into the shelter. "Boiling water. Where is it?"

Rebecca jumped to her feet. Why hadn't she thought to have it ready? "In a moment! I'll have it in a moment!"

Crow Woman took charge like a chief or a general. "Put baby down and let him sleep!" she cried to Two Fires. "A nice sharp blade! I need a blade!"

Two Fires laced Walks-Tall back into the cradleboard. "You!" The old woman pointed to Peshewa. "You hold him down. When he feels blade, he fight us with all his strength."

"Now? You're going to dig out the musketball now?" Rebecca paused in the act of stoking up the fire.

"The longer we wait, the weaker he gets!" The old woman shrilled. And Walks-Tall woke up just then and began wailing, but Two Fires had no time to tend to him now.

No sooner had she handed Crow Woman her

425

sharpest blade, when the old woman barked out another series of commands. Rebecca couldn't understand all of them, but her heart leapt with a sudden joy. Maybe the old crone knew what she was doing after all!

Crow Woman tossed her a clump of roots and stems that did indeed resemble a horse's tail—for it was thicker and bushier at the bottom than at the top of the spiky plant. "Boil it. We make both poultice and tea. I use Horse Tail plenty for curing sores with pus and also for cleaning pots—it good strong medicine."

Curing sores and cleaning pots! Rebecca's confidence took a nose dive into icy waters of doubt. Would the old woman cure Kin-di-wa or kill him? His wounds were far worse than mere runny sores! And as for cleaning pots—!

But soon, the little caldron was bubbling merrily as it hung over the fire on its tripod of sticks. Rebecca dropped in the plant and stirred with a piece of wood. Crow Woman handed her the bone-handled knife she planned to use on Kin-di-wa. "Stick in fire—then let it cool. Later, we heat it again."

Rebecca plunged the blade into a lick of flames. She didn't know whether she could bear to watch Crow Woman cut into Kin-di-wa's flesh, but she supposed she had no choice. It was either that or watch him die.

When Crow Woman was finally ready to begin her operation, she held out her hand to Rebecca.

Rebecca removed the knife from the flame, but as she pressed the handle into the old woman's claw, she had a moment of fearful hesitation. "Couldn't —couldn't we wait until morning?"

Crow Woman nodded to the east. "Morning," she grunted. And Rebecca saw a faint graying light far distant through the marsh and surrounding trees.

Peshewa knelt by Kin-di-wa's head, leaned over him, and pinioned his arms. Two Fires knelt beside Crow Woman, ready to mop up Kin-di-wa's blood with a strip of thick homespun material she'd dug out of a basket. It was a piece of some white woman's skirt, but where on earth had she gotten it, Rebecca wondered, as she made ready to do whatever Crow Woman commanded next.

The old woman glanced at Rebecca, eyes shining like bright black stones in her withered face. Her breath was fetid as she whispered, "If he does not cry out, he good as dead, even though he breathes. Watch closely then, and we see how much life be left in him."

Rebecca, who'd been hoping Kin-di-wa might somehow remain unconscious through the entire thing, now began to hope for exactly the op-posite—and she wasn't disappointed.

As soon as Crow Woman began probing into his shoulder wound, Kin-di-wa's body jerked. He opened his eyes and turned his head. The brilliant blue was startling in the pale moon of his face. "What are you doing?" he rasped in English.

"We've got to get the ball out," Rebecca explained. "You must lie very still."

"No!" He cried with great forcefulness, and then again, "No! No!"

"Lie still!" Rebecca pleaded.

"Hold him!" Crow Woman hissed, and Peshewa leaned the full weight of his body down against Kin-di-wa's arms. Rebecca held down his legs. He began to kick and shout, "No! No!" over and over. She had to sit on his legs to keep him down, and he began to bleed harder from his stomach wound, the blood gushing out to stain her doeskin even worse than it was stained already.

"There!" Crow Woman held up a tiny lead ball—too tiny and oddly misshapen to be responsible for so much damage. Rebecca looked past the old woman's bloody fingers to the torn flesh of Kin-di-wa's shoulder. Crow Woman handed her the knife. "Heat it again."

Rebecca inched off Kin-di-wa's legs and hurried to plunge the knife back into the fire. Kin-di-wa was lying more quietly now, his blue-tinged lips set in a thin straight line. She knew he must feel ashamed to have fought beneath the knife, for that was Kin-di-wa's way, the way of all his people: suffering was to be borne in silence.

But she wanted to tell him it was all right if he screamed. He needn't be courageous on her account or anyone else's.

When the knife was ready a second time—glowing white hot from the flames, Rebecca gave it back to Crow Woman, but Crow Woman wouldn't take it. "You do it!" she commanded. "I am old woman. I am tired."

"But—I can't!"

"Lay it on open wound. That all you have to do. Knife will do the rest."

Kin-di-wa's eyes were closed. His whole body was trembling in helpless anticipation. Two Fires moved down to sit on his legs. Shaking with fear, Rebecca positioned the knife blade so that when she lowered it onto Kin-di-wa's shoulder, it would sear the open edges of the wound.

"Do not take it up too quickly," Crow Woman cautioned. "Wound must be completely purified. Hurry now, before it cools!"

With a quick downward motion, Rebecca held her breath and laid the white-hot blade on Kin-di-wa's shoulder. His body jerked and twitched, but he never made a sound. She took the blade away. The wound was sealed with the imprint of the knife. And the smell of burnt flesh filled the air.

"There—it is done," she breathed.

Kin-di-wa's eyes flew open. They looked stunned—and glazed with suffering. His lips formed a single word, "Cat-Eyes!" but no sound came out. Then he lapsed again into unconsciousness.

"Now, poultice," Crow Woman said. "Undo pad from his stomach."

Rebecca untied Kin-di-wa's waist thong and plucked away the pad. Fresh blood trickled freely, and now Rebecca could clearly see the path the bayonet or saber had taken. The line of Kin-di-wa's bottom rib looked slightly uneven. There was a yellowish lump in the middle of it that was turning black and blue. Here, the bayonet had struck, its impact breaking the rib. Then it had glanced off and pierced his abdomen. The wound itself was not so deep as she'd expected, but it had caused a great loss of blood.

"Bring caldron!" Crow Woman cried to Two Fires.

Two Fires lifted it from the fire and set it down nearby on a small flat stone. Crow Woman took the piece of wood Rebecca had used to stir with and poked around in the pot. "Get other stick!" she barked, and Two Fires pulled one out of a little stack of firewood and handed it to her. Crow Woman attempted to lift the mass of Horse Tail between the two sticks, but her hands were shaking so with fatigue or nervousness she couldn't quite manage it.

"You see what it is to be old?" she snapped. "Here—you do this too."

"Do what?" Rebecca cried. "Surely, you don't mean to take that out of boiling water and put it on the wound! Haven't we hurt him enough already?"

"Pah!" The old woman grunted scornfully. "He not a child. He prepare for this day from the very hour of his birth. Were he captive of Shawnee or Iroquois, they kindle fire on his stomach—and like any Miami warrior, he tell them it not be hot enough.''

"Savages. Barbarians," Rebecca muttered, but she took the two sticks from the old woman, and lifting the steaming mass of stems, held them dripping for a moment. Then she hoisted them onto Kin-di-wa's stomach wound.

"Aaaaaaah!" he moaned, twitching from head to foot.

"I'm sorry!" Rebecca cried. "Dear God, I'm sorry!"

The sticks fell from her hands as a fit of shuddering overcame her. She scrambled to her feet and lurched away from Kin-di-wa's pallet. "You'll have to do the rest. I can't hurt him anymore."

"Pah!" Crow Woman grunted. "White women have weak stomachs. Get awl and length of sinew. I sew up other wound myself."

Rebecca stumbled out of the lean-to, fighting sudden dizziness. She had to get away. She couldn't help it. Nothing in her life had prepared her for this; she was unsuited for it. But she stood there, breathing deeply, and thinking: in a moment, I'll go back. He needs me so I *must* go back.

In an effort to get hold of herself, she walked a short distance to the banks of Swan Creek. The morning air was still, and to the east, the sky glowed a fiery red. The day promised to be warm but less humid than it had been. In the depths of the marsh, waterfowl were calling. Wings whirred nearby, and a flock of honking geese tilted up into the sky.

How is it possible life can go on as if nothing has happened? she wondered. A man lays suffering—possibly dying, while all around him life hurries onward.

A wood duck and its mate glided across the smooth surface of the stream. The hen was a dark mottled brown with a distinctive white ring around each of her eyes, and her chin, throat, and belly were also splashed with white.

But it was the male who arrested Rebecca's attention: much showier than the female, the drake wore a crest of irridescent plumage on its head with two parallel white stripes from its bill to the tip of its crest. His eyes and the base of his bill glowed reddish orange, and a V-shaped white patch extended from his chin up the sides of his head.

Fingers of black and white separated his wine-colored chest from his bronze-colored sides, and his back and tail—of deep dark purple—contrasted sharply with his white breast and belly.

How beautiful he is! she thought, like a Miami warrior in all his war paint and feathered finery.

But, unlike watching a man decked out for war, she felt a sense of peace watching the wood duck skimming effortlessly across the water. She knew that after the first frost, he and his mate would wing their way. south, returning again in the spring to make their nest along the creek.

She wished she and Kin-di-wa could live so simply—disturbed only by the passage of the seasons. But of course, the wood duck had his enemies too, the greatest of whom was man. In man's quest for a tasty meal or a sheltered home, he became the enemy of nearly everything—most of all of himself. For a place to plant his crops or bury his dead, he'd kill even his own brother.

Sighing, she turned to go back to the lean-to. Even such refreshment as nature provided was lost when she considered the nature of man. But she would try now to be much stronger. She'd pray every day for more strength. Kin-di-wa would need her badly in the days and weeks to come. She mustn't shame him with her weakness.

And suddenly, she couldn't bear the thought of Crow Woman or Two Fires touching him. She herself would provide for all his needs. After all, *she* was the wife of his heart—not just of his body. And Two Fires would have enough other things to keep her occupied.

She broke into a run and came to the lean-to just in time to find Crow Woman tying off the last stitch in Kin-di-wa's upper arm wound.

"So. Your courage return. Has it not?" Crow Woman cocked her grizzled white head.

"Yes. I can do whatever needs doing now." And Rebecca was amazed to discover she *did* feel stronger. The walk in the marsh had been exactly what she needed.

"You help bind up his rib then." The old woman passed several lengths of rawhide under Kin-di-wa's back, while Peshewa lifted him slightly. She showed Rebecca how to pull each one tightly across his chest and how to knot them around a small stick, which could then be twisted to draw the bands even tighter.

Kin-di-wa lay limply, as if feeling little—and for this Rebecca was grateful. It was easier to work over him now, when she wasn't causing pain.

Crow Woman grunted her satisfaction. "There —we finished. Now, it up to Manitou."

"Isn't there anything else?" Rebecca studied Kin-di-wa's stomach wound, wondering if the poultice was helping.

"Tea." The old woman gestured to the caldron. "Give him tea—a mouthful—whenever he awakens. Later, we make poultices from bark of the slippery elm to put on all his wounds. Slippery elm keep away rot. And when fever comes, we use another herb for that."

"Fever? Will he come down with fever too?"

Crow Woman's head bobbed. "Fever always follow wounds. I must find Five Finger Grass and Birth Root too. If Horse Tail doesn't stop bleeding, we try remedy for bleeding in child birth. Birth Root very good, and not so hard to find. But first, I eat. Then lie down and sleep. You care for him now? You feeling better?"

"Yes," Rebecca admitted. "And I won't run away again."

"That good," the old woman grinned tooth-lessly. "We make Miami squaw out of you yet."

She got to her feet and moved off toward a mat Two Fires had spread out in a corner of the lean-to. Two Fires gave her some dried berries and vegetables to eat, then the old woman curled up, sighed deeply, and was instantly asleep.

Peshewa came up to Rebecca as she sat watching Kin-di-wa's chest rise and fall with a jerky uneasy rhythm. She looked up to find him watching her intently.

"You sleep too," he said. "Two Fires watch Kin-di-wa."

Rebecca shook her head. "I want to watch him myself."

"Two squaws in lodge. Two young squaws and one old one. Two can sleep while one watches."

"I—I'm all right now. I'm not even tired."

Peshewa leaned over and touched Kin-di-wa's forehead with his palm. "No fever yet. You must save strength for fever."

Under the war paint and dirt which were smeared together, Peshewa's face looked strangely gentle, as if a mask had dropped away—or perhaps she was merely seeing him closely for the first time. Even his bright red quills struck her as somehow less absurd.

"Until Kin-di-wa hunt again, I keep this lodge in meat," he promised. "I help build new lodge too—make ready for winter. But—" He held up his hand to forestall her protests. "I no longer send presents."

"Oh, Peshewa!" She hardly knew what to say to this man she had first insulted with false flattery and then rejected. What *could* one say—when he was now proving his kindness and friendship far more than was really necessary or expected?

"Presents all destroyed by Chenoten anyway," he grunted. "And *Sieur de Richardville* no can ask white woman to share his lodge without presents."

"Of course. I understand. Kin-di-wa is indeed fortunate to have a friend such as you, Peshewa. And the woman you one day marry will also be very fortunate."

"I go now. Come back later with meat."

Rebecca thought of the two beautiful wood ducks on the creek but didn't mention them. At the moment, game was still plentiful, and she'd hate to see them killed. Then, as Peshewa left the lean-to, Two Fires came up and sat beside her, offering her a handful of dried berries.

So here we are, Rebecca thought. Two wives watching over one husband. But surprisingly, she could summon up no resentment or jealousy. If Kin-di-wa lived, it would be as much because of Two Fires and Peshewa—two people she had no right to scorn—as because of herself or Crow Woman.

Two Fires idly smoothed back Kin-di-wa's hair, her lovely face betraying less emotion than a flower.

436

But does she feel about him as I do? Rebecca wondered. Or am I once again misjudging?

She herself smoothed back his hair, deliberately refusing to acknowledge the possessiveness of the gesture. What did it matter how Two Fires felt? Only *one* thing mattered: Kin-di-wa *must* not die.

Sixteen

On the fourth day, Kin-di-wa's fever set in. Rebecca had somehow hoped to avoid it by spending three whole days dribbling tea down his throat, flooding his stomach wound with tea, and almost hourly changing his poultices, until even Crow Woman objected: the patient might die from over-care.

Horse Tail, Birth Root, Five Finger Grass— Rebecca tried them all, then hounded Crow Woman for more. But nothing seemed to stop the fire building up within him.

"Don't you know any remedies to *prevent* this fever? Two Fires knows herbs to keep us from getting the fever the Saginwash suffer from!"

"This fever different," Crow Woman insisted. "Is test of Kin-di-wa's strength. If he strong, he live. If not, he die. When body suffer great injury, fever always follow. Is nothing we can do to stop it—but now, I go find herbs to *cure* it!"

And off she went again into the marsh and forest, leaving Rebecca to lay cool wet cloths on Kin-di-wa's burning brow and to murmur endearments when his eyes flew open, and he cried out in the throes of a feverish nightmare.

The mere thought of fever filled Rebecca with terror. Mama had died of it, though her fever had been one more closely related to the debilitating summer malady suffered by the British. Rebecca well remembered the alternating horrors of fiery heat and icy cold to which the victim was subjected.

All day, she watched helplessly as Kin-di-wa's skin grew hotter and redder, as if his blood were boiling. And no matter how often she moistened his lips, they grew drier—so dry, they cracked.

No longer did he recognize her, as he had once or twice when he awoke—white-lipped with pain and groping feebly for her hand. Now, his blue eyes were so glazed over, they reminded her of the eyes of a china doll Aunt Margaret had once sent for her birthday.

Rebecca examined each of his wounds hourly, searching for some sign of infection or "rot" as Crow Woman called it. But she found no swelling, no pus, and no smell of spoiling flesh. At least, the bark of the slippery elm tree seemed to be doing its job. Crow Woman claimed her poultices drew out evil spirits, but if pus *did* appear, she planned to suck the wound, another good Indian remedy.

Of course, Crow Woman also claimed her incantations were assisting Kin-di-wa, but Rebecca placed no more faith in them than she did in her own prayers. Where was God—Manitou, the Great Spirit, or whatever He was called—through all of this? she wondered. Why did He allow such suffering?

In the following days, Kin-di-wa's fever took on a pattern. In the mornings, he had fits of shivering that no amount of skins or furs piled atop him could allay. His eyes grew sunken, his hands cold and clammy, and his teeth chattered so loud Rebecca could hear them. Even his fingernails turned blue.

But by the afternoons, he had grown hot again, and by the evenings, he was burning up. Sometimes, Rebecca had to tie his hands to keep him from tearing out his stitches or clawing open his slowly healing wounds.

Sometimes, she had to send Two Fires after Peshewa to help hold him down. For at such times, Kin-di-wa ranted and raved as if he'd been bitten by a mad dog. Usually, Rebecca could make no sense of his ravings—but once, she knew he was reliving the day his mother had been murdered.

Over and over, he called her name, *"Min-gi-a!*

Min-gi-a! Mother! Mother!"

The sound echoed through the marsh like the cry of a lost man-child, and even Two Fires was unable to stand it. She snatched up little Walks-Tall who'd been watching and listening in wide-eyed fascination and hurried out of the lean-to.

On any given day, the fever would die down after midnight, result in chills by dawn, and then begin its slow steady climb back upward. Rebecca took to sleeping curled up next to Kin-di-wa so she could warm him with her own body when he began to shiver or cool him with splashes of water when he began to burn. She couldn't bear to leave him—even for a moment.

But by evening of the tenth day, Rebecca was so exhausted her hands were shaking, and the world outside the perimeter of sturdy saplings, covered over with mats and branches, looked blurred and unreal—almost dreamlike.

Sweet Breeze came into the lean-to, knelt down beside her, and shook her head. Rebecca, knowing she must look terrible, vainly tried to straighten her torn doeskin and smooth down her braid.

"Here," Sweet Breeze said. "I bring you new doeskin. That one shame you. It stained with blood and torn so bad it not worth keeping."

"Thank you," Rebecca mumbled. "I'll change into it later."

"Cat-Eyes . . . you must let Two Fires care for

442

Kin-di-wa. You half-dead from kneeling here—not sleeping. Not much eating.''

"If Kin-di-wa can stand this suffering, so can I."
Rebecca reached over and determinedly adjusted a pad of damp rawhide on Kin-di-wa's forehead. Kin-di-wa tossed his head restlessly, muttering snatches of a chant.

"But Kin-di-wa belong to Two Fires too. It be her right to care for him.''

"Has she complained to you?" Rebecca asked.

"No—but she proper wife. I know what she thinking!"

Rebecca wondered if anyone could know what Two Fires was thinking. "Two Fires *is* caring for him," she argued. "In her own way. She does all the food gathering, except for the meat Peshewa brings us, and she does the cooking. She also cleans the lean-to and takes care of little Walks-Tall. And she's helping Peshewa build a lodge for us. She has enough to do!"

Sweet Breeze moved a small caldron of water closer to Rebecca so she wouldn't have to reach so far to dampen her rawhide. "Then why you no let Crow Woman watch over him—while you sleep?"

"Crow Woman has been very helpful too. I don't know what we would have done without her. But people come here everyday, asking for her—she can't spend *all* her time on Kin-di-wa.''

"But Crow Woman sleeps here. Does she not? Why you no let her take turns watching Kin-di-wa at night?"

"Crow Woman is very old!" Rebecca snapped. "She gets very tired—too tired to treat wounded warriors all day and still sit up with one all night."

"Then *I* come sit with him from now on."

"No!" Rebecca's patience was at an end. "You shouldn't even suggest it. Do you think I don't know what work there is for *you* to do? The whole camp was destroyed. Hundreds of braves were killed, and I don't know how many more were wounded! The crops have all been burned, and no one but us has shelter. Haven't you enough to keep you busy? Must you come and lecture me as if I were a child?"

Sweet Breeze looked away. "Your tongue grows very sharp, Cat-Eyes. Mayhap, I should not come here at all."

"I—I'm sorry," Rebecca apologized. "It's just that I want—I *need* to look after Kin-di-wa myself. Wouldn't you feel the same if *Apekonit* had been wounded?"

Sweet Breeze nodded grudgingly. "You right. I no let anyone touch him but me. But I know Two Fires love Kin-di-wa too. It *not* right you keep her from him."

"I'm *not* keeping her from him. We share the same lean-to. She can sit with him anytime she wants!"

444

"But you no let her sit with him alone. When she sit, you sit too. Same time." Sweet Breeze pointed out.

Rebecca sighed. What was the use of arguing? In her heart, she'd made peace with the idea of sharing Kin-di-wa—but until his fever broke, she'd leave his side as little as possible. "Tell me what is happening with Chenoten and the Saginwash. And your father too."

Now, it was Sweet Breeze who sighed. "Chenoten gone, taking all his Long Knives with him."

"Gone! Already?"

"What need for him to stay? There be no more war parties now. Starving Indians do not fight."

"No one's starving yet! I should think he'd want to remain just to make certain the Saginwash don't try to reorganize the tribes."

"Saginwash! Pah! Not one of them fight— excepting Colonel McKee, Simon Girty, and a few others. But not Major Campbell or his soldiers. And now, they stagger around Fort Miamis, falling down with fever. Chenoten know he need not be afraid of Saginwash."

"And the tribes? Is there no one willing or able to lead them?"

"Turkey Foot dead. Blue Jacket take his Shaw- nees and go back home. Tarhee, the Crane, take his Ottawas, and Buckongahelas his Delawares. There be no one left but my father—" Sweet Breeze's voice broke, and Rebecca thought sadly of Little

Turtle whom she hadn't seen since the day of the battle.

What had happened to him? Had this defeat—which he'd tried so hard to prevent—made him ill or sick at heart?

Sniffing, Sweet Breeze recovered her composure. "Miamis no longer have home to go to, or we be gone now too. Kekionga destroyed—all our lodges, corn, vegetables—everything. There be nothing left."

Rebecca's heart twisted with sympathy. "What are your people going to do? I mean, what are *our* people going to do?"

"We stay here through winter. Live as best we can. It no use now try to rebuild Kekionga. Too many wounded . . . And not enough time before winter. Besides, maybe Saginwash give us food and blankets."

"But won't there be a treaty council? There still needs to be a written agreement between the tribes and the Long Knives—even if it's just a formality confirming what lands have already been taken!"

"Chenoten say he send for us—after winter. He call treaty council in summer, after crops be planted."

"Oh!" Rebecca snorted. "You mean if the Miamis survive starvation, he'll gladly meet with them—to say *he* now owns the crops they've planted!"

"Yes," Sweet Breeze whispered. "He win. We lose. Now, we must pay. And if anyone still feel desire to fight Chenoten, winter take it out of them."

That night, Rebecca sensed Kin-di-wa had reached a point of crisis. His fever soared so high it burned her hand to touch his forehead. He tossed and turned and moaned on the pallet, jerking his head from side to side.

"Ka-ta-mon-gli! Ka-ta-mon-gli!" His hoarse cries filled the air. Before, in his delirium, he'd called his dead mother—now, he called his dead brother.

Rebecca looked up from sponging off his body to find Two Fires staring at him, her eyes twin moons of shock and fear. Walks-Tall, alarmed by his mother's expression, clung to her skirt, wailing. But before Rebecca could say anything, Kin-di-wa suddenly jolted upright to a sitting position, oblivious to his injuries.

"Ka-ta-mon-gli!" he screamed. Then he looked at Rebecca and asked clearly, "Where is my brother, Black Loon?"

"Lie down," she begged, pressing him back down onto the pallet. "You'll hurt yourself even more."

Kin-di-wa clutched his broken rib and fell backwards, groaning through parched lips. "When I find the man who murdered my brother, I

447

will kill him!'' His glazed blue eyes opened and closed. Opened and closed.

Then, they opened and focused on Rebecca. "Hah! I know you! You are he—the one who killed my brother!''

"Kin-di-wa, hush now. Be still. It's me—Cat-Eyes! Don't you know me?''

Kin-di-wa's hand shot up and grabbed her braid which was hanging down over her shoulder. "Why do you wear this necklace of fingers—if you are *not* the one I seek? My brother's murderer wore such a necklace!''

For one so ill, Kin-di-wa's grip was unbelievably strong. Rebecca sought to disengage his hand. "That's no necklace. You're holding my hair! Let go, Kin-di-wa, let go, and I'll bring some herbal tea to soothe you.''

But Kin-di-wa held fast to her braid. "Do you think I shall free you now—when I have found you at last? Where is my knife? Where is my war club? Prepare to die, you dog!''

"You must lie still!" Rebecca cried as Kin-di-wa tried once more to sit up.

She was about to call for Peshewa or Crow Woman to help restrain him, when she remembered that there was no one else nearby but Two Fires and little Walks-Tall. Crow Woman had gone to stay the night with the family of another wounded brave at the new camp, and Peshewa was at his mother's new lodge on the river—where he was also building a new lodge for them.

"Two Fires!" she called. "Can you come and help me? He won't lie still, and he's got hold of my braid!"

She twisted around to see if Two Fires had heard her. The girl was standing there silently, watching, her wailing son hanging onto her skirts. She seemed to be frozen with some raw emotion: fear or grief or both.

"Two Fires!" Rebecca repeated. She suddenly realized she'd been speaking in English, and she switched instead to the Miami tongue. "Come and help me!"

Then Kin-di-wa pulled so hard on her braid, Rebecca's head was forced down. His other hand came up and reached around her throat. His thumb pressed into her windpipe, and she caught sight of his brilliant blue eyes—glittering like a mad man's. "T—Two Fires! Hurry! He means to kill me!"

But the last half of her plea was shut off, along with her air, as Kin-di-wa pressed in sharply with his thumb.

How was it possible he could be so strong! Or was she merely too weak to fight him? She struggled to pull his hand away, afraid of falling on him and reopening his wounds, but his thumb pressed harder and harder, reminding her of that awful day when Simon Girty had almost choked her.

A shower of sparks fell over her—twinkling like tiny stars. A roaring assaulted her ears. She made one last effort to pull away, to fight off the waves of blackness. Then blackness swooped over her like an outflung bearskin, and she felt herself falling—falling, and her head struck something hard. There was a moment's lance of pain, then—nothing.

Rebecca heard a baby crying in the far off distance. The sound came closer, and she knew it was Walks-Tall, crying as he never did. What was wrong? What was happening? Two Fires never allowed him to cry like that. At his first whimper, she usually came running. Then Rebecca heard another sound: the abandoned weeping of a woman.

Kin-di-wa is *dead!* she thought. The only reason Two Fires would weep so terribly is because Kin-di-wa is dead.

She opened her eyes and found herself lying beside Kin-di-wa's pallet, her body across his one arm and an overturned caldron beside her. She rolled over and took his hand; it felt so cool! And he was lying so incredibly still, his head turned away from her, his body relaxed.

He *must* be dead, she thought. Before, he'd been burning up with fever, and every breath he took had rattled inside his chest.

Over and over, Two Fires moaned, "Ka-ta-mon-gli! Ka-ta-mon-gli!''

Rebecca's heart skipped a beat. Two Fires was mourning Black Loon—not Kin-di-wa!

She got to her knees and bent over him, but the fire had so died down, it was difficult to see him clearly. She placed her ear to his chest. His heart beat was strong and steady, his breathing calm and regular. A soft sheen of perspiration lay across his forehead and upper lip. He wasn't dead—his fever had simply broken.

"Kin-di-wa!" she cried joyfully.

He turned his head. His eyes fluttered open. In the dim flickering light, they shone a clear lucid blue. "Cat-Eyes, little Cat-Eyes . . ." he whispered, then he closed his eyes again and fell into a long deep sleep.

Each day after that, Kin-di-wa grew a little stronger. His color improved, his eyes looked less sunken, his bones protruded less through his skin. But he remained as weak as a newborn baby. Any movement at all exhausted him.

Rebecca fed him herbal teas and broth—from whatever meat Peshewa brought them, and she pounded berries, roots, and acorns into small flat cakes, wishing she had more to give him. But Two Fires's store of dried corn and vegetables had dwindled down to nothing, and there was little else to be found.

Two Fires herself was once again calm and quiet

and industrious, her feelings carefully re-hidden. But Rebecca sometimes watched her covertly. How long had the girl kept her emotions sealed up tightly inside her? Was this the first time she'd actually wept over her dead husband?

The mere mention of his name on Kin-di-wa's lips had somehow unleashed a storm of grief that ought to have been spent a long time past. What other feelings was she holding back? What *was* she thinking behind those enormous, black-fringed eyes?

Any other time, Rebecca might have held it against Two Fires for not responding to her cry for help, but if Kin-di-wa himself had died, she wondered how it might have affected her.

Nor did she worry that Kin-di-wa had almost killed her. The fever had made him crazy, "loco" as Crow Woman called it. But now, the craziness and delirium were behind him, and despite the shaky future ahead, Rebecca felt recklessly confident.

She nursed and fed and cared for Kin-di-wa, as if he were indeed a newborn baby—and she a brand new mother. No task was too large or too small. Hoping to draw a wan smile from him, she even tried to do things for him before they became necessary.

"Can I bring you another cake? Would you like more tea? Can I comb your hair? Is there anything else you want?" she would ask.

He'd only taken a mouthful of the first cake, a single sip of his tea, and she'd combed out his hair twice that day already.

No, he would shake his head, but he rarely smiled and more rarely spoke, though, as he grew stronger, his eyes followed her everywhere. Often, she awoke to find him lying there and watching her. And for the moment, it was enough.

Then the day came when she began to think of moving into the new lodge. The previous night had been shivery cold, and the morning fog was thick as stew. Rebecca guessed it must be late September or early October for the trees were splashed with red and yellow, and she was suddenly seized with foreboding: time was slipping away so quickly.

Soon, the trees would be stripped and bare, the winds would blow cold, and the creek would freeze over. There was so much still to be done before winter; the moving must take place this very day.

First, everything had to be carried out of the marsh and down to the river, where the bare bones of the new lodge awaited them. She sent Two Fires and Crow Woman on ahead, laden as heavily as pack horses. Then it was time to deal with Kin-di-wa.

She knelt down beside him and smiled encouragingly. "Shall I send for Peshewa now? The two of us carried you here all the way from the fort, so we can surely carry you back to the river."

Kin-di-wa's mouth set stubbornly. "It is time I walked."

"But you are still so weak!" Rebecca protested. Kin-di-wa had been sitting up and feeding himself, and once he'd gotten to his feet and swayed there dizzily, but he wasn't yet ready for walking.

"I am a man—not a child. Remember?"

And Rebecca was reminded of Crow Woman telling her the exact same thing. "All right," she agreed. "But if you feel dizzy, you must lie down again, and I will get Peshewa."

"If I feel dizzy, I shall wait till it passes—but I will *not* lie down again."

Rebecca helped Kin-di-wa to his feet, noticing that his lips blanched white with pain, as he leaned against her body. He stood still for a moment, taller than she remembered, but thin and gaunt as a skeleton, his once vibrant black hair hanging limp on his shoulders.

Then he shook his head as if to clear his vision. "You *are* dizzy!" she exclaimed. "This is foolishness. Come lie back down and I'll go get help."

"No!" he muttered between clenched teeth. "Let go! I don't need help."

Stung to the quick, Rebecca stepped back. Kin-di-wa swayed but didn't collapse. He took a step, then two steps. She backed out of the lean-to in front of him. His face was white as birch wood, and he held onto his wrapped broken rib as if the pain were excruciating. "Kin-di-wa, this isn't necessary! What do you have to prove?"

His eyes glowed with a spark of their old deep-shadowed fire. "Pick up the rest of our things," he ordered. "You will walk ahead of me to our new lodge. And if I stumble and fall, you will not turn back. You will not stop and wait. Of what use is a man who must lean on a squaw?"

Rebecca had many answers to give this question, but they were answers that would make sense only to another woman. She stomped back into the lean-to, picked up the remaining bundles and folded mats, and set out ahead of him on the path.

By the time Kin-di-wa made it down to the river on his own, the new lodge was complete in all its comforts. Indeed, because of Two Fires's foresight in hiding their belongings both underground at Roche de Boeuf and later in the marsh, the lodge was more complete than any others in the camp.

Rebecca almost felt guilty as she helped Two Fires lash the last reed mat in place. Most of the other new lodges in the immediate vicinity—fifty or sixty of them—still lacked enough mats and skins to keep out heavy weather.

But as she saw Kin-di-wa coming toward her, step by weary step, her sense of guilt evaporated. Every muscle in her body wanted to run and help him, but she held herself in check. At least, if he insisted on walking—through sheer determination rather than strength!—there was now a warm sheltered place for him to lie down and rest, and a pot of broth bubbling over the lodge-fire.

Kin-di-wa made his way to the pallet inside the lodge and lowered himself down with a deep ragged sigh. Rebecca ran to dip out a bowl of steaming broth with bits of meat swimming in it. "Here! Peshewa found an elk last evening. Now, we have food aplenty to make you strong again."

He took the bowl in an unsteady hand. "Take the meat he gave us and divide it among the others."

"Others?"

"My people," he grunted. "Other squaws and children whose husbands and fathers are dead. I am still alive—and from this moment on, my family will eat no meat but what I bring home to them."

"Kin-di-wa, that doesn't make sense! You can't go hunting yet! And Peshewa *has* been dividing his meat. He brought only enough to feed you and me and Two Fires and Crow Woman. With some left over for Walks-Tall—but he doesn't eat much."

Kin-di-wa glared at her between slurps of broth. He finished the bowl and put it down. "Go and tell Two Fires to divide the meat. She will know who

needs it most. Then go and find Peshewa. It is time
I made my plans.''

Plans! Rebecca was so shocked she couldn't
argue. What plans could he be thinking of? He'd
just climbed off a pallet upon which he'd nearly
died, and already he was talking plans! Without so
much as saying please or thank you—or anything
else!

Blinded with sudden tears, she arose and stalked
out of the lodge. How could he be so insensitive—
so—so hopelessly savage, stubborn, and uncaring?

Down to the river bank she went. If he is now so
strong, she thought, he can go find Peshewa
himself.

But as she came to the river, where the trees were
turning golden, and the murmur of the creek
could be heard as it flowed out into the Miami of
the Lake, the anger drained from her. She stopped
and wiped away her tears, looking about with
surprised recognition. Somewhere near here, upriver further, Simon Girty had surprised her two
days before the battle.

Simon Girty. Whatever had happened to him?
She'd been so busy worrying about Kin-di-wa,
she'd practically forgotten the man who raped her
while she lay unconscious. And thinking of him
made her think of Will: they belonged together in
the same awful thoughts.

Her hands flew protectively up to her breasts.
Her body was now sheathed in new soft doeskin,

the smock Sweet Breeze had somehow found for her, but still, for a moment, she wanted to race back to Kin-di-wa. She wanted desperately to feel his arms around her, to know the peace and safety she remembered having always found there.

There was only one problem: since that night when he'd made love to her before the battle, he hadn't *put* his arms around her.

She'd been waiting and longing for him to do so, but thus far he hadn't even told her how much he appreciated all she'd done for him. Now— when he was feeling better—did he no longer need her? Somehow, the last thing she'd expected from him was this sudden resentment and hostility—as if she were responsible for everything that had happened.

The thought arose unbidden: *did* he hold her responsible? Was he transferring to her all the anger and hate he must feel toward her people?

No, she argued with herself, Kin-di-wa could never be so unfair. He only resented his helplessness. And knowing him as well as she did, she ought to be more understanding. A man so brave and proud and strong as Kin-di-wa must find it doubly hard to discover himself only human.

She wandered along the bank a short distance, finding peace and comfort in her surroundings. The scenery still bore scars from Anthony Wayne's awful vengeance, but even the smoke-blackened trees and grasses seemed to speak to her as she passed. "We will grow strong again," they promised. "We will grace the land with our beauty."

She came to a solitary tree, flaming crimson among the gold, and paused beneath it—allowing herself to feel one with the river, the tree, and the sky. This land was part of her now, she reflected. She'd been earning her place in it with every moment of sadness and suffering she'd experienced since she crossed the mountains with Papa!

What was it Kin-di-wa had said to her once? "You will find that my land is beautiful, worth fighting for, worth dying for. It has always been so—the land will claim you. In time you will feel as I do. In time, you will love this land."

I *do* love it, she realized. I love it more than I ever thought possible. And suddenly, she understood what Kin-di-wa was doing by making plans. He was acclaiming to her and to everyone that he had not been defeated. The battle had been lost, the Miamis brought low. They had even been betrayed. Their villages and crops and more than half their young men were dead and gone. *But the land itself was still here!*

The land was strong. The land endured. And Kin-di-wa, whose soul and spirit was in this land, was also looking forward—not back. Did he mean to reorganize the tribes himself? To somehow devise a peace strategy?

459

Kin-di-wa! Her brave strong Kin-di-wa! After all he'd been through, he refused to give up.

Back along the riverbank she went, racing for the lodge. If Kin-di-wa could pull himself together and make plans, she could surely do the same. She'd never even told him she'd changed her mind about going back to Philadelphia.

Of course, he must assume it—after all these weeks, how could he not? But now, he must hear it from her, and he must share with her what he was thinking. Whatever he wanted to do, she'd be right there at this side: his wife and help-mate, the way she was meant to be.

She skidded into the lodge, breathless from surging happiness. How good it felt to be filled with purpose! Then she saw Peshewa, seated beside Kin-di-wa.

The two men looked up, and Kin-di-wa grunted reproachfully. "I had to send Two Fires to bring my friend, since *you* would not bring him to me."

"I'm sorry. I—forgot."

He motioned for her to come closer. "But it is well you returned when you did. Now, you will be pleased to hear what has been decided about your future."

"My future?" Her heart thudded with glad anticipation. She didn't even mind they weren't alone!

"It is time I kept my promise, Cat-Eyes—time I took you home. But since I cannot take you myself,

460

Peshewa has agreed to take you. You leave as soon as possible: tomorrow—when you awaken."

"What? What did you say?"

Kin-di-wa's blue eyes were unwavering. "Tomorrow," he repeated. "Tomorrow, you are going home."

Seventeen

Rebecca could only stand there, too stunned to object or argue. Two Fires came in behind her, bringing Walks-Tall by the hand. At sight of her, the baby crowed a greeting and grabbed hold of the fringed edge of her doeskin.

"You had best prepare your things," Kin-di-wa said. "Peshewa wishes to leave early."

"I—I have nothing to prepare," Rebecca mumbled. "I came with nothing, have you forgotten?"

"But it is a long journey back. You will need a buffalo robe or a blanket. Also, a good knife. Two Fires will give you whatever you need."

"Where—where will Peshewa take me?"

"Back to your cabin. I have told him where it is. Or if you prefer, he can take you further down the Muskingum to Fort Harmar. From there, you can find someone who is going to Philadelphia."

Rebecca looked around the lodge. How could she speak freely in front of Two Fires and Peshewa? Yet she must. "What if I don't want to go?"

Kin-di-wa's lip curled scornfully. It didn't seem to bother him one bit that other eyes were watching. "Before the battle, when I was strong and whole, you made it clear you could never stay here. Now, when I am weak and broken, how is it you have changed your mind?"

Walks-Tall tugged at her skirt, demanding her attention. Rebecca looked down at the baby's bright eyes, his happy smile, then back at Kin-di-wa's scowling face. "Kin-di-wa, I don't think now is the time for us to discuss this. You are only just getting better! We've just moved into a new lodge, and we have to prepare for winter. We haven't even had any time alone—to talk, to plan, to even think!"

"It is the only time to discuss it. Winter will not wait on a woman's foolishness. Soon, the water-fowl will all be gone. The deer and elk will move further into the forest. Already, they are disappearing. I myself have a wife and a son to feed— and someone must take care of Crow Woman. I have no need of another hungry mouth!"

Rebecca felt as if she'd been struck. Was that what she had become to him—a hungry mouth?

But before she could respond, Kin-di-wa lifted his hand in a despairing gesture. "Once, I thought it could be different between us. I thought your heart could be won by a proud Miami warrior. But I am proud no longer. My eyes have been opened by defeat. You do not belong here, Cat-Eyes. Go home to your people. If you stay with us, you will only starve."

Rebecca found her voice at last. "But I *want* to stay! I *have* changed my mind, Kin-di-wa! I was coming back just now to tell you this."

Kin-di-wa's eyes turned icy blue. "Do you speak from your heart—or from your pity?"

"Kin-di-wa! I—" Forgetting about Walks-Tall clinging to her skirt, Rebecca took a step forward, and the baby tumbled backward. Unthinkingly, she swept him up as he let out an angry howl.

"Give the child to his mother, Cat-Eyes. He belongs to her—not to you."

And Rebecca heard the unspoken implication: so also did Kin-di-wa.

She shoved the howling baby into Two Fires's arms. The girl looked startled, not triumphant, but Rebecca was too close to the edge of hysteria to wonder what she was thinking. "Take him then!" she shouted in the Miami language. She spun around to face Kin-di-wa. "Take *both* of them! I hope they break your heart as you've broken mine!"

Then she dashed out of the lodge.

She spent a miserable cold night in the old lean-to in the marsh, refusing to go back until morning. But in the cold clear light of dawn, after hours of

465

alternately raging and weeping, she came to realize Kin-di-wa was right. She did not belong among people who didn't want her, people who threw away love and friendship as soon as disaster struck.

She'd been prepared to accept it all: defeat, hard times, the bitter cold of winter—and sharing him with Two Fires. But he could not accept her. His foolish arrogant pride would not allow her to love him unless he was all that he had been. To him, she was still the outsider, one of the enemy who'd stolen his lands and defeated his people. Now, when he was hurt and wounded, he retreated among his own and deliberately shut her out.

As she retraced her steps through the marsh, she thought about how he'd even made it impossible for her to plead with him to let her stay. How clever he had been! If she begged to stay now, she'd be taking food right out of their mouths. Yes, his strategy had been faultless. What a fine successor to Turkey Foot he would make—now, that it was too late for anymore strategies!

She found Peshewa, Two Fires, and Crow Woman awaiting her at the lodge. Peshewa was already dressed in leggings for the journey. He carried a wrapped bundle under one arm, and a musket, bow, and quiver, slung across his back. When he saw her, his red quills shook impatiently, signaling that he thought it long past time to be leaving.

Kin-di-wa was nowhere to be seen. Was he

hoping to avoid any last moment arguments?

Two Fires handed her a *mocuck,* filled with food and other provisions, and gestured to a rolled up buffalo robe. She kept her eyes and her face lowered, unwilling as usual to betray her feelings.

But Crow Woman came up sorrowfully. The wrinkles around her mouth and on her forehead slanted downward in a frown. "I am sad to see you go." She took Rebecca's free hand and turned it palm upwards. "This hand be made for healing. It only wanted for you to find your courage."

And Rebecca was reminded of how often she'd been sickened by the sight of physical unpleasantness—but yes, she'd finally found her courage. Even more surprisingly, she saw now that she actually *did* enjoy learning about herbs and healing. "But without you," she hastened to point out, "Kin-di-wa would have died."

"Pah!" Crow Woman scoffed. "What I did was nothing! Kin-di-wa fortunate he had you to care for him . . . It too bad I no can teach you more: how to treat burns and broken bones, how to cure falling down sickness and body aches, how to deliver babies. You learn fastest of anyone I ever know."

Wishing she *could* learn more, Rebecca smiled at the tiny ugly woman with her toothless grin and wispy white hair. "You have taught me so much already. Your wisdom will travel with me—along with the moccasins you gave me once. Remember?" She lifted first one foot, then the other, to show she still wore them.

The old woman's eyes crinkled. She clawed at the pouch dangling around her neck. "I keep your hair always. Good strong medicine. Each time I use, it remind me of you."

Walks-Tall toddled over to her then, grinning as if yesterday's tears had never happened. Rebecca put down the *mocuck* and picked him up. His naked round body was warm in her arms. She studied his bright black eyes, the curve of his cheek, and his thatch of unruly black hair. A lump rose in her throat. She'd never see him again.

She pressed her cheek quickly to his and set him down on his own two feet. He stood there confidently, without wobbling, and she knew his name was well-chosen. Walks-Tall. She would remember him walking tall. Then she picked up her robe and her *mocuck* and turned to Peshewa, "I'm ready now, but—where is Kin-di-wa?"

Peshewa could not meet her eyes. "He take knife and go hunting."

So Kin-di-wa had not even waited to say goodbye. He'd gone off hunting instead. This did not surprise her, but his choice of weapons did. "He took only a knife?"

Peshewa shrugged. "Kin-di-wa can no draw back bow yet. No can fire musket. He take knife to cut vines and build snare. That he can do sitting down. Then he only need to wait."

Yes, she thought, he *would* know how to hunt, regardless of his weakness. At least, she'd been right about one thing: Kin-di-wa wasn't totally defeated.

She started to follow Peshewa out of the lean-to, then stopped and turned to Two Fires. "Goodbye, Two Fires. I'm sorry for what I said yesterday. I spoke in anger. And I wish you only happiness."

Two Fires lifted her face, her eyes luminous with unshed tears. "Rain," she said clearly in English. "Thank you."

Rebecca was stunned. After all that had happened, how could Two Fires remember those two single words she'd taught her? It seemed so long ago! And now that she and Two Fires were no longer rivals, Rebecca felt a surge of affection for the girl. "Yes, *wi-nik*. Thank you, *Wi-nik* for everything."

Rebecca hurried out of the lodge, following Peshewa through the clearing where the new lodges stood clustered like beehives. But they hadn't gotten far when someone called out behind them, "Cat-Eyes, wait!" Sweet Breeze came running after them.

Rebecca turned to Peshewa. "How did she know I was going? I—I hoped I wouldn't have to say goodbye to her!"

"I tell her," Peshewa grunted. "It no be right you leave without her knowing."

Sweet Breeze ran up breathlessly. "Cat-Eyes! I never forgive you if you leave without say goodbye!"

Rebecca dropped her belongings and reached

out to her friend. "Oh, Sweet Breeze, I'm sorry. But you were the last person I wanted to see."

Abandoning all her reserve, Sweet Breeze threw her arms around Rebecca, while Peshewa looked away uncomfortably.

Sweet Breeze sobbed in her ear. "Miami squaws not supposed to weep—to show feelings! But today I feel like white woman."

Stifling her own sobs, Rebecca drew back. She attempted to keep her face passive—the way Two Fires almost always managed. "No, it is right to conceal your feelings. Feelings are—nothing in the end."

Sweet Breeze's head jerked up. Her black eyes snapped. "Cat-Eyes, you must not be bitter because Kin-di-wa send you away."

"If he loved me, he wouldn't send me away."

"It for your own good, Cat-Eyes. He no want you to stay here and suffer. The rest of us—we Miamis. Have no place to go. Have no choice. But *you* have choice! So he send you back among your own people, where you be safe from harm."

Rebecca struggled against rising irritation. How could Sweet Breeze defend Kin-di-wa? Would she send her own husband away "for his own good?" Why did everyone set one standard for themselves—and a different one for her?

With an effort, she forced herself to remain calm and reasonable. "Let's not argue when we must say goodbye, my friend. I'm going to miss you too much as it is. I could never forgive myself if we parted in anger."

A tremulous smile hovered about Sweet Breeze's lips. She nodded to Peshewa who was waiting more or less patiently to one side. "My father wish to say goodbye to Cat-Eyes. You wait here a moment more?"

Peshewa grunted assent, and Sweet Breeze took Rebecca's hand and hurried her off into a grove of young elm trees. "My father have gift for you. Here . . ."

And Rebecca saw Little Turtle standing beneath a golden canopy of leaves and holding the reins to the halter of a small white war pony.

The old man was dressed as she'd first seen him: in embroidered leggings and breech clout, with silver earrings, brooches, and necklaces for ornament. Only his ceremonial feathered headdress was missing—and he looked a hundred years older.

Defeat had taken its toll on him in the final graying of his once black hair, the slight stoop in his once straight shoulders, and the haunted look in his once proud eyes. "So, little white woman. The time has come for you to leave us."

Rebecca shivered. Only the sound of his voice retained all the grandeur she remembered. It had even, if possible, grown deeper and more impressive. "I'm sorry to have to go," she said simply.

Little Turtle nodded. "But it is good you return to your people. When they speak of Fallen Timbers, tell them we fought bravely. Tell them

471

why we fought—why so many of us died. Four hundred, Cat-Eyes. Four hundred of my people, and thirty-three of yours."

Rebecca hadn't known until that moment the exact number of dead. "You may be sure I will tell them," she whispered fiercely. "I will tell them everything."

Little Turtle's eyes glowed in his weathered face. "That good. We need someone to tell our story. No one must forget Fallen Timbers—or the battles that went before. We fought only to keep what was ours: the land Manitou gave us. Tell your people Miamis not savages, as they call us. We flesh and blood—the same as you."

"I will do what I can," she promised. "But my people are very proud—and sometimes very stupid. They may not want to believe it."

"Even if you are only one voice—in your lodge, in your village—it better than none. Here . . ." he held out the reins to the pony. "You must take him on your journey. He will carry you a far distance, and if you cannot find game or other food, his flesh keep you alive."

Rebecca shook her head, refusing to take the reins. She fought to conceal the tears rushing to her eyes. "A Miami war pony should stay among the Miamis. You need him more than I do . . . goodbye, Little Turtle."

"Goodbye, little white woman, go with Manitou."

Rebecca hugged Sweet Breeze quickly, one last

time, then turned on her heel and hurried away. It was time she left—before her dignity shattered and she succumbed to the desire to throw herself on the ground, screaming and weeping with bitterness and lonely frustration. Oh, Kin-di-wa! Kin-di-wa! she wanted to cry. How can you send me away?

Two days later, she knelt in a grove of flaming crimson trees, collecting wood for a fire. It was late afternoon of a crisp and sunny October day, the Moon of the Falling Leaves, and Peshewa had left her to follow the delicate heart-shaped track of a white-tail.

Suddenly, she heard the gobble of a turkey calling its mate, and she looked up with sudden interest.

If Peshewa were not too far away, he might have heard it too! Her growling stomach would settle for turkey as well as venison. She straightened up and listened. The leaves behind her rustled. Something snorted. That was no turkey! She wheeled around.

A tall warrior on horseback was approaching. As the pony picked its way between the trees, the man swayed slightly, his warrior's body a dusky bronze, but lean and gaunt as a hungry wolf's.

Heart thudding wildly, she watched him come. His eyes shone a brilliant blue, and lines of fatigue edged his mouth and forehead. Two white feathers protruded bravely from his long black hair, and an embroidered band of rawhide neatly held the hair back from his face.

He kneed his pony toward her, one hand clutching his ribs which seemed to hurt him whenever he moved. Her glance fell on the fresh scars crisscrossing his entire body—livid streaks of red contrasting sharply with the pale dull white of older scars.

She longed to trace those scars with her fingertips, to gently kiss them and soothe away the memories of pain and suffering. She thought to herself: some would say his handsomeness had been destroyed, his strength reduced to a whisper, but I would say he's the most beautiful man I've ever seen.

He came up to her on the pony, then brought the animal to a halt. The leaves of the tree whose branches framed him were the color of a blood-red sunset. He gazed down at her, his eyes bluer than the October sky. "I cannot let you go, Cat-Eyes," was all he said.

She leaned her body against the pony's side and laid her head against the brave's wounded forearm. She was trembling from head to foot. "What will happen to us, Kin-di-wa?"

She felt his hand come down on her hair—stroking gently, smoothing back the wisps that had escaped her braid. "I do not know, little Cat-Eyes. Only Manitou can know our tomorrows."

"Will you send me away again—when next you are hurt or wounded? When your people face new difficulties? Whenever there is some part of your life you don't want me to share?"

"No. Never," he answered in a husky voice. "Without you, I have no reason to live. No reason to go on."

Tears slid down her cheeks as she lifted up her face. "Whatever the future holds, it is enough, Kin-di-wa. It is enough we are together."

He brushed the tears from her face with his thumb. "Yes," he whispered. "It is enough."

The wind gusted suddenly and blew down a swirl of crimson leaves, as if reminding them of the coming winter. Rebecca stepped over her pile of firewood, leaving it where it lay, and picked up her bundle and her robe. Then she set them down again, bent over, and made an arrangement with sticks on the ground.

"What are you doing?" Kin-di-wa asked.

She was surprised. He of all people ought to have guessed. "I am leaving a message to tell Peshewa where I have gone. You see?" She pointed to the arrangement of sticks. "They point in the direction of home—our home."

"That is an old Miami trick," he smiled. "But I do not remember having taught it to you."

She went up to him and took his hand. "Do you think you taught me everything? Some things I have learned on my own!"

He tilted up her face, bent down with a grimace of pain, and kissed her on the lips. Injured and weak, he might still be, she thought, but his kiss was firm and strong and possessive.

"Ah," he murmured. "There is still much I have to teach you, Cat-Eyes. As soon as I am able."

She slid her arms around his back to brace him, then returned his kiss with one of her own. And in it, she strove to remind him of the promise of the future—of joys and sorrows to come.

"We'll learn together," she whispered. "We'll experience it all—*together*."

Rebecca took the reins to the pony's halter and turned him around. She walked beside Kin-di-wa as they started their journey homeward. And all about them the forest flamed with glory—raining down swirls of crimson-gold leaves, like scattered jewels across their path.

THE BEST IN HISTORICAL ROMANCE

EXCITING BESTSELLERS FROM ZEBRA

PASSION'S REIGN by Karen Harper   (1177, $3.95)

Golden-haired Mary Bullen was wealthy, lovely and refined—and lusty King Henry VIII's prize gem! But her passion for the handsome Lord William Stafford put her at odds with the Royal Court. Mary and Stafford lived by a lovers' vow: one day they would be ruled by only the crown of PASSION'S REIGN.

HEIRLOOM by Eleanora Brownleigh   (1200, $3.95)

The surge of desire Thea felt for Charles was powerful enough to convince her that, even though they were strangers and their marriage was a fake, fate was playing a most subtle trick on them both: Were they on a mission for President Teddy Roosevelt—or on a crusade to realize their own passionate desire?

LOVESTONE by Deanna James   (1202, $3.50)

After just one night of torrid passion and tender need, the dark-haired, rugged lord could not deny that Moira, with her precious beauty, was born to be a princess. But how could he grant her freedom when he himself was a prisoner of her love?

DEBORAH'S LEGACY by Stephen Marlowe   (1153, $3.75)

Deborah was young and innocent. Benton was worldly and experienced. And while the world rumbled with the thunder of battle, together they rose on a whirlwind of passion—daring fate, fear and fury to keep them apart!

Available wherever paperbacks are sold, or order direct from the Publisher. Send cover price plus 50¢ per copy for mailing and handling to Zebra Books, 475 Park Avenue South, New York, N.Y. 10016 DO NOT SEND CASH.

EXCITING BESTSELLERS FROM ZEBRA

MORE RAPTUROUS READING!

LOVE'S FIERY JEWEL   (1128, $3.75)
by Elaine Barbieri

Lovely Amethyst was on the verge of womanhood, and no one knew it better than the devilishly handsome Captain Damien Staith. She ached with passion for him, but vowed never to give her heart.

CAPTIVE ECSTASY   (738, $2.75)
by Elaine Barbieri

From the moment Amanda saw the savage Indian imprisoned in the fort she felt compassion for him. But she never dreamed that someday she'd become his captive—or that a captive is what she'd want to be!

AMBER FIRE   (848, $3.50)
by Elaine Barbieri

Ever since she met the dark and sensual Stephen, Melanie's senses throbbed with a longing that seared her veins. Stephen was the one man who could fulfill such desire—and the one man she vowed never to see again!

WILD DESIRES   (1103, $3.50)
by Kathleen Drymon

The tempestuous saga of three generations of Blackthorn women, set in the back streets of London, glamorous New Orleans and the sultry tropics of the Caribbean—where each finds passion in a stranger's arms!

ISLAND ECSTASY   (964, $3.50)
by Karen Harper

No man could resist her delicate beauty and sweet sensuality. But only one man kindled the flames of desire in the heart of Jade—the one man who resisted her!

Available wherever paperbacks are sold, or order direct from the Publisher. Send cover price plus 50¢ per copy for mailing and handling to Zebra Books, 475 Park Avenue South, New York, N.Y. 10016. DO NOT SEND CASH.